MW01602217

RAGE

A Dark Romance Anthology for Reproductive Rights

Volume 3

Jo Brenner   Poppy Jacobson   MT Addams   Heleva Risque

Mae K Knight   Rianne Burnett   Adelaide King

Torrence Robb   L.R. Douglas   Inara Gage   K. Rose

Beatrix Hollow   Molly Briar   Lucy Smoke   O'Junea Brown

C.B. Frey   Jenn Bullard   Sherelle Green   Aiden Pierce

Ashley Pines   A.H. Monroe   Amanda Cessor   Marla York

C.J. Willis   Britt Bee   Sarah Daniels   B.L. Brown

Cassia Quinn   C. Hallman   Theia Luna   Maisie Kane

L.B. Martin   Shar Khan   Evie Dawn & Ava Kade

Rebecca Rathe   M.M. Riott   A.B. Daniels-Annachi

Sarah Bale & Everleigh Blake   Maree Rose   ED Crowe

Mira Raven   Skylark Melody   Allie Maddox

Kenya Goree-Bell   Cait Alvarez   Lily Prince   R.K. Pierce

Daniela Romero   Pandora Cress   Cover Designer: Baddies

Illustrated by Sarah Seidel

Illustrated by Snowarox

Illustrated by Luaartiste

Wet Ink Publishing House, LLC.

Each story in this anthology is copyright © 2025 the individual author(s).

Good Villain copyright © 2025 Jo Brenner
Savage Thieves copyright © 2025 Poppy Jacobson
Summoned copyright © 2025 MT Addams
Your Twin Was Better copyright © 2025 Heleva Risque
Daniels' Rage copyright © 2025 Mae K. Knight
Blood and Pleasure copyright © 2025 Rianne Burnett
Before Christmas Ends copyright © 2025 Adelaide King
Icicle copyright © 2025 Torrence Robb
Picture You copyright © 2025 L.R. Douglas
Beauty Within the Beast copyright © 2025 Inara Gage
Making A Monster copyright © 2025 Beatrix Hollow
Happy Hunting copyright © 2025 Molly Briar
Imperium copyright © 2025 Lucy Smoke
A River Red copyright © 2025 O'Junea Brown
An Omega's Revenge copyright © 2025 Jenn Bullard
Bound to the Brothers copyright © 2025 Sherelle Green
Swallowed By The Tide copyright © 2025 A. B. Daniels-Annachi
Rapture & Reckoning copyright © 2025 Theia Luna
Crimson Dress copyright © 2025 A.H. Monroe
The Traveling copyright © 2025 Skylark Melody
Circus Psycho copyright © 2025 Aiden Pierce
Sin & Sacrifice copyright © 2025 Shar Khan
The Untaming of Ivy Allaway copyright © 2025 Allie Maddox
Cover for Me copyright © 2025 Ashley Pines
Night Sister copyright © 2025 B.L. Brown
Sins Of The Father copyright © 2025 Rebecca Rathe
Malevolence copyright © 2025 Sarah Daniels
How The Shadows Fell copyright © 2025 Britt Bee
Taming His Lady copyright © 2025 Sarah Bale and Everleigh Blake
Paper Ring copyright © 2025 C. Hallman
Witch's Revenge copyright © 2025 R.K. Pierce
Her Spark copyright © 2025 C.J. Willis
tHERapy copyright © 2025 Pandora Cress
Toothtaker copyright © 2025 Cait Alvarez
One Night of Vengeance copyright © 2025 Cassia Quinn
The Torment That Scared Me copyright © 2025 Mira Raven
Wicked Devil copyright © 2025 Daniela Romero
The Mafia's Queen: Uprising copyright © 2025 E.D Crowe
Taste Of Vengeance copyright © 2025 Maree Rose
Sinfully Unfaithful copyright © 2025 Evie Dawn & Ava Kade
Fateful Vengeance copyright © 2025 Marla York

Trust Me Not copyright © 2025 K. Rose
Savage Heirs copyright © 2025 Maisie Kane
The Viper and Chef copyright © 2025 Kenya Goree-Bell
Twisted Help copyright © 2025 Lily Prince
Shattered Silence copyright © 2025 L.B. Martin
Devil In The Details copyright © 2025 Amanda Cessor
The Taste Of Venom copyright © 2025 C.B. Frey
Son of Sin copyright © 2025 M.M. Riott
I Hope They Serve Dick In Hell copyright © 2025 Jo Brenner

Illustrators:
Medusa: Stages of Rage, a collaborative art piece by S.seidel.art, Snowarox and
Luaartiste
All Other Illustrations done by S.seidal.art

Cover Designer: Daniela with Baddies

All rights reserved. No portion of this book may be reproduced in any form without
permission from the publisher, except as permitted by U.S. copyright law. For
permissions contact authormtaddams@gmail.com.

Contents

Foreword

Organizers' Note

Rage, by itself, is easy. After all, there is so much to rage about—racism, misogyny, queerphobia and transphobia, Islamophobia, anti-semitism, xenophobia, bigotry of all kinds. But how do you confront a cruel and unequal world, and channel that rage to affect change, rather than shake your first at the sky, railing against injustice?

We can't always fight darkness with darkness. We can't always fight darkness with light, either.

But what we can do is help the people already doing the work. No one person, no one *anthology*, can fix this. But there are organizations out there that have been fighting this fight for years, day in, and day out, making sure that folks who need access to reproductive care get it. As anthology organizers, readers, authors, and artists, it's not our job to reinvent the wheel—our job is to put our money where our mouths are, and support those who got that wheel rolling long before us.

The Chicago Abortion Fund provides financial, logistical, and emotional support to those denied access to abortion care in the midwest. They, in their own words, "boldly affirm a person's right to bodily autonomy"—and so, dear reader, do we.

And we hope you do, too.

Within these pages are standalone stories, bonus scenes, and epilogues from previously published novels. They run the gamut of relationship types and perspectives. But what they have in common is twofold: Our deep-rooted rage, and our determination to give you and everyone happily ever afters. (Or happily for nows, in some cases, but the point still stands.)

We are so grateful to you for supporting the Chicago Abortion Fund with your purchase and page reads, and helping us help the CAF get abortion care to those who need it. We invite you to donate on your own, as well.

Thank you so much. Together, we can make sure that the true bad guys don't win so easily. Together, we can fight.

Sometimes, we need to write our own villain origin story.

This is ours.

In solidarity,
      Jo, Poppy, and MT

Volume 3

One Night Of Vengeance

By: Cassia Quinn

A Twisted Arrangements Story

About One Night Of Vengeance

Your past comes back to haunt you in the most unexpected of places.

I'm out for a fun night at a new sex club, with my husband, when a devil from my past reappears. But this time, I'm not the victim he once knew.

I'm stronger.

I'm braver.

I'm ready to reclaim the part of my soul that he stole all those years ago.

Content Note:

Mature content. For readers 18 & older. Attempted sexual assault, torture, dismemberment, gore, mutilation, strong language, graphic sex, rope bondage, verbal abuse, misogyny, trauma, PTSD, nightmares, terror, revenge, power imbalance, D/s themes, suspension, dark themes.

Relationship type: MF

Chapter One
Ginevra

The blue satin dress hugs my every curve, and I straighten to my full petite height. I'm feeling more comfortable in my own skin than I have in forever—maybe even for the very first time in my life. I've worked through a lot of my issues in this past year. It's been quite the healing process.

My hand tightens around Blake's arm, and he glances down at me. "Are you all right, magpie?"

I nod, offering him a genuine smile. We're at the grand opening celebration for the most stunningly opulent sex club I've ever seen. Owned and operated by one of Blake's associates, we have to attend and congratulate him, not to mention see what all the fuss is about. The owner's been posting vague but alluring teasers across social media for months now.

All around us, couples—and trios—are dressed to the nines, while scantily clad men and women move seductively on platforms placed throughout the main room. At both ends, there's a bar, with booths and tables occupying the perimeter, spaced out between ornate pillars that give varying amounts of privacy.

We approach the bar and Blake orders for us. "Glenlivet, neat, and a lemon drop with extra sugar on the rim."

Warmth spreads through me as Blake orders my favorite cocktail, without a disgusted sneer on his lips for once. I'm not the only one who's changed in the last year or so.

Our drinks arrive and Blake lifts his in the air, clinking the glass against mine. "Here's to a night of debauchery. I can't wait to test out one of the private rooms."

I sip my drink, blushing, my heart rate picking up at all the naughty images flitting through my imagination. What does Blake have in mind for tonight?

"I thought this was just a social call, then we'd be heading home."

A wicked glint shines in his bright blue eyes. "That was my original plan, but now that we're here, why don't we indulge a little?" He leans closer, his breath hot in my ear. "I want to tie you up, magpie, and fuck you until you scream my name. How does that sound, Mrs. Baron?"

"Yes," I breathe out. Butterflies flutter in my stomach every time he calls me *Mrs. Baron*.

"In that case, let's—"

His phone rings. Without looking, he pushes the button to ignore the call. It immediately starts ringing again.

"Fuck." Glancing at his cell, his luscious lips form a tight line. "I have to take this. Privately. Stay in this room."

"I'll be fine. Find me when you get back."

With a frown drawing his brows together, he nods, then makes for the exit. Hopefully, he won't be gone for too long. I'm already trembling with anticipation of how the rest of this night will go.

Not so long ago, the mere idea of being tied up and helpless threw me into a panic. Until Blake changed everything for me. I trust him. I know he'll never hurt me unless I ask him to, and even then, the pain feels so good. I love how he takes control, how I can let myself go in his hands. Never did I think that could be possible until now, until him.

I loiter at the bar, studying the unfamiliar faces in the sea of people around me. The room is packed. Seems like this grand opening is a hit.

A group of partiers surge toward the bar, so I step aside to make room for them. That's when I notice the walkway around the perimeter of the room, behind the seating areas. I step into the less crowded space and sip my cocktail while studying the art on the wall. Each piece is tall and narrow, framed with molding.

Further down the walkway, a soft click catches my attention, and one of the pieces of art swings open to reveal a private room beyond. Are each of these panels actually a door? Clever.

"Ginevra Pontrelli?"

I whirl around at the sound of my maiden name, coming face-to-face with a tall, dark-haired man. He seems familiar, but I can't think of his name.

At my silence, he says, "It's me. Carl Jones the third." When I continue to draw a blank, he leans closer, his cologne cloying. "You rode my dick at Greer's party two years ago."

I'm not sure if it's his vulgar description of what we did or the jarring scent of his cologne, but the faintest of memories surface. *The spitter.* That's right, this guy shoved me into the pool house and couldn't wait to get me wet, so he spit on his cock and fucked me. I was so wasted I'm surprised I even remember that much about the encounter.

Carl Jones III grins down at me. "It's good to see you again, Gin. Especially in a place like this. Want to get a room? We can have another go at it."

That idea makes me queasy.

"No, thanks. I'm actually here with someone."

"That's too bad." He crowds me, maneuvering me closer to the wall of doors. "Who are you here with? Looks like you're all alone to me."

"I'm here with my hus— Hey!"

Carl bumps my drink. The sweet, sticky liquid splashes down the front of my dress.

"Oops." His expression is a mask of concern. "Let me help you."

He grabs my wrists and pushes my back up against the wall, a wall which, seconds later, gives way and I'm stumbling backward. My heart pounds in my ears. I'd fall, except for the iron grip Carl has on me. He kicks the door closed behind him and we're engulfed in silence.

Releasing me, he clicks the lock into place. Anxiety and fear prickle across my clammy skin.

We're all alone in a dimly lit, adult play room. A bed sits centered against the far wall. On one side, shackles dangle from a large wooden structure, and a swing hangs from the ceiling on the other side. If I was in here with Blake, I'd be intrigued, but with Carl, I'm terrified.

He takes a step toward me, and I throw my cocktail glass at him, then dart away, trying to put some distance between us until I can get to the door.

The glass nicks his forehead, then shatters on the wall behind him, raining tiny shards of glass everywhere. He curses, coming after me as I dodge behind the wooden bondage frame, momentarily out of his reach.

"There's nowhere to hide, Ginevra. Just be a good little slut and come here and suck my dick. You're not leaving this room until I'm finished with you." He leers at me.

"Get away from me or you'll regret it." I scream as he lunges for me, quickly scurrying across the bed to the other side of the room. I manage to put a tall bench between us. "Leave me alone. No means no."

He scoffs. "Only stupid bitches think that. Your body, my choice."

The phrase sends a shudder of dread through my entire body as reality sinks in. I'm not getting out of here until Carl finishes using me. Until he rapes me. He honestly thinks he has the right to do whatever he wants.

Thinking back, I'm pretty sure I told him *no* in that pool house, but he didn't care then either. For men like him—rich and powerful—there are no repercussions, no consequences for what they do to women.

My gaze flits to the door, the floor covered in glass, the impossible distance between where I am and the only exit. I'm fucked.

Blake, where are you?

Though with the well-hidden doors, even he might not be able to find me. I'm on my own.

My heart hammers against my chest and my hands shake. Do I try to fight him? He's much larger than I am, stronger too. He could really do some damage if he wanted. Do I give in and let him have my body? Maybe he'll be quick, then he'll let me go.

I'm torn, truly not knowing which of my two options is the best.

Anger rushes through me, igniting a fire in my belly. I shouldn't even be in this situation. I shouldn't have to choose between bad and worse. This is fucking bullshit, all because of one entitled prick. But I'm so damn helpless. It's unfair.

I search for anything to use as a weapon, while Carl rounds the bench, and I sprint to the other side. We're at a standoff again.

"Having fun yet?" Carl lunges, catching me by surprise this time. "I'm going to make you pay for every second that you're making me wait, bitch."

His massive body collides with mine, taking us to the floor. I scream for help, not that anyone can hear me, and scramble to get out from under him, losing a shoe in the struggle. I'm almost free, but Carl drags me back, pinning me under his weight. I can't breathe. Panic flairs, bringing older, more horrifying memories to the surface. I squeeze my eyes closed against the onslaught.

"That's right." Carl hovers above me, pressing me into the floor. "Just stay still and take it. You know you want it. No matter how much you fight me, you want my dick. You're such a whore."

He tries to kiss my lips, but I turn my head away. His mouth lands on my cheek, wet and sloppy, and I cringe. Between us, he fumbles with his belt, trying to free his erection.

I can't let this happen to me again. Opening my eyes, I scan for my lost heel, locating it at my side. I reach for it, get a good grip, and then forcefully drive the stiletto into Carl's back. He howls in pain, but I don't let up. I hit him over and over until he rolls off me. The tip of my heel drips blood.

Scrambling away from him, I try to get my footing, but Carl reaches out and grabs my ankle. I yank my foot away and he's left with only my shoe.

Barefoot, I stand up and sprint toward the door. The crunch beneath my feet is the only warning I get before pain blossoms on my soles, but I don't stop. I leave bloody footprints in my wake, desperate to get to the exit.

I make it to the door, my fingers slick against the lock as I try to turn it. I almost have it, I'm nearly free. The deadbolt clicks open, and I reach for the handle.

Suddenly, Carl slams into my back, wedging me between his body and my door to freedom. He presses up against me so hard that I can't move, can't draw in air, can't escape him.

"Not so fast," he snarls. "You want me to do you up against this door, then that's what I'll do. There's no getting away, Ginevra. So stop trying, for fuck's sake!"

I gasp as he leans away far enough to undo his trousers and lift my dress up to my waist. Cool air briefly hits my backside. His heavy breath in my ear. His bruising touch assaults my ass, my breasts, my thighs. He shoves a knee roughly between my legs.

I close my eyes, willing all of this to go away, searching for an escape somewhere deep inside my psyche. I just want it to be over.

"Told you I'd make you pay," he grunts.

I whimper, clawing at the wooden door, desperate to get away from him. Bile rises in my throat. Mentally, I attempt to brace myself for what's coming next. Not only for the pain, but the humiliation and the shame. The powerlessness.

I've made so much progress on working on myself, on my trauma, and this is going to set me back to square one. I'll have to start all over again. And who's to say this will stop here, that this time will be the last?

Suddenly, he's jerked away. Cool air replaces his body heat. There's a thud, followed by a grunt.

Peeling myself off the door, I spin around, eyes wide, heartbeat raging. Agony shoots through the bottoms of my feet, then relief swells in my chest with such staggering force that I sway.

"Blake."

"Magpie." He gazes down at an unconscious Carl, his shoulders rigid with tension.

I must be in shock because I can't seem to move my limbs. I just stand frozen in place and ask the first question that comes to mind. "H-how did you get in here?"

Blake lifts his eyes, meeting mine, and the fury in them sends shivers of ice through my veins. He jerks his chin toward one wall. "Hidden exit."

"O-oh." My voice trembles.

When Blake approaches me, his gaze softens, but his tone remains steely. "He hurt you."

I nod, even though it wasn't a question. He reaches for me and the numbness I'm feeling fades away, leaving me a shaking, sobbing mess in my husband's arms. He doesn't shush me, he just holds me close as I cling to him. He came for me. Of course he did. I never should have doubted that he'd find a way to get to me.

"*Christ*," Blake curses, picking me up and carrying me away from the glass-riddled floor where I've been standing. "Baby, your feet are bloody." He glances over my head. "Get me doctor. Now."

For the first time, I notice that we're not alone. A man hovers near us. It takes me a second to put a name to his face. Jet black hair, green-grey eyes, foreboding presence... Greyson Hyde, owner of

Leonidas Gentleman's Club, as well as this new establishment. While everyone knows his name, and has seen his picture in the papers, this is the first time I've seen him in person.

"Doctor's already on her way," Mr. Hyde growls. His gaze lands on Carl's prone form. "I'm assuming you want to deal with that in your own way."

Blake nods. "Put him on ice for me, will you?"

"Consider it done."

I glance questioningly between the two men. "Y-you can't. Don't you know who he is? His father—"

"He's Carl Jones the third, and when I'm through with him, there won't be a fourth." Blake sits on the bed, setting me on his lap while we wait for the doctor to arrive. "He could be the most powerful man on this planet and I'd still make him pay for what he's done to you, magpie. You're my *wife*. No one touches you."

I melt against him. He holds me closer, wrapping his strong arms around me, and inhales the scent of my shampoo.

"I'm sorry I wasn't here sooner, my love," he murmurs.

"You're here now. That's all that matters." I nestle into him, doing my best to ignore the pain I'm in.

The doctor arrives at the same time as two men dressed in black. The men lift Carl's unconscious body between them and drag him from the room. Mr. Hyde disappears with them, leaving me with my husband and the doctor.

Blake remains close to me, growling at the doctor every time I hiss as she plucks shards of glass from my soles. He holds me while she examines the bruises on my body. Though she scowls at him, she efficiently does her job, gives me meds for the pain, and eventually tells me I can go home to rest and heal.

There's no point in getting the police involved. This isn't going to court. Carl got caught. We are his judge, jury, and executioners. If he survives the week, I'll be surprised.

Chapter Two
Blake

Gin wakes me up three nights in a row with her nightmares. Her screams and sobs wreak havoc on my heart, batter my soul, and I'll take each one of her tears from Carl Jones III's flesh. Eventually.

I hold Gin to my chest, her legs tangled with mine, as her breathing evens out and she falls to sleep again.

Greyson Hyde always keeps his word. Carl's been on ice, waiting in a creatively constructed version of hell on earth while I tend to my wife this week. My best torturer has visited him daily just to keep things interesting, but I've made it quite clear that he's to be kept alive.

The media is all over the case of the missing millionaire heir, Carl Jones III, with pleas from his grieving parents saying they'll pay any ransom amount. Except this is one situation that won't be fixed with money—not this time. Carl's not going to get a slap on the wrist and pay a fine instead of going to prison because jail time would destroy his promising future.

He has no future.

He's one less predator in the world now.

The Joneses may suffer at the loss of their son, but they deserve it. It's punishment for raising such a monster. If I'm feeling merciful, I might send them a gift, a piece of their beloved child, so that they can have closure once he's dead.

That's a big *if*. Mercy's not a state of mind that comes easily or often to me these days.

Right now, I'm filled with rage. Perhaps I should slip away tonight and release my anger on Carl, and end this. But this isn't about me, it's about my sweet wife. This needs to end in a way that leads to her healing, to her regaining a sense of empowerment and strength. She must get her vengeance.

* * *

It's another couple of weeks before Ginevra's healed enough to walk on her scarred feet. While the physical damage quickly heals, I know her mind and soul continue to suffer. Which means today is the day I've been waiting for. Today, this ends.

"Magpie," I call, finding her in the kitchen, her favorite room in the house.

She glances up from the mixing bowl, a dusting of flour smeared across her cheek. Adorable. "Yeah?"

"It's time."

"Time for what?"

"Time that I give you a choice about what to do with Carl." I lean against the kitchen island, my gaze pinned on her, so I don't miss her most subtle reactions. She flinches slightly at his name.

"What can be done with him?" Her gorgeous brown eyes widen. "He's not still alive, is he?"

I nod. "I've been keeping him alive for you, in case you wanted to kill him yourself, or help me, or watch. Whatever your heart desires, it will be done. What do you want, baby girl?"

She abandons her baking, going to wash her hands in the kitchen sink. Her silence tells me she's thinking, considering her options before she makes a decision.

"I don't want him dead." She turns to face me. "I want him unable to hurt anyone again. Death is not justice, it's too final. I want him to suffer for the rest of his life, just like those he's hurt."

A wicked smile curves my lips. I wrap my arms around her and nuzzle her neck. "Then that is what you shall have, my love. Come. Let's do this now."

Chapter Three
Ginevra

Of all the places I imagined Blake would keep this piece of shit, the basement of Leonidas Gentleman's Club wasn't one of them. Yet here we are, beneath the glamorous Greek-style columns, crystal chandeliers, and gold leaf paint, in the dark bowels of earth and rough stone.

The space is dry, like an ancient tomb. Electric sconces set into the walls illuminate this torture chamber that's well-equipped with shackles and chains, a drain in one corner that emits a rank odor.

In the middle of it all, Carl dangles from his restraints, stretched onto his tiptoes. His chains vanish into the vast space of darkness above him. He's naked, his entire body one enormous bruise. In fact, I'm pretty sure his bruises are bruised. The layers of discoloration, some fading, others fresh, saturated color, make my stomach roll.

Completely at odds with the scene before me is a black velvet throne-like chair on a small platform, positioned a few feet away from Carl. Gold scroll work decorates the arms and high back. It belongs in a Renaissance castle, not down here.

I glance at Blake. "What's with the chair?"

"That's for you." He takes me around the waist and lifts me into the enormous seat. My feet don't even reach the floor. "I had them bring this down here for you. You should be a queen on your throne while you deliver punishment to this vile creature."

I stare at Blake for a long moment. He really is slightly unhinged. I love it. Things like this... this is how I know he loves me.

"I love you," I tell him.

He drops a kiss to my forehead. "I love you more."

I settle onto the throne, feeling like a fucking queen up here. The velvet's smooth beneath my fingers. I sit up straighter. I'm in charge here, and this is my court. A new sense of strength rushes through me and I feel more like myself than I have in weeks.

Blake comes to my side so that we're both facing Carl. He hasn't moved since we entered the room, and I wonder if he's actually still alive or not.

"What shall we do with him?" Blake keeps his voice low, even though it's just us down here. "How do you want me to hurt him, magpie?"

I let all my anger, all my hurt, and the sense of being violated course through my body and embrace all the emotions that rise. Letting my imagination run wild, I think of stabbing him over and over until he bleeds out, of cutting off his dick and making him choke on it, of having someone take him against his will until he's bloody and sobbing.

The fantasies, the possibilities keep coming. Though are they really fantasies when I can utter the word and make any of them a reality?

A sensation of dark empowerment sings in my veins. I was victimized by Carl, but I'm not the victim here today. I'm the Angel of Death and Vengeance. I'm the Queen of Revenge. I'm Carl's worst nightmare—a powerful woman.

Which is why I don't want to kill him, as temporarily satisfying as that would be. He needs to be a living example of what happens to men who have no respect for women, to men who think they're untouchable because of their position in society.

Finally, he stirs. His puffy eyelids open, his gaze landing on me. The chains rattle as he struggles against the restraints. "Gin, you little bitch. You can't do this to me! Tell them to let me go!"

Hmm. Why don't his pleas move me? Maybe because he's such a fucking asshole.

Blake steps up to Carl and backhands him across the face. "Don't you dare speak to my wife like that."

Carl's eyes widen. He glances at me, then at Blake, and back again. "You're his w-wife?"

I bob my head.

Apparently, he didn't get the memo that I'm now Ginevra Baron, wife to the notorious and feared man called The Black Baron—for the lack of light shining in his soul.

"I-I didn't know." Too little, too late, Carl. I'm annoyed how he's only afraid now because of my relationship with Blake. He's only cowering because he's afraid of my husband. That's about to change. I want him to be terrified of me.

Behind every great man is a vengeful woman.

"Blake, darling, pull out your knife." I instruct from my cushy throne. "You'll also need something to cauterize the wounds."

"Wh-what?" Carl tugs at his chains. "What are you going to do?" His panicked gaze darts between me and my husband, as Blake's knife appears in his hand. "Tell him to stop, you crazy bitch!"

"Cut out his vile tongue."

Blake grabs the tongs, forces Carl's mouth open and stretches out his tongue. In one fluid motion, he brings the knife down and slices through the spongy meat. Carl screams, choking on his own blood. He screams even louder when Blake presses a red-hot iron to the gushing wound.

I barely give Carl a moment to recover before catching Blake's eye. Pointing at Carl's flaccid dick, he nods, then cuts it from the man's body.

This time, Carl passes out. The abrupt silence soothes my jagged nerves. I'm not a violent person—usually. Blake cauterizes the wound, then diligently cleans his knife.

I lean back in my chair. "You can have him returned to his parents now. Just make sure he knows that if he tries to come after us, we'll kill him."

"I think he's bright enough to understand, but I'll make sure of it." Blake sneers at Carl's limp, blood smeared body. "Do you want to keep anything for a souvenir?"

"Are you serious?" The idea of having even a drop of Carl's blood on me is repulsive, much less anything... larger.

Blake shrugs. "I just want to give you everything and anything your heart desires. There's no limit to what I'll do for you, or what you can have. Some people like to collect pieces."

"I'm definitely not one of them. But there is something..."

"Anything." His brilliant blue gaze steals my breath away.

"I want to go back to the club, to that room where it happened."

"Are you sure?" His brow furrows.

I swallow down the lump in my throat and nod. "I need to face what happened or it will haunt me forever. I'm done with Carl, but that room and everything that happened there, I need to be there again."

"Then let's go." He lifts me from the throne. I slide down his hard body, inhaling his spicy cologne, until my feet touch the floor. Blake drops a kiss on the top of my head, then takes my hand and we walk away from the mutilated man, almost like this is an ordinary day. I've known violence all my life, but I never thought I'd be the person dealing out justice in this way.

Being in this room sends a shiver through me as my memory replays everything that happened here. The pain and fear Carl put me through, the glass shards in my feet, and even how Blake came to my rescue—again.

But that's not what I want to remember at this club or in this playroom.

I face Blake. "Let's make new memories here." I glance around the space, taking in all the fun possibilities, and knowing immediately which one we'll enjoy the most. "Tie me up and fuck me. Make all the painful memories go away."

"That, I can do." Taking me by the shoulders, he presses a kiss to my mouth. "Do you remember your safe word?"

"Cupcake," I murmur against his lips.

"Good girl. Now I'm going to do something to you I haven't done before."

I frown up at him in confusion. "You've tied me up before."

"Not like this." He steps away from me, gathering up a bunch of coiled ropes. "This will take a little while, but it will be worth is, so be patient."

I eye the rope. In the past, he's preferred binding me with his silk ties, or even handcuffs, but never actual rope.

"Do you trust me, magpie?" he asks, his intense gaze boring into mine.

"Yes. Completely."

"Good. Take off your clothes, then I want you on your knees."

I do as I'm told, stripping, then sinking down onto the plush carpet. Blake positions me where he wants, then slides the first section of rope across my chest. It's not as coarse as it looks. The fibers glide over my skin with silky softness. I release the breath I was holding and relax into my husband's touch.

He expertly binds my breasts in a series of knots that form a criss-cross pattern over my chest and shoulders. My arms he folds behind my back, then secures them in place with short lengths of rope. Moving lower, he creates intricate knot-work on my torso, between my legs, and round my thighs.

Each glide of the rope feels like a lover's caress, each knot a firm embrace. I thought at first that the bondage might make me feel too constricted. Instead, I'm surprisingly able to let go, emotionally, mentally, and physically. I give myself over to Blake with complete trust.

The feeling is freeing, liberating in a way I've never fully experienced before.

When he has me bound the way he wants, a satisfied hum vibrates from his chest. He's still fully dressed, while I'm not only naked but restrained and at his mercy. The power imbalance sends a thrill through me.

I let out a surprised squeak when Blake lifts me into his arms. He carries me over to the suspension frame, where I'm secured by my chest, waist, and ankles until I'm floating in the air. Suspended, the sense of weightlessness and surrender shoves the remains of my negative thoughts from my mind.

I'm completely present, submitting to the here and now.

"Good girl." Blake caresses my sensitive flesh, and I shiver. All sensation feels heightened right now. Dipping his fingers between my spread thighs, he finds me wet. "Perfect girl. The binding was foreplay for you, wasn't it?"

I murmur an incoherent response, too lost in all the sensations to form a clear thought, much less words.

Blake teases my clit, and an orgasm hits me out of nowhere. My entire body tightens and shudders, and a long moan leaves my parted lips. Coming while bound and suspended is unlike anything I've felt before—total vulnerability.

My husband barely gives me a chance to catch my breath before he lines himself up and pulls my soaked, throbbing pussy onto his cock. He rocks us, gently swinging, until I take every inch of him. He's in control of our pacing and the angle. Wrapping my hair around one of his fists, he eases almost all the way out before pulling me onto his hard length again, over and over.

Slowly, he continues his seductive torture. Every nerve ending in my body flames to life, verging on sensory overload as he diligently, reverently fucks me.

I whimper and moan his name, begging for more, until he finally snaps. The room fills with the lewd sounds of our flesh slapping, his grunts and my gasps. When he pinches my clit, fireworks explode behind my eyelids and white-hot pleasure steals my breath away. My cunt pulses around him and he follows me over the edge, tensing, he spurts hot cum deep inside me.

This, all of this, is exactly what I needed. This experience overrides everything else about this place, overshadows my past trauma so thoroughly that what happened before is a distant memory. One that can no longer haunt me unless I give it the power to do so.

I may be forever fucked up, but therapy has made me stronger, more resilient, and capable. I'm no longer ruled by the traumas of my past. They don't cut as deep as they once did.

And this man, my husband, has helped me through so much. His love and devotion fill all my gaping wounds, making me whole in a way I never thought possible.

Catching our breaths, Blake buried deep in my pussy, he slowly rocks us. His deep voice growls in my ear, "Round two. Come for me again, magpie."

Not ready to say goodbye to Blake and Gin yet? Read their story in FOREVER FAKE, get it here: https://books2read.com/ta-3

About the Author

Cassia Quinn writes dark billionaire and mafia romance. Find her online: www.CassiaQuinn.com/links

The Torment That Scared Me

By: Mira Raven

A Dark Romance

About The Torment That Scared Me

I've been killing men together with my husband for as long as I can remember. But now that we have three children, there's even more rage inside me. More fury that needs an outlet. I'm crippled by the thought of something happening to my family, so this thirst for blood gets fueled by my fears. I don't know who else than my husband can make me stop. But nowadays, not even he can reach me.
I feel lost.

Content Note:

Mature content. For readers 18 & older. This story is an extended epilogue of the Heartbreak series and ends in a HEA. This book contains sensitive material relating to: Blood/Gore, Explicit Language, Torture, Violence, and Explicit Sex

Relationship type: MF

Chapter One
Echo

Every time I kill a man I can't help but fall in love even more with the silence that comes after he gives his last breath. The whole process is a symphony, it starts with them whimpering and begging, negotiating for something they know deep down I'd never offer. Then comes the crescendo, the screaming, the cursing, the crying, and the wailing. And then, it's just the sweet silence.

And dear Larry makes no exception. Larry, who hit his wife for the last time tonight. Larry, who screamed at his seven-year-old to fuck off one last time a couple of hours ago. Larry, whose blood is now pooling at my feet, staining my Loubutins. *Fuck Larry. That makes me hate you even more.*

Wiping my shoes on his shirt and stepping on his back, I start walking towards my husband. Ian is looking at me from across the room with a look that says he's as proud as ever when he sees me murdering someone.

"Stepping on corpses is beneath you, baby."

"And flattery won't win you extra points, Ian Beckett." I smile when I reach him, grabbing his collar and kissing his cheek. "Besides, we both know the only man alive who deserves to feel my heel pressing on his skin is you."

He stays silent, giving me the smile that sent shivers down my spine the first time I saw him. It's not only mesmerizing, but there's a cruelty in it that everyone can see, but only a few people perceive. And while it's terrifying to see what hides behind the mask, I can only consider myself incredibly lucky. Honored, even. Honored that I got to witness the horrendous things my husband is capable of while feeling more protected than ever.

Flipping me around and pushing my back against the wall, Ian gets closer. Closer, closer, and closer until I can feel his breath on my neck, his inhales and exhales as accelerated as ever when he can barely hold himself together. I know he's hanging by a thread every time we kill a man. Because he constantly fears that somehow I'll end up being that man's victim. I only wish he would realize there's no reality where that could happen. Not only because I'm sure he would give his own life to protect me, not only because we always work together and outnumber our targets, but also because I would never leave him or our children.

The only death I wish for is the one of all abusers in the world. And if I could live forever and make my family immortal, I would do it in a second just to have the chance to spend eternity and forever surrounded by them.

"Take me home, Ian," I say breathlessly. "Please, just take me home."

"I want to take you right now, Echo Whitlock." He bites the skin of my neck, the sound of it tearing making me even wetter. "I want to take you, break you so I could put you back together for the millionth time just to remind you who owns you, and whom you own."

"Ian—"

"No." He cuts me off. "You know we can't go home until we get rid of the body, and I'm not sure I can last that much longer without feeling your cum dripping from my skin."

It takes him no more than a couple of seconds to lift my skirt, push my panties to the side, and make me moan loudly when he shoves two fingers inside me and starts moving them in a come-hither motion. His thumb is pressing on my clit, massaging it in circles, my eyes rolling to the back of my head.

"Don't, pretty girl," Ian says in a threatening voice. "Let those greens see what I do to you. Let them see how I can make your perfect pussy soak my fingers and how I can make you scream my name over." He gives me a hard thrust. "And over." Another one. "And over again."

"I love how well you know me," I whisper, barely able to make the words come out. "I love how you know exactly how to touch me, and how to fuck me so you can make me come all over you."

"Then be a good girl and show me." His hand starts moving even faster, the pressure he applies on my clit becoming too much to be able to hold back.

I come screaming his name from the top of my lungs looking into the blue eyes that have been holding my soul captive for more than six years. My whole body is shaking and my knees are close to giving in, especially since seeing my husband licking my cum off his fingers is an image that will always drive me insane.

"Ian," I swallow. "I need us to get rid of Larry and go home."

"Of course, baby," he says, kissing my forehead. "Do you miss the kids that much?"

His question gives me pause. Because I know the answer to it, yet I'm not comfortable admitting it out loud. But if there is one thing I know Ian Beckett would do is judge me. And not only I hate lying to him, I don't see a reason to. Not now, not ever. He earned my loyalty and my trust time and time again, and I don't think we would've been where we are today if we were nothing but truthful.

"I do miss them," I say in a tentative voice, looking into his eyes. "But I—" I hesitate, nodding to reassure myself. "I miss feeling you inside me in our bed more." Tears are flooding my eyes and my chin is shaking when I ask my own question. "Does that make me a bad mother, Ian?"

He takes a step back, frowning and looking at me from head to toes. I feel so vulnerable, so exposed, so liable to be judged and broken. I know my husband loves me, I do. I know he would move Heaven and Earth to make me happy, no matter if that translates to buying me flowers on a rainy day or helping me kill a man. I know all of that, but my children, my relationship with them, and the one with their father is something that I feel very conflicted about.

"You're the best mother to ever haunt this world, Echo Beckett." His voice reverberates in the empty storage room, making me feel like his words are searing into my eardrums. "Our children love you with everything they are, not because they're conditioned to do that. It's because they know how lucky they are to have you as a parent."

Clearing my throat, I wrap my hair in a ponytail, looking into his eyes when I continue.

"And I love them. With every particle of my body, baby. I am absolutely and insanely obsessed with all three of them." I take a deep breath, blowing my cheeks and letting the air out before resuming. "But I don't want them to hate me when they grow up because I want to spend time with their father and not them."

"Pretty girl," he cups my face, rubbing his thumbs over my cheeks, "they will be functional adults *because* you want to spend time with their father. They're learning love, a healthy definition of it, not the one we grew up with. And this way neither Noah, nor Corbin, nor Hayden will ever tolerate the behaviours we used to tolerate."

I know he's right. I know I tolerated abuse in my previous marriage and in most of the relationships I had. That's why I killed my ex husband. And that's why Ian killed my ex lover. To some extent, that's why we are still killing people similar to them even after all these years.

Maybe we haven't forgotten the way our close family and people who swore they loved us treated us, and maybe we'll never be able to forgive them. Despite the fact that what we are doing is completely illegal, I can't help but wonder if it's immoral. Or unethical.

Is it so wrong that we don't want to see more people going through what we did? Is it so wrong to defend the ones who can't defend themselves? I don't think we're heroes, not in any way, shape, or form. But I do believe we're vengeance incarnated mixed with a spectrum of emotions that glue us as a couple and keeps our family together.

I don't reply to what Ian said with anything else than a nod and a kiss. And he doesn't need more, that's one of the many things I love about him. He takes my hand and guides me to where Larry is still bleeding.

"This one was easy," he says.

"Boringly so."

"Do you think we should start torturing them more?"

"It depends. I don't want to let these monsters rob me of the seconds or the breaths I could spend with my family. But, from time to time, when the kids are with Nora, we could have a fun date that involves some scissors, hammers, or any other sharp objects."

"Do you want to cut their fingers?"

"I want to cut their balls."

He laughs. That deep, rich laugh that never fails to brighten my days. The same laugh I love waking up to when he's playing with the twins and their older brother. The laugh that gives me purpose and the laugh I crave hearing the same way a junkie craves their next hit.

"Come on, pretty girl. Let's wrap Larry up and feed him to the pigs."

"Do you think someone will eventually start wondering why a lawyer and a stand-up comedian decided to have a farm 50 miles from their home?" I ask, starting to undress Larry and scrunching my nose in disgust when I see his dick.

"Maybe." He shrugs, gently pushing me aside and continuing what I started. "But even if they do, you know we're brilliantly covering our tracks, baby. We've been doing this for years."

"I guess."

"Echo, look at me." His voice leaves no room for negotiation so I lower my gaze to look into his eyes. "You're coming up with reasons to worry for absolutely no reason."

"There *is* a reason." I lift my hands only to smack them on my thighs. "I don't want our children to grow up visiting mommy and daddy in jail. And I don't want us to die in there either."

"Then we'll stop doing this."

"It's not that simple and you know that."

"Why? It really is. One day you're killing someone, the other you don't. You can find a different hobby. Might I suggest crocheting?"

"Stop it." I snarl, clenching my jaw.

"Or maybe some cute DIY projects? I'm sure you can find some housewives who would absolutely *love* to help you build a Christmas tree from toilet paper tubes."

"Ian, I'm warning you—"

"You're warning me?" He lets out a mocking laugh. "You don't want to go to jail for killing random men who should've been a stain on someone's sheets, yet you would go to jail for murdering the father of your children? So. Maybe pick up fishing?"

Deciding to not feed his mockery anymore, I grab Larry's hair and start dragging him towards the exit, ignoring my husband and trying to settle my anger. I know why he did that, I know all the tricks Ian Beckett has in his proverbial hat and I know how many aces he has up his sleeve. And usually I admire that about him. But now, I'm angry that he decided to use them on me.

I can hear Ian saying something behind me, but I'm too angry to pay attention to him. I hate that he doesn't take in consideration the risks, that the fact that we now have a family and three mini versions of us to take in consideration before making decisions. And I can't believe that less than an hour earlier I was worried I'm not a good enough mother, when those children couldn't have a more reckless father.

Taking a butcher knife from the wall of the pig stale, I start chopping his body, throwing the pieces behind me. I can feel the dirt and the pebbles digging in my skin, I can feel the blood on my hands and the drops falling on my face, but I don't care. I just need to get this done and go home to my children. Their father can do whatever he pleases, but he'd better stay away from me if he doesn't want to end up like Larry. Because right now jail doesn't sound that much of a bad idea if that would mean Ian never mocking me again.

I can feel Ian's hand gripping my hair, but I choose to ignore it. I might be a lot of things, but a fool I am not, so there is no way I will fall for the same tricks just to calm down and forgive him for goading me. It's not what he said—not at all—it's the fact he chose to treat me as a regular person. As somebody he just likes to poke and have fun with. And that is something I'd never tolerate, especially not when it's coming from my husband who knows damn well that I have been treated like this by too many men. And the fact most of those men are now pig shit or fish food might be a hint of what I'm capable of when somebody doesn't give me the respect I think I deserve.

"Enough, Echo," he murmurs in my ear, my head going backward when he pulls my hair so hard I can hear it crack. "You made your point."

"I don't think I did," I retort while I keep cutting Larry into small pieces even if the only thing I can see now is my husband's face upside down.

Letting go of my hair, he grabs my arms and makes me stand, gently pushing me away. It all happens in a blur. Ian takes a canister from his left, pours its contents on Larry—or what Larry used to be—lights a match, and throws it on the ground. He turns around, the flames behind him making him look even more menacing than he usually does. Ian Beckett is the brightest angel that Hell could have ever housed, and now he looks the part.

My body is screaming to go to him and kiss him. To forgive and forget, and to focus on everything he's done for me throughout the years. But I refuse. Besides the fact that I'm not letting him win this easily, I have to admit that this is the most fun we've had in months.

I straighten my back and arch an eyebrow, crossing my arms over my chest. My heart is beating so fast I can hear it drumming. Because anticipation means excitement, and my husband means redemption. And I'll have all of that on a silver platter simply because I worked hard to get them.

"Now that Larry's been taken care of maybe we can talk?" The right corner of his mouth lifts slightly when he asks the question.

Frowning, I spit, "No. You've done enough talking for tonight."

"This is not who you are, Echo." Ian shakes his head in disappointment. "This is not who *we* are."

"You don't get to tell me who I am and who we are," I say in a deadly voice. "Not after mocking me and joking on my account."

"I was actually goading you. Making you realize *exactly* who you are and what you stand for. Because there are too many questions, too many thoughts running rampant in your head and I'm not the one to answer them. *You* are."

"You could help!" I raise my voice, walking towards him, anticipation and excitement completely replaced by pure rage. "Because it's not the first time when I've felt lost and incapable of finding my way back to who I know I am. The only thing that's different is that this time a murder or two or ten won't fix it. So now the great Ian Beckett doesn't know how to handle this so he chooses the path he knows too well. Belittling. Manipulation. The only problem with that, *husband*, is that you chose the wrong person to inflict it upon."

His gasp is audible and the way his eyes grow bigger with every word I say makes me think he's surprised by what he just heard. But he shouldn't be. Not in my opinion, at least.

"I think you're overreacting, Echo."

"Wrong fucking answer, Ian."

Chapter Two

Ian

From the united front that we were, I now feel like there are miles between us. And it's tearing me apart. My heart is in shambles and, for the first time in my life, I have this daunting feeling that I can't reach my wife.

That she decided to shut me out for months or maybe years, and that now is the time when she'll completely shut that door and let me be alone in this cold, dark room that life without her is.

I thought she's enjoying our endeavours. I thought she's as keen on punishing the abusers in this world as I am. Until I realized she isn't. Or not in the same way or for the same reasons as she did. There's a fear that guides her mixed with the determination I saw in her eyes all those years ago when she killed her ex husband. And that fear makes her reckless and makes both of us vulnerable.

And maybe I was wrong to goad her. Maybe I should've tried talking to her and put her demons at rest. Maybe I should stop playing games just to get the result I want, especially when it comes to my wife. But for that I need to know what scares her to this extent. Is it the fear of losing me? Losing our children? How could that be possible since she knows I would never allow that to happen, and I proved that to her time and time again.

"Talk to me," I say, pulling my seatbelt and ignoring the way my wife reves the engine.

I'm met with silence.

"Baby—"

"Do *not* baby me, Ian." Her voice is laced with venom, and I feel the poison dripping on my heart. "I'm not in the mood to argue."

"We've never argued." I scoff, waving my hand dismissively. "Ten years. Not a single argument."

"That's a lie and you know it."

"Do I?" My head turns abruptly looking at my wife. "Because I'm not sure what I know or what I don't anymore."

"We argued, Ian." She sounds exasperated. With me. And it's killing me. "We argued when you found out I killed Gabriel. And we argued even worse after that. We argued when I was pregnant with the twins. We argued when we were in Romania trying to keep our ghosts from haunting us only to create new ones to add to the collection. We argued for a lot of times."

"Not like this," I sound just as exasperated as she does. "Never like this."

The silence in the car is deafening, the tension so thick not even the sharpest knife could cut it. I feel it and I know she feels it too. I see it in the way her jaw ticks and in her bottom lip that's already bleeding from how much she bit it.

It's a battle of egos and of wills, but I'm not one to keep fighting these types of wars. Not with my wife. So I clear my throat before saying,

"I want to know what is it that torments you, pretty girl. And please don't say it's me. I might have contributed to it, but you and I both know that's not the case. So tell me." I lower my voice. "What is it that makes your heart bleed, and what can I do to make that wound form a scar?"

Her chin is trembling and tears are pooling in her eyes. I *hate* seeing her like this. Absolutely loathe it. But if we want to move past this, to sort out everything in our hearts and souls, we need to walk on this dark road.

"I—" she inhales sharply. "I think I lost myself along the way."

"Meaning?"

"I want to kill so, so many people, Ian," she whispers. "I can't seem to stop. I have all this," she waves her left hand chaotically, the diamond on her wedding band shining brightly in the otherwise dark car, "*rage*. It's building and boiling inside me more and more with every day that passes, and I'm starting to wonder if this is what a mother should feel."

"Baby—"

"Let me finish. Please, just let me finish."

I nod and stay silent, my head tilting to the side so I can see her better.

"I have all these thoughts running rampant in my head. That a mother shouldn't be a serial killer, but at the same time a good mother should do anything to protect her children. We have a daughter, Ian!" she says the last sentence louder, pushing the acceleration pedal even further. "We have a daughter and I have dreams about her going through what I did. Or worse."

"That could never happen." My hand instinctively goes to the collar of my shirt, pulling it hard so I can breathe. Because what my wife just told me made me feel like I'm suffocating.

I know I told her that could never happen, but I don't believe that. I just said it to reassure her. But deep down, I know that our Corbin could easily become a victim of an abuser. It just takes one wrong person to fall in love with and it all goes downhill from there. And no matter how we raise her, no matter how much we try to protect her, at the end of the day she'll be the only one to take care of herself once she grows up.

"And two boys," she continues, completely ignoring what I've just said. "Three innocent souls that are susceptible to going through all the horrendous things we did or even more. So I want to kill everyone who might hurt them before that actually happens. Is it immoral? Most probably. Am I going completely insane? Absolutely. But I can't control it, Ian. And I think the best thing to do is stop altogether because otherwise this thirst, this *need*, only grows and grows and fucking grows. Before we had the twins every kill satiated something in me. Like a junky who got their hit and for a while they're happy. But now I feel the exact opposite. I kill Larry and the next things I want is to see my children and make sure they're safe, have sex with you, and then go find the next Larry."

"So why did you get so upset with me?" I voice the question that's been haunting my mind for the past hours. "Just because I made a joke? Just because I tried to lighten the mood or make you see things for yourself? I've always tried to help you, Echo."

"I know." She nods swiftly. "I know, Ian. But I guess I can't tell right from wrong anymore. Because again, I have all these emotions running through my bloodstream and I'm losing control over them more and more with every day that passes."

"I need you to let me in, baby," I whisper, flinching when I'm met with silence.

I don't know what else to say. If she decides to shut me down for the first in her life, so be it. But this isn't the way we function. We've always been a well-oiled machine, a tandem dance taken to perfection. Suddenly, I don't feel like that anymore. And now I'm the one who has a spectrum of emotions that he can't handle.

"You *are* in," she finally says, and her voice—just her voice—soothes my soul and makes my demons scream less. "But if I don't know who I am anymore, how could you possibly be familiar with this place you are in?"

"Because I know you, Echo Beckett." Determination is dripping from my voice when I unfasten my seatbelt, grateful that we are finally home. "I know you better than you know yourself. And I know you're scared and vulnerable and raw now because you sense this shift inside you. I *know* that shift. That's what happens when you decide to bring small versions of yourself into this world. You change because it's not about you anymore. It's about innocent lives that you would sell your soul to the highest bidder for. I know that shift because I've felt it too."

A pensive look takes over her face, and I let her sit with that. I let her remember the times when I was going through the same thing as she is now. I had the same thoughts when Noah was born, but I reacted differently. I wasn't enraged, I was scared out of my mind that something would happen to her or to my boy. And because of that fear, I tortured the corpses of the people we killed just to make sure they were dead and stayed dead.

I was scared, yet my beautiful, strong woman is enraged. I've always said she's far better than I am from all the perspectives one might think of. And this is just proof that I'm right. Because instead of letting her dark thoughts scare her, she takes them and twists them, turning them into something productive and into something that helps us make this world a better place.

I know a lot of people disagree. I know according to the law we deserve to rot in jail. I know all of that, and I'm sure she knows it too. But we also know that at the end of the day, we are doing this world a service. And if before that was reason enough to cover our tracks and never become suspects in any of these murders, now we have more important reasons for that. Reasons made from our flesh. Reasons that have our blood circulating through their veins. Reasons created by our love for each other and the desire to bring more good people on this planet, to try and tip the scales in the direction of what we consider as decent.

Getting out of the car, I run towards her side, opening the door before kneeling next to her. The light on our porch is bright enough to allow me to see the tears pooling in her eyes and the way her nose is scrunching, the inner conflict she's going through bright as day.

"I think I know what I want, Ian," she whispers, turning her head in my direction. "I think I want to wait for them to grow up and teach them how to continue our legacy."

I feel my stomach churning when I hear her words, but I can't say she's completely wrong. Because no matter how much we do our best to protect them, there will come a day when they will need to protect themselves and—hopefully—each other.

"Do you want to teach our kids how to kill a man without leaving tracks?"

"I want them to learn everything you taught me. I want them to know that killing your abuser—hell, any abuser—is the right thing to do, consequences be damned. I want them to fight, Ian. I want our children to never allow others to step over them and their dignity, and I want them to punish the ones who even dare to dream of that."

"Okay." I nod, standing up and taking her hand, pulling her out of the car. "Okay, baby, let's do that."

And then she kisses me. The type of kisses that melts my heart and mends my soul, bending it to her will. The type of kiss that reassures me that everything will be alright. That come what may our small world we fought so hard to build will stay together. And if telling our children everything we did is the way to achieve that, then so fucking be it.

About the Author

More about this author:

Mira is a lover of loyalty, equality, watermelon, and Formula 1. Her Kindle is almost always next to her, and her notes are full of random thoughts she plans to put in her books.

She'd love nothing more than to connect with her readers, so make sure to follow her:

Instagram: @author.mira.raven

TikTok: @author.mira.raven

Or join her Facebook group where she promises to be more than active and give you snippets from her latest work in progress: Mira's Miracles

This is an extended epilogue of the Heartbreak series, so if you want to know the original story of Ian and Echo, you can start with The Heartbreak That Birthed Me (Heartbreak #1)

Wicked Devil Epilogue

By: Daniela Romero

Bonus Story
Roman's POV

About Wicked Devil

I'll do anything to protect her—even if it means losing myself.

When the man who hurt Allie escapes real justice, I make a deal with Andrés DeAnde, a dangerous ally with the power to make things right. It's messy, illegal, and could destroy me.

But Allie's worth it. Always.

For her, I'll cross every line and burn the world down. Because love isn't just a promise—it's vengeance.

Content Note:

This story contains themes of sexual assault, violence, and vigilante justice, including graphic depictions of physical harm. Reader discretion is advised.

Relationship type: M/F

Chapter One
Roman

"All rise for The Honorable Judge Mayhew."

Everyone in the room stands. Allie's hand is small in mine, and I squeeze her palm, letting her know I'm here. She squeezes back, her grip almost desperate. The judge walks into the room, his black robes billowing as he takes his seat behind the podium.

"You may be seated."

As we sit on the wooden bench, I pull Allie close, but she remains tense, her shoulders stiff, knee bouncing. I place a hand on her thigh, and she freezes. Her eyes meet mine, offering an apologetic smile.

I kiss her temple. "You good, vanilla?" I whisper.

She nods, but we both know it's a lie. That's okay. After today, she will be. I'll make sure of it.

The trial against Miguel has been grueling. He's not being charged for the rape, which infuriates me. But Pops is right—if Allie pressed charges, it'd be her word against his, with no evidence to back her claim. She never completed the rape kit at the hospital and refused to talk to the police once Janessa showed up. That decision still pisses me off, even if I understand her reasoning.

Janessa thought she was protecting Allie, sparing her from a flawed justice system. I get it, at least I try to. But it leaves a bitter taste in my mouth. Without the rape charge, the case against Miguel is cleaner: first-degree securities fraud, money laundering, and extortion. Each charge carries a minimum sentence of five years. He deserves much more, but with his plea deal, he's looking at six years, maybe less with good behavior.

I suck on my teeth, anger simmering beneath my calm exterior.

I glance at Allie. Her eyes are fixed on Miguel, who sits there smug and unrepentant. My blood boils, but I keep my cool. Allie needs me calm. I can punch a wall later. As the judge reads the sentence, Allie trembles beside me. I tighten my grip on her thigh, a silent reminder she's not alone. We brace for the verdict.

"Ten years, with the possibility of parole."

"Fuck," I curse under my breath.

Allie exhales shakily, her shoulders trembling. "Ten years," I mutter. It's not enough, but it's something. He didn't walk free.

"It's more than I expected," she confesses, her sad smile breaking my heart. "It's over."

It isn't, but I don't tell her that. "Yeah, vanilla. It's over." I press my lips to her temple, hugging her close. She's been through so much. Ten years feels like a slap on the wrist, especially with parole. But I have a backup plan. If all goes well, Miguel won't see the light of day again.

The courtroom empties. People file past with murmurs of approval or dissent. We wait until Miguel is led away in handcuffs before standing. My father might be the chief of police, but I've never cared for what happens after they bag the bad guy. It never feels like enough, and it's why I won't follow in his footsteps, despite my parents' wishes.

Allie stands on shaky legs, and I place my hand on her back, guiding her toward the exit. She's too lost in her thoughts to notice the lone man left in the room, who thankfully stays silent.

"I'm going to hit the restroom before we head out," I tell her, brushing a lock of hair from her face. "I'll meet you in the car?"

She nods, too drained to argue, and makes her way to the exit.

Once she's out of sight, I scan the courtroom. Andrés DeAnde stands in the same spot, his gaze narrowed and calculating. I wasn't sure he'd show up today, and I don't know if I'm anxious or relieved. Regardless, I need his help.

"Andrés," I say, approaching him.

"Roman," he replies, his voice curious. "I take it what you need has to do with today?"

I nod. "Ten years isn't enough."

Andrés leans back against the wall, hands in his pockets. "For money laundering and extortion? Seems sufficient."

"Ten years with parole. He'll be out in three."

Andrés quirks a brow. "Tell me why I should care?"

I inhale deeply. "Miguel raped Allie earlier this year. He wasn't charged, but he did it. Y este cabrón" —*this fucker*— "deserves to pay. She's your cousin. Tu sangre y tu familia." *Your blood and your family.* "That's why you should care."

Andrés stiffens, a menacing aura falling over him. For the first time, I sense just how dangerous he can be.

"Run that by me again," he demands.

"Miguel attacked Allie at SVH. My pops found her afterward. She refused the rape kit and didn't file charges. Her father's assistant convinced her to walk away."

"Esa maldita perra." *That fucking bitch.* He curses.

"I want him to pay," I tell him. "Can you help me with that?"

Andrés rubs his jaw, considering me. "What are you asking?"

"Whatever you're thinking, that's what I'm asking."

His eyes narrow further. I hadn't considered what to do if he refused.

"We can't have this conversation here."

"Alright. Where should we have it?"

"I'll text you the address. For now, go home. Take care of my cousin."

Chapter Two
Roman

I stare at the screen of my phone, my fingers drumming against my leg when the text finally arrives.

It's about damn time.

Andrés has kept me in the dark for six fucking days. I've been crawling out of my skin waiting for word from him.

"Everything okay?" Allie asks as she steps into the room, her eyes searching my face.

Smoothing out my expression, I slip my phone into my pocket and widen my stance. "Yeah. Dom's just bitching about shit with Kasey," I lie smoothly.

Allie rolls her eyes. "Those two are always at it. I don't know why Dominique doesn't just tell her how he feels already. They'd stop fighting if he admitted he wanted her, and she could tell him she feels the same."

I chuckle, a hollow sound. "Why don't you tell him that and let me know how the conversation goes."

She huffs out a laugh, and as soon as she's close enough, I tug her down onto my lap.

"Roman—" she laughs, pushing against my chest. I wrap my arms around her tighter, holding her until she finally relents.

"You're ridiculous," she mutters. "I was going to sit next to you."

"Not close enough," I grumble. She makes a sound of annoyance, but I know it's all for show. Allie sinks into my embrace, her body melting against my chest.

"How are you feeling today?" I press my nose into the crook of her neck, breathing her in. Cinnamon and vanilla. I'm fucking addicted to this girl.

Allie leans forward, but I tighten my arms around her. "Fine," she says. Her fingers trace the lines of the anchor tattoo on my hand. "It's just..." She hesitates. "I don't know." Her mouth curls into a frown, and I resist the urge to kiss it away, needing to hear her thoughts.

"I thought I'd feel different. Maybe happier or relieved, but..."

"I get that," I say softly. "Give it time. You'll get there."

"Maybe," she mutters, unconvinced.

With my thumb and forefinger, I turn her chin toward me and capture her lips with my own. She sighs into the kiss, her lips parting as some of the tension leaves her body. "It's going to take time for things to go back to normal," I remind her.

"I know," she grumbles. "I just want to be me again, you know? The old me that wasn't like this." Allie makes a frustrated noise in the back of her throat.

"I like this version of you," I tell her. "You're perfect. And he's behind bars. Give yourself a chance to let that sink in. He can't hurt you."

She nods and rests her head against my shoulder, her body curling into mine. "What about when he gets out?" she whispers, finally voicing her deepest fear.

"He won't," I say firmly.

She doesn't argue, but I already know what she's thinking. She's thinking that he will. That Miguel behind bars is only a temporary reprieve. She doesn't want to get comfortable. But she needs to. Because I've got her. I won't let anyone or anything hurt her again.

"What's on your agenda today?" she asks.

Running my hand up and down her thigh, I consider pushing my meeting with Andrés, but I know I can't. This might be my only shot. "I need to swing by the field. Coach wants to talk to me about next year," I tell her. "I won't be gone long. Do you want me to call one of the girls to—"

"No," she interrupts quickly, then more calmly says, "No. I'm okay. I don't need a babysitter."

Allie untangles herself from my hold and stands. I scowl, disliking the distance, but I wasn't lying when I said I needed to run by the field. It just isn't Coach I'll be meeting.

Chapter Three
Roman

He stands in the middle of the field, his back turned, eyes fixed on the goalposts. The empty expanse makes my skin prickle. The stillness of the stadium feels out of place for a meeting like this.

"Is this supposed to be more inconspicuous?" I ask as I approach.

Andrés turns to face me, a slight smirk on his lips.

"I'm not sure a guy like me and a suit meeting on a football field on a Saturday will go unnoticed."

He shrugs. "I don't care if people see us," he says. "I care if there are ears listening. And here," Andrés waves around the field, "there are none."

Fair point.

"So—"

"One moment," he interrupts. "We have one more arrival."

I follow his gaze and see a man walking across the field toward us. He's dressed similarly to Andrés in dark slacks and a white button-up shirt with the sleeves rolled up. He has the same dark brown hair and cold brown eyes. The closer he gets, the more their similarities become evident.

"A relative?" I ask.

"My brother," Andrés says. "Adrián," he introduces. "Adrián, this is Roman. Alejandra's..." he considers me. "What are you to our cousin? You're the boyfriend, right?"

I don't like the way he asks that, as if 'boyfriend' isn't sufficient. Maybe it isn't. We're young, but Allie is endgame. I won't rise to the bait.

"Yep," I tell him. "I'm the boyfriend. Nice to meet you."

I hold out my hand and shake Adrián's as he scrutinizes me.

"You're also the son of the chief of police in Sun Valley," he comments. "So, do you want to explain why you're asking my brother to commit a crime?"

I cock my head. I hadn't considered that angle.

"I'm not asking your brother to commit a crime," I tell him. "I'm asking him to help me commit one. I don't have the resources to get to Miguel now that he's behind bars. But I assume you do?"

The brothers exchange looks. "We might," Adrián hedges.

"Okay. That's all I need. If you can get me to him, or him to me, I can take it from there."

They don't look convinced. "You're what, eighteen?" Andrés asks.

"Nineteen." In another two weeks, but he doesn't need to know that. "Your point?"

"You've got your whole life ahead of you, kid," Andrés says. "Allie tells me you play ball. You want to go pro after college."

I nod. "That's the plan. But that doesn't change the fact that this needs to be done. Miguel needs to be put down. He was given a deal he didn't deserve, and I'm not going to sit back, waiting for my girl to fall apart when that fucker is inevitably set free."

Andrés rubs his chin. "There's no going back after something like this. Taking a life, no matter how deserved, it leaves a stain on the soul. One you can't wash away."

"I can handle it," I tell him.

Adrián chuckles beside him. "Me gusta este cabrón. Alejandra eligió bien." *I like this fucker. Alejandra chose well.*

My chest puffs up at his statement. I don't need their approval, but it doesn't hurt to have it.

"Sí, lo hizo. Pero él es joven. No sabe en lo que se está metiendo." *She did. But he's young. He doesn't know what he's getting into.*

Irritation prickles beneath my skin. He's talking about me like I'm not here.

"Te entiendo," I tell them. *I understand you.* "I don't care if you think I'm too young. I know exactly what I'm asking. Alejandra means everything to me. She's the air in my lungs and the blood in my veins. My heart beats for that girl, so will you help me or not?"

Both men sober as they consider my request.

"Sí," Andrés says. "We'll help."

"But there will be a price," Adrián adds.

"Name it."

Adrián chuckles. "It doesn't work that way," he says. "We help you, and when the time comes and we need a favor, you help us. Tú entiendes?" *Do you understand?*

Loud and clear, and I don't like it. But I'm not in a position to decline.

Jaw clenched tight, I nod. "Yeah. Okay."

"Good," Adrián says. "You'll meet a group of our men here," he hands me a card with a scribbled address. "Tomorrow night, 11:00 PM. Don't be late, and come alone."

"Your men?" I question with a frown as I look over the address, ignoring the anxious knot in my chest.

"Yes," Andrés repeats. "My men. Do you have a problem with that?"

Shaking my head, I tuck the card in my back pocket. I assumed Andrés would be there but this works just the same. "No. It's fine."

"Good. Now go home. Get your shit in order. Everything should go smoothly, but if it doesn't," he shrugs his shoulders, "it's always better to be prepared."

Chapter Four
Roman

I stand by the bed, watching Allie sleep. Her breathing is steady, her face relaxed. It kills me to leave her, but I have to do this. Bending down, I press a soft kiss to her forehead and whisper a silent promise that I'll keep her safe. She mumbles something in her sleep before rolling over, her shirt shifting to expose the smooth skin of her stomach. Need thrums through me, but there will be plenty of time for that once this is over.

Taking one last look at her, I leave our bedroom and slip silently through our home. Once outside, I move quickly through the quiet streets to my car. The drive to the address Adrián gave me is short but feels like an eternity. Less than two miles from the Sun Valley jail, it's an abandoned warehouse.

The building looms, dark and foreboding. Four of Andrés's men are already there, waiting for me outside. Each man is dressed similarly—dark denim paired with black sweaters. Parking my El Camino, I shove my hands into the pockets of my black hoodie and make my way over to them, ignoring the chill that runs down my spine as I near.

"Hola," one of them says. "Ven por aquí." *Come this way.*

I follow the man inside, keeping my head tucked low as the rest of the men follow behind me. Inside, I find a man bound to a metal chair. He's dressed in prison orange, his arms bound behind his back and his ankles tied to the front legs of the seat. There's a black sack over his head, but this has to be him.

My heart pounds, rage boiling beneath the surface. One of the men hands me a black and white skull mask and instructs me to put it on. "En caso de que lo dejes vivir." *In case you let him live.*

Not happening, but I slip on the mask anyway and thank him. "Gracias."

The mask is cold against my skin, a stark contrast to the fire burning inside me. When they yank the bag off Miguel's face, I finally see him for what he is—a pitiful, broken man. Tears streak down his cheeks, mingling with the snot running from his nose. The smug arrogance is gone, replaced by raw, naked fear.

"It's him," I say, my voice low and deadly.

"What's happening?" Miguel sputters. "Who are you? Why am I here?"

I ignore his questions.

The man who handed me the mask steps forward. "You have ten minutes to do what needs to be done. After that, we have to return him to the jail where his body can be found."

"Body?" Miguel jerks in his seat. "What the fuck are you talking about?" He pulls at his restraints, but whoever strapped him down did one hell of a job because Miguel can hardly move.

"Thank you," I tell the man, grateful for his help. He and the others keep their masks in place as they walk away, giving me privacy to handle this. But before the last of them reaches the door, he turns and makes a sound, drawing my attention.

"Here." He throws something in my direction, and on instinct, I reach up to catch it. "When you're done with your fists, you can use this to finish the job."

I look down at my hands and take in the smooth metal folding knife. Flicking it open, I admire the sharpness of the blade. This will do.

I thank them with a curt nod and return my focus to Miguel. He stares at me with wide eyes, confusion and fear mingling in his gaze.

"Do you know why you're here?" I ask, my voice dripping with menace as I step closer. "You should. You hurt someone I care about. It's only fair that in return, I hurt you."

Miguel struggles against his bonds, but it's no use. Without giving him the chance to brace for it, I swing my fist, and it connects with his jaw, the impact sending a jolt up my arm. Pain blooms, but it's nothing compared to the satisfaction of hearing his pained cry for help.

Drawing back, I punch him again. This time, my fist connects with his nose. Bone crunches and blood pours down his face.

"Whatever you think I did—"

I strike him again and again, not giving him a chance to speak. "You deserve this," I tell him. "You deserve this and so much worse."

Each punch is cathartic, a release of all my pent-up rage. This man hurt the one person who is precious to me. He broke her spirit. He took away her safety. He made her feel weak and helpless. Fuck. He made me feel helpless. I couldn't fix what he did. I couldn't take away her pain.

I think of what Allie was like when it first happened. How withdrawn she became. How she was suddenly afraid of even the people she knew. People she was friends with. Like Dom and Emilio and even me. It took months for Allie to come out of her shell. For her to smile again. For her to feel safe.

And this asshole is the reason behind it.

Fuck him. Rotting in a prison cell is too good for him. He needs to rot in hell.

I channel every ugly emotion swirling inside of me into every blow, again and again, until my hand goes numb and my knuckles are split and bleeding.

A sharp whistle draws my attention, and I look over my shoulder.

One of the men makes a motion with his finger, signaling me to wrap it up. Chest heaving, I stumble back on my feet.

Miguel's face is a mess of blood and bruises, but I'm not done. Not yet.

"Please," he sputters, his teeth stained in blood. "Have mercy."

I pull the knife from my pocket, the blade glinting in the dim light. He whimpers, a pitiful sound that only fuels my determination.

"Mercy is ending your pathetic life before making you suffer the same pain you've inflicted on others," I snap, plunging the knife into his side. My heartbeat pounds in my ears, my vision narrowing to the sight of my own hand and the blade now buried in Miguel's stomach.

His scream echoes through the empty warehouse, and I grit my teeth. Finish this.

I twist the blade, and Miguel cries out again, this time softer. His chest heaves at first, but as the seconds pass, his breathing begins to slow. I tear the knife out, and he gasps as I step back, the knife now dripping at my side.

Andrés's men return, their expressions hidden behind their masks. They look at Miguel's unmoving form and nod in approval. One of them claps a hand on my shoulder. "You finished it," he says, his tone pleasantly surprised. "Good for you."

I nod, feeling a grim sense of satisfaction. It's over. This wasn't the justice my girl deserved, but I'll settle for vengeance.

As two of the men carry Miguel away, the other two lead me to a large barrel with a fire burning bright inside of it. "Strip and burn your clothes here," one of them says. The other holds up a small bundle of items. "Toss it all in, and we'll make sure no evidence remains while our guys return Miguel to where he belongs."

Swallowing hard, I do what he says, tearing my shirt and hoodie over my head and tossing them into the waiting flames along with the skull mask. Kicking off my sneakers, my jeans are next.

"Shoes too," the other man says.

Gritting my teeth, I toss those in as well along with my socks until all that I'm left in are my black boxer briefs. "Here." He opens a container of wet wipes and hands them to me one at a time. I scrub the blood from between my fingers and hiss at the sting of alcohol against my split skin. "Shower when you get home. Be thorough."

I nod, and with my hands as clean as they're going to get, I accept the small bundle of clothes and slide into a pair of unfamiliar sweatpants and a gray t-shirt that's a size too small. As soon as I'm dressed, one of the guys heads to his waiting vehicle. He returns with bottles of bleach in either hand and starts pouring it on the ground, both on and around the chair Miguel was previously tied to.

"Go home," the other says to me. "We've got it from here."

Swallowing hard, I thank them one last time and walk away. Back to the waiting arms of my girl. The one place I belong.

About the Author

Daniela Romero is a USA Today and Wall Street bestselling author and the owner of Baddies, an indie book shop and monthly book box. You can learn more by visiting her website www.daniela-romero.com or check out her shop www.baddiesbookshop.com for signed copies of her books.

The Mafia's Queen: Uprising

By: E.D Crowe

About The Mafia's Queen: Uprising

At age five, I learned my father was a ruthless clan leader in the Irish Mob.

At age eight, I learned I was his heir. Only he never wanted me, a *girl*, to take his place.

At age thirteen, he gave me to his second-in-command as his future wife. I was made to endure unspeakable acts and forced to bear it with gratitude. I am, after all, just a *girl*.

Now, at twenty, I'm taking back my control. Taking back my freedom. My power.

I never planned on Killian Linwood getting in the way. I never planned on letting him steal the key to my heart. But he took it anyway—and he's determined to keep me, whether I want him to or not.

First, I'll burn this clan down to ashes, let the smoke clear, and remake it into my image.

For I am its Queen. And this is *my* throne.

Content Note:

This story has a Happy for Now (HFN) ending. Both main characters have questionable morals (varying ranges of grey to black) with complicated reactions to intense circumstances. This is not a happy world and they react accordingly. Questionable consent, off-page rape of a minor by the villain are expressly referenced and mentioned, murder, blood play, organized crime hierarchy, descriptive sexual acts, trauma, gore, hurt/comfort with snark and violence occur within. Mature content. For readers 18 & older.

Relationship type: M/F with mentions of previous same-sex couplings.

Chapter One
Maeve

7 years ago

I *hate that fireplace.*

It's a monstrous black brick fireplace with deep green tile, surrounded by dark walls. The flames lick at the edges, scorching it with tarnished soot. The dark stained wood of the mantle is nearly black against the wallpapered walls of green forests and golden accents, of dancing nymphs and flying birds.

This place is a spot of power in my home. In my *father's* home.

This office is the bane of my existence. It's where my father rules his empire, it's where I sit and listen to his decrees.

A decree that he's now going to give to me.

I shouldn't have been given one, not yet. Decrees are given at twenty-one to those in the clan; if you wanted to stay within the family, then you were given a place to fit. That could be as simple as what your job in the clan would be, like enforcer or soldier, or what the Captain needed from you.

My younger sister Collins will get her decree at twenty-one, just like everyone else. My father has always envisioned her as the clan doctor, and that's what he'll tell her on the eve of her birthday. My youngest sister Sloane will be told to marry and produce children, her relationship leveraged as a way to strengthen the family. As for my brother Briar, though still an infant, he'll likely be groomed to serve as hired muscle or a hitman. Most of the men born into the clan are used the same way.

That leaves me, the heir, to know of my fate.

Once the decree is leveled, it's either take it with gratitude or walk away from the family. There is little else I can do.

I'm thirteen. I can't go anywhere. This is my home, my legacy. Whatever my father has planned, I have no choice but to follow through.

Leaning back into his chair, my father is a massive man. Dark locks, the same shade as my own, with muddy, beady eyes. His hands are like mallets, and his body is thick like a tree trunk. His pale cheeks are ruddy, his Irish complexion still not used to the cold of Boston during the winter.

In two weeks, I'll be fourteen. I wonder if he even remembers.

My father is a good businessman, running his clan with an iron fist. But he's a shitty father.

Puffing on his cigar, I don't turn as the door behind me opens and then closes quietly. It could be anyone. Looking away from my father is a death sentence, though. He expects loyalty at all times. Always from me.

A body moves to perch itself on to my father's massive desk. It's just as dark as the room, with a cloud of smoke lingering above us. I hate the smell but it isn't my home. It's *his*. Always his.

Locking eyes with Michael Langston, my father's second-in-command, I stop the urge to recoil. Michael is a normal fixture in my father's rebuilt castle, a mockery to the ones that litter the Irish coasts. He's always lurking around, enjoying my father's best wine or his expensive cigars. What he does for my father is anyone's guess; he doesn't run the product, he doesn't do the books, and he certainly doesn't kill the competition.

I would know. Because I do it.

Thirteen years old and I have already taken a life. I've done all sorts of terrible things for this clan.

I am, after all, my father's daughter.

When Michael continues to stare at me, I turn my gaze to my father, shooting him an annoyed glare. I would never openly disagree with him, but here, in his office, I am as stubborn as him. He knows I have no fear of him.

Soon, I'll replace him on this throne and control the clan that belongs to me. With his death, I'll be Captain.

"Well?" I drawl. "I'm here. What did you want?"

He stubs out the cigar. "It's time for you to know your place in the clan."

I brace myself. My father is not a fan of women; he's made that abundantly clear. I had to work harder, faster, be more ruthless than anyone else in his crew in order to get just a scrap of admiration. But this is my birthright.

He's naming me as his heir. *Finally.*

Nodding, I plant my feet shoulder-width apart, bracing myself as if readying for battle. My leather jacket is a bit too big for my slender body, my combat boots too scuffed to belong to a mafia princess. But I don't rely on my father to buy me things. I never do.

My shoulders tense as he stands. Ferguson O'Brien dwarfs me easily.

"You are to be betrothed."

The wind rushes from my lips silently. My body locks, fight or flight mode activating as adrenaline surges through my veins.

"Betrothed?" I could not have heard him right.

Sloane was to be married. Collins was to be a doctor. Briar was to be a soldier.

I'm supposed to be Queen.

"Yes." My father claps Michael on his shoulder in a show of some familiarity. They're the same age, having come to America from Ireland decades ago.

Michael chews on the butt of his cigar and his blue eyes turn malicious.

Something is niggling at me, in the back of my head, a nail poking a festering wound. I need to pay attention here. But my focus is entirely on my father. On the indescribable feeling of *wrong*.

Swallowing, my hands fist at my sides. *Breathe.* "And what of my birthright?" The words sound hollow.

Ferguson snorts. "Birthright?" He shakes his head, temples barely grey. "Your birthright is what I tell you it is."

"I'm your oldest. Your *heir*," I stress the word. *Heir*. Birthright. This clan is *mine*.

If not, why was I on the streets, selling drugs? Why did I know what it was like to take a life, hands warm from freshly spilled blood? What was the point of it all if he's just going to sell me to the highest bidder?

"You are my heir," he says slowly. "But you will never lead this clan, Maeve. There is no way a woman could be what this clan needs at its head."

I rear back as if struck. He thinks, because of what was between my legs, that I can't rule effectively. That I can't be the person who strikes fear into the men of this clan, that I cannot wield my power like an untouchable *man*.

How very fucking wrong he is.

"Instead, the clan will continue in our name, through you." He gestures to my body, still developing into girlhood. I haven't even started my period yet, and he's already discussing the use of my uterus to this family.

"You're going to give the clan to an outsider." Someone who is not an O'Brien.

My father spent decades building this clan into the powerhouse it was now. We have two rivals in Boston who we fight on the regular for territory. We went from nothing to *something* and he just wants to give it away.

He claps Michael again. "Not an outsider. To someone in the family."

My green eyes land on Michael and everything goes eerily still.

Him. My father is giving me to *him*.

Michael, who my little sisters call Uncle Mike. The man who my father goes to strip clubs with and who pays prostitutes to lower themselves to their knees for him. The man has a beer belly and usually wears a stained white shirt and dirty jeans. He's balding with yellow teeth and gives me the absolute worst creeps.

He's to be my husband.

I feel sick.

"No." I shake my head. "*No.*"

Ferguson grabs my upper arm, hauling me close. At his nearness, I can see the flecks of gold in his brown eyes—the same ones I have—and I can feel his power in his hands. One flick of his wrist and he can break my thin arm without a second thought.

"Yes," he hisses. "You will marry Michael. You will be a good, *obedient* wife to him and produce heirs to our clan. And you will do it all with a fucking smile on your face. That is my decree. Or," he breaks off, tossing me back. My feet stumble over the stationary chair I had refused to sit in. "You could leave, Maeve. Walk away. But I will say that if you do, someone will still be Michael's wife."

"Someone?" I lick my dry lips, glancing from his second to him. "Who?"

My father shrugs. "I have two other daughters. They're more than willing to serve the clan, their father, without question."

On the outside, I'm a mask of cold disinterest. Inside, my chest feels as if it's been sliced open with a rusted blade.

If I don't take his decree, he'll impose it on one of my sisters. My beautiful, bright, sisters who don't know an ounce of darkness in this world. Because I've kept it from them, let them live ignorant lives. I took the hits so they could thrive.

My father would shackle one of them to this monster before me and at their ages, they would agree. Just to make Ferguson happy.

I can't let that happen. I can't let my father break them. Not like how he broke me.

Lifting my chin, I snarl at them both, "Fine. I accept your decree."

It's better if it's me, instead of them. I can handle the abuse, the shame.

Because even though Michael would control me, I'm not done fighting.

Once I have a plan, I'll take back my power and my throne from them both.

Chapter Two
Killian

4 years ago

"Rough night?" I ask, teasing slightly.

Maeve looks up at me, bored.

There are dark circles under her eyes and her dark dripping strands fall across her oversized band tee. I don't have the heart to tell her that it's mine. Probably a mix-up from the housekeeper.

I came into the O'Brien clan at fourteen years old. At the time, Maeve was barely thirteen and yet, she was a legend on the streets. Cold, ruthless, she ran the boys better than men four times her age.

Her father took me in, gave me a bed and hot food. More than I had on the streets, where he found me, covered in some guy's blood. It was a justified kill; the man had tried to take from another girl and as much as I didn't care, I did.

Ferguson began to train me from that night on. I could defend myself, but he taught me what it took to live in this life, to be as cruel as those who would take from you. I became a protégé of sorts to the Captain. I gladly lapped up the attention and the status in his ranks.

Maeve and I got on as well as fire and gasoline.

Now, at sixteen, she was a powerhouse in her own right. The heir to a lucrative business, Maeve was poised to take over for her father. She ran the books, knew of all the shipments and could control all the main players without breaking a sweat. She was good with a gun but better with a knife.

I would never tell her this, but she scared me a little.

Maeve didn't like me and I didn't really care. She was a rival, one who I knew intimately well. I knew how she took her coffee. I knew her favorite poet. I knew her favorite bug. I made it my life's work to know Maeve O'Brien.

"Something like that," she deadpans, flipping a page in her book. A steaming mug of coffee sits at her elbow and the early morning light filters into the kitchen, highlighting her big green eyes. They look like twin emeralds, sitting in a pale, elfish face.

I see the slice in her cheek as she moves, the purple imprints along her long neck.

Fingerprints.

Someone grabbed her neck—a neck no one should have been touching.

Going to the fridge, I wrap a towel around some ice and hold it to her neck. She winces and I can't tell if it's from pain or fear.

Maeve doesn't fear anything. She never has; she certainly never fears me like she should. Whatever she experienced has left a lasting impression.

I shouldn't care. She's my childhood rival, someone I work to unnerve. Do you know how hard it is to work at every single skill because a girl younger than you is just better, naturally?

A better shot. A better leader. Better at everything.

But I do. We have an uneasy competitive relationship. And she hates me for usurping her place.

At least, I think she does. She did threaten me the first night I showed up. But that's just Maeve.

This is new for me, offering to help.

She takes the towel, pulling away from me. My hand hovers, not sure I should move away just yet.

Maeve has been nothing but a hindrance since I got here and yet...

I hate seeing the haunted look in her eyes. It's far from the calculating heir I've watched grow over the years.

"Anything you want to tell me, Princess?"

She glares, but it's lacking its fire. Maeve hates the nickname, and I learned early on that the best way to unnerve her is to piss her off.

After all, she's the heir to a king in this world. Princess seems fitting.

"No."

I tsk, rocking back on my heels. I run a hand through my dark locks, smirking as her eyes narrow.

"That's not very nice." I gesture to the towel. "And even after I tried to help."

"I never asked for your help, Killian." She stands, throwing the towel back at me. Ice scatters all over the white tiled floor. "Stay out of it."

My smirk just grows at her irritation. Pissing Maeve off is an art form that I enjoy too much to be healthy.

Instead, I wink. "As you wish. But..." I lick my lips, watching as her eyes linger on my tongue. "You might want to ice that down. Only one person is allowed to wring that pretty little neck, and it's not some guy you met on the street."

She knows I'm teasing, but her cheeks flush. "Fuck off."

Maeve shoves past me and I inhale her violet and juniper scent like it'll give me strength. Years ago, Maeve was my rival in so many ways.

Now I can't stop the rage from filling my chest at someone hurting her.

Chapter Three
Maeve

2 years ago

I whimper against the grinding of my aching ribs.

Ribs I'm pretty sure Michael broke earlier that day.

I'm eighteen, far from the stubborn thirteen-year-old my father gave to his best friend. Now I'm considered a woman, and forced to endure unspeakable acts as is my place in this world.

Unfortunately for my future husband, I don't go without a fight.

Today is just another endless day where Michael acts like he owns my body. For my refusal, he stomped my ribs and crushed my left hand. I'm right-handed, but I shoot better with my left so this is an annoyance at best.

He knew what he was doing when he aimed. It's not enough to take my body, he's trying to break my soul.

Leaning back on the white suede couch, I pull my black shirt up over my stomach, seeing the first signs of bruising around my sides. If they're not broken, they are certainly bruised.

Fuck, it hurts. I can barely breathe.

"We have to stop meeting like this."

I groan, even though I don't want to. Any bit of movement kills.

Killian leans against the doorway, a black bag at his feet.

I shoot him a dark look. "Don't you have a flight to catch?" I'm not bitter about his ability to leave the house. His freedom to go about his life, killing in far off exotic locations.

Because that's what Killian was trained to do. He's a reaper, a hitman, and he's damn good at it.

I am desperately, terribly bitter.

After my decree, my father forbade me from leaving the state. I was expected to be a good, *obedient* wife to Michael. That meant serving him in ways only a wife should and not traveling like Killian.

Killian, the boy who my father took off the street, who he allowed into our home. The boy who took my spot. Once Killian was here, I became obsolete.

I try turning to ignore the reaper but I wince, pain radiating through my torso. *Definitely bruised.*

Dropping to the spot next to me, Killian tugs at the hem of my shirt. "Let me see."

"Fuck you," I growl. This is a dance we've done before; Killian finds me broken and heals me. It's not something I particularly like.

This means vulnerability. And I can't be vulnerable in this life.

I lean away from his touch, but I don't get far. Everything hurts too much for me to actually do anything. Black spots dance in my vision and the world turns on its side.

Killian is on me before I can argue, yanking my shirt high.

He sucks in a deep breath.

Those cold black eyes shift from my face to my bandaged hand, then to my exposed ribs.

I see the flash of anger before he smothers it.

"What happened?"

I shake my head. "Nothing." I lie.

Killian is my rival for my father's affection, the son he wished he had with his first—the son he wishes he still had.

He'd use this against me. Tell my father. Tease me for it. Hell, he might even judge me.

I carry enough shame; I don't need Killian Linwood adding to it.

He sits next to me, ignoring my protest as he lifts my shirt to inspect me closer. He pokes my side, and I yelp in pain before I can control it.

Probably cracked. Dammit.

"Someone used you as a punching bag, Princess."

Glaring, I kick out with my boot-covered foot. The reaper easily bats it away with his shin. "Don't fucking call me that."

Leveling me a bored look, Killian pokes my ribs, earning a harsh shriek of pain for his effort. He smirks. "No."

Digging into his bag, the reaper pulls out wraps and metal clasps.

He doesn't look remorseful as he gestures to my ribs. "I'll need to wrap them."

Lifting my chin, I glare at him. "I can handle it."

"I have no doubt about that, Princess."

Adjusting my shirt under my bra, Killian begins to tightly wrap my ribs, keeping me stable with the other. I bite my bottom lip to keep from screaming. The pain is torture.

Killian works in silence, his eyes trained on my torso. Gone is the boy from his youth, emancipated and scrappy. Now, Kilian is nineteen, tall and strong. He reminds me of a sitting viper, with his raven-colored messy locks and almond black eyes. No light enters them; they're as soulless as the night.

Right now, though, he looks downright murderous as he finishes my ribs.

"Going to tell me what happened?"

"No," I snap, earning a harsh chuckle from the man in front of me.

"Of course not." His smirk is hollow. I never tell him where the wounds come from, but he always asks.

It annoys him. Years of being in the same house as him and I know him better than I know myself.

Once he's done, he clasps the ends, pulling my shirt down with a harder touch than necessary. My body jerks forward, and pain flares along my ribs.

Fucking prick.

"Simon will need to see these."

Swallowing, I nod. The clan doctor won't be able to do anything. Michael will just break me again and again. This is the decree I decided to take at thirteen.

I plan on getting out of this arrangement soon. Killian doesn't need to know about it, though.

Standing, I feel his hand whip out, grabbing my wrist.

In that simple act, I know a few things for certain.

One, Killian is powerful. His touch is enough to keep me incapacitated. No matter that I am his equal, that I have a knife strapped to my thigh and can slice his throat, I know he could easily overpower me.

And two, the look in his eyes makes my stomach drop.

Fear, pain, and rage all simmer in those cold eyes turning them into burning coals.

"Tell me who did this, Maeve."

Licking my lips, I shrug. "Why? It's already done. Let it go, Killian." I twist out of his hold, relief singing through me as I put distance between me and the reaper. "Goodnight."

"Goodnight, Princess." Those emotions are gone from his face and all that stares back at me is the face of a killer.

And strangely, I feel comforted by it.

Chapter Four
Killian

1 year ago

She's bleeding again.

She thinks I don't see it, all of it, but I do.

Her lip is split, her eye bruised. I see the blood seeping through the thin white shirt. Her lacy black bra underneath catches my attention, but I focus on the red.

"If I didn't know any better, I'd think you were in an underground fight club."

My words startle her, but she tenses when we meet eyes in the mirror—big, swimming green eyes that could double as uncut emeralds. Breathtaking, haunted.

I smirk, leaning against the doorway. "Tell me you at least won."

She throws the discolored rag into the sink. I see blood still coating her chin, her chest. Someone got her nose good.

This isn't the first time I've seen her bleeding and broken. Certainly not the second, either.

Dozens of times, I've seen this: Maeve injured from something she won't tell me about. It's always when I'm leaving. Tonight, I went looking for her, just to make sure she was still alive. She stopped caring for her wounds in the common areas leaving me to chase her.

Much like her, the bedroom is a dark fortress of gothic books, pictures, and taxidermized bugs. She's always had this beautifully dark, poetic side, a part of her where I somehow felt oddly at home. Her darkness is like mine; there, under the surface, ready to take us under if allowed.

But we fight it back, give it just a little taste with every heinous act in this life, enough to keep it happy. Enough to let us live without succumbing to it entirely.

"Get out," she demands, throwing her hair over her head. A few dark strands cup her sharp jaw.

Ignoring her, I grab the rag. "Here. Sit." I push her toward the toilet.

She stares at me, glaring. Maeve isn't the most trusting, and she's injured. She'll strike out like a scared, cornered animal if I push too much. Something she's done on more than one occasion.

Oh, well, I've always been a little off. Her fight is as intoxicating as the drugs her father pushes.

"Get the fuck out of my room, Killian."

I cross my arms, eyes daring her. "No."

She turns, readying a punch. I see it coming. Before she can make contact, my hand goes to her throat and the other locks her arms down at her sides.

"Easy, Maeve. I'm not here to fight."

"Could have fooled me," she spits. She is all hellfire and rage and I lap it up. She is a sight.

Shoving her onto the toilet, I narrow my eyes.

"Shirt. Off," I command. She snorts, crossing her arms defiantly.

I see the wince. Her back is soaked red, damaged flesh pulling with each movement. How much more of this can she endure? If she doesn't listen, she'll get an infection.

"So you can see me in my bra?" She shakes her head. "Not happening."

Lowering to my knees, I part her thighs, positioning between them.

She tries to bar my entrance, but we both know I'm stronger. My fingers dig into her legs, and she hisses out a curse, relenting.

She's nineteen and I'm barely twenty. This isn't exactly the best position to be caught in. Hell, I should really hit up a few of the clan cousins who are so keen to share my bed. Keith has always been willing, and Angie has been begging for just one night. At least it'd kill some of this coiled tension inside me whenever Maeve is around.

But I'm drawn to her, always have been. Even when I thought of her only as a rival.

"I could take it off you myself, Princess." My voice has dropped, and I see the reaction—the goosebumps, licking her bottom lip, the intrigue in her eyes even as the pain masks it. "I thought I'd at least give you the chance."

"You wouldn't..." Her eyes narrow.

My smirk grows into something sinister. "Oh, I most certainly would." Gladly. Anything to help her.

Biting her bottom lip, she wrestles with her decision. It's a brief moment, and then she whips the shirt off, tossing it over my head. Better to get it done and over with. "Happy?"

Exceedingly so. The lacy black bra is a bare scrap of fabric holding her full chest. Her dusty nipples pucker just out of reach.

For being so petite, Maeve's body is meant for sin.

Gulping, I focus on my task. She's the heir and I'm a reaper, I have to remind myself. This isn't my place. Looking at her would be just wrong.

Even if a pretty blush has covered her cheeks and her green eyes are bleeding black with desire.

Clearing my throat, I start cleaning the blood around her collarbone.

"So. Did you win?" I ask, voice tight. I keep my fingers from touching her skin. If I do, I won't be able to stop.

A simple touch, and I'd be a goner—if I wasn't already.

I'm here to heal her, that's all, I remind myself. Anything more wouldn't be fair, not in her current condition.

"Win what?" She's looking over my shoulder, avoiding my eyes.

"The fight." There's a lot of blood.

I love how it paints her skin, makes her seem dangerous and forbidden, the bright red against the pale white of her skin, like a blemished rose in the snow. It's beautiful.

She's beautiful.

It's been a long time since Maeve has only been my rival. A very long time.

She shoots me a glare. "I'm alive, aren't I?"

I chuckle darkly. "A good standard to judge winning by, Princess." I move her to the side, cleaning her back. It's sliced to hell. "Someone use a knife?"

Her body stills just long enough for me to look back at her.

She tries to play it off, but her foot taps. A sure sign she's uncomfortable. She's done it since we were kids.

"Yes."

"Did you disarm them?"

She glares. "Don't patronize me."

The marks on her back are long, superficial, as if they just wanted to see her skin break. Someone wanted to hurt her, make her suffer.

Dark fury rolls through me, but I focus on cleaning her wounds. There's only one person who should be allowed to mark her skin and that someone is *me*. As dark as the thought is, it feels right.

When the blood stops, I put on creams and gauzes, intent on covering her as much as possible. It's my way of making sure no one else sees her like I have.

I am a reaper, but I am also the one person allowed to heal the great Maeve O'Brien.

When she's done, she pointedly sits back, letting me have my fill of her. She's all pale skin, body covered in various bruises and cuts from a hard life running drugs, from beating men three times her size, from torture and mayhem.

Old scars, lines that have been broken into her body, glow under the harsh bathroom lights.

Yet, she is the most incredible creature I've ever seen.

Her eyebrow raises. "Need something, Killian?"

This vixen is going to be the death of me.

Standing to my full height, I swipe something from the floor, running the opposite hand through my roguish hair.

"You should rest." I throw the rag into her trash, ignoring the jerking at my crotch. She's not the one for me. What can I offer the heir to an Irish clan?

Nothing.

Tell that to my body.

Because who wouldn't want her? She's a warrior goddess meant for slaying and loving under bloodred skies.

I exit her private suite, inhaling her dark violet and juniper scent.

I shove the bloody shirt into the bag I left in the hall, knowing that this obsession with her wasn't going to end any time soon.

Chapter Five
Maeve

Present day

On the eve of a clan member's twenty-first birthday, they're given a decree.

I was given my decree at thirteen.

Now, I stand in my room, staring at the white wedding dress hanging in my closet, fear and rage holding on with an icy claw into my chest.

I'm to be married on my twenty-first birthday. *Tomorrow.*

I don't bother to plead to my father to change his mind. He and I have very little in common but our stubbornness is the same. He won't bend and he won't yield. But neither will I.

So, I'll show him the daughter he created. The monster I became to survive the hell he put me in.

Dressed in a short red leather skirt, I tug the black corset top into place. My full lips are painted a deep burgundy, and my dark locks are curled down my back.

I even stole a pair of Sloane's designer red heels, the arches so sharp I have to pray to whatever God will listen not to let me fall on my ass.

Ferguson might have sold me to Michael, but I'm not going without a fight.

This is my life, my clan, my power.

Slipping a knife into my thigh holster, I put another between my breasts. A gun would attract attention, but a knife I can hide.

There's a brief moment of pause. Doing this, going through with this, would be close to clan suicide. I would put a target on my back, risk the wrath of my father in exchange for my freedom.

I'll gladly risk it.

Exiting my bedroom, I turn to the grand staircase. My sisters each have a wing on the second floor, whereas I have one on the third. Even now, I realize my father has been separating me from the family, so as not to allow me the opportunity to lead. My sisters were allowed to be children, allowed to experience love whereas I was stuck in serving his second. My only existence was to populate the next generation of the clan because of when I was born.

I'm not going to be that person. That is not my future.

What I don't expect to find is Killian.

He takes in my appearance, all the way down to the sharp heels, and dark rage contorts his handsome face. His sharp features are twisted, the blacks of his eyes so dark, not one flicker of light enters them. He looks possessed.

This is the face of the infamous killer. This is the man everyone is afraid of.

"Where are you going, Princess?" He rakes his eyes over me again. It feels like a physical touch, making my nipples pebble, my nerves stand on end.

The entire house is empty, save for me, Michael, and now the reaper. I didn't expect him home, not after traveling so many days this month.

The air crackles with tension. It's also been there between us.

This need pulsates and throbs whenever we're alone. It simmers just under the surface, begging to be released.

Shifting, I move to the hallway. "Somewhere."

Killian is on my heels. "Anyone I know?" There's an edge to his words. I ignore it. If I think too hard, I'll lose my focus.

I can only focus on my plan. My revenge. My freedom.

"Not now, Killian." I stop at the hallway, facing where Michael's room lies. "Feel free to go. I forgot something."

Killian steps into my space. I inhale, breasts pushing into his chest, his body heat scorching me.

He's death in human form—dark tight sweater, dark jeans that hang low on his hips, a pair of black combat books that make him even taller. His inked hands clench at his sides, as if trying to halt the urge to grab me.

Under his collar, there's more ink, just asking for a touch.

I want him. I want to feel him close, his skin against mine, his hands in my hair, kissing his lips. Every single inch of his body I want pressed to mine in the most intimate of ways. I need it like I need air.

At some point, my annoyance and anger at the reaper turned into something hotter, more wicked. It could have been the many times he healed me and stitched me back together. It could have been when he left me gifts before leaving the mansion—simple treasures like drawings he would doodle in a notepad before departing in the night.

Or it could be because I see that inner darkness in him. The same one that lives inside my chest, that's festered and grown with every day I ignore it. The darkness that begs me to release it onto my enemies, to scorch the earth for anyone daring to hurt me.

I feel the same urge inside Killian, an unhinged deadly presence that he can barely control. Control that seems to snap and break in my presence.

Licking my lips, I see his attention on my mouth.

"Killian."

Slowly, he drags his black eyes up, and what I see steals my breath.

So many emotions. Lust, rage, possession. Everything I've ever wanted from him shines at me in those endless depths.

"Who is it, Maeve?" His words are rough, pained. "Give me a name."

I swallow. "There's no one."

"No one," he echoes.

He looks down again, rubbing his bottom lip with his thumb.

"If you were mine, I'd never let you out of the house like this," he whispers, a hand curling around my throat, as if to hold me closer.

My stomach drops.

Another restriction. Another man who thinks he can control me.

I long for freedom, for the power, for my control of this clan. This is what I'm fighting for, what I survived for. Another man is not going to keep me from achieving it.

"Because you don't want others to see me like this?" I sound bitter.

He smirks, and it's positively devilish. "Because I wouldn't be able to keep my hands off you long enough to let you leave." His lips brush mine, and sparks ignite over my skin. I almost whimper. "Let them look, Princess. I'll pluck out their eyes, rip out their throats, and then fuck you on top of their corpses. Because you'd be *mine*."

Wetness coats my panties, causing me to shift uncomfortably. Killian's words should not be turning me on, but it figures his dark unhinged fantasies would stir something in me.

I live in the dark, embracing the evil that thrives there. Killian does the same. We are two broken souls who took the dark and made it ours.

I wish I could forget my plans and climb into that fantasy, cling to Killian's bones and make my home in his heart.

But I have a plan and I need to follow it through.

"Killian..."

"Whoever it is, will pale in comparison to me, Maeve. I promise you that." His fingers flex at my neck, pulling me close.

Without warning, we shift, and he wraps a lean arm around my back, slamming us into the wall. The force pushes me against him, and he cages me to the wall, one long leg parting my thighs to hold me captive.

This is the first time I've ever felt happy to be caught. Killian's weight feels too good to fight, his knee sending waves of friction all over my body. I gasp as he leans closer, rubbing just enough to heat my skin.

He inhales at my neck, scenting me. "Fuck, Maeve. You don't know how long I've wanted this. Your legs wrapped around my hips. I bet you are a fucking sight when you come."

"I don't—" He bites my neck, making me moan at the spike of pain, even as his knee moves to offset the sting. This is escalating fast, and I don't want it to stop. "I've never done that."

He chuckles and licks at his bite mark. Ownership—that's what this is. He's marking me as his. "Then you're fucking a boy. If you were mine, you'd be screaming my name all night."

I want to give in. My body has always belonged to someone, and now, I want to give it to him. I want him to bring me the pleasure I've fantasized about, wished for. With him. *By* him.

But I can't. Not yet.

"No, Killian." I push lightly at his chest. "I can't."

He stills, pulling away. Dark eyes are clouded with lust, but more than that, he looks wounded. "No?"

"No." I sigh, chest heaving.

There's a brief pause, and he pulls away. Without him, my body goes cold.

My legs tremble as I stand, leaning against the wall for support, nails digging into the wood. Killian looks ready to say something, to argue, but instead, he just runs a hand through his hair and turns on his heel. He's down the stairs before I can call him back.

I want to. But I can't.

Blowing out a deep breath, I turn right to walk to Michael's room. Right now, the only thing I can do is finish my plan. I can't marry Michael tomorrow, and I will never be a good *obedient* wife. Never.

I walk the distance to the far room with a singular light. Knocking once, Michael pulls open the door, smiling wickedly.

My body goes cold.

"Well, well, it seems it's my lucky night. Hello, *fiancée*."

I ignore the nausea and enter his Godforsaken room.

Chapter Six
Maeve

This room is a testament to the power Michael wields with my father.

Rich drapes, expensive sheets and a crackling fireplace all show off his status within the clan. Michael likes expensive things and enjoys having people think he's important. He's embraced his role and willingly took me as a future bride because of what it will give him.

He stole my innocence and gave me back only darkness.

I'm not letting him get away with it.

Sitting on the bed, he lets the towel part. I don't take the bait. His dick isn't that impressive.

For years, I've endured. I was made to take the punishments and smile with gratitude.

Never again.

"You came to me on your own. I didn't even have to call a guard this time. You're learning." He smiles wide. He's praising me like a pet who learned a new command.

There aren't any guards left at the house. They're spread thin covering the family as they make one last holiday romp through downtown Boston while I stay here. With Michael.

I can't help it. I smile back.

"I thought it was time to accept my fate," I say, words dry. A fate I would make my own.

"You're almost twenty-one." He nods, leaning back. His belly is so big, walking has got to be difficult for him. "I'll admit, I do miss that young body of yours, but this version certainly comes with perks."

Bile rises hard and fast up my throat. I have to breathe through my nose to settle it back down.

"Perks?" I move closer, letting my hips sway. This isn't easy for me. I don't do seduction well. I'm too tough, too brash.

"That ass of yours." His beady eyes lower. "Much better now. And those tits? Fuck." He bites his lower lip, and it takes everything in me not to visibly react.

"Lay back," I purr. It's now or never. He does so without question.

I follow, hiking my skirt high on my hips for better leverage. My fingers graze the pearl inlaid handle against my thigh like a dinghy in the storm. The heaviness of it eases my heart at being so close to a monster.

"Do you know what I think about when I'm all alone?"

Michael shakes his head, eyes glued to my form. This is his fantasy come to life. "No, what?" His voice has lowered, as if enjoying my little act. As if I've actually agreed to this punishment.

I smirk.

"How good I'll look covered in your blood."

There is a pregnant pause, the words ringing out loudly around us. Swiftly, as if I had rehearsed it, I grab the knife from my skirt and arch it over my head.

I plunge. One, two, three strikes before I lose count. I don't bother to remember them, just feel the movement of my arm, my body swaying with each stabbing like a memorized choreography.

Dozens and dozens of marks litter his body, ruby red staining the sheets under him. I watch the trails of blood splatter against the walls, hitting the ceiling with a frenzy I didn't know I possessed. But it was there, under the surface, buried along with my rage as I finally surrendered to it.

I always dreamed of the sounds he'd make as I cut him into tiny pieces. It's even better in real life. Sweet. Loud. Agonizing.

Pulling back slightly, I lick the knife, tasting the copper tang of his blood. It's sweet. It tastes like melting cotton candy on a hot summer's day. Like promises and a bright future where I lead.

"Your blood tastes almost as good as your death, Michael." I smirk, lips bloody.

He gurgles something horrible and my smile grows feral.

"You'll never touch me again. You'll never touch *anyone* again." I strike again, slicing into his throat. It's a hard hit, lodging on bone. "You thought you could take my power, my clan? This is my birthright and I will lead. Without *you.*"

A death hiss releases from his mouth, his body deflating, cold eyes rolling up to the ceiling. My words were the last things he heard. The minute his soul leaves the room, it grows brighter, my chest lighter.

It's done. *He's gone.*

A sob catches in my chest. Relief so heavy surrounds my heart and my eyes well.

"Maeve."

Glancing to the bedroom door, I see Killian gripping the sides of the threshold as if to physically restrain himself.

Shit.

Chapter Seven
Killian

Maeve didn't want me.

Maybe whoever she was going to see, dressed like *that*, was someone she loved.

I had half a mind to follow her and slice the fucker's neck to rid me of the competition.

How dare someone have what is *mine?*

Maeve is mine.

Since we were kids, I was drawn to her. Since I saw the marks on her body, healed her wounds. She was *mine*.

And seeing her in that outfit? *Hell*.

That outfit looked better on the floor next to my jacket. Her moans would drift over it as I went back to her, time and time again, making her forget whoever she was going to see. I'd have her begging, wishing for me to stop, but I wouldn't be able to.

Because once I had her, I'd lose myself completely in her.

Fuck. My cock twitches against my zipper.

The idea that someone gets *that,* gets *her,* and it's not me, is unfathomable.

Spinning on my heel, I dart back upstairs. No way in fucking hell was I going to let her go to someone else like that. I don't care if she's in love. She belongs with me and only me. She'll love me too. Eventually. Even if I have to force her.

The landing is empty, but a light down the hall pulls my attention. Voices drift out and I know Michael is there.

When I get close enough, I hear his words, fury lining my hands.

"You're almost twenty-one. I'll admit, I do miss that young body of yours, but this version certainly comes with perks."

My vision narrows, chest heavy as ruthless rage boils up, tasting of black tar and promises of retribution.

All the cuts. All the broken bones. Everything slips into place.

I'll slice him into tiny pieces for ever thinking he had a right to Maeve.

I dart into the bedroom, ready to do whatever it takes to end this *now*.

I stop short, momentarily shocked at what I see.

Maeve straddles the man, towel pooled under her. If not for the knife hanging in the air, I might have shot the man dead and dragged Maeve away by her hair, consequences be damned.

She plunges and stabs relentlessly, with a ferocity that can only be described as religious. She's expunging her demons, making Michael take them to hell. Blood sprays around her in a holy arc, flowing over the entire room. It hits lampshades and curtains, covering walls and the clock by the mantle.

It's fucking poetic.

Her barely clothed body is painted with it.

She looks absolutely *breathtaking*.

When she stops, she stumbles off him. She sobs once, but it's a broken laugh of relief more than one of sorrow, relief that her tormentor, the man who used her, defiled her, is dead.

How did I not see it until now?

How could I? I was never here. She never told me. But I should have seen it. I should have known. Because I know *her*.

"Maeve."

She spins, her wide green eyes wavering as she looks at me in fright. Her bottom lip trembles, and her hands shake as she drops the knife.

"Killian, I—" Her words fail. She tries again, voice hoarse, as if the words are being forced out. "I won't apologize for what I did."

Why should she? It was justified.

I grab her, pulling her body close. With the adrenaline spiking and dropping, she's a shaky mess of limbs, and I hold her face between my palms. She smells like vengeance and wrath and, *fuck*, if that doesn't make me want to drop to my knees for her.

"You don't need to apologize." I shoot the dead body a glare that I hope his soul feels in the fires of Hell. "He deserved so much worse than this."

"He deserved to suffer," she agrees. Her words are brutal, much like the small woman in my arms. "But I needed to end it. All of it. Before my birthday."

I nod once, rubbing my thumbs over the blood quickly drying on her skin. Of course. The decree. I was lucky enough not to be born into the clan and therefore missed the tradition.

That meant Ferguson knows.

"Why didn't you tell me?"

Her green eyes flash. Shame. Embarrassment. Everything she hides behind her tough girl exterior shines there, if only anyone looked long enough to see.

"Everyone knew," she whispers, broken. "No one cared. I thought you knew and just—"

"Didn't care?" I pinch her chin, making her look at me as I say the next part. I need her to understand. "No, Maeve. I didn't know. If I did, his head would have been cut off and nailed to the front *fucking* door for ever daring to touch *you*."

I watch as she glances back at the body, shoulders sagging. "Do you think I'm a monster?" In my silence, she turns back. "After what he did to me, what I did to him... I feel broken."

I wrap my arms around her gently, not caring if the blood stains my clothes. Blood never scared me.

"We're all broken, Maeve, every single one of us. But this? This doesn't make you broken. You did exactly what you needed to do to take back your power. You avenged yourself. You *saved* yourself. And you're fucking magnificent."

She's a force of nature, a fury sent to destroy those who would hurt women. This isn't revenge, it's justice.

Tenderly, I brush my nose to hers. I need to comfort her even if it's a small touch of skin.

She shakes her head. "No." Watery eyes blink at me. "No, don't be gentle with me."

A pained laugh leaves my lips. "Trust me, Princess, I would like nothing more than to fuck you until you forgot everything, but I don't think that's a good idea." Not after years of abuse. Not after killing her abuser. Not after *this*.

Fuck, Ferguson will notice his second-hand being gone. I'll have to clean this up.

Fisting my shirt in her small, deadly hands, she glares at me darkly.

"You said I'm not broken, so don't treat me like I am." She presses her entire body against mine, and I groan. She feels good like this— thick curves, fuckable breasts, strong legs. "Please, Killian. Make me forget. Replace his hands with yours."

I wanted to help her forget all the hurt he caused, all the ways he used sex to control her, twisting something meant to be good and pleasurable into something dark and painful.

She wants me to replace those memories with *us*.

My heart pounds loudly in my ears. This is everything I've ever wanted.

Grabbing her throat, I hold her with enough pressure to stutter her breath.

"I need a safe word, Maeve." Before I go too hard and hurt her.

I'll never forgive myself if I do. "When you say it, this stops. Every-thing stops."

She nods, watching me under thick eyelashes. "*Mors.*"

Latin for death, the word inked onto my knuckles holding her tight.

The grin I give her would make a nun sin.

"Against the wall, Princess. Let me see those pretty panties so I can take them off with my teeth."

Chapter Eight
Maeve

I stumble against the wall, my abuser's dead body bleeding to my left as Killian kneels in a puddle of blood in front of me. My leather mini skirt is pulled high, twisted into my fists.

He is a sight, death willing to submit for me.

"Right here?" I ask, eyes wide. I'm literally covered in another man's blood, his corpse next to us.

"Can't think of a better place." He runs his hands over my legs, nails raking over my skin as he pulls the fishnets lower. They pool at my feet, and he carefully takes them off.

He doesn't stop to remove my heels, dragging one leg over his shoulder, pressing close to my center. Only a thin piece of red silk separates us, and I'm ashamed to admit how wet I am.

Killian sees it, though. He inhales at my pussy, smiling against me.

"You're fucking soaked."

"It's the adrenaline," I bite out, watching as he kisses my inner thigh. Close, but not where I want him.

"No. I think it's more than that." His teeth surprise me, dragging over the fabric, leaving my knees trembling. "I think you like seeing me kneel at your feet. Like a war goddess, covered in the blood of your enemies, being pleasured by your dark god. Does this turn you on?"

The images are fucking hot. Beyond hot. They're molten. The idea that this man, this killer, would worship me is a power trip.

I grow wetter, and he chuckles. *Fucking bastard.* He knows what he's doing to me.

He reaches up, snapping the strings with a bite of pain. Before I can object, he places them in his jeans.

"Souvenir?"

"Definitely. I'll need something for later when I'm fucking my hand to the memory of your wet cunt."

My pussy hums as his tongue darts out to take a long, languid lick. My head falls back, ecstasy and relief mixing with budding pleasure. He groans against me.

"You were right. His blood was sweet but not as sweet as this pussy." He goes back again with long licks that leave me breathless, toes curling.

Deep pleasure starts to well inside of me. He latches onto my clit, lapping at it with hard strokes and, finally, I moan low in the room.

Who cares if the door is open and a dead body is next to me? Killian Linwood is tongue fucking me against a wall, and it feels so fucking right. The world could burn to ashes around us, and I wouldn't move from this spot.

"That's it, Princess." He smiles, chin wet. "Let this entire house know who makes you feel this good." He goes back, lifting my other leg so only his shoulders and the wall are supporting me.

His tongue flicks and strokes against my sensitive flesh. Teeth nibble around my core, soothing and wicked. My whole body begins to burn. Soon, one finger enters me, and I clamp down.

The intrusion is hard, bringing painful memories to the front.

Of being forced on my back, legs pulled wide...

"Eyes on me, Maeve." My eyes flicker open. He kisses my inner thigh almost lovingly. "You stay here, with me. He doesn't get this. This is for us."

No, Michael doesn't get this. He's dead, killed by my own hand. I'm covered in his blood.

I'm taking this back.

Nodding, I lick my lips, mind resolved. "I'm with you."

"Good." He locks eyes with me as his mouth descends on my clit and another finger enters me. My body tries to accommodate it, not used to relaxing at the stretch, but I breathe and think through it.

With Killian here, eyes open, I can only see him, think of him, smell him—cool mint and a bare trace of cigarette tobacco—and see the desire in his eyes. Desire for *me*.

His tongue moves faster in time with his fingers, and soon, my hips are grinding against him, chasing my release.

A fire rages in my gut, dancing up my spine. My vision darkens, focused on the man before me as my body tightens. A loud groan releases from my throat, and the orgasm crashes into me like a thunderous burst, dams weakening, core melting from his touch.

Killian doesn't stop, moving and drawing it out until a small one shakes me, and I push at his arms. "No, enough."

"No, Maeve. I don't hear that safe word." He continues to lick and suck, drawing a pained moan from my lips. It burns, drawing my body tight again. I want to move away, but I can't. I won't. "If you need to stop, use it."

I don't want to stop. I can't. Having Killian's mouth on me is the sweetest torture, and like hell am I going to use the safe word. *Stubborn* will be written on my gravestone.

That's the first orgasm I've ever had that wasn't self-induced. Words can't describe how fantastic it felt, knowing Killian was actually here, enjoying this as much as me.

"I want another one, baby. Give me one more."

"Killian, I *can't*." There's no way I can come a third time, not so quickly.

"You can." A third finger enters me, and I have to breathe against the ache. My body heats, hips following his fingers. He sucks on my clit, a beautiful mixture of pain and pleasure as my body withers.

Pleasure builds, tempered by the pain of exhaustion, of too much too soon. It rolls through me, hitting my core like a bullet, taking me under. Killian doesn't stop, moving his mouth lower, tongue spearing into me.

Fuck, I'm going to come *again*.

"God, Maeve, you taste so damn good." He sucks harder, pulling my throbbing clit between his teeth. My hips buck, and I whine, moans puffing from my lips. "That's it, Princess. Just let go."

His words, his encouragement, unlock something in me. Another hard orgasm rocks my center, wetness leaking from me as Killian laps it up. This one robs my breath, blackening my vision. My body shakes violently, Killian kissing my thighs as I come down.

He drops my legs, standing to his full height.

Fuck. If that's what he meant by forgetting everything but his name, he wasn't kidding. I can barely stand.

Crushing me against the wall, Killian's lips descend on mine. I can taste my release,—tobacco, and mint on his tongue. Unlike Michael, this is sweet, intoxicating. *Him.* Greedily, I dig my hands into his hair, pulling him closer. I need more—more of him, more of this feeling between us.

Because Killian isn't my hero. He's the villain who recognizes the villain in me. He's my harbor, my place to rest my weary head, where I can drop my armor and bask in the dark.

He handed me the knife and stood back, letting me reap my own salvation.

No judgement. No conviction. Just understanding.

He sucks my bottom lip into his mouth, tugging sharply.

"You alright?" He's panting, cock painfully hard against my lower belly.

My mouth waters thinking of him inside me, how thick he feels, hearing his moans as he comes inside me. I need him naked *now*.

"More than alright." I smile, watching as his dark eyes glimmer.

"Good."

Grabbing a fistful of my hair, he wrenches me closer, pulling off my skirt and undoing my corset while his mouth nips and licks my neck.

"Get on the floor, Maeve."

I do as he commands, not waiting long before his powerful body covers mine. *This.* This is what I needed to banish the bad memories of this room.

Michael would abuse me in this room. The way Killian kisses me, worships my breasts, crushes my hips in his hands as if I'm something to treasure, is nothing like that. This is desire and lust wrapped up into the promise of safety. These are the memories I needed.

His soft lips trace the scars on my shoulders and on my lower stomach. Every past hurt, he erases with his mouth, as if he can take all those bad memories away.

He drags his shirt off, kicking off his pants and boots.

Black-blue ink catches my eye: intricate designs of a Grim Reaper over his left arm with his Scythe, on the other side a bouquet of funerary flowers on a casket. Over his back are black wings of death, reaching up his neck and over his shoulder blades.

Pierced nipples glint in the roaring flame's light, and I play with one as he lowers himself over me.

Once his cool skin meets my heated flesh, I hiss in relief.

A gold pendant catches my attention, swinging in my face as the fog of arousal thins.

"What's that?" I lick my lips, holding it close.

A Dead Head Moth pendant glints in the fire light.

Something foreign wells in my throat. It's my favorite bug. He would know this because he knows *me*. He has for years.

"It reminds me of you." His words are whispered, afraid to be spoken where anyone could hear. "Wherever I go, you're with me."

I capture his lips in a hard kiss, saying everything I can't speak. Emotions and thoughts, things that cause me too much pain to repeat, are forced through our lips, communicated with our tongues. If I could rip open my heart and give it to him, I would.

Everything I have, I would gladly give to him.

He enters me with one, fluid slide. I groan into his mouth, and he swallows it down, greedily keeping it for himself.

"Maeve," he murmurs into my mouth, pulling back to stare down at me, at where we're joined. "You have no idea how badly I've wanted this."

"Enough to fuck me in a puddle of blood?"

The smirk he gives me is twisted and deranged. "You look delicious covered in blood, Princess." He licks my throat, over his bite mark from earlier. "Fuck, I've dreamed of having you for years. Under me, over me, however I could have you. I just wanted *you*."

The thought is intoxicating that this man, this killer, has only ever wanted me. He draws out before slamming back into me. It's hard and rough, exactly what I needed. The carpet cuts into my back, his nails ripping into the thin skin of my hips.

My body used to carry the marks of my abuser. Now, I'll gladly carry the reaper's marks.

He grabs a clump of my hair, wrenching my head back, arching my body.

"If only you could see what I see." He bites one breast, thrusting his hips into me. I feel so full, body stretched to the point of pain around him. "You're fucking perfect."

Flesh slaps together in a messy tangle of sweat and blood. The heat of the fire is bathing us as Killian pumps into me, holding me still. The pleasure is building, but I need more. I need him.

"Killian, I need—" I moan as he shifts his hips, releasing my hair. He holds my neck, pulling me closer. "I need—"

"I know what you need, Maeve." He steals a kiss, fist tightening around my throat. My vision darkens before he lets up. Fuck, my pussy clenches around him with every squeeze, making his movements sloppy. "Remember that, Princess. Only I know what you need. I'm the only one who can make you feel this good." It's possessive but I don't hate it.

Because he does. He knows exactly what I need. He always has.

His other hand finds my engorged clit, rubbing small hard circles in time with his hips. God, it's too much. Too much pleasure, too much pressure. There's no way I can survive this. I'm going to explode.

"Killian, I... I can't—" I'm going to die like this—the hold on my neck, the friction, the feel of him. It's all too much. My words are failing me. "*Fuck,* Killian."

"That's it, Maeve. Scream my fucking name." He smiles like the Devil into my neck, inhaling. God, he's loving this lapse of control. As close as I am, I know he must be. His thrusts are harder, faster, driving me across the carpet. "Let this whole house hear you. Let *him* hear you in the underworld."

I clamp down. Let *him* hear how he doesn't get this. This is my pleasure, my body. I get to experience this without him hanging around.

I hope he can hear it from wherever he is. This was never his. It was always *mine*.

My chest heaves, heart thumping as my body tightens.

"Fuck, fuck, fuck," I chant, letting the wave crest.

"There she is." He chuckles as my pussy tightens and my mouth opens on a guttural moan. "This pussy is mine. *You* are mine. Forever. Don't you *ever* forget that."

He thrusts with a savage rhythm, growling his release into me. He collapses on top of me, one hand curling into my hair, the other around my neck.

Ownership. Possession. Safety. That's what Killian is offering.

And it's something I want—desperately.

Chapter Nine
Killian

I left Maeve in her bed, naked, freshly washed and snoring lightly.

If it was up to me, I'd keep her painted in blood. She is a fucking sight covered in the blood of the man who hurt her. It's dark justice.

But instead, I had a body to clean up.

It doesn't take me long. Years of cleaning up my kills, some messier than Maeve's, have made me an expert, and Ferguson is too trusting to doubt my lies.

After cleaning the blood with the chemicals I keep on hand, I change the sheets and clean Michael up. Then, I dress him, asking Simon to lie about the cause of death.

It takes considerably more control not to slice Michael into pieces for even thinking Maeve was his to touch.

"He's going to know," Simon whispers, pushing black glasses up his nose. Greying blond locks dust over his skull. "If he sees the body, he'll know this isn't a heart attack."

"Well, it's a good thing he won't see the body." I smirk, my eyes narrowing on the guy. He has only been in the clan a few years, and he'll be on the way out soon enough.

This life is hard. Most can't handle it.

After the room is staged, documents signed, I wait in Ferguson's office.

I sure as hell don't want to be here. I want to be in Maeve's bed, feeling her cunt around my cock again.

I meant what I said. She's mine and I'm hers. I have been since the moment her green eyes caught me and her knife cut into my throat as children.

Ferguson enters, throwing his jacket on to a rack by the door.

His glare disappears the minute he sees me.

"Ah, Killian. I was wondering when you'd be back. All good in Arizona?"

"It's taken care of."

He nods, pouring two large glasses of whiskey. He hands me one. "Good man. I knew you'd be an asset the moment I saw you in that alley."

The night he saw me kill someone. Normal people would think I was a murderer, Ferguson just saw a promising pupil.

Sipping from the glass, I sit on his desk casually. "We have another situation."

"Oh?"

"Michael's dead."

Ferguson holds the whiskey on his tongue before swallowing bitterly. "One of the families?"

"Oddly, no. Heart attack. Wasn't exactly a healthy man." I tsk, even as everything in me wants to bring the asshole back just so Maeve can kill him again.

Seeing her so savage does something to me. I feel a kinship to what lives in her, two black halves of one shriveled black heart. Maeve is made for me.

Rubbing the bridge of his nose, Ferguson nods. "Fuck."

He sits behind his desk heavily. "That screws everything up."

"Such as?" I finish the booze, hating how it gets rid of Maeve's taste.

Like fresh berries and soft whipped cream. *Fuck*. I'm such a goner.

"Michael was supposed to take over." He throws his beefy hand around. "I was grooming him to take over once Maeve turned twenty-one." Which is today.

The day that should have been met with love and celebration, was going to be about giving her to a monster. I clear the emotions from my face as I stand to pour another glass. I figured as much, but to hear it from my mentor, a man I killed for...

"You gave Maeve to him."

Fury, the kind that could scare the Devil himself, threatened to overtake me.

If not for Maeve's safety, I would have blown the fucking Captain's head off, mentor or not. All that matters is Maeve.

"Of course, I did." He scoffs. "Only a man can lead a clan. Maeve being the eldest was the best way to keep the O'Brien blood while getting a man to lead."

"What about Briar?"

He slaps the desk. "That fucking ungrateful boy. He had the nerve to tell me I was ruining this family. Left last night for God knows where. He couldn't do what it takes to lead."

Sipping the freshly poured glass, I let the liquor burn my throat.

"So who will take the reins now?" I can't offer Maeve. She's the best choice for this, but he won't listen to that.

Ferguson hates women, thinks them weak. I've seen the marks on his pseudo-wife. Unfortunately, he probably raised the scariest woman to ever walk this Earth.

"No fucking clue." He leans his head back, dark hair grey at the temples.

I chew on my cheek, finishing the whiskey. A plan slowly forms in my mind. "Give me a list. I'll work through the names, see who's suitable." And kill every single person who thinks they can have something that belongs to me.

I couldn't protect Maeve before, but I can now.

"Ah, good man. I'll have it for you in the morning." He looks over my shoulder down the darkened hall. "Where is my oldest daughter, anyway?"

"Her room." I hold his curious look, not giving anything away. Ferguson is a brute, but he isn't stupid. He's noticed me *noticing* her. He's smart enough not to mention it. "Once I have the names, I'll handle it right away."

He doesn't need to know that this clan will never go to an outsider. Only Maeve will sit on its throne. I'll make sure of it.

Chapter Ten
Maeve

A warm body slides into my bed behind me, wrapping a strong arm around my waist.

I freeze as his lips brush my ear—mint, tobacco, and the soothing citric smell of good whiskey. "It's me, Princess."

Immediately, I relax. Only Killian would ever come into my bedroom, would feel comfortable enough to be in my sanctuary. Everyone else was too afraid to go into unwanted territory.

His firm body is a welcoming weight, a leg sliding between my bare ones, holding me close.

"What happened to the body?" Sleep is trying to pull me back under, but I nestle closer to Killian. I need to make sure things are settled.

Michael is gone and a weight has left my shoulders. Free, relaxed, I feel like I can do anything.

"Handled." He moves my legs, his hardening cock lodging against my backside. "Your father is home."

His lips trail over my neck, and I move, allowing him access.

Although I'm tired, my body heats as the hand on my stomach slides lower. I had him hours ago, and I want more. This desire has never been here before. My pleasure has always taken a backseat to survival. Now, it's back with a vengeance. My breathing picks up, and I lean against him, breasts pushed out as I seek his fingers where I need him most. I'm aching for his touch.

He chuckles. "Did you miss me already?"

"Killian," I warn, trying to push his hand further south. He's not having that, which infuriates me.

Quickly, I flip us over, straddling him as he adjusts to sit. I know I'm not as strong as the hitman, but he certainly acts as if I have all the power. That's something I've always wanted—the power, the control, the safety that comes with it.

Because I'm sadistic, I hover over his bare pelvis, not letting him anywhere near me. He's completely nude, and it's a glorious sight: coiled muscle, inked skin, and pale scars. He's beautiful.

The smirk he gives me is teasing, edged with desperation.

I like this Killian. Eyes beg me to lower, hands crushing my hips as he restrains himself from forcing me closer. A girl could get used to this.

"What did he want?" I ask, lips brushing his jaw, nipping at his chin. There's a sharp intake at the bite of pain, but he moves his neck, allowing me more access.

"Nothing to interrupt this right now." His words are pained as I lower my head to his chest. Taking one silver piercing in my mouth, I tug it with my teeth, and his hips buck. "Maeve..."

"I've decided," I say suddenly, sitting up. My wet core is just out of reach as he hungrily takes everything in. "This clan needs to change."

"And I'm sure you know exactly what kind of changes we need, don't you, Princess?"

Sinking onto him, slowly, tauntingly so, I watch how his eyes roll back into his head. He curses darkly, neck flexing with his restraint.

This is power I've never had. I've never been allowed ownership of my body, of my pleasure, never allowed to set the tone, never allowed to ignite or deny. Killian is offering this to me on a silver platter, letting me use his body as I see fit, and I'm holding on to it with both hands.

"I want to watch it burn," I whisper into his mouth, stealing a hard kiss. "I want to watch my father bleed out for thinking I wasn't good enough to lead. I want to wipe that fucking smile off his face when he sees the daughter he sold to a monster became what he feared most. Powerful. In charge. *Captain*."

He growls, fisting my hair, letting my hips set the punishing rhythm. Skin slapping, I can feel my body tighten, need coiling through me quickly as the release rises on the horizon. Harder, harder, I ride him, chasing that high.

"*Captain*," he purrs under me. God, it sounds good coming from his lips. His hands move with my hips, never halting my progress. He's long and hard, allowing me to lead while adding the right kind of pressure between my thighs. "I like the sound of that."

"Can you follow me, Killian?" I pant, rolling forward. Sweet friction burns at this angle, and my eyes flutter. I tweak one nipple, rolling the other in my hand, head falling back to enjoy the rush. He's watching me with bold desire. "Can you have me as your leader?"

I don't know what would happen if he couldn't follow a woman. Couldn't follow *me*. The O'Brien clan has never had a woman leader. If he didn't fall in line, the great Killian Linwood, no one would.

"I will happily let you burn this entire organization to the ground and walk over the charred ashes just to be at your side. Then I'd build it back up in *your* image." My orgasm crests, him surging under me, thrusting on every beat, his words muffled and strained. "There's nothing I would love to see more than you sitting on the throne of your empire, your family's clan under your control, and you, covered in blood, forcing everyone who ever doubted you, ever *hurt* you, to their *fucking* knees."

The images are enough to drive me on, and I shout in relief, feeling him grip me tighter. I moan his name as his release barrels into me, following me over the edge in a tired, fully satisfied state.

I drop to his chest, body spent, warmth spreading through my chest.

"I'll follow you to the ends of time, Maeve. Just say the word. I'm yours to command."

Nuzzling into his neck, I breathe him in. Mint, tobacco, sweat, and danger. I'm sated, safe in a killer's arms.

This is love, safety, and freedom, all rolled into one. And Killian is mine.

Tomorrow, we can worry about taking over the clan. I can worry about my father and the consequences of my actions later. Right now, in his arms, this is where I belong.

We can face everything else together tomorrow.

THE END

If you enjoyed this spicy, dark romance, check out: https://linktr.ee/authorecrowe for the continuation of this series, with The Mafia's Bride, debuting May 2025!

About the Author

E.D Crowe is a debut author who runs on coffee, chaos, and unhealthy amounts of dark chocolate. When not writing, she can be found howling at the moon, crafting potions in her kitchen or swooning after the deranged villains. She has two Australian Shepherds who think they're lap dogs, three feral children, and a golden retriever husband who is as far from the villain as possible.

Taste of Vengeance

By: Maree Rose

About Taste of Vengeance

Beyanka Harvey's life shatters the night she is dragged into the woods and left for dead. When she wakes, it's to the quiet strength of Jasper Baker—a man as dangerous as he is tender. As Bee recovers, shadows of that night return, reigniting a hunger for vengeance. Jaz, no stranger to darkness, becomes her unlikely guide. Together, they hunt the men who destroyed her. But retribution is a patient beast, and on the anniversary of her assault, Bee will make them bleed.

Content Note:

There are mentions and memories of prior SA and physical assault, the revenge is bloody but also not detailed. If these things are an issue please be mindful of your mental health and skip this one, my writing isn't for everyone and I completely support you putting yourself first.

Relationship type: MF

Chapter One

Consciousness claws its way back into my grasp, a spiteful cat leaving claw marks of pain across the landscape of my mind. My head throbs in a persistent cruel rhythm, each pulse a hammer blow against the fragile shell of my skull. My body echoes the torment with sharp aches that carve their presence into every limb, branding themselves deep within my flesh.

I muster the strength to pry my eyes open, but they betray me, rebelling with nothing more than slits against the harsh light. I try again, desperation clawing at the edges of my newly awakened, terror filled consciousness. The world around me swims in a blurry haze, shapes and shadows melding into a canvas of confusion. I'm adrift in a sea of disorientation, my senses mutinous, refusing to report anything but fragments of reality.

With each laborious attempt to focus, my frustration mounts—a silent scream in a void where no one can hear. Vulnerability wraps around me like a shroud, heavy and suffocating. I want to shout, to demand clarity from the murky haze that holds me captive, but my voice is a prisoner too, locked somewhere deep inside.

A shard of memory pierces the fog in my mind, cruel and uninvited. It's a hand—no, hands—everywhere, grasping, taking, stealing what isn't theirs to claim. My breath hitches in my throat as the images cascade over me: the trees, the scent of the ocean nearby, the weight of a body pressing down on mine. The sounds of my own screams drowned out by the music and crash of the waves.

"Please, no," the desperate cry escapes from my lips, barely more than a whisper as I try to shake away the flashes that fracture my sanity. I feel the ghost of their touch, rough against my skin, igniting a raw panic that coils around my spine like barbed wire. The terror is a live thing inside me, squirming and clawing its way up my throat.

"Shhh... You're safe now." A deep, gentle voice slices through the chaos of my mind, the tone rich and unexpectedly comforting.

I flinch at the sound, instinctively recoiling from the masculine timbre. But there's something inexplicably soothing about it, like a balm applied to a burn. The voice is a stark contrast to the shrieking of my memories. It resonates within the hollows of my despair, stirring an odd sense of security amidst the storm.

"Try to breathe with me. In... and out." The voice instructs, rhythmically, insistently.

I cling to the cadence of those words, letting them become the heartbeat I synchronize with. The presence is a warmth in the cold dread that has settled in my bones. I don't know this man, I don't recognize this voice in the dark, but for reasons I can't begin to fathom, I find myself wanting to believe him, to trust in the protection his tone promises.

"Good, you're doing great," the voice encourages, a thread of something like pride weaving through each word.

The sound envelops me, wraps me in a cocoon, shielding me from the jagged edges of my own fractured thoughts. With each spoken word, the tide of fear recedes a fraction more, leaving me adrift in a strange calm that I hadn't dared hope to find again.

The timbre of his voice, deep and reassuring, is a strange lullaby that stills the tempest in my mind. The man's voice should be a threat, yet it isn't. Instead, it's a paradoxical caress against the jagged edges of my psyche, and it both terrifies and comforts me.

"Who are you?" I want to scream, but the words knot up in my throat, unvoiced whispers of distrust wrestling with the unexpected solace that blankets me.

My body, a sea of agony, betrays me at the first attempt to move. Pain arcs down my spine; sharp, searing pain that splinters through me, anchoring me back into the unforgiving present. I gasp out a strangled sound. My limbs are leaden, uncooperative, and the effort to command them is like shouting into a void. Helplessness swamps me, a tide of despair threatening to drag me under again.

"Shh, easy," the voice murmurs, closer now, a lifeline amid the throbbing hurt that holds me captive. There's a gentle touch against my arm, featherlight, a contrast to the invisible weights pinning me down. The tender care from hands that belong to someone unknown slices through the fog of my confusion, sharpening my focus.

"Let me die," I whimper, tasting the metallic tang on my tongue. The plea is a blade, cutting through the remnants of my former self-assuredness, laying bare the raw, bleeding need for salvation. Each syllable is an admission of defeat and a cry for rescue all at once.

"Let you die?" There's a pause. "How will you take your revenge if you're six feet under?"

The word 'revenge' ignites something within me, a spark in the darkness that threatens to consume everything. It's a match struck in a room full of gasoline, dangerous and intoxicating all at once.

Move, I command myself, channeling what remains of my willpower into the simple act of lifting an arm. Agony laughs at the effort, a cruel reminder of my plight. But beneath the physical torment, there's an ember of resolve that refuses to be extinguished. This pain will not define me. I will not allow it.

"Stay still, you're safe," he says, the undertone of authority mingling with concern threading through the darkness. A peculiar curiosity flickers to life, a beacon amidst the desolation. I want to know this stranger whose voice seems to hold the power to soothe and disarm the demons that have taken root in my soul.

The voice drifts back to me, a lifeline thrown into the churning sea of my consciousness. "I won't hurt you. No one will hurt you ever again." Each word is a balm, seeping into the cracks of my fractured spirit. They are soft and strong at once, like sturdy vines that I instinctively grasp, allowing them to anchor me to the present, away from the abyss that threatens to swallow me whole.

"Who—" My attempt at speech is a rasp, a harsh sound scraped from the depths of my throat. The effort sends a fresh wave of pain through me, but I'm determined to break through the silence that cocoons me. I need to hear my own voice, however broken, asserting its right to be heard.

"Shh... don't talk. Save your strength," he urges gently.

"Name..." I manage to croak out, demanding, needing the power that comes with knowing. Names hold sway, a modicum of control, and if I am to navigate this shadowy limbo between victim and avenger, I must arm myself with knowledge.

"My name's Jasper Baker, but you can call me Jaz," comes the reply, simple and unadorned. Jaz. The name is a new beginning, a chapter yet unwritten, and it fortifies me with a sliver of strength I didn't know I had left.

The coolness of a damp cloth ghosts across my forehead. I flinch, an instinctive recoil, but the touch is persistent—gentle, almost reverent.

"Easy," he murmurs, his voice a low rumble. His fingers brush against my arm, light as moth wings. His hands are deft as they tend to me, movements practiced and precise. Why does he care? Why is this man trying to heal my battered form?

"Who are you?" I finally rasp, curiosity warring with the caution that prickles beneath my skin.

"Someone who wants to help," he replies, and there's a weight to his words, a promise.

I force my eyes open wider, fighting against the swollen lids and stabbing light. The world slowly comes into focus, revealing a face hovering above me. Dark, intense eyes bore into mine, framed by a strong jaw and sharp cheekbones. Inky black hair falls in disheveled waves, and intricate tattoos creep down his neck, disappearing beneath the collar of his shirt. His features are a study in contradictions—hard lines softened by concern, danger tempered with gentleness.

"Why?" I croak, my voice still raw and unfamiliar.

A shadow passes over Jaz's face, something dark and primal flickering in his eyes. "Because I know what it's like," he says softly, his words heavy with unspoken history. "To be broken. To want vengeance more than air."

The intensity of his gaze overwhelms me, and I have to close my eyes again. The darkness behind my eyelids offers no respite, instead becoming a canvas for my pain to paint itself anew. Every nerve ending screams, a symphony of agony conducted by my battered body. My skin feels aflame, as if I've been dragged across miles of broken glass and left to bleed under a merciless sun.

Another shard of memory pierces through the haze—darkness, a stifled scream, the cruel grip of hands that don't belong. I flinch, my breath hitching as the scene plays out in jagged fragments before my mind's eye. The sharp tang of fear floods my senses anew, and I whimper, trying to steel myself against it. I need to remember, to piece together the splinters of what happened, even if it razes my soul to ash.

"Easy." Jaz's voice is a low thrum. "Talk to me."

"Jumbled..." My voice comes out ragged, a testament to the turmoil within. "The memories are jumbled."

"Let them come, but don't chase after them. They'll make sense in time." There's wisdom in his words, wrapped in the velvet of his tone.

I nod, or at least I think I do—it's hard to tell when my body feels so disconnected from my will. A shiver courses through me, not from cold but from the effort of holding onto this sliver of clarity. I want to recoil from his touch, to reclaim the space around me as my own untainted sanctuary. But the truth is, I'm adrift and right now, Jaz is the only lifeline I can discern through the fog.

"Thank you," I whisper, the words scraping against my throat like gravel. I'm grateful, yes, but there's an undercurrent of something else too—something dark and twisted that coils within me. Gratitude born from necessity has thorns, and they prick at me with every beat of my heart.

"Nothing to thank me for," Jaz replies, his hands moving with purpose as they tend to my wounds. There's a ritualistic quality to his movements, as though every action is both calculated and sacred. His fingers brush against my skin, leaving trails of fire in their wake, but it's a different burn than the one etched into my memory. This one doesn't sear with malice; it's complicated, tinged with a pain that's almost... cleansing.

"Rest now," he advises, and I realize that my eyelids are heavy, my consciousness waning once more.

"Stay," I manage, the word barely more than a breath. It's a plea, a command, and a whisper of fear all at once. In this room where shadows dance along the walls and secrets linger in the corners, Jaz is an enigma I cannot solve, yet I can't seem to push him away.

"Always," he assures, and there's a promise in his voice that feels older than time.

I let the darkness take me again, but it's different this time. There's an edge to it, a sharpened resolve that wasn't there before. I won't just be a victim of my past, a plaything for fate. No, I'll forge my future with iron and blood. And if Jaz is willing to stand by me? Then so be it.

For now, his presence is the guardrail on this precarious bridge I'm crossing back to life. For now, that will have to be enough.

Chapter Two

Days blur into nights, a hazy tapestry of pain and fleeting lucidity. Jaz is my constant, a shadow that never strays, his presence both comforting and unsettling. He tends to my wounds with a gentleness that belies the strength in his tattooed hands, applying salves that sting and soothe in equal measure.

I drift in and out of consciousness, my mind a broken kaleidoscope of fractured memories. Each shard cuts deep, leaving me gasping and trembling. Jaz is always there, his voice a lifeline in the tempest of my thoughts.

"You're safe, little fighter. I've got you," he murmurs, over and over, until the words become a mantra that anchors me to reality.

"You... you keep calling me that," I say.

A small, sad smile tugs at the corner of Jaz's mouth. "You didn't have any ID on you when I found you," he explains. "And I didn't want to push for your name until you were ready."

I take a deep breath, feeling the weight of the moment. "It's Beyanka," I tell him. "Beyanka Harvey. But... most people call me Bee."

Jaz's smile grows warmer, a spark of something like affection in his eyes. "Bee," he repeats softly. "My little Bee."

His words hang in the air, a gentle claim that should make me bristle but instead wraps around me like a warm blanket. I let the silence stretch, savoring this moment of calm before the inevitable storm of reality crashes back in.

His fingers, calloused yet impossibly gentle, brush a wayward strand of hair from my face. The touch sends a shiver down my spine, a mix of instinctive fear and something else—something I'm not ready to name.

"Bee," he says again, his voice low and careful. "There's something we need to discuss."

I tense, bracing myself for whatever's coming. "What is it?"

Jaz takes a deep breath, his dark eyes searching mine. "I know this is difficult, but we need to consider your health. After what happened... it would be wise to test for sexually transmitted diseases."

The words hit me like a punch to the gut, dragging me back to that night on the beach. I squeeze my eyes shut, willing the memories away.

"And..." Jaz hesitates, his usual confidence faltering. "We should also check for... pregnancy."

A hysterical laugh bubbles up in my throat, but I swallow it down. "I have an IUD," I manage to say, my voice steadier than I feel.

Relief flashes across Jaz's face, quickly replaced by concern. "That's good, but we should still test for other things. STDs, infections... just to be safe."

I nod, grateful for his matter-of-fact approach. "Okay," I whisper.

Jaz reaches for my hand, his touch feather-light. "I can draw the blood myself," he offers. "You won't have to go to a clinic or explain anything to strangers."

Curiosity pricks at me. "You know how to do that?"

A shadow passes over his face. "I have... experience in many areas. Not all of it pleasant."

I don't press for details. We all have our demons, and Jaz has been nothing but respectful of my boundaries. I owe him the same courtesy.

"Alright," I agree. "Let's do it."

Jaz nods, squeezing my hand before standing. He moves with fluid grace, gathering supplies from a nearby cabinet. I watch him work, marveling at the contrast between his imposing physique and the delicate way he handles the medical equipment.

As he prepares my arm, swabbing the crook of my elbow with alcohol, Jaz clears his throat. "Bee," he begins, his voice hesitant. "I hope you don't mind me asking, but... if you didn't have the IUD, what would you have done?"

The question hangs between us, heavy with implication. I meet his gaze, unflinching. "I'm just glad it's my body and my choice," I say simply. "That I have the free will to take care of that." My words hang in the air, heavy with unspoken meaning.

Jaz nods, a flicker of understanding passing through his dark eyes. "I respect that," he says softly, his voice a low rumble that sends shivers down my spine. "Your body, your choice. Always."

He turns his attention back to my arm, his fingers tracing the delicate network of veins beneath my skin. The touch is clinical, but there's an underlying tenderness that makes my breath catch in my throat. I watch as he selects a needle, the metal glinting in the soft light of the room.

"This might pinch a little," Jaz warns, his eyes meeting mine. "Ready?"

I nod, steeling myself for the pain. But when the needle slides in, it's with such practiced precision that I barely feel it. Jaz works quickly and efficiently, filling several vials with my blood. The crimson liquid seems to glow in the dim light, a stark reminder of my vitality--and my vulnerability.

As he withdraws the needle, Jaz presses a cotton ball to the small puncture. His thumb rubs gentle circles on my skin, the motion soothing and intimate. "You did great," he murmurs, his praise warming something deep inside me.

I watch as he labels the vials, his handwriting a scrawl of barely legible letters. "How long until we know?" I ask, hating the tremor in my voice.

Jaz pauses, considering my question. "I have connections," he says carefully. "People who can run these tests quickly and discreetly. We should have results in a day or two."

The word 'connections' piques my curiosity, but I don't press. There's so much about Jaz that remains a mystery, layers of complexity I've only begun to scratch the surface of. Instead, I focus on the immediacy of the moment, on the strange comfort of his presence.

"Thank you," I whisper, the words feeling inadequate for all he's done.

Jaz's eyes soften, the hard edges of his face smoothing into something almost vulnerable. "You don't need to thank me, little Bee," he says, his voice rough with emotion. "I told you, I'm here to help."

A lump forms in my throat, threatening to choke me with the weight of my gratitude and fear. I reach out, my fingers brushing against the intricate tattoos on Jaz's forearm. He goes still at the contact, his muscles tensing beneath my touch.

"Why?" I ask, the question that's been burning inside me finally spilling out. "Why are you doing all this for me?"

Jaz is quiet for a long moment, his eyes fixed on where my hand rests on his arm. When he finally speaks, his voice is low and intense. "Because I've been where you are," he says. "Lost. Broken. Thirsting for vengeance."

The room seems to shrink around us, the air thick with tension and unspoken truths. Outside, a gentle rain begins to fall, its patter against the window a soothing counterpoint to the storm brewing within these walls.

I swallow hard, gathering my courage. "Did you... did you get it?" I ask, my voice barely above a whisper. "The vengeance you wanted?"

A small smile plays at the corners of Jaz's mouth, a dangerous curve that sends a shiver down my spine. It's not a smile of joy or mirth, but something darker, more primal. His eyes flicker with a memory and for a moment, I see a glimpse of the man he must have been—raw, wounded, driven by an all-consuming need for retribution.

"I did," he says simply, his voice low and rich with satisfaction.

The admission hangs between us, charged with possibility. I lick my dry lips, heart pounding. "How did it feel?" The question escapes me before I can stop it, a mix of fear and fascination coloring my words.

Jaz's smile widens, revealing a flash of white teeth. His eyes lock onto mine, intense and unblinking. "It was the best feeling," he says, each word dripping with dark pleasure. "Like finally scratching an itch that's been driving you mad for years. Like taking your first breath after being underwater for too long."

I shudder, not entirely from fear. There's something intoxicating about the raw honesty in his voice, the way he doesn't shy away from the darkness within him. It calls to something deep inside me, a part I've kept locked away and hidden.

"Even now?" I press, unable to stop myself. "Do you still feel that way?"

Jaz's expression shifts, becoming more guarded. He studies me for a long moment, as if weighing how much to reveal. Finally, he lets out a slow breath. "I'll be honest with you, Bee," he says, his voice dropping to a low rumble. "I still get that feeling every time I kill someone."

The admission hits me like a physical blow. I gasp, my eyes widening as I process his words. Jaz watches me carefully, his body tense, as if preparing for rejection or recoil.

"Does that scare you?" he asks, his voice gentle despite the weight of his confession.

I take a deep breath, forcing myself to really consider the question. The old me, the Bee from before that night on the beach, would have been terrified. She would have recoiled in horror, fleeing from this dangerous man and his dark confessions. But I'm not that girl anymore. The waves washed her away, leaving behind someone harder, someone with jagged edges and a thirst for retribution that threatens to consume me.

"No," I whisper, surprised by the steadiness in my voice. "It doesn't scare me."

Jaz's eyebrows lift slightly, a flicker of surprise crossing his face before it settles back into careful neutrality. "Why not?" he asks, his tone gentle but probing.

I close my eyes, letting the darkness behind my lids become a canvas for my thoughts. The memories of that night surge forward, a tidal wave of pain and rage that threatens to drown me. But instead of fighting it, I let it wash over me, through me, until I'm trembling with the force of it.

"Because," I begin, my voice low and raw, "I think I understand. I think... I think I want to feel it too."

The admission hangs in the air between us, charged with potential. When I open my eyes, Jaz is watching me intently, his dark gaze boring into mine. There's something in his eyes--not judgment or disgust, but a spark of recognition, of kinship.

"It's addictive," he says softly, his words a caress against my skin. "That feeling of power, of control. Of making them pay for what they've done."

I nod, a shiver running down my spine. "I have some memories but not their faces," I confess, the words tumbling out in a rush. "But I hear their laughter, feel their hands on me. And I imagine... I imagine making them suffer."

Jaz reaches out, his calloused fingers brushing against my cheek. The touch is electric, sending sparks skittering across my skin. "Tell me," he urges, his voice a low growl that resonates deep in my chest.

I lean into his touch, letting my eyes flutter closed again. "I want to hear them beg," I whisper, the words feeling like a prayer and a curse all at once. "I want to see the fear in their eyes when they realize what's coming. I want to make them feel every ounce of pain and terror they inflicted on me."

When I open my eyes, Jaz's face is inches from mine. His pupils are dilated, his breathing shallow. There's an intensity to him that should frighten me, but instead, it fans the flames of my own desire for vengeance.

"I can help you," he says, his voice rough with promise. "I can teach you how to make them suffer, how to extract every drop of pain they deserve."

My heart pounds, a mix of fear and exhilaration coursing through my veins. Jaz's words paint vivid images in my mind--dark, violent fantasies that should repulse me, but instead ignite something primal within. I lick my dry lips, voice barely above a whisper as I ask, "How?"

Jaz's eyes darken, a predatory gleam flickering in their depths. He leans in closer, his breath hot against my ear as he murmurs, "First, we find them. Then, we make them regret ever laying a hand on you."

A shiver runs down my spine, equal parts anticipation and apprehension. "But how will we find them?" I ask, frustration edging into my voice. "My memories are still so fragmented."

Jaz pulls back slightly, his expression softening. "It'll come back to you, little Bee. And when it does, I'll be here to help you piece it all together."

His confidence is infectious, and I find myself nodding. "Okay," I breathe, steeling my resolve. "So what's the first step?"

Jaz's eyes soften, a hint of tenderness breaking through his hardened exterior. "The first step, little Bee, is to heal. To get stronger." His hand finds mine, his calloused fingers intertwining with my own. "Your body needs time to mend, and your mind... well, that's a different kind of healing altogether."

I nod, feeling the weight of his words settle over me like a warm blanket. The rage still simmers beneath my skin, a constant companion, but there's wisdom in his approach. I can't exact my revenge if I'm broken and weak.

Chapter Three

Days turn into weeks, a blur of healing and revelation. Jaz becomes my constant, my anchor in the storm of recovery. He tends to my wounds with practiced care, continuing to apply his salves that sting and soothe in equal measure. His hands, calloused and strong, are infinitely gentle as they ghost over my bruised skin.

Slowly, painfully, my body knits itself back together. The bruises fade from violent purples to sickly yellows, then vanish altogether. But the marks on my soul remain raw and weeping.

I wake screaming some nights, phantom hands grasping at my flesh. Jaz is always there, and when I beg him to hold me, his arms become a fortress against the terrors that haunt me.

As my strength returns, so do the memories, replaying like jagged shards of glass, cutting deep. They come in flashes, vivid and cruel. The bonfire's warmth on my skin. The sweet taste of the drink in my red cup. The dizziness that wasn't just from alcohol. Three faces, leering and predatory, emerging from the shadows between the trees.

I come to consciousness screaming again, clawing at phantoms.

Jaz holds me, his embrace both a cage and a sanctuary. "Let it out," he whispers fiercely. "Your pain is your power. Use it."

And so I do. I rage, weep and curse the universe for its cruelty. Jaz weathers it all, a rock against which my storm breaks.

Time passes, measured in small victories. The day I can sit up without assistance. The first steps I take, wobbling like a newborn fawn. The morning I look in the mirror and recognize the face staring back at me, battered but unbroken.

Jaz becomes my protector, my confidant, my dark angel. He teaches me to channel my pain into purpose, to forge my anger into a weapon.

"Revenge isn't just about violence," he tells me one night, his eyes glinting in the lamplight. "It's about reclaiming what was taken from you. Your power. Your autonomy. Your future."

I absorb his words like a sponge, letting them fill the hollow spaces inside me. With each passing day, my resolve hardens. I will not be defined by what was done to me. I will rise, and I will make them pay.

It's on a quiet evening, as Jaz changes my bandages, that the final pieces click into place. The scent of antiseptic hangs in the air, sharp and clinical. His fingers brush against my skin, and suddenly, I'm there again. The bonfire. The trees. The laughter that turned to screams.

"I remember," I whisper, my voice hoarse with the weight of revelation. "I remember their faces."

Jaz's hands still, his dark eyes locking onto mine. "Tell me, little fighter," he urges softly.

The words spill out of me like blood from a wound, each memory a fresh cut on my psyche. "The bonfire... it was a party, a bunch of us from the same college. I can see the flames dancing, hear the music pulsing. My red cup... the drink tasted off, but I ignored it. Everything went fuzzy after that."

Jaz nods, his jaw clenched tight, a muscle ticking in his cheek as he listens. His fingers resume their ministrations, gentle yet grounding.

"There were three of them," I whisper, my voice cracking. "They... they followed me when I stumbled away from the party. Into the trees."

I trail off, choking on the words. Jaz's hand finds mine, squeezing gently. "You're safe now," he reminds me. "Keep going. Let it out."

Drawing strength from his touch, I press on. "They took turns. I could smell the ocean nearby, hear the waves crashing. But no one heard me. No one came." Tears stream down my face, hot and bitter. "When they were done, they beat me. Fists and feet and cruel laughter. Then... nothing. Just darkness."

Silence falls between us, heavy with shared understanding. Jaz's thumb traces soothing circles on the back of my hand. "I found you there in the morning. You survived," he says finally, his voice thick with emotion. "You're stronger than they could ever imagine, little fighter. And so damn brave."

I nod, a shaky breath escaping my lips. "They were in some of my classes," I whisper, the words tasting like ash on my tongue.

Jaz's eyes widen, a spark of dangerous interest igniting in their depths. "You know their names?" he asks, his voice low and urgent.

I close my eyes, letting the memories wash over me. The lecture hall comes into focus, its tiered seats filled with faceless students. But three faces stand out with cruel clarity, etched into my mind like a brand.

"Yes," I breathe, my voice barely audible. "I know their names."

The room seems to shrink around us, the air growing thick and heavy. Outside, the wind picks up, whistling through the trees and rattling the windowpane. It's as if nature itself is responding to the tension building between us.

Jaz leans in closer, his presence both comforting and intimidating. The scent of him—sandalwood and something darker, more primal—envelops me. His breath is warm against my cheek as he speaks. "Tell me, little Bee. Give me their names."

I open my eyes, meeting his intense gaze. The world narrows to just us two, everything else fading into insignificance. My heart pounds in my chest, each beat a war drum urging me forward.

"Tyler Matheson," I say, the name like poison on my lips. "He sat two rows behind me in Psych 101. Always cracking jokes, acting like the class clown."

Jaz nods, his expression hardening. "Go on," he encourages softly.

"Marcus Delgado," I continue, my voice growing stronger. "We shared a Creative Writing seminar. He... he used to compliment my stories. Said I had a way with words."

A bitter laugh escapes me, the irony of it all threatening to choke me. Jaz's hand finds mine, his grip firm and grounding.

"And the third?" he prompts gently.

I take a deep breath, steeling myself. "Ethan Reeves," I spit out, hatred coursing through me. "Captain of the lacrosse team. We had Calculus together. He was always surrounded by his adoring fans."

As I speak their names, it's as if I'm casting a spell. The air around us seems to crackle with energy, dark and potent. Jaz's eyes glitter dangerously, a predatory smile curving his lips.

"You've done well, little fighter," he murmurs, pride evident in his voice. "You've given us the key to your vengeance."

I shiver, both from the intensity of his gaze and the weight of what we're about to embark on. "What happens now?" I ask, my voice barely above a whisper.

Jaz reaches out, his calloused fingers tracing the line of my jaw. The touch is electric, sending sparks skittering across my skin. "Now," he says, his voice a low rumble that resonates in my chest, "we plan. We prepare. We become the nightmare they never saw coming."

His words ignite something primal within me, a dark flame that threatens to consume everything in its path. I lean into his touch, craving the strength and certainty he exudes. "How?" I whisper, my voice trembling with a mix of fear and anticipation.

Jaz's eyes soften, a hint of tenderness breaking through his hardened exterior. "First, we gather information," he explains, his thumb brushing gently against my cheek. "We learn their routines, their weaknesses, their darkest secrets. Knowledge is power, little Bee, and we're going to arm ourselves to the teeth."

I nod, drinking in his words like a parched traveler in the desert. The room around us seems to fade away, leaving only Jaz and the promise of retribution hanging between us. Outside, the wind howls, a mournful sound that echoes the turmoil in my soul.

"What then?" I ask, my voice stronger now, fueled by the growing resolve within me.

A slow, dangerous smile spreads across Jaz's face, his eyes glinting with dark promise. "Then," he says, leaning in close enough that I can feel his breath on my skin, "we strike. We take everything from them, piece by piece, until they're left with nothing but the knowledge of their own depravity."

His words paint vivid pictures in my mind—Tyler, Marcus, and Ethan brought low, stripped of their arrogance and false bravado. I see them cowering, begging for mercy they don't deserve. The images should horrify me, but instead, they fill me with a fierce, terrible joy.

"Will it hurt?" I ask, surprising myself with the eagerness in my voice. "Will they suffer?"

Jaz's smile widens, revealing a flash of white teeth. "Oh yes," he purrs, the words dripping with dark satisfaction. "They'll feel every ounce of pain they inflicted on you, magnified a thousand times over. We'll make sure of that."

A shiver runs down my spine, not entirely from fear. There's something intoxicating about the darkness Jaz offers, a seductive pull that I'm powerless to resist. I find myself leaning closer, drawn into his orbit like a moth to a flame.

His hand slides from my jaw to the nape of my neck, his grip firm but gentle. "Tell me about them," he urges, his words a caress against my skin. "Every detail you can remember. Their habits, their weaknesses, their sins."

I close my eyes, letting the memories wash over me. The lecture hall comes into focus, its tiered seats filled with faceless students. But three faces stand out with cruel clarity, etched into my mind like a brand.

"Tyler," I begin, my voice barely above a whisper. "He's always late to class, rushing in with some elaborate excuse. He sits in the back, surrounded by his cronies. They laugh too loud at his jokes, preen under his attention."

Jaz nods, encouraging me to continue. His thumb traces soothing circles at the base of my skull, grounding me in the present even as I delve into the past.

"Marcus," I say, my voice growing stronger. "He's quieter, more calculated. Always has his nose in a book, but his eyes... they wander. I've seen him staring at girls when he thinks no one's looking. There's a hunger in his gaze that makes my skin crawl."

A low growl rumbles in Jaz's chest, his grip tightening slightly. The sound sends a thrill through me, a mix of fear and something darker, more primal.

"And Ethan?" Jaz prompts, his breath hot against my ear.

I shudder, memories of that night threatening to overwhelm me. Jaz's presence anchors me, his steady heartbeat a counterpoint to my racing pulse.

"Ethan's the worst," I whisper, hatred coating my words. "He struts around campus like he owns it. Girls fawn over him, guys want to be him. But there's a cruelty in him, barely hidden beneath the surface. I've seen how he treats people he thinks are beneath him."

As I speak, it's as if a dam has broken. Words pour out of me, a torrent of observations and suspicions I didn't even realize I had. I tell Jaz about Tyler's drug habit, poorly concealed and eagerly indulged. About Marcus's obsession with a freshman girl, his eyes following her with a predatory gleam. About the rumors swirling around Ethan— hushed whispers of other girls who've stumbled away from parties, dazed and confused.

Jaz listens intently, his dark eyes gleaming with each new revelation. His fingers card through my hair, the gentle touch at odds with the violence brewing between us.

"You've done well, little Bee," he murmurs, pride evident in his voice. "This is exactly what we need."

I lean into his touch, craving the comfort and strength he offers. "What's next?" I ask, my voice steady despite the storm of emotions raging within me.

Jaz's lips curve into a dangerous smile. "Now," he says, his voice low and rich with promise, "we start to build our web. We'll gather more information, create a detailed picture of their lives. And then, when the time is right, we'll begin to dismantle them piece by piece."

A shiver runs down my spine, equal parts fear and anticipation. "How long will it take?" I ask, impatience coloring my words.

Jaz chuckles, the sound dark and velvety. "Revenge is a dish best served cold, little fighter. We can't rush this. It needs to be perfect."

I nod, understanding the wisdom in his words even as frustration burns in my chest. "I want them to suffer," I whisper, surprised by the vehemence in my voice.

"And they will," Jaz assures me, his eyes glittering dangerously. "I promise you, by the time we're done with them, they'll be begging for death."

His words should horrify me, but instead, they send a thrill of dark satisfaction through my body. I lean in closer, drawn to the promise of vengeance like a moth to flame.

"Teach me," I breathe, my lips barely brushing against his. "Show me how to make them pay."

Jaz's breath hitches, his pupils dilating with desire—for revenge or for me, I'm not sure. Maybe both. He cups my face in his hands, his touch gentle yet possessive.

"Are you sure?" he asks, his voice rough with emotion. "Once we start down this path, there's no turning back. You'll be changed forever."

I meet his gaze unflinchingly, steel in my voice as I reply, "I'm already changed. They saw to that. Now it's time to show them exactly what they've created."

A slow, dangerous smile spreads across Jaz's face. "Then let the lessons begin," he purrs, sealing our dark pact with a kiss that tastes of vengeance and forbidden desire.

As his lips claim mine, I feel something shift inside me. The last remnants of the old Bee—naive, trusting, vulnerable—crumble away. In her place rises someone new, forged in the fire of pain and trauma.

Chapter Four

The weeks become months, each sunrise bringing me closer to the reckoning I crave. Jaz is my dark guardian angel, guiding me through a metamorphosis both beautiful and terrifying.

My body heals, scars fading to silvery reminders of what was stolen from me. But it's my mind that undergoes the most profound transformation. Jaz teaches me to hone my pain into a weapon, to channel my rage into cold, calculated purpose.

We spend hours poring over information, piecing together the lives of my attackers like a macabre jigsaw puzzle. Tyler's drug habit proves easy to exploit--a whispered word in the right ear, a strategically placed bag of white powder. Within weeks, he's spiraling, paranoia etched into the dark circles beneath his bloodshot eyes.

Marcus's obsession with the freshman girls becomes our key to unraveling him. Anonymous tips, fabricated evidence, and suddenly he's facing a restraining order and whispers of "stalker" follow him across campus. His carefully cultivated image of the sensitive writer crumbles, revealing the predator beneath.

Ethan proves the most challenging, his golden-boy facade seemingly impenetrable. But even Teflon can't withstand the acid we drip onto his life. Rumors spread like wildfire, fanned by strategically leaked photos and whispered confessions. His teammates start to eye him warily, his adoring fans drifting away one by one.

Through it all, Jaz remains my anchor. He holds me when the nightmares come, his strong arms a fortress against the terrors that haunt me. His voice, low and soothing, talks me through the panic attacks that leave me gasping for air, convinced I'm back on that beach with sand in my mouth and cruel hands on my skin.

"Breathe, little Bee," he'll murmur, his fingers tracing soothing patterns on my back. "You're safe. I've got you. They can't hurt you anymore."

And slowly, painfully, I start to believe him. The flashbacks come less frequently, the panic attacks lose their paralyzing grip. In their place grows something new--a steely resolve, a hunger for justice that burns away the last vestiges of the girl I used to be.

Jaz teaches me self-defense, his hands guiding my body through forms and strikes. There's an intimacy to these sessions that goes beyond the physical. With every blocked punch, every perfectly executed throw, I reclaim a piece of myself that was stolen that night on the beach.

"Good," Jaz growls as I pin him to the mat, his eyes dark with pride and something else, something that sends a shiver down my spine. "You're getting stronger every day, little fighter."

Our training sessions grow more intense, the line between violence and intimacy blurring with each passing day. Jaz pushes me to my limits, his hands alternating between brutal strikes and gentle caresses. I learn to read the tension in his muscles, to anticipate his movements before he makes them.

One day, as we grapple on the mat, something shifts. I pin Jaz beneath me, my breath coming in ragged gasps. His eyes lock onto mine, dark with a hunger that has nothing to do with combat. For a moment, we're frozen, the air between us crackling with electricity.

"Good girl," Jaz growls, his voice low and rough. The praise sends a shiver through me, igniting something primal in my core.

I'm not sure who moves first. One moment we're staring at each other, chests heaving, and the next his lips are on mine. The kiss is brutal, all teeth and tongue and pent-up desire. I taste blood, unsure if it's his or mine, and find I don't care.

Jaz's hands roam my body, no longer gentle but demanding, possessive. I arch into his touch, craving the burn of his calloused fingers against my skin. He flips us over, pinning me beneath him, and I feel the hard length of him pressing against my thigh.

"Tell me to stop," he pants, his eyes wild with need and a hint of desperation. "If you don't want this, tell me now."

I answer by pulling him down for another kiss, pouring all my rage, pain and desire into it. Jaz groans, a sound that reverberates through my very bones. His hands make quick work of our clothes, leaving us bare and panting on the training mat.

There's nothing gentle about what follows. It's a clash of bodies, a battle for dominance that leaves us both bruised and gasping. As Jaz enters me, the world narrows to just this moment--the stretch and burn, the fullness, the exquisite pleasure-pain that shoots through my core. I cry out, my nails raking down his back, leaving angry red welts in their wake.

"That's it, little Bee," Jaz growls, his voice rough with desire. "Let me hear you."

He sets a punishing pace, each thrust driving me higher, closer to the edge of something I can't quite name. It's revenge and healing, punishment and absolution all at once. I meet him thrust for thrust, my body singing with sensations I'd thought lost to me forever. Jaz takes me hard and fast, his fingers digging into my hips hard enough to leave marks. I welcome the pain, relish in it, using it to ground myself in the present.

"Look at me," Jaz commands, one hand gripping my chin. "I want to see your eyes when you come undone."

I obey, locking my gaze with his. The intensity I see there--the raw need, the fierce protectiveness—pushes me over the edge. When I come, it's with a scream that's part pleasure, part release of all the pent-up emotions I've been carrying. Jaz follows soon after, his body shuddering against mine as he buries his face in the crook of my neck.

We lay there for a long moment, sweat cooling on our skin, neither of us willing to break the silence. Finally, Jaz props himself up on one elbow, his dark eyes searching mine.

"Are you okay?" he asks, a hint of vulnerability creeping into his voice.

I nod, surprised to find that I am. For the first time in months, I feel truly present in my own body. The constant undercurrent of fear and shame that's been my companion since that night on the beach has quieted, replaced by a sense of power and control.

"I'm more than okay," I tell him.

Jaz's eyes soften, a rare vulnerability flickering across his face. His hand comes up to cup my cheek, thumb brushing gently across my cheekbone. "You're incredible, little Bee," he murmurs, his voice rough with emotion. "So strong, so fierce."

I lean into his touch, savoring the warmth of his skin against mine. For a moment, we stay like that, suspended in a bubble of intimacy that feels both fragile and unbreakable.

But the real world intrudes, as it always does. A car horn blares outside, shattering the silence. Jaz tenses, his body coiling with sudden alertness. I feel the shift in him, the return of the hardened warrior.

"We should get cleaned up," he says, already moving to stand. "We have work to do."

I nod, pushing myself up from the mat. My body aches in a dozen places, a delicious soreness that reminds me I'm alive, I'm here, I'm fighting back. As I gather my scattered clothes, I catch Jaz watching me, his dark eyes unreadable.

"What?" I ask, suddenly self-conscious under his intense gaze.

A small smile tugs at the corner of his mouth. "Just admiring my handiwork," he says, gesturing to the constellation of bruises blooming across my skin. "You wear them well, little fighter."

Heat rises to my cheeks, a mix of embarrassment and pride. These marks are different from the ones that came before. These, I chose. These, I earned.

We shower separately, the sound of running water a poor substitute for the intimacy we just shared. When I emerge, skin pink from the heat and hair dripping, Jaz is already dressed and bent over his laptop.

"Come here," he says, not looking up from the screen. "I think I've found something."

I pad over, curiosity overriding any lingering awkwardness. Jaz's fingers fly across the keyboard, pulling up documents and social media profiles faster than I can process.

"Ethan," he says, his voice hard. "He's planning a party this weekend. Big one, out at his family's beach house."

My breath catches in my throat. "The same place where..."

Jaz nods, his jaw clenched tight. "The very same. Seems our golden boy likes to revisit the scene of his crimes."

A cold fury settles in my chest, icy tendrils wrapping around my heart. "What are you thinking?" I ask, though I already know the answer.

Jaz turns to me, his eyes glittering with dark promise. "I'm thinking it's time we crash a party, little Bee. What do you say? Ready to face your demons?"

Fear and anticipation war within me, but I push them both aside. I meet Jaz's gaze, steel in my voice as I reply, "Let's do it," I say, my voice steady despite the storm of emotions raging inside me. "It's time to make them pay."

Jaz's eyes darken with approval, a slow smile spreading across his face. "That's my girl," he murmurs, his hand coming to rest on the nape of my neck. The touch sends a shiver down my spine, a potent mix of comfort and excitement.

We spend the next few days in intense preparation. Jaz drills me on every aspect of our plan, his patience seemingly endless as he walks me through each step. We go over contingencies, escape routes, signals. By the time Friday night rolls around, I feel like I've memorized every grain of sand on that cursed beach.

As I stand before the mirror, applying the finishing touches to my makeup, I barely recognize the woman staring back at me. Gone is the soft, vulnerable girl from before. In her place stands someone harder, sharper. My blue eyes, once wide with innocence, now hold a predatory gleam that matches Jaz's. My hair hasn't seen a hairdresser since the attack, so instead of the shortened bleached bob it's now back to its normal honey blonde, the waves falling down to my waist.

"You ready, little Bee?" Jaz asks, appearing in the doorway behind me. His eyes rake over my form, appreciation evident in his gaze.

I nod, smoothing down the front of my dress. It's black, form-fitting, with strategic cutouts that show just enough skin to be enticing. A far cry from the bright pinks and light colors I used to wear, from what I wore that fateful night. But then again, I'm not the same person anymore.

"Let's go hunt some monsters," I say, my voice low and dangerous.

The drive to the beach house is a journey through memory and shadow. Jaz's sleek black car purrs down the coastal highway, headlights cutting through the gathering dusk. The ocean stretches out beside us, an inky expanse that seems to swallow the fading light. I watch the waves crash against the shore, each one a heartbeat of anticipation.

"You okay?" Jaz asks, his eyes flicking between me and the road. His hand finds mine, fingers intertwining with a gentle squeeze.

I nod, not trusting my voice. The closer we get, the more vivid the memories become. I can almost taste the salt in the air, feel the sand between my toes. It's been exactly one year since that night, a fact that hasn't escaped either of us. There's a poetry to it, a symmetry that feels both terrible and right.

"Revenge is a dish best served cold," I murmur, more to myself than to Jaz.

He chuckles, a low sound that sends a shiver down my spine. "And we've let this one chill for a full year," he agrees. "It'll be positively glacial by now."

The metaphor should be comforting but instead, it makes me shiver. I think of the pain I've carried for the past year, the rage that's become my constant companion. It hasn't cooled; it's crystallized, sharpening into something hard and deadly.

As we round a bend in the road, the beach house comes into view. It's a sprawling structure of glass and wood. Lights blaze from every window, and even from here, I can hear the thump of bass. My stomach clenches, a mix of fear and anticipation roiling within me.

My breath catches in my throat as I spot the bonfire on the beach below. The flames dance in the darkness, casting long shadows across the sand. It's so similar to that night, yet everything has changed.

"Remember," Jaz says, his voice low and intense. "We're in control. Every step, every moment--it's all on our terms. You say the word, and we're out of there. No questions asked."

I nod, grateful for the reminder. I take a deep breath, centering myself. "I'm ready," I tell him, and I'm surprised to find that it's true.

We make our way down to the beach, the sand cool beneath our feet. A massive bonfire blazes some distance from the house, casting long shadows across the sand. Figures move around it, their silhouettes distorted by the flames. The scene is eerily familiar, like a nightmare come to life.

"Look," Jaz murmurs, nodding towards a group near the fire.

My breath catches in my throat. There they are—Tyler, Marcus, and Ethan. They're laughing, red cups in hand, looking for all the world like normal college guys enjoying a party.

Chapter Five

My eyes lock onto them, a cold fury settling in my chest. Tyler, with his shaggy hair and lazy grin, looking more haggard than I remember. Marcus, his eyes darting nervously, a far cry from the confident predator of my nightmares. And Ethan... my fists clench at my sides as I take him in. He looks unchanged, still radiating that easy charm that once fooled me. They look so normal, so carefree. As if they hadn't shattered my world a year ago on this very beach. The injustice of it burns through me, igniting a rage that threatens to consume everything in its path.

Jaz's hand on my lower back grounds me, his touch a reminder of why we're here. "Easy, little Bee," he murmurs, his breath hot against my ear. "Remember the plan."

I nod, forcing myself to take a deep breath. We make our way towards the bonfire, blending in with the crowd of partygoers. The music pulses around us, a primal beat that seems to sync with my racing heart.

As we draw closer, I catch snippets of conversation. Ethan's voice carries over the din, boastful and loud. "...and then I told her, 'Baby, you know you want it,'" he laughs, his friends joining in with raucous approval.

The words hit me like a physical blow, memories threatening to overwhelm me. But Jaz's steady presence keeps me anchored in the present. I feel his muscles tense beside me, barely restrained violence in every line of his body.

"Soon," he promises, his voice low and dangerous. "Very soon."

We circle the bonfire, keeping to the shadows. I catch Tyler's eye as we pass, and for a moment, I think he recognizes me. But then his gaze slides away, dismissive. I'm just another pretty face in the crowd to him now.

The realization steadies me. We have the element of surprise on our side. They have no idea what's coming for them.

As the night wears on, we watch and wait. Jaz slips away at one point, returning with a predatory gleam in his eye. "It's done," he murmurs. "Now we wait."

The party reaches its peak, a frenzy of dancing bodies and drunken laughter. And then, one by one, our targets begin to falter. Tyler stumbles away from the crowd, his face pale and sweating. Marcus follows soon after, clutching his stomach.

Ethan holds out the longest, but eventually even he succumbs. I watch with grim satisfaction as he staggers towards the house, his golden boy facade crumbling.

"Now," Jaz says, his voice tight with anticipation.

We move swiftly, following Ethan into the house. The music fades behind us, replaced by the sound of retching coming from upstairs. We climb the steps silently, predators on the hunt.

The bathroom door is ajar, light spilling out into the darkened hallway. Ethan is hunched over the toilet, oblivious to our presence. Jaz moves first, swift and silent. Before Ethan can react, he's pulled back, a cloth pressed over his face.

The night air chills my skin as we drag the unconscious men into the trees near the house. My heart pounds, a mix of fear and anticipation coursing through my veins. The familiar surroundings bring painful memories flooding back but I push them aside, focusing on the task at hand.

Jaz secures our captives, his movements efficient and practiced. "I'll be right back," he murmurs, pressing a gentle kiss to my temple before melting into the shadows.

Left alone with my rapists, I study their slack faces in the dim moonlight. They look so ordinary, so harmless. But I know the monsters that lurk beneath.

The distant thump of music grows louder, revelers oblivious to the dark drama unfolding in the trees. Jaz returns, a duffel bag slung over his shoulder. His eyes gleam with dangerous intent as he unzips it, revealing an array of tools that make my breath catch.

"Remember," he says softly, "this is your revenge. I'm just here to guide you."

As we stand over our captives, the gravity of the moment settles over me. Jaz gently guides my hand to one of the tools—a sharp knife that glints in the moonlight. "Do it like I showed you. Start slow," he murmurs. "Make them feel every moment."

With trembling fingers, I make the first cut across Tyler's chest. He jerks awake with a muffled scream, eyes wild with fear and confusion. The sight of his pain ignites something primal within me.

Jaz's hands steady mine as I work, his low voice in my ear providing instruction and encouragement. "That's it, little Bee. Make them suffer."

One by one, they wake to a nightmare of their own making. Their pleas for mercy fall on deaf ears as I extract my pound of flesh. With each cut, each scream, I feel a piece of myself returning. The power they stole from me that night flows back into my veins.

As their cries grow weaker, my resolve strengthens. Jaz watches with dark approval, occasionally stepping in to demonstrate a particularly cruel technique. The sounds of their suffering mingle with the distant bass of the party, creating a macabre symphony.

When it's over, when their broken bodies lie still on the blood-soaked ground, I feel reborn.

And turned on.

The adrenaline coursing through my veins ignites into something else--a primal, desperate need. I turn to Jaz, my body thrumming with dark energy. His eyes lock onto mine, pupils blown wide with a hunger that matches my own.

Without a word, I launch myself at him. My lips crash against his, teeth clashing as I pour every ounce of rage and pain and twisted desire into the kiss. Jaz responds instantly, his strong arms wrapping around me as he devours my mouth.

We stumble backwards, away from the carnage we've wrought, until my back hits the rough bark of a tree. Jaz's hands roam my body, no longer gentle but demanding, possessive. I arch into his touch, craving the burn of his calloused fingers against my skin.

"Please," I gasp against his lips, not even sure what I'm begging for.

Jaz understands. With a growl, he picks me up, pressing me firmly against the tree. His body covers mine, hot and hard, and I wrap my legs around his hips. I feel the thick length of him pressing against my entrance as his lips trail fire down my neck.

"Is this what you want, little Bee?" he rasps, his voice rough with need. "To reclaim this place? To wash away their touch with mine?"

"Yes," I moan, grinding against him. "Please, Jaz. I need-"

My words cut off in a gasp as he hikes up my dress further, cool air hitting my overheated skin. Jaz's fingers trace the edge of my panties, teasing me. "So wet for me," he murmurs approvingly. "Such a good girl."

In one swift motion, he tears the delicate fabric away. I cry out at the sting, pleasure spiking through me. Jaz's hand comes up to cover my mouth, muffling my cries.

"Shh," he whispers, his breath hot against my ear. "Can't let anyone hear us, can we? Don't want anyone interrupting us."

I nod frantically, beyond words. Jaz keeps his hand over my mouth as he positions himself at my entrance. With one hard thrust, he's inside me, stretching me to the point of pain.

There's nothing gentle about what follows. Jaz takes me hard and fast, his hips snapping against mine with bruising force. Each thrust drives me against the rough bark of the tree, the pain only heightening my pleasure. Jaz wraps a hand around my throat, not squeezing, but applying just enough pressure to remind me of his strength. The possessive gesture sends a thrill through me. His dark eyes bore into mine as he pounds into me relentlessly.

"You're mine now," he growls, his voice rough with exertion and something deeper, more primal. "Say it."

"Yours," I gasp out, the word muffled against his palm. "I'm yours, Jaz."

His grip on my throat tightens fractionally, cutting off my air for just a moment before releasing. The brief deprivation makes my head spin, heightening every sensation.

"Again," he demands, his hips never slowing their punishing rhythm.

"Yours!" I cry out, not caring if anyone hears. Let them come. Let them see what we've done, what we've become.

Jaz's movements grow more frantic, his control slipping. I can feel my own release building, a tidal wave threatening to overwhelm me. The rough bark of the tree scrapes against my back, pain and pleasure blurring until I can no longer tell them apart.

"Come for me, little Bee," Jaz commands, his voice a low growl that vibrates through my entire body. "Let me feel you."

His words are the final push I need. I shatter around him, waves of pleasure crashing over me as I cry out his name. Jaz follows soon after, his body shuddering against mine as he spills inside me with a guttural groan.

For a long moment, we stay like that, panting and trembling in the aftermath. The distant sounds of the party filter back in, a stark reminder of the world beyond our dark cocoon. Slowly, Jaz lowers me to my feet, his hands gentle now as they smooth down my dress.

As the last tremors of pleasure fade, reality crashes back in. The coppery scent of blood mingles with the salt air, a grim reminder of what we've done. Jaz's eyes lock onto mine, a silent question in their depths. I nod, no words needed between us.

We move swiftly, gathering our tools and erasing any trace of our presence. The bodies of our victims lie still and broken in the shadows, their unseeing eyes staring up at the star-strewn sky. A part of me wants to linger, to savor this moment of triumph. But Jaz's hand on my arm urges me forward.

"We need to go," he murmurs, his voice low and urgent. "Someone will come looking for them soon."

The walk back to the car feels surreal, like wading through a dream. The sand beneath my feet is cool and damp, so different from the scorching grains that burned my skin a year ago. The distant thump of music grows fainter with each step, the revelry of the party a stark contrast to the dark deed we've just committed.

As we reach the road, I pause, turning to look back at the beach house. Its windows still blaze with light, silhouettes of partygoers visible through the glass. How long before someone notices the absence of the three golden boys? How long before their broken bodies are discovered among the trees?

Jaz's hand on the small of my back guides me into the car. The leather seat is cool against my overheated skin as I sink into it. For a moment, we sit in silence, the weight of what we've done settling over us like a heavy blanket.

Then Jaz starts the engine, its purr a comforting rumble in the stillness of the night. We pull away from the curb, leaving behind the scene of both my greatest trauma and my ultimate revenge. As we merge onto the coastal highway, the ocean stretches out beside us, an inky expanse that seems to swallow the moonlight.

"Where to now?" Jaz asks, his eyes flicking between me and the road ahead.

I gaze out at the endless horizon, feeling a sense of lightness I haven't experienced in a year. The burdens I've carried for so long--the fear, the shame, the burning need for vengeance--have been left behind on that blood-soaked beach.

In their place is a vast, exhilarating emptiness, a canvas waiting to be filled.

"Anywhere," I reply, surprised by the steadiness in my voice. "As long as it's with you."

Jaz's hand finds mine, his fingers intertwining with mine. The touch is gentle now, a stark contrast to the bruising grip of our earlier passion. I look over at him, taking in his profile illuminated by the dashboard lights. The sharp angles of his face, the fullness of his lips, the intricate tattoos creeping up his neck--he's beautiful in a dangerous way, like a predator at rest. His dark eyes flick to mine, a small smile playing at the corners of his mouth.

"Anywhere it is, then," he says, his thumb tracing circles on the back of my hand. "The world's a big place, little Bee. Lots of monsters out there waiting to be hunted."

His words send a thrill through me, a mix of excitement and trepidation. We're fugitives now, I realize. There's no going back to my old life, to the person I was before. But as I watch the familiar coastline fade into the distance behind us, I find I don't want to.

The girl I was died on that beach a year ago. The woman I've become was forged in fire and blood, tempered by rage and vengeance. And now, with the deed done and justice served, I feel... free. Unburdened. Ready to embrace whatever comes next.

"Tell me about these monsters," I say, turning to face Jaz fully. "Where do we find them?"

Jaz's grin widens, predatory and proud. "Oh, little Bee," he purrs, "they're everywhere. Men who think they can take what isn't theirs, who prey on the vulnerable and believe they'll never face consequences. But we know better, don't we?"

I nod, feeling a familiar fire ignite in my belly. "We do," I agree, my voice low and dangerous. "And we'll make them pay."

Jaz's eyes gleam with approval and something darker, more primal. "That's my girl," he murmurs, his hand squeezing mine gently.

We drive through the night, the familiar coastline fading into unfamiliar territory. The rhythmic purr of the engine and the gentle rock of the car lull me into a state of calm reflection. I think about everything that's led me to this moment—the pain, the rage, the dark transformation I've undergone.

A year ago, I was a different person. Innocent. Naive. Vulnerable. Now, I'm something else entirely. The old Bee would be horrified by what we've done tonight. But the woman I've become? She feels only a grim satisfaction.

"What are you thinking about?" Jaz asks, breaking the comfortable silence.

I turn to look at him, taking in his profile illuminated by the dashboard lights. "About how much I've changed," I admit. "About how I should feel guilty, but I don't."

Jaz nods, understanding in his eyes. "Guilt is for those who haven't suffered," he says softly. "You paid your dues in pain and blood. Now it's time for the monsters to pay theirs."

His words settle over me like a warm blanket, soothing away any lingering doubts. I lean back in my seat, watching the world fly by in a blur outside the window. The future stretches out before us, unknown but full of so much dark promise.

About the Author

Maree lives on the East Coast of Australia with her wonderful husband, her son, and her two gorgeous squishy british bulldogs.

When she is not writing, she is working in a financial career (for something completely different to the creative side) or she is working on her photography (which is just as hot as her books).

If you enjoyed this story, make sure you check out her novella Dead Devil's Night, you can find it here: books2read.com/deaddevil snight

Or check out her dark contemporary why choose standalones The Darling Games, filled with masked unalivers and the women who bring them to their knees. You can find the first one here: book s2read.com/huntmedarling

Access all of her books and social media links here: https://linktr. ee/mareeroseauthor

Sinfully Unfaithful

By: Evie Dawn & Ava Kade

About Simply Unfaithful

Katherine

After my husband foolishly provoked Dimitry, the infamous Zaytsev bratva boss, he decided to retaliate by taking me.

I had always been a loyal wife. Yet no matter how much I tried, I couldn't ignore how dangerously attractive Dimitry was. Towering and commanding, cloaked in raw power, his piercing gaze was enough to leave me breathless.

He was vicious and ruthless. His name alone made men tremble.

I was his captive, not just his enemy's wife. I should've focused on escaping, but every time he looked at me, my body betrayed me in ways I'd never felt before.

I knew I should resist him and remain faithful to my husband. But how could I, when his touch made every nerve in my body spark to life, when his voice sent shivers down my spine, and when he whispered that I would soon beg him to claim me?

I should've thought of my husband. I should've fought harder. I should've run.

But what if I didn't?

Dimitry

When I ordered my men to bring me Chernov's wife, I expected another pawn. A means to an end.

What I didn't expect was a wild, defiant kitten. Or for her to tempt me like no one ever had.

She was proud, stupidly brave, and utterly irresistible. Thoughts of what I could do to her consumed me—ruining her, taking her body in ways her husband never could, and sending her back to him shattered.

I thought she'd be a fleeting distraction. A pet I'd tire of after a few nights.

But instead, I found myself wanting more. I wanted to break her and watch her offer herself willingly, begging for me.

That should've been the end of it.

Except it wasn't.

The more time I spent with her, the more I craved her. I wanted to protect her, keep her as mine.

These feelings weren't me. They were dangerous. Vulnerabilities like this spelled disaster in my world.

I needed to stick to the plan. She was meant to be a weapon, not my weakness.

But what if I couldn't let her go?

Content Note:

This extra spicy story has a HEA, is light on dark, and features a morally grey hero and a strong, defiant FMC. Contains cheating, dubcon, body betrayal, violence, and murder. All characters in this story are 18 years of age or older. Mature content. For readers 18 & older.

Relationship type: MF

Chapter One
Katherine

"He's making mistake after mistake, Papa!" I said, pacing the room before dropping into a chair.

I braced my elbows on the table, taking a deep breath. My father stayed silent, fidgeting with his glass.

"You need to talk to him," I insisted. "Maybe one of his brain cells will kick in long enough to listen to you."

"He should listen to you, Katherine. You're his wife."

My father's voice was level, but I knew him too well to miss his frustration. For the last five minutes, he'd been tracing the glass rim, staring blankly at it. His brows were furrowed, a vein bulged on his temple, and new lines creased his forehead, signs he only showed when tense.

"But he doesn't listen," I replied, with a huff. "I'm tired of constantly cleaning up his messes. I married him to strengthen our position, not to babysit him. And until now, his mistakes were at least manageable. But this time, he screwed up. Badly."

I'd married Ivan two years ago, when I was nineteen. He was in his thirties but lacked even a shred of the maturity he should've had, always impulsive, aggressive, and flat-out stupid.

The only redeeming quality was his inheritance, the Chernov bratva, which controlled the north while my father ruled the east of the region. Of course, a marriage seemed obvious, and I'd agreed to it.

Ivan was good-looking, and back then I thought he was smart enough. Too bad that after his father died a year ago and he truly got the reins, I started to see what a walking disaster he was.

I'd had to lean on my father and my own contacts to save his ass a few times. But now I honestly had no idea how the hell I was supposed to do that. Ivan's latest "brilliant" plan was to expand into the south and west.

The problem? That was Dimitry Zaytsev's territory.

I'd never met him, but I'd heard enough to know he was a man you didn't provoke. My husband, of course, didn't see it that way. He had contacted a few cartels and offered them better deals to work for him.

The next day, Dimitry had sent every one of Ivan's men back to our doorstep, in pieces. And now, instead of making amends, Ivan wanted to push further by sending even more people into Dimitry's territory.

My father dragged his hands over his face with a deep sigh.

"I'm sorry, Katya. I should never have proposed this alliance with Ivan, but I didn't realize he was such an idiot. And now..."

My heart ached seeing him like this. Dad had always been an unbreakable source of strength, always calculated and in control. But now, he suddenly looked older, worn down. And, for the first time, scared.

I shouldn't have burdened him with all of this. I reached across the table, covering his hand with mine.

"Don't worry, Papochka," I said. "I'll fix it somehow. I'll talk to Ivan again, and maybe he'll realize how much he's fucked things up this time. I'll make him apologize to Dimitry."

I spoke in a calm, affectionate voice, hoping he wouldn't notice the fear that had crept inside me since I learned what my idiot husband had done. The way my father looked at me told me he saw right through it, though.

"Maybe you should stay here, Katya. This is your home, after all. And we guard our territory better than the Chernovs."

It surprised me to hear him use Ivan's last name. The coldness in his voice sent a shiver down my spine. Despite his rough exterior, my dad had always treated Ivan like family. But now, he practically spat out his name.

I squeezed his hand, offering a soft smile.

"Don't worry, Papa. I'll be fine. One way or another, I'll make Ivan apologize to Dimitry. I'm sorry for dragging you into this. I probably overreacted and made it sound worse than it is."

I could tell he didn't believe a word. Neither did I. Yet this was my and my husband's problem, and I shouldn't have brought it to him. I started to stand, but my dad gripped my hand.

"Stay here, Katya. Please."

"I can't, Papa. I'm Ivan's wife, I should be with him. Idiot or not, he's my husband. But don't worry, everything will be alright."

He tried to convince me a few more times, but I held firm. I wasn't going to bring all this trouble home. Maybe now I was Katherine Chernova, Ivan's wife, but before that, I was Katherine Romanova. Husband or not, Ivan wasn't my priority. My father and my bratva were.

After a few more words, I left the villa, followed by my bodyguards. I waved goodbye as the driver started the car, my mind drifting as I stared out the window, lost in thought.

Then I heard the explosion.

And everything went black around me.

Chapter Two
Katherine

My heart thumped as they brought me into the room. Judging by the massive, imposing table and the sheer number of chairs, I assumed it was used for meetings. The place was vast and austere, minimalist decorated, giving me a feeling of cold elegance.

It also reminded me of a luxurious cage, and I asked myself if this was only because of the position I had found myself in, or if it was something every person who had ever been here had felt.

The brute that led the group of men yanked me toward the middle of the space.

I glanced at him, and I took some pride in seeing the marks I'd left on his face. Whatever Dimitry was going to do to me, at least I knew this one was going to remember me every time he looked in the mirror.

They hadn't covered my eyes while bringing me here, so I'd known instantly I was in Dimitry's home. I easily recognized the region, and it wasn't as if I didn't expect something like this.

If I get out of this alive, I'm going to cut Ivan's balls off for dragging me into his mess.

The funny part, if there could be one, was that Dimitry had put more effort into this kidnapping than my husband had put into our entire marriage.

I heard voices nearby, and judging by the tension among the men around me, I assumed they recognized their boss.

My pulse quickened, and I needed all my willpower to keep my fear from showing on my face. I dug my nails into my palms, focusing on my breath. I wasn't going to give them the satisfaction of knowing how fucking scared I truly was.

The door opened, then slammed shut as he entered. The men straightened, confirming my suspicion. This was Dimitry.

He stopped right in front of me, leaning against the table as he took in the room. He didn't say a word, yet I felt the energy shift as his gaze swept over his men.

They're afraid.

I took my chance to study him. He was older than me, almost the same age as my husband, somewhere in his early thirties. Despite my attempts to not focus on that aspect, he was handsome. Tall, ripped, with a groomed beard and short, raven hair, he was a walking temptation.

His black suit blended with the dark glass of the table. He braced his palms against the glossy surface and relaxed, his legs falling open as he leaned back. My eyes fell for a moment to his crotch. Given the tent in his pants, he was huge.

Fuck! I have to focus on getting out of this shit somehow, not on how hot this man is.

"Chernov's wife," he said in the end, looking at me.

His voice was calm and controlled, almost friendly. But I knew better. His hazel eyes were intense, and my heart beat wildly as I held his gaze. Whatever whirl of emotions was inside me, I wasn't going to let him see them. Even if the way he looked at me made me feel as if he was seeing right through me.

"Katherine," I said. "My name is Katherine."

I hoped my fear wasn't obvious in my voice. Dimitry smiled and gave me a once-over. I could decipher a mix of curiosity and lust in his eyes.

A spasm of electricity coursed through me as his gaze fixed on my deep cleavage for a moment. I mentally slapped myself as my nipples hardened under his attention.

Fuck, no! Focus Katherine! People always confuse fear with arousal, so stop it! Focus!

"Katherine," he repeated.

Butterflies fluttered in my stomach as the word rolled off his tongue. It sounded like a purr, and for a damn second, I imagined him moaning my name. I mentally kicked myself, again.

Actually, maybe this wasn't such a bad idea. If he was more focused on how I looked instead of what I was doing, maybe I could find a fucking way to escape him.

Dimitry stood up, and the calculated way he approached me reminded me of a hunter. I could tell he was gauging my reactions while closing more and more of the space between us with each step.

I thrust my breasts forward, drawing his attention to them. Arousal spiked through me, too, as lust coursed through his eyes, but I was still going to count that as a victory point.

The brute fidgeted next to me and took a step backward, offering his boss more space. Dimitry walked around me, the close proximity making me feel as if electricity danced through my veins.

Focus, Katherine! You need to get the fuck out of here before he...

Before he what?

Sends me in multiple parts back to my husband?

Fucks me?

I dreaded the first option, but I wasn't sure I liked the way that I shivered at the second or the wave of warmth that washed over me. I avoided Dimitry's gaze, and as I angled my head, I noticed the brute's knife, tangling at his belt.

Maybe...

Fuck, this was both stupid and crazy, but if I managed to at least hurt him, or better, kill him, his men should be panicking enough for me to run away. Dimitry continued to circle around me. An electric shock zinged to my clit as he trailed his fingers through my long hair.

He barely touched me, but it had been enough to cover me in goosebumps and make my body react in ways I wasn't sure I liked. For fuck's sake, he was hot, but I couldn't be attracted to him. I had to focus on my escape. This was only me confusing fear with arousal, nothing else.

And yet, I could feel my panties dampening with every swirl of his fingers.

Dimitry stopped on my left, mere inches away. A rush of heat flushed my face. God, I needed to concentrate on what I had to do. I glanced at the knife again. I could do it. It wouldn't be the first time I had to attack someone to save myself or someone close to me.

I stopped thinking and let my instinct guide me.

The brute didn't even have time to react as I leaned toward him and stole the weapon. Dimitry did, though, and exactly as I tried to stab his neck, he grabbed my hand.

His calmness shocked me, his reaction contrasting with the way my heart pounded so wildly that I thought I was having a heart attack.

I missed. I'm fucked.

Dimitry smiled, and God, his grin scared me more than if he had been angry, yelling, kicking, and throwing things around. He tightened his hold on my wrist enough to make me whimper and drop the knife, and yet, not enough to hurt me.

His men moved toward me, but he barked them an order and all of them froze. My mind was in overdrive searching for solutions, and I was sure at this point my fear was visible, no matter how much I was trying to control it.

"Such a bad kitten," Dimitry murmured in that calm, soothing voice that pricked my hair. "Give me the knife."

It took my brain a moment to realize he had given that order to me. He released my hand and waited. Was he serious about this?

What was the catch? He wanted me to give him the weapon just for him to kill me with it?

If I took it, I could attack him again. Maybe this time I could actually manage to hurt him. No, he wouldn't have given that order to me if I had really been a danger to him.

What does he want to prove with this?

Dimitry seemed to love my turmoil. He kept silent, watching me with amusement and curiosity written all over his face.

Swallowing hard, I knelt in front of him and retrieved the knife. Fuck, the position made me stare at his crotch, and my pussy clenched. What the hell was wrong with me? He could have killed me at any moment and I was thinking about fucking him.

Thankfully, the coldness of the metal brought my senses back enough to make me stop staring at that huge bulge in his pants and asking myself how big he was. I stood up slowly, my fingers tightening around the handle.

Should I attack him again? Is this a test?

Dimitry waited calmly, his face indecipherable. I swallowed hard and offered him the weapon, looking directly into his eyes. If he was going to kill me with it, at least I could take some pride in dying with my head held high.

His fingers touched mine as he took it from me. Tingles ran up my arm, and the tension inside my core jerked and spread. He inched closer, the distance between us so small now that I could feel his minty breath against my face.

"You failed me," he said. "And I don't like to be failed."

He was looking at me, but didn't seem to talk to me. His eyes didn't leave mine as his hand moved, and the next moment I heard a loud thump behind me.

Swallowing hard, I glanced over my shoulder. The brute was dead, the knife buried inside his neck. I didn't even know what to feel. Shock? Remorse? Pity? I didn't care about that man, and I had bigger problems on my hands right now.

"Now, what should I do with such a bad, crazy kitten?"

Dimitry grabbed my chin and made me look at him again. My legs quivered as his eyes captured mine, the intensity shining in them making fear and arousal blend within me. Or maybe it was only fear, but I was too overwhelmed to correctly distinguish between them. I had no idea.

It was as if my brain stopped working, and having him touching me wasn't helping either. All my nerve endings were tingling with electricity, and all my senses were on high alert. I could feel the other men's eyes on us.

"I think this bad kitten needs to be punished."

I should have been scared as hell, and I was, but the seductiveness that dripped from his voice made me react to the word "punished" in ways I didn't expect and couldn't comprehend. A fresh wave of wetness soaked my panties and my pussy throbbed with desire.

I gasped as he yanked my hand and dragged me toward the table. My heart leaped to my throat as he bent me over it, with my ass toward the group of men in the room.

Is he going to fuck me in front of them?

My body flushed with heat. Oh, God, what the hell was I doing, thinking or feeling? This was a fucking psycho who kidnapped me to seek revenge on my husband. Yes, husband, because in case my pussy forgot this little detail, I was married. Maybe Ivan was an idiot, but I was still his wife. A loyal one.

My traitorous body didn't seem to care about that, though.

A hum of illicit pleasure coursed through me as he lifted my dress up around my waist. I should remind him that I was married, but that would have probably made him even more eager to fuck his rival's wife.

My system overheated, and my body fought with my mind about what I should feel about this. I squirmed, unsure of what I was trying to do. Run? Tease him? Attack him again?

Dimitry pressed one hand on my back, pinning me in place. I fixed my eyes forward, my heart pounding wildly.

Whatever he was going to do, I couldn't let him see the mix of emotions flooding me. Maybe I couldn't tell which was which, but I knew I didn't want him to have the chance of using any of them against me.

"A bad kitten like you needs to learn to behave," he growled.

I yelped as his palm landed hard on my ass. Pain radiated through me, making the arousal pulsing within me surge. Before I could process it completely, a new slap followed. Embarrassment turned my cheeks red.

I was the heir of a powerful bratva, married to a brava boss. Yet here I was, being spanked by a ruthless rival of my husband, in front of his men. What was worse, though, was the way each spank made my pussy clench with need.

"Bad. Kitten."

I mewled and squirmed as he continued to slap my ass cheeks in turns. I could feel the drenched fabric of my panties glued to my skin, and I knew he could see how aroused I was.

His men could, too.

My ass felt as if it was on fire, and my face burnt with shame and frustration. Why was this so arousing? No one ever did something like this to me, and my body was reacting in ways I would have never expected.

A thrill of pleasure coursed down my back as a new pang of pain rolled through me when he spanked me again. I clenched the table edges, biting my lower lip to stifle the moans that threatened to rip from my throat.

To my complete embarrassment, I found myself lifting my ass in an attempt to meet the slaps sooner.

"Your cheating cunt is so wet, kitten," he said.

I couldn't hold back a whimper of joy as he ceased his assault and skimmed his finger along my pussy. I wanted to deny it, I wanted to protest, but the only sound that left my mouth as he pressed on my clit had been a loud moan.

Why does it feel so good? I shouldn't...

"Maybe I should tell your husband how wet his wife is for me. And inform him I'm going to turn her into my whore."

The threat and the filthiness of his words should have disgusted and scared me, but instead of that, I felt a new wave of warmth spreading through my core.

This shouldn't feel so good!

Dimitry teased my clit a few more times before resuming his attack on my ass.

I shuddered every time he landed a rough, hard hit. With each new slap, he dragged me toward the edge, and I could no longer hold back my moans.

Fuck, no, this couldn't be possible. This should be the fear, and my body was confused. That was the only explanation I was going to accept.

I tightened my hold on the table edge as I whimpered and thrashed at each spank. It took my brain a few seconds to realize he was no longer pinning me down. Yet, I didn't move away, and the embarrassment of that realization gave me the final nudge over the edge.

"Oh, fuck!"

I cried out as an intense wave of ecstasy coursed through me. My legs buckled, and I writhed as my orgasm rolled along my body. Dimitry landed a few more hits that intensified my burning pleasure, making my toes curl.

Once I stopped spasming, the slaps ceased, too. My brain was still buzzing, and I refused to accept that I had come while being spanked by him in front of his people.

What is this man doing to me?

I let out a weak mewl as Dimitry caressed my burning ass. I clenched, unsure of what he was going to do. Was he going to fuck me now? Was he going to spank me again?

He sank his hand into my hair and yanked me up. As Dimitry turned me around, I tripped on my high heels and braced myself on him in an attempt to not fall. He kept his hold on my hair and wrapped his other arm around my waist, steadying me.

His grip on my body reminded me how powerless I actually was. Under his control. I should be clawing at his face and kicking him, screaming and trying to escape.

Yet, I didn't put up a fight as he pressed me into him. My palms were on his chest, and I could feel all his muscles jumping under my fingers as I moved them up and down.

I would have liked to say I was trying to push him away, but that wasn't true, my gesture feeling more like a caress than anything else. He smirked and tightened his hold on my hair.

"I'm going to have so much fun showing your husband and everyone else how his cheating wife is begging for my cock."

His words awoke the proud bratva wife within me enough to whisper, "That's never going to happen."

"But it will. I promise this to you."

The threat frightened and aroused me at the same time.

I'm fucked.

Chapter Three
Dimitry

S he was on my bed, leaning on one side, with her hands handcuffed on one of the bed's edges. I had ordered Petrov to do that. After the show she had put on, I didn't trust her enough to only lock her inside the room.

Katherine was still wearing her short black dress, and I let my gaze linger along her long legs. She was no longer wearing her shoes. Petrov had told me she'd tried to stab him with the heels, so he took them and locked them in the wardrobe. I smiled.

Crazy kitten.

Her breathing was equal, and she seemed to be sleeping. I carefully approached her, making sure to not wake her up. Maybe she was pretending. It wouldn't have surprised me to have her feigning sleep only to attack me again.

Like a little wild cat.

When I had first seen her, my first thought was about fucking her. She was gorgeous. Tall, thin, with big tits, round ass, maddening curves, and long, black hair, she looked like a goddess. And I wanted her.

What had surprised me, though, had been her behavior.

Surrounded by my men, she looked as if she was commanding them, not like their captive.

The kitten has an attitude.

She was scared. It was visible in her green eyes despite her attempts to hide it. And proud. So fucking proud. But her fear didn't stop her from attacking me. Or maybe that was what had pushed her to do it.

I'd had enemies who had been too afraid to attack me directly, and yet she had done it without thinking twice. When she had lashed on me there hadn't been an ounce of hesitation in her eyes.

What I didn't expect had been the way I reacted and the realization that had struck me as I stopped her. She could have stabbed me and I would have still wanted her.

I want to tame her.

And then, as I'd spanked her ... all I craved had been to fuck her. To bury my cock in her pretty, wet pussy.

At first, I had intended to put on that show for my men since I was leaving her alive, but as I'd seen her squirming and moaning under each slap, I could barely hold myself from shoving my dick inside her cunt.

But she'll have to beg for that honor. And she will.

I stopped right next to the bed and studied Katherine. She seemed to be truly sleeping. Her hair cascaded over her face, and I couldn't hold myself from brushing it away. Something stirred inside me as I took her in.

She had cried.

Her expression was tense, and I could distinguish dried tear streaks on her cheeks. There was a damp spot on the pillow, and the skin around her nose and cheeks looked a little blotchy.

I didn't like the way it made me feel seeing her like that. Or the strange sudden need to protect her.

She quivered and whimpered in her sleep as I trailed my fingers along the line of her face. I glanced at the handcuffs and something spasmed inside me.

Fucking crazy kitten!

How the hell I didn't notice earlier? Her wrists were bruised, red, and inflamed. I muttered a curse as I leaned in and released her arms. She squirmed and let out a soft sigh as she cuddled in her sleep and tucked her hands to her chest.

As she moved, my eyes fell on her wedding ring. That piece of shit didn't deserve her. No one did. A wave of jealousy washed over me as I stared at the jewel, surprising me. I slipped it off her finger and tossed it aside, the ring landing on the floor with a faint chime.

I crossed the room and took the medical aid from the drawer. As I returned to her and applied some cream on her wrists, I asked myself what the fuck was I doing.

She was going to be a good fuck, that was obvious. And I wanted to bury my cock inside her cunt. Katherine was also the perfect leverage over her husband, and I planned to use her to both humiliate him and make him bow to me.

But there was more, and it frustrated me to not be able to exactly name it. Maybe I should just fuck her, use her against Chernov, and throw her away. Sooner I got rid of Katherine and made her husband grovel, the better it would be.

Yet, the contrast between how vulnerable she looked right now and how defiant she had been despite her fear not only turned me on like hell but also made me want to keep her around.

I just want to break her. To tame her and see her begging for my cock.

Yes, that had to be. She was entertaining. Nothing more.

I threw the bottle of cream back in the drawer and got on the bed. Katherine was lying with her back to me. I hugged her thin frame and pressed her into me. Just to be sure the crazy kitten wasn't going to try to escape during the night.

My heart stopped and my cock twitched as she instinctively molded against my body. Was she imagining I was her husband? The mere thought of Chernov's hands on her made me want to rip his head off.

How many times had that piece of shit fucked her? Had she begged for his cock? Had she acted like a whore for him?

I squeezed her fragile frame, and she let out a soft purr. Electricity rushed through me as she pressed her ass into my crotch. My dick throbbed and jerked, and I had to remind myself I wasn't going to fuck her.

Not until she begged me to.

I smiled as I remembered the defiance in her gaze as she had provoked me. Katherine moved again, and I pressed my face into her hair and took a deep breath. She smelled like vanilla and jasmine, and my balls tingled as I inhaled her feminine scent.

She will beg. All of them do it in the end. And then I'll give her the fuck of her life and after that finally get rid of her.

But until then, she was mine.

Only mine.

Chapter Four
Katherine

I stretched and squirmed, snuggling more into him. Ivan wasn't cuddly, and most of the time I wasn't in the mood for him, either, so we never had these kinds of mornings. I could feel his muscles pressing into my back. That was new. Did he start working out?

His cock twitched against my ass when I teased him with a wiggle. A wave of arousal floated through me, and I smiled. Maybe we could have a quickie. It had been some time since we fucked, given how much Ivan had annoyed me in the last few months.

He wasn't the best lover, but maybe I could use him as a dildo well enough for me to finish this time.

The sun caressed my face, and as I took a deep breath, I felt the sandalwood notes of his cologne and his masculine scent.

Wait a moment...

This wasn't Ivan.

And I wasn't home.

The memories of the last night crashed on top of me like a cold shower. My heart leaped to my throat, choking me, as I realized who the man I was currently glued to, the man who was hugging and pressing me close to him, actually was.

Dimitry.

No. No. No. This couldn't be happening. I should find a way to get the hell out of here. I slowly moved my hand.

Did he release me?

I remembered the handcuffs and the frustration I had felt as I couldn't break them last night. I cried myself to sleep while still dragging at them. It had hurt so fucking much, but now ... I looked at my hands. Some bruises were still visible, but the pain was gone.

Why did he do this? What, he prefers to be the one breaking his toys? Is this his way to remind me he's the one in control?

I furrowed my brows as I noticed my wedding ring missing.

Did he send it to my husband?

That wasn't important, anyway. All that mattered was for me to find a way to escape. Dimitry moved in his sleep, hugging me tighter. I cursed the surge of desire that zinged through my core.

When his cock throbbed, my pussy fluttered with interest and once again I had to mentally remind myself that this psycho was my husband's enemy and that he'd kidnapped me.

Hot or not, I should stay away from him. Not only because I was fucking married, but also because he could decide to get rid of me anytime.

I could feel his warm breath against my neck, causing a quiver of pleasure to ripple through me.

Fuck! Stop it, Katherine!

I didn't care about my body's opinion. I knew what I had to do.

Listening to his regular breaths, I looked around, trying to find anything I could use as a weapon. He was physically stronger, so it would be stupid to try a one-on-one fight against him. But maybe I could balance that. My eyes fell on the lamp on the bedside table.

Perfect!

My back was pressed to his chest, and I didn't dare to glance at him, but I hoped his sleep was deep enough for him to not notice my movements. I slowly and silently squirmed away, leaning toward the lamp.

"Don't even think about it."

I froze with my hand in mid-air. All my muscles tensed, and for a moment, I stopped even breathing. Dimitry didn't sound angry, but that didn't mean he wasn't going to decide to send me back to my husband in multiple boxes.

Especially since I didn't actually trust Ivan to save me.

Maybe Papa learned about this, too...

I knew that using my father's name might help me at least a little, but I didn't want to drag him into this. Dimitry hated Ivan, but he had nothing against Romanov bratva. He wasn't known for stupidly attacking or provoking other mafia bosses, but still, I didn't want to make him focus on my dad and my people.

I was on my own. Like always.

I swallowed hard and put my hand down. Dimitry sighed and moved his palm over my flat stomach, toward my breasts.

The loyal wife in me whispered that I should push him away, that I should put up a fight at least, but the shudder of pleasure that coursed through me as he cupped my tits and massaged them silenced my mind.

"It's so early in the morning, and you, little crazy kitten, are already trying to do stupid things," he murmured in my ear and chuckled. "What the fuck should I do with you?"

"Release me?"

He laughed. I let out a soft moan as he pinched my nipples through the fabric of my dress. I put my hand over his, and I wanted to believe I was trying to push him away, but the truth was I didn't. Why the hell was it so hard to even think when he was touching me like that?

"Where is my wedding ring?" I asked. "Did you send it to my husband as a threat?"

I hoped talking about Ivan was going to wake up the loyal wife within me enough for me to at least try to shove him away. It didn't happen.

It seemed to have an effect on him, though.

Dimitry didn't say a word, but I could feel his muscles tensing. His movement turned rougher, and as he stroked my breasts, the hotness blazing within me intensified. My face burnt with a mix of guilt and shame as I pressed myself more into him and moaned.

"The ring is somewhere on the floor. I don't need to send it to Chernov to make my point clear."

His voice was cold as ice. Great, so I'd somehow pissed him off. I knew he already disliked Ivan, so that wasn't unexpected, but I couldn't understand his sudden change. Was his disdain so intense that he hated even hearing my husband's name?

And fuck, it was so hard to focus on anything else but the way he was kneading my breasts.

"But maybe I should send him a video of you," he added, and his timbre changed, taking again that raspy, seductive note. "I bet he would love seeing you begging like a whore for my cock. Asking me to fuck you."

My nipples hardened at his filthy words. I closed my eyes, trying to ignore the delicious sensations he was sending through me as he stroked my body. I had no idea how the fuck he was making me react so strongly to him, but I wasn't going to give him the satisfaction of knowing that.

"That's not going to happen," I mewled.

"Are you sure?"

Dimitry moved one hand along my body, toward my legs, while he continued to use his other one to play with my tits. My breath grew labored as he advanced along my thigh, and despite any rational thought, I found myself spreading my legs for him.

What the hell am I doing? I shouldn't ... I'm Ivan's wife, and ...

A foggy pleasure flooded my head as he moved his fingers along my pussy lips, making my brain blip out. Even through the fabric of my panties the sensation was surreal.

My heart beat faster, and all my cells hummed in arousal. I tried once again to think about my husband, but as Dimitry teased my clit, his existence vanished from my mind.

"Maybe I should send Chernov your soaked panties, showing him how wet his wife is for me."

I moaned as he tugged at the fabric, ripping it. I wanted to protest, to deny the obvious truth, but the fresh wave of ecstasy that washed over me as he rubbed my nub rendered me silent. Dimitry tugged at the upper part of my dress, releasing my breasts.

The temperature in the room was perfect, but the air felt cold as it caressed my heated body. The contact of skin on skin drove me wild as he played with me, each touch leaving me craving the next one.

I'm married. He's a fucking psycho. I shouldn't feel so good.

And yet I couldn't deny how wonderful it was. My breath came out in short, little pants. Electric currents coursed through me as he tormented my breasts with one hand while using his other one on my nub.

"You're so responsive and wet. Let me guess, Chernov isn't satisfying you," he murmured in my ear.

Fuck, he was right, but I wasn't going to let him know that. Ivan wasn't bad, but ... mediocre at best. He could barely find my clit, let alone any other pleasure point, and always focused more on himself than on me.

Even when I guided him step by step, he always finished so fucking fast that I barely had time to feel anything.

"He does!" I lied through my teeth. "And he's better than you. With him, I would have already come."

Dimitry laughed and pinched my nipples in turns, drawing a cry of pleasure from me. I thrashed and pushed myself into his hand, tingles of ecstasy jumping through me.

"You're such a bad liar," he said with a chuckle. "Poor little kitten, you should be so unsatisfied with him."

My eyes opened wide and I let out a loud moan as he slipped his fingers inside my channel. While thrusting them, he used his thumb on my clit. I writhed against his frame, spreading my legs as much as I could for him.

What the fuck am I doing? I should push him away... but fuck, this feels so good... but Ivan...

The storm of thoughts cut off as he kissed my neck. The roughness of his beard covered me in goosebumps. I lifted my hand and tangled my fingers into his hair, but instead of pushing him away, I pressed him into me. I knew I shouldn't, but still, I did it.

My entire body flushed with heat. Fuck, he was so good, and the asshole knew what he was doing. He changed the rhythm and the angle based on my mewls, and when he curled his fingers and massaged my G-spot, stars played in front of my eyes.

"Oh, God! Fuck! Fuck!" I panted.

The mix of sensations overwhelmed me. The way he kneaded my tits, the rough thrusts inside my pussy, the teasing of my clit, the hotness of his lips on my skin. Everything pushed me toward the peak.

I shuddered with every new wave of pleasure and pushed myself into him as much as I could. His lips curled into a smile, and fuck, I didn't need to look at him to guess how much he enjoyed it.

That didn't mean he won, though. He was a good dildo, I had to give that to him, but that didn't mean I was going to beg for him. No matter how good it felt, I wasn't going to give him that satisfaction.

Or let him use it against Ivan.

Idiot or not, that man was still my husband, and I was supposed to be loyal to him.

"Fuck!" I whimpered, clenching around his fingers as I felt myself gnawing at the edge.

I was so close, so fucking close. I tightened my hold on his hair, shivering with each new tide of wildfire that traveled along my body.

"Do you want to say something, Katherine?"

I whined in frustration as he slowed down his movements. I

bucked, trying to tease my clit against his hand, but he took his touch away entirely.

"Dimitry!"

"Yes, kitten?"

He continued to play with my breasts and fluttered his fingers over my pussy, but that wasn't enough. My body tensed, every cell of me humming in discomfort. I had been so close! I fucking needed to come.

I released his hair and tried to touch myself, but he caught my hand and pressed it against my stomach. Dimitry laughed as I let out another mewl of protest.

"Fuck you!"

I thrashed, trying to hump his arm, leg, blanket, fucking anything. With the little touches he granted me, he kept me right on the edge. My breath grew labored, the need within me intensifying with every passing second.

Fucking asshole!

"Please!" I whined.

I cursed myself as that word left my mouth. His satisfied groan sent shivers down my spine. My vision blurred as he thrust his fingers again inside my pussy and used his thumb on my clit.

"Yes! Yes! Yes!" I moaned.

Pleasure, frustration, guilt, and shame mingled within me. Fucking jerk. I shouldn't have murmured that word, but I fucking needed him to let me come. I didn't remember the last time when I'd felt so good. Damn, I didn't think I ever felt like that with Ivan.

But that didn't mean Dimitry won.

And I knew how to take my power back.

As I spiraled toward my orgasm, my inner brat saw the opportunity and decided to take it. I knew it was stupid and that I shouldn't provoke him like that, but fuck it, the proud bitch within me needed to make things even.

"Ivan! Fuck! Ivan! Yes! Yes! Ivan, yes!" I screamed as my climax shuttered my entire being.

His annoyed growl should have probably frightened me, but at that point, I was probably as crazy as him because it only aroused me even more. I spasmed against him as I rode out the waves of my release, my entire being buzzing alive.

Dimitry grabbed my hair and pulled hard, angling my head enough for me to see him. Yeah, he was pissed off, and that brought me some form of satisfaction.

I had no idea how this man was making me feel so many crazy things, but fuck it, he could have killed me right then and there and I would be delighted to know I'd provoked him so much.

"You did it on purpose, you little slut."

My pussy clenched instinctively around his fingers. Ivan had tried to call me names in bed, but it didn't arouse me. But now, hearing those words from Dimitry turned me on like hell.

What the fuck is wrong with me? How does he have such an effect on me?

My heart thumped wildly as he tightened his hold on my hair while he pulled his fingers out of my pussy. I could smell my desire and pleasure as he brought them to my face.

"It wasn't that pathetic piece of shit you married who made you feel like this, kitten. I did."

I moaned as he pressed his digits against my lips. I parted them without even thinking. My pulse quickened and heat colored my cheeks as I sucked on them. I could taste myself on his skin, and that made me feel like a whore. To my complete shock, I loved it.

I looked into his eyes while swirling my tongue around his fingers, and for a fucking damn second, everything around ceased to exist.

I no longer had an idea what I felt or what I was doing. Just that it felt good. It was as if I was surrendering into a state of blissful submission, and for a moment, I stopped worrying, fighting, or thinking.

I just enjoyed it.

The tension left my body as I sucked on his fingers. My pussy ached as I fantasized about how it would feel to be his cock instead in my mouth. If he knew to use it half as good as he used his hands, it would probably be the best fuck of my life.

No ... Ivan ... I'm married ... Fuck! C'mon, Katherine, have some self-respect!

I released his fingers and looked away. He allowed me to. Dimitry brushed his lips against my neck, and I closed my eyes, scolding myself for showing any sign of weakness to him. A spasm of pleasure danced through me as he dragged his tongue along my throat and chin.

"You're mine, crazy kitten. And one way or another, I'm going to tame you. And after that..."

After that what? Give me back to my husband if he grovels? Kill me?

He didn't finish the sentence, and I wasn't sure I actually wanted him to do it, either. He released me and got off of the bed without another word.

Chapter Five
Dimitry

"She's Romanov's daughter!?"

Sergei swallowed hard, shifting his weight from one leg to the other. He'd told me he informed Chernov that Katherine was with me. The bastard not only sent a message back, saying he didn't care about the "whore," but also killed the man who delivered him the news.

Part of me thought I should respect him for that. Especially given how badly things had ended for my father when he'd let his emotions take over.

My father had been head over heels in love with my mother. When she got caught in a war between him and a rival bratva pachan, he'd sacrificed everything to save her. And it still hadn't been enough.

That pachan had killed them both, and at nineteen, I was the one left to avenge them and reclaim our territory. I learned one thing that day: never be so foolish as to fall in love and let someone use your emotions against you.

But now... there was no respect to be had for this piece of trash.

That pathetic excuse for a man was lucky enough to have

Katherine as his wife, yet instead of protecting her, he threw her away like garbage. He called her a "whore."

I wanted to break his neck just for that.

And my stupid, crazy kitten had the nerve to scream his name just to annoy me. I sniffed my fingers. I'd taken a bath earlier, but damn if her scent didn't still cling to me. Made me want her even more. I'd nearly come when she'd moaned, "Please."

I could see the constant battle playing out on her face. I knew Katherine craved me, but she was too proud to admit it and still trying to stay loyal to that idiot.

But she will give in. One way or another, I'll make her surrender, make her beg me to fuck her. And she'll moan my name. Not his or anyone's else. Mine.

I still couldn't understand everything she made me feel, but I knew I wanted to make her mine. I wanted her to surrender to me. I had no idea what I'd do with her after that, but I was going to tame her.

A "whore" ... he dared to call his own wife that.

"That's what the message said," Sergei stammered. "Romanov also sent this."

Sergei signaled to Andrei and Mikhail, who brought in ten bags and dropped them on my desk. I opened a few, finding them stuffed with cash.

"He said he's offering you however much you want to give Katherine back."

This was needlessly complicating things. I fiercely protected my territory, that was the whole reason I'd started this fight with Ivan. The pathetic fool thought he could play games with me and cross into my domain.

But I hadn't planned to start a war with others. Neither Romanov nor Chernov was a true threat on their own, but together, they could cause trouble.

She should have told me she was his daughter.

Not that it would've changed much. But I could have planned things better.

I looked at the money again. At least Romanov valued her enough not to insult me with a small offer. But the idea of putting a price on her disgusted me, and my stomach twisted.

I'm not letting her go. Not for money. Not until she begs, and I turn her into my pet. Then I'll decide what to do with her.

"Send the money back."

"Are you sure, boss? He might feel insulted, and…"

Sergei shut his mouth when I shot him a look, then ordered the men to remove the bags.

"Should I tell him anything?"

"No."

It was clear he had more questions, but I didn't have time for that. I needed to talk to my crazy kitten, make it clear I don't like being lied to, and find out what other secrets she might be hiding.

She's going to tell me everything, whether she likes it or not.

Chapter Six
Katherine

I adjusted the red lingerie set, making sure it highlighted all my assets. Earlier, after he'd taken a bath, Dimitry had left me in his room. He hadn't locked me up but pointed out that his men were around.

After I'd showered, I found an array of clothes, jewelry, and cosmetics in the room, presumably brought in by his men.

As I applied my makeup, I looked into the mirror. Dimitry might be in control, but that didn't mean I was helpless. Even if I'd felt that way a few times. But not anymore. After all, I was Katherine Chernov.

Katherine Romanova.

My dad had taken good care of me, but he'd always been busy with the bratva. After my wedding, I'd tried not to burden him with my troubles. And Ivan ... maybe he was a good choice as a husband for his heritage, but I couldn't trust him enough to rely on him for support or protection.

I'd always been on my own, and I knew I could only rely on myself.

That's what I'm going to do now, too.

A shiver rushed through me as I applied lipstick. I could still feel Dimitry's touch on my skin, the taste of his fingers and my own pussy juices on my tongue. I still couldn't understand why I reacted to him this way.

Was it the lack of sex between Ivan and me?

Was my body confusing fear with arousal?

Was it simply because he was painfully attractive and experienced?

All of that? None of that?

I could still feel his hands on my body, and it turned me on like crazy. Even now, the mere thought of him made my pulse quicken and my body ached with need.

It was wrong. I was married, and I shouldn't want him, but he made me feel things I'd never felt before.

Yet I could use this to my advantage.

He was a man, after all, visibly attracted to me. Why shouldn't I lean into that, using all my wiles to make him do exactly what I wanted? If he thought with his other head, it would be easier to escape.

I glanced at my wedding ring, and a pang of guilt twisted in my stomach. I didn't love Ivan, but I had been faithful to him. Before Dimitry, no other man but my husband had touched me.

I'm doing this because I have to. I need to save myself, to escape.

At least, that's what I told myself as I dropped my wedding ring in one of the drawers. There were a few more objects in it, but a hidden photo caught my attention.

It was of a couple, maybe in their fifties. The man looked like an older version of Dimitry, and the woman had the same striking hazel eyes.

Are these his parents?

Footsteps in the hallway jolted me from my thoughts. I quickly put the photo back and closed the drawer.

Dimitry stepped inside and slammed the door closed behind him.

He froze and narrowed his eyes when he found me only in my lingerie. I'd planned on seducing him, but now, watching him, I could tell something was off.

He was irritated by something.

His jaw was clenched, and his shoulders were rigid and squared. His nostrils flared slightly, and yet, despite all of that, I could see lust in his eyes as his gaze traveled along my body. I had no idea what had frustrated him so much, but I knew my plan could still work.

I swayed my hips toward him, making sure he had a perfect view of my breasts. He watched me like a predator watches its prey, and that sent butterflies fluttering in my lower belly. Fuck, I had to control myself. I was the one playing the game now, I had to be careful.

"I was waiting for you," I purred, moving my palms along his torso, toward his shoulders.

He didn't move. I knew the change had been too sudden for him to believe that I had suddenly fallen in love with him or something like that, but maybe if I was a little honest with him, it would be enough for him to let his guard down.

"I felt good earlier," I admitted. "And I thought we might do it again."

I leaned into him, pressing my tits into his chest. The warmth of his body enveloped me as he wrapped his arm around my waist. My clit throbbed and my nipples hardened as I caressed his body.

I rubbed against him like a shameless slut, electricity rushing through me as his cock jerked. That was perfect, he was aroused. Dimitry pressed me into him and brushed my lips with his.

I leaned in to kiss him, but he pulled away.

"Tell me something, kitten. Do you think I'm an idiot?"

Fuck!

"Of course not." I avoided his eyes and played with the buttons of his shirt. "It's just ... I felt good. Better than ever. Ivan never made me feel like that."

That was true. Guilt swirled inside my body, but I ignored it. I didn't like shaming my husband, but if that was going to make my plan work, it was worth it.

"I'm sure of that. That's why you moaned his name."

Fuck, I didn't expect him to turn that little dig against me.

"That was..."

"Yes?"

I could tell based on the tonality of his voice that he was toying with me and that my frustration amused him. That irritated me even more. I was supposed to be the one in control here. I fixed my gaze on his chest, trying to find my next words.

"Dimitry..."

"Yes, Katherine Romanova?"

Fuck! Fuck! Fuck!

My eyes shot to his. I swallowed hard and tried to take a step back, but he tightened his hold on my waist and kept me close to him. My mind was in overdrive, searching for solutions, but I had no idea what I should do or say.

"Please don't involve my father in this," I whispered.

My voice came out weaker and more vulnerable than I intended. I clenched his shirt in an attempt to compose myself, but I knew my emotions were visible on my face.

"He involved himself when he offered me money in exchange for you. But that's not the important point now."

I gasped as he pushed me against the wall and braced one hand against it while keeping his other one around my body. Trapping me there, he pressed his body into mine, the position making me feel more helpless than any time in my entire life.

And also, more aroused than I had ever been.

What the fuck is wrong with me?

"Let's make one thing clear, Katherine. I don't like to be lied to. And you did it twice. First, you didn't say you're Romanov's daughter."

"You didn't ask," I cut him off.

My heart was pounding wildly. I knew he was irritated, I knew I wasn't the one in control, and yet, I couldn't stop myself from provoking him. He snorted and pushed himself more against me. I felt his erection through his pants, and my pussy pulsed in anticipation, making me mentally curse myself.

"First, you didn't say you're Romanov's daughter," he repeated. "Second, you took me for an idiot and tried to seduce me."

"I didn't, I..."

"That's the third lie, kitten. But don't worry, I think I know exactly what I can do with your lying mouth."

I yelped as he grabbed my hands and pushed me to the floor, making me kneel in front of him. I could feel my heart thumping in my ears as Dimitry unbuckled his belt and unzipped his pants. Heat surged through me. I stared at his crotch as hypnotized as he released his cock.

Oh, fuck!

A throbbing need pulsed along my body and my mouth watered as I looked at his shaft. He was huge, so long and thick that my entire being buzzed. Definitely bigger than Ivan. Veins slithered from the base to the tip in irregular patterns, and the swollen mushroom head was dripping pre-cum.

Without even thinking I wrapped my fingers along his length, feeling how heavy and hot he was. I mentally slapped myself for that. He groaned and his cock throbbed against my palm.

"Go on, kitten, suck me off," he ordered.

His voice was commanding, and a flutter of excitement rushed to my clit. I glanced at Dimitry as I stroked him. He seemed satisfied by my behavior, and for a moment, I remembered once again I wasn't supposed to want this.

"Do you realize your cock is in my hand right now?" I asked, tightening my grip on him. "Are you sure you want to risk being so close to my teeth?"

He let out a mix between a laugh and a groan and thrust his hips, sliding his cock through the circle of my fingers. I instinctively moved my hand faster, making him moan.

"Yes, I'm sure, little slut. You're a crazy kitten, not a stupid one."

A pang of desire darted through me as he sank his fingers into my hair and tugged at it hard enough to arouse me, and yet, not to hurt. My clit swelled with need and I couldn't stop the whimper of plea- sure that left my mouth.

"You just forget sometimes that I'm the one in control, kitten. But don't worry, I'll make you understand and remember that."

He used his grip to push me down toward his cock and it shocked me how eager I actually was to obey. I wrapped my lips around him, moaning as his taste washed into my mouth. Fuck, he was deliciously salty.

I swirled my tongue around him, making Dimitry shudder and groan. More pre-cum filled my mouth, and I purred as I savored it. I pulled back, and to my surprise, he didn't stop me. My hair was still in his hand, but he allowed me to move freely.

What's his plan? Is he toying with me? What does he want to prove?

Dimitry was staring at me through hooded, lust-filled eyes, but apart from that, I couldn't distinguish anything on his face. I chan- neled my attention on his cock. I should bite him.

But would that really help me escape?

I wanted to believe it was the rational part of me the one that made me lean in and suck on the tip of his cock instead of doing anything to hurt him. That was the only explanation I was going to accept.

A thrill of submission rolled down my back as I started to lick him, from the base to the mushroom head, coating him with saliva. I used my hand on his shaft at the same time with my mouth, and the way he groaned and throbbed sent pulsing pleasure through my entire being.

I had rarely done this for Ivan. Maybe once or twice at the beginning of our relationship. I had no idea why, but the position annoyed me, so when he'd tried to convince me to blow him again, I'd pushed him away.

I expected to feel the same disgust now, too, but it didn't show up. I couldn't even understand what I felt. Or why it actually was ... good? Fuck, what the hell was wrong with me? I couldn't actually enjoy this.

Even if I did.

I let more saliva drip down his length and used my tongue and hand to spread it along his length. His scent was intoxicating, and my pussy clenched with desire. It was a mix of his masculine musk and a minty scent from his shower products.

"Katya," he groaned, pushing himself more into my hand.

The pet name he used stirred something deep inside me. Aside from my dad, no one ever called me that. It should have annoyed me, but it didn't. For whatever reason, I liked hearing Dimitry say it almost as much as I enjoyed him calling me "kitten."

I shouldn't, but I did.

His cock throbbed, and I didn't even think before taking him again in my mouth. Making my tongue flat, I teased the underside, making him spasm. I bobbed my head, welcoming more and more of him every time he slid between my lips.

"You're such a good cocksucker," he moaned. "A perfect slutty kitten."

Those words should have frustrated me, but instead, they made me feel stronger. I purred, and he groaned at the vibrations.

Being on my knees in front of him, with his cock in my mouth, made me feel powerful. What the fuck was wrong with me?

I couldn't comprehend it, but I liked knowing I was the one making him feel like that. The one bringing him so much pleasure and controlling his ecstasy. I instinctively doubled down on my efforts, sucking him with gusto.

Guilt twisted inside me. I'd never put so much passion or been so sloppy with Ivan. I shouldn't do this now, I shouldn't want it, I shouldn't enjoy it, I shouldn't...

"Fuck, Katya. You're amazing."

Dimitry tightened his hold on my hair, the pang of pain pulling me out of my thoughts. He fisted my long locks into a makeshift leash and used it to move me. I moaned as he started to slam me against his pelvis, burying my face into his pubic hair at every stroke.

"So good," he grunted.

I braced my palms on his legs in an attempt to balance myself while he face-fucked me. God, I should have been angry, annoyed, humiliated. No one had ever treated me like this. But instead of that, I felt good. Powerful and in control. Knowing I was the one that brought him into such a state of desperate need.

I gagged as he shoved himself down my throat, so deep that I could feel him hitting the back. Tears of effort ruined my make-up, but instead of pushing him away or fighting against his grip, I surrendered myself to him.

My neck strained. My glurgs and slurps seemed to spur him on given that his movements turned even more frantic. The pleasure that washed over my body shocked me. I hummed around his cock, the vibrations sending visible ripples of euphoria through him.

"Fuck, kitten!"

Dimitry treated me as a rag doll, turning my mouth into nothing more than a hole he used for his pleasure. My pussy pulsed with need, my entire being humming with arousal.

With every slide of his shaft between my lips I felt myself succumbing into a mindset of being nothing more than a fucktoy, melting into a state of blissful submission.

It shocked me how good it felt.

My brain shut off and nothing else existed. For a delightful second, I stopped thinking, worrying, fighting. I only felt. Pleasure coursed through me as an electric shock, Dimitry's roughness pushing buttons inside me that I hadn't even been aware of before.

The warmth in my stomach jerked and spread through me as I

felt him swelling and twitching in my mouth. I could tell he was close, and shame, guilt, and arousal blended inside me as I realized how much I wanted to taste him.

I glanced at him, a shiver of ecstasy rushing directly to my clit as I noticed the possessiveness and lust in his gaze. He hissed and his cock throbbed as he moved me faster.

I let out a whine of protest as he pulled me away from his cock. My face burned with shame while I fought against his hold in an attempt to reach his shaft. I acted like a desperate whore, but I didn't care.

Dimitry's grip had been unyielding, though, and he kept me at a few inches from his dick.

"Stay," he ordered.

My compliance shocked me. I obeyed, remaining on my knees, with my eyes fixed on his swollen cock. He jerked himself off, and my body ached as I realized what he wanted to do. Fuck, no one ever did something like that to me.

The proud brat within me told me to disobey, but my inner submissive slut I had no idea existed was stronger. I opened my mouth and darted my tongue out, moaning in anticipation.

Dimitry's eyes widened, and the low, raspy growl that ripped his throat turned me on like hell.

A wave of cum rained on top of me, covering my hair and face. The sticky warmth dripped down along my skin as he spurted rope after rope. A few drops landed on my tongue, and I moaned as I tasted his salty sweetness.

When he unloaded the last streams of cum, he took a step back, watching me. I held his gaze, both of us panting. I expected a wave of anger and humiliation to hit me, but that didn't show up.

Why the hell did I like this? Why does it make me feel so good?

He didn't say a word, and I couldn't read anything on his face. A flutter of pleasure shot through me as he caressed my hair, the gesture making me feel like an obedient pet. He trailed his fingers along my face, cleaning me up.

Without thinking, I tilted my head and dragged my tongue along his palm, greedily swallowing more of his cum.

What am I doing? What is this man doing to me?

Dimitry groaned and took another step back. He turned around without a word and left the room, leaving me there, more confused and shocked by my own actions than in my entire life.

Chapter Seven
Katherine

I played with my wedding ring, twirling it between my fingers.

I fucked up. I cheated on Ivan.

Because no matter how much I tried to convince myself that I had to do it, deep down, I knew the truth. I wanted it. And I craved to have more of him.

I had taken a long bath after Dimitry had finished on me, but I could still feel his taste on my tongue.

The way he had taken control, using me as if I was a fucktoy and nothing more ... God, it had turned me on more than anything else. Even now, at the mere thought of him and his dominance my body buzzed alive.

I never felt something like that before, such a primal, raw desire. I actually wanted to please him. Ivan didn't care about my pleasure, and so, I'd long since stopped caring about his. Our sex life, as much as it existed, was ... mechanical. Clinical. Cold.

But with Dimitry, fuck, it had felt surreally perfect each time. He'd easily made me feel so good, even when I knew I shouldn't have allowed myself to. It was wrong, not just because I was married, but also because I was his captive.

I still could lie to my husband. He didn't need to know what I actually felt while sucking on Dimitry.

I cuddled up in a ball and hugged myself, keeping the ring in my fist. I'd wanted to put it on, but the guilt stopped me. It was also obvious to me that Dimitry hated seeing me wearing it. Why would he have it taken off that night, otherwise?

I wasn't sure which reason was stronger, or maybe I didn't want to admit what I already knew.

The sound of the door opening caught my attention. Dimitry entered, carrying a tray of food. My stomach rumbled as the delicious aroma filled the room. Chicken breasts, creamy mashed potatoes, and Medovik. My favorites.

I'd refused to eat earlier. No matter how Dimitry had treated me, I didn't trust him or his men enough. I was pretty sure he wasn't going to poison me, but what if he or anyone else decided to drug me? I couldn't lose the little control I still had.

A small part of me insisted he wouldn't do something like that. Still, I'd forced myself to refuse the food they had brought. No matter how much my weaker side begged, I'd listened only to reason.

Dimitry placed the tray beside me, and my stomach let out another growl.

"These are your favorites, aren't they?"

I narrowed my eyes as he sat on the bed.

"How do you know?"

"I have my sources. Eat."

That had definitely been an order, and that irritated me and made my inner brat snort. Why was he so eager to see me eating this? Did he put something in it? I glanced again at the food, and my stomach churned.

Fuck, it looks so good.

"Katherine. Eat!"

"No, thank you," I replied coldly.

How the fuck does he know these are my comfort foods? I don't remember eating them when outside, our chef was always preparing them for me at home. Does he have spies in Ivan's house?

Dimitry took the knife and fork, cutting the food into slices. I swallowed hard, realizing I'd noticed the cutlery earlier but hadn't even thought of using it as a weapon. Shouldn't that have been my first instinct? To try to hurt or kill him?

Dimitry took a few pieces of chicken breasts and mashed potatoes, his eyes fixed on mine as he chewed. Once swallowing, he made a perfect bite for me and brought it to my lips.

"I don't poison or drug people or whatever you imagine, kitten. I kill directly, and if I wanted you dead, you would already be. Now eat."

His voice was level, the authority in it making me feel a strange mix of arousal and irritation. Why did he care if I ate or not? That was my problem, not his. My stomach protested, but I held my ground.

"Katya."

I knew it was safe to eat, and yet, the fact that he was ordering me to accept it strengthened my stubbornness. As I crossed my arms across my chest, I accidentally dropped the wedding ring.

Before I could pick it up, he took it from me. A pang of guilt hit me as I realized I didn't care. Another pang hit me as I realized I wasn't thinking just about the ring.

"I'll give it back after you eat."

I looked at him again. What the hell was his plan? Did he just want to make sure I wouldn't starve to death and ruin his scheme against my husband?

Dimitry sighed and rolled his eyes.

"We can stay all night and debate this, but you're going to end up eating something."

I raised a brow, my inner slut suddenly awakened. Before I could stop myself, I asked, "Something?"

Fuck, what the hell was I doing? Was I flirting with him? Well, a naughty part of me had some lewd ideas about what I could eat, though. My eyes fell to his crotch, and a flush of heat claimed my neck and face as I saw his bulge growing right under my gaze.

Okay, I had to admit, that made me feel powerful.

"God, you're going to be the death of me," he groaned, exasperated. "Katya, I'm serious. Eat. Now."

He brought the food again to my mouth, the delicious smell making my stomach growl. I wasn't sure if it was my hunger or the authority on his voice, or the filthy thoughts that had floated through my head earlier, but I parted my lips and took the bite.

"Good girl."

Fuck!

I almost choked on the food. Tingles of electricity ran under my skin and slickness flooded my pussy. Why was it so arousing to hear him say those two words to me? Dimitry smirked, and I cursed myself realizing he had noticed my reaction.

Yet, as he brought another bite to my lips, I obeyed. Partly because I was starving, partly because a slutty side of me wanted to hear him saying them again. Yeah, I refused to acknowledge that side of me.

I tried to take the fork from him, but he held it firmly.

"No. Let me. Just in case you decide to try and stab me with it," Dimitry said with a chuckle.

"The knife would be a better option," I said, touching the cold metal.

Dimitry laughed and fed me another mouthful, completely ignoring my hand on the knife. I had no idea what he was trying to do or prove. What was he thinking? This man was a fucking dark mystery, and I mentally kicked myself once again realizing how drawn to him I was.

As he fed me, I waged a mental battle with myself. I shouldn't let him do this. It felt too intimate, too vulnerable. It scared me. Ivan had never done anything like this for me. Neither had I for him.

"Good girl," Dimitry said with a triumphant, arrogant grin as he fed me the last one.

I flushed, avoiding his gaze as a rush of warmth jumped through me. Desperate for distraction, I picked up the dessert spoon and took a piece of Medovik. But instead of eating it, I brought it to his mouth.

I wanted to believe it was because I needed to be sure it wasn't poisoned. He didn't taste the cake, after all.

But another part of me knew that I just wanted to do it. I felt the need to ... to what? To feed him? To take care of him?

Fuck! What the hell is wrong with me? What was the medical term? Stockholm syndrome? Yeah, I'm going to blame it on that!

Dimitry stared at me for a second before accepting the mouthful. Tingles swirled through me as he wrapped his lips around it and my mind instantly went haywire with filthy fantasies about having his mouth on me.

God, I'm married! I have to stop this.

But instead of that, I found myself offering him a second one. Electricity pricked my hair as he wrapped his fingers around my hand and guided it to my lips.

"Your turn, crazy kitten."

I obeyed, moaning as I tasted the honey sweetness. It had been some time since I had asked our chef, Aleksei, to make it for me. Something vibrated inside my core as he guided my hand again and again, feeding me more of the cake.

"How did you know these are my favorites?" I asked again.

I expected him to give me the same answer. Dimitry accepted the next mouthful I offered to him, and given the way he looked at me, I could tell he was studying me.

"Some of your husband's men work for me," he said in the end.

I stopped with my hand in mid-air. Dimitry smiled and gently took the spoon from me, feeding me the last bites. While I accepted them, he continued to talk.

"Your chef, Aleksei. Your driver, Yuri. Your maid, Alina. Your bodyguard, Vasiliy. And more."

I opened my mouth to say something, anything, but no sound left my lips. Those people had worked for Ivan for years. He could have ordered them to kill me and Ivan anytime.

Why didn't he?

"I prefer direct confrontations, Katherine," he said, almost as if he had read my mind. "But I like to stay one step ahead and know everything about my enemies."

"Do you have spies in my father's house, too?"

I didn't expect an honest answer, but I hoped I could gauge his reactions enough to guess the truth. Dimitry surprised me as he nodded.

"Tatyana, Yakov, Yuri and Marina. Romanov hadn't been on my radar, so I rarely asked for information from them. That was a mistake, since if I did, I would have known you're his daughter."

The confession shocked me. Why was he honest? Assuming he actually was.

Is he going to kill me? After all, now that I know this ... does he have more people in Papa's house? He was clear about being more in Ivan's, but ...

"Katya," he murmured, and the gentleness in his voice surprised me.

He trailed his fingers through my hair, the gesture covering me in goosebumps. He skimmed them along the line of my face, and as he cupped my cheek, I instinctively leaned into his touch.

I shouldn't have done it, I knew, but the wave of warmth the feeling of his hand had sent to me had been too strong.

I wasn't used to this kind of tenderness, and it surprised me to have him, of all men, showing it to me. Ivan barely knew the notion of foreplay, let alone anything else. I closed my eyes, and for a moment, all the chaotic thoughts and emotions stopped.

"Katya, I have a question. I want you to be honest."

I opened my eyes and looked at him. Dimitry's voice still held that note of gentleness, stirring something deep inside me. He straightened and pushed the tray aside. I didn't move as he shifted closer.

"Do you know your father is sick? After Sergei told me about it, I asked Tatyana, and she confirmed that he has chronic kidney disease."

The words hit me like a punch. No, I didn't know. The last time I saw him, he seemed tired, but I'd chalked it up to age and stress. Tears pricked my eyes, blurring my vision. This couldn't be happening. Not him.

Papa...

"Katya, kitten," Dimitry whispered.

The softness in his voice broke me. Dimitry tensed as I threw myself into his arms, sobbing. He stayed motionless for a few seconds before hugging me tightly and pressing me to him.

"Tatyana told me he's under treatment and that he'll be getting a new transplant soon. The Romanov Bratva has money problems, but he'll be fine."

"A *new* transplant!?" I whimpered.

God, how many things had my dad hidden from me? Since when was he fighting with this problem? He should have told me! At least I wouldn't have bothered him with my fucked-up marriage. I would have supported him. I could have made sure he had enough money so he wouldn't have to stress about it. If necessary, I would have throttled Ivan until he gave him any sum of money he needed.

"Tatyana said he already had one, but something went wrong. She didn't know exactly what happened, but the doctor said he needed a new transplant. Your dad is looking for a new donor."

Oh, God...

I fisted his shirt, nestling myself against his chest as I let my tears out. He should have told me! I was his daughter, for fuck's sake. I would have been there for him, no matter what!

And fuck, Dimitry had told me Dad had offered him money in exchange for my freedom. If our bratva was already in a bad place financially ... God, did he still have enough for the treatment?

Dimitry caressed me, making soothing, slow circles on my back with his palm. I hid my face in his neck, still sobbing. And then I realized who he was. In whose arms I actually was right now.

He's going to use this moment of weakness against me. Against Papa. Against anyone he could.

"I'm sorry," I said, leaning back. "I shouldn't..."

Dimitry hugged me again and pressed me into him. Despite knowing better, I let him do it. It was just for a moment. One single moment of weakness, nothing more. I buried my face in the crook of his neck and allowed him to caress and soothe me.

"He will be fine, Katherine," he said in a calm voice. "I promise you, he will be fine."

Chapter Eight
Dimitry

I dropped myself on the bed and stared at the ceiling. I could hear the water from the shower, and I knew she was still inside the bathroom. Katya had gone there one hour ago, and when I left the room, I heard her sobs.

She was broken.

It hadn't been my intention, but I wanted to know if she knew about it. If she was once again lying to me. I didn't expect her reaction, nor the way it had made me feel. When she had thrown herself in my arms, crying, it had killed me.

Not once in my life, have I felt such a strong need to protect someone. I'd wanted to take and hide her from everybody, to keep her safe.

To keep her as mine.

She had looked so vulnerable and helpless. Defeated.

I'd planned on breaking her, but not like this. It should have made me happy to see her in such a state of vulnerability. I knew I could make her do anything when she was like this. I should enjoy it.

But I didn't.

Her pain hurt me.

I ran my palms over my face and sighed.

What the fuck am I doing to myself?

This woman was trouble, and she fucking made me feel things I shouldn't. But I couldn't deny the truth.

I wanted her. Badly. Entirely.

I glanced at the bed, where she had left her wedding ring. I clenched my fist around the jewel. That fucking piece of shit didn't deserve her. Katya shouldn't be his.

She's fucking mine.

But I wanted her to choose me. I knew she was attracted to me, but I didn't want to force her. A slide show with images of her offering herself to me played in front of my eyes, causing a shiver of pleasure to crawl down my back.

I pictured her telling me how much she needed and wanted me. Yes, that would be wonderful.

I threw a disdainful glance at the wedding ring. Katya wasn't going to wear it again. Not because I would take it from her, but because she would realize that pathetic excuse for a man didn't deserve her as his wife.

And after that, she'll be only mine.

I placed the ring on her bedside table. Yes, soon Katya will realize I was the one owning her, not that piece of shit she had married. Or anyone else. She was mine. Only mine. And she was going to learn and accept that soon.

I knew it was stupid to allow myself to feel like this. To let myself get attached. To care. But no one needed to know what I actually felt. Not even her. It would probably scare her anyway to realize what an obsession she had become.

I could barely function or think rationally since she had stepped into my life. I'd thought it was lust. It should be only lust, but everything happened too soon and too fast.

One day. One. Fucking. Day.

She had been here since yesterday night.

And she had made me feel more than I felt in my entire life.

It was the worst thing I could do, but I would make sure it was my secret. Neither Katya or anyone else had to know what I actually felt for her. They all could assume she was my new fucktoy and nothing more.

Maybe I would tell her the truth at some point. But only after she already offered herself to me. Until then, no one had to know how important Katya truly was. I wasn't going to allow anyone to use her against me.

But first, I had to fix her. I needed to see my feisty kitten smiling again. And I was going to keep the promise I'd made to her.

I had already contacted everyone I needed regarding her father's transplant. It was just a matter of time until they found a donor. And given the exorbitant sum of money I'd offered to anyone compatible with Romanov, there was no way to not have someone quickly accepting it.

My breath hitched as she stepped out of the bathroom. Fuck, she looked like a goddess. A delicious tension made my balls tingle as I took her in. Katya was wearing only an extra-short blue nightdress with spaghetti straps.

I bet that if she bent or stretched, I would have a perfect view of her pretty cunt. I remembered the feeling of her pussy milking my fingers and my cock throbbed as I fantasized about being inside her.

For a second, I asked myself how many times Chernov had fucked her. I wanted to rip him apart for that mere thought, for knowing that he was her husband and he had the chance to be inside her warm cunt whenever he wanted.

The fucking bastard called her a whore and didn't bother to do anything to save her. I should tell Katherine about that, but she wouldn't believe me.

I bit my lower lip as I looked at her deep cleavage. Fuck, I wanted to bury my face between her large tits, to have her under me, writhing and moaning in my arms.

Screaming my name. Mine, not his. Not anyone else's. Mine. Again, and again.

I gave her another once-over, but even if I tried, I couldn't look at her like she was only a piece of meat, a beautiful object I wanted to add to my collection, a sex toy to use for a night.

Katya was different, and I couldn't exactly pinpoint what or why, but she made me feel more than lust. I didn't care about her just because she was a good fuck. It was stupid of me, but it was true. I wasn't sure I liked that, but it didn't matter. I craved her.

Katherine walked toward the bed, and my heart ached as I looked at her face. Her eyes were puffy and red, her nose was swollen, and her skin was pale, completely drained of color. I wanted to hug her, but I wasn't sure if that would help her or would make things worse.

She glanced at me as she joined me on the bed. Katya studied me for a few seconds, and the look on her face reminded me of a hurt, scared deer. My heart thumped as she slowly crawled closer.

She hesitated for a moment before dropping herself right next to me. I immediately wrapped my arms around her. She felt so fragile and vulnerable. Something pulsed inside my soul as Katya placed her head on my chest. I snuggled her into me.

"Dimitry," she whispered, tilting her head and looking at me.

Even her voice sounded broken. It killed me to see her like this.

"Can you help him? Please. I'll do anything. I'll give you anything you want."

A part of me loved that she asked for my help. A part of me wanted to celebrate her surrender. But I couldn't. I didn't want her to do it because she felt she had no other choice. I wanted her to need and desire me. To trust me. Not to accept me now just because I was her best bet.

And a part of me was disgusted that she thought I would take her offer. What kind of man did she imagine I was?

"I can. I already promised you that he'll be fine."

I kept my voice equal as I explained to her what I'd already done. I saw her face changing with every word I said, and my heart beat faster as I noticed light returning into her eyes.

"Thank you."

Those two words and the honesty in her voice ruined me. I didn't remember the last time when someone said those words to me and meant them. And coming for her, they tingled something deep inside me.

She shifted and crawled on top of me, straddling my body. My cock jerked, and goosebumps covered my skin as she moved her palms along my bare chest.

"Katherine, what are you..."

"I'm thanking you."

A kick in the balls would have hurt less. So that was what she actually thought about me. That I was a monster helping her now only to fuck her. I didn't give a shit about what my enemies thought about me. I'd built myself that image, the one of a ruthless beast.

But it stung to have her thinking that, too.

She leaned in to kiss me, but I grabbed her neck and stopped her before her lips could touch mine.

"I don't want you to thank me like a whore would."

Chapter Nine
Katherine

I felt so numb as I stepped out of the bathroom. Not once in my life have I felt so helpless and lonely. It was clear to me that Dimitry was going to keep me here until he solved things with Ivan, and since my husband was a complete moron, that could take a while.

Papa had already offered Dimitry money. Did he still have enough for his treatment? Was he at least focusing on his health? I wished he wouldn't have known about me being taken by Dimitry. Now I was sure he was worried and scared, and that would only make things worse.

I was used to being alone and taking care of things on my own. But fuck if I couldn't use a hug and someone telling me everything was going to be alright.

Like Dimitry did.

I was sure he was manipulating me and playing his own game. But it'd felt so good, though. I glanced at him as I approached the bed. He was laying on his back, watching me, and in a strange way, his mere presence there, so calm and so in control, was comforting.

Crawling toward him, I swallowed hard. I shouldn't do this. Not only that my husband would probably die in shame to know I was acting like this for another man, but I knew Dimitry was going to use any sign of weakness against me.

But I needed it.

I needed it so much.

I just craved a moment of weakness, in which I didn't have to fight. Or at least to not fight alone. I was just tired.

Biting my lower lip, I dared to drop myself next to him. I knew it was a mistake, but I didn't care. The moment he hugged my body made me melt into him, and despite knowing better, I placed my head on his chest.

The warmth of his body enveloped and lulled me. I closed my eyes, listening to his heartbeats, and for a moment, my brain shut down. I wasn't sure why he had this effect on me, but it was comforting.

Dimitry caressed my back and a wave of blissful calmness washed over me. As I focused on his touches, I let my mind drift away. Ivan wasn't going to help my father, and because of his mistakes, I couldn't either. He was too immature, too self-centered, too impulsive and stupid.

Maybe...

I couldn't believe I was thinking about this. I shouldn't trust Dimitry enough to ask for his help. But if he didn't... I glanced at the wedding ring on my bedside table. I didn't remember placing it there, but probably Dimitry did.

Guilt swirled through my body. A loyal wife shouldn't even be thinking about this. But what other choice did I have? And yet, what scared and hurt me the most was that I wasn't so sure I wanted to do it just because I needed his help.

No, I'm doing it for Papochka. Only for him.

"Dimitry," I whispered. "Can you help him? Please. I'll do anything. I'll give you anything you want."

He stayed silent for a few moments, making my pulse quicken.

"I can. I already promised you that he'll be fine."

My brain barely could keep up as he started to tell me what he had already done. I couldn't understand why he'd put all those things in motion so fast, but I assume he saw the opportunity and took it.

It didn't matter, anyway. Whatever plan he had, knowing that my dad was going to be alright made all my worries vanish. It was all I wanted and needed.

My heart clenched as I realized that his actions were more than my husband had ever done for me. And that he had also done them even before I asked.

He even gave Papa his money back.

Maybe it was his plan to make my father owe him or something like that, but that wasn't important to me. My dad was going to be fine.

I was honest as I whispered, "Thank you."

The little smile he gave me made all my cells vibrate. He trailed his fingers along my spine, and that tiny gesture had been enough to set me alive. I was making a mistake, I knew it. I was betraying Ivan. And yet, I didn't care.

Before thinking twice, I straddled Dimitry's body. A wave of wetness flooded my pussy as I felt his cock twitching. Oh, he was hard, and I couldn't keep myself from dry-humping him. Fuck, I wanted him.

Maybe it was the unexpected relief of knowing that he was going to help my father and how grateful I was. Maybe it was that illicit desire that had burned within me since I'd met Dimitry. Maybe it was the way he had made me feel every time he'd touched me.

I didn't know.

I didn't care.

I wanted him.

Dimitry moved his palms to my hips, and my inner slut shivered in response to his touch. Screw Ivan, I could lie to him if needed. If I was going to spend some time with Dimitry, I could very well make the best of it.

"Katherine, what are you..."

I opened my mouth wanting to tell him the truth. That I craved him. But that would give him even more power over me than he already has.

"I'm thanking you."

It was partially true, after all. I leaned in to kiss him, but my breath hitched as he grabbed my neck and stopped me. What was he doing?

"I don't want you to thank me like a whore would."

The coldness in his voice felt like a slap. Wasn't this what he wanted? To have me offering myself to him?

Dimitry held my gaze as he muttered, "But maybe I should be the monster you think I am and use you like the cheating slut you are."

My heart stopped as he pulled me closer for a kiss. He roughly parted my lips with his tongue and shoved it inside my mouth. I moaned and squirmed as he used his other arm to force me to melt against him.

Every cell of me buzzed back to life. His dominance, his anger, and the way he took control scared and aroused me at the same time. Or maybe the emotions blended too much for me to correctly distinguish between them.

I yelped as he suddenly toppled me. A pang of pain zinged to my clit, making it throb as he bit on my lower lip. I whimpered and writhed, grinding against him as he channeled his attention from my mouth to my neck.

His lips against my skin felt like molten lava, forcing out a stream of connected moans as he kissed me there.

"Maybe I should fuck you, brand you as mine, and then sent you back to your husband. With my cum still inside you."

My pussy clenched at the filthiness of his words. God, why was this so arousing? I roamed my palms along his back as he nibbled at my neck. Fuck, my entire being hummed when he trailed his mouth along my shoulders, licking and kissing me.

"And once you're together with that idiot you call your husband, once you're in his bed, I'll come and take you right then and there. Right next to him. Until you scream my name."

I whimpered and dug my nails into his back as he bit my neck hard. Pain and pleasure mixed within me, hotness flushing my body. More slickness pooled between my thighs, and my heart beat faster as he glanced at me.

I could see the annoyance in his eyes, but I still couldn't understand what had irritated him so much. I didn't have too much time to think about it, though. His demanding kiss swallowed my moans and made my brain mushy. I instinctively deepened it and wrapped my hands around his neck.

Fuck, he was a good kisser. Our tongues entwined, and my entire being pulsed as we made out, the taste of him overwhelming my senses. My toes curled as he moved his hands all over my body, stroking and groping. I was breathless when he finally broke the kiss.

"If you want to give your body to me as a price for my help, like a cheap cheating slut, then so be it. I wanted to fuck you since I saw you, so I should take what I want after all."

I yelped as he roughly turned me around. He yanked my body, placing me on my hands and knees. The mattress dipped as he shifted behind me. I looked over my shoulder and saw him pushing his pants and boxers down.

My pussy fluttered in anticipation as he released his cock. He was exactly as huge as I remembered, and a shiver of pleasure floated through me as I imagined him stuffing me.

Dimitry guided his length at my entrance, the sensation of his tip pressing against it sending pulsing spirals of fire through my core. A loud cry of pain and pleasure left my mouth as he slammed inside without warning.

I jostled forward, but his grip on my hips kept me in place. My inner walls quivered, stretched more than they had ever been, but he didn't bother giving me a moment to adjust to his size. Dimitry immediately started to thrust in a frantic rhythm that turned the warmth within me into a blazing inferno.

"Oh, God!" I gasped, each stroke sending rippling waves of ecstasy through me. "Fuck! Yes!"

I still had no idea what had pushed his buttons like this, but I liked it. I mirrored his movements, fucking him back as much as he fucked me. I could feel his anger in every mind-shattering thrust. I could tell he was focusing only on his pleasure, chasing his own orgasm, and yet, this was the best sex of my life.

I wasn't sure if it was his experience, his dominance, or what else, but he was feeding the fire within me with each stroke. The lewd wet sounds of his thighs slapping my ass, making my flesh ripple, echoed in the bedroom.

"You give me your body for my help," he grunted. "If I wanted only this, I could have taken it from the first day."

The air left my lungs as he pressed on my back, making me collapse. Dimitry leaned on top of me, trapping and squeezing me under the weight of his body while he relentlessly jackhammered into my pussy.

My mind tried to process his words, but God, when he changed the angle and repeatedly massaged my G-spot at every impale, my brain blipped out. My moans mingled with his grunts as he ravished me like a beast in heat, so rough that I thought he wanted to brand himself on my inner walls.

"Fuck, yes! Fuck! Oh, God!" I panted.

"If I wanted you as my whore and nothing more, you would have already been," he growled in my ear.

I fisted the bedsheets, my vision blurring as he slammed his hips against mine so fiercely that I believed he might fuck me through the bed. The pleasure within me became so intense that I was sure he had just pushed me to my body's limit for rapture.

"Fuck! Fuck! Fuck!"

My release crashed on top of me with the force of a billion orgasms, making my entire being shudder. I cried out as I rode out the shockwaves, spasming and trembling under his delicious assault.

Dimitry continued to fuck me through my orgasm, using me as if

I was a rag doll. His growl covered me in goosebumps as he came inside my pussy. Ecstasy coursed through me while he coated my insides white, filling me up with his hotness.

I moaned as I felt him shifting on top of me. Dimitry leaned toward the bedside and grabbed my wedding ring. His breath was as labored as mine, and while he moved, my face burnt realizing I wanted nothing more than to have him holding me in his arms.

Why am I feeling this? Why do I crave him in such an intimate way?

I clenched and gasped when I felt him shoving the jewel inside my pussy.

"Congrats, Katherine. Your cheating cunt paid for my help regarding your father."

Those words hit me like a punch in the stomach. What the hell was wrong with him? I turned around to face him, but he was already getting out of bed. I missed the warmth of his body the second he moved away.

"Dimitry," I started, but all I heard was the slam of the door as he left the bedroom.

What the fuck!?

Chapter Ten
Dimitry

I shouldn't have done this. I shouldn't have fucked her. Now I wanted her even more.

And she sees me as a monster.

I kicked the chair, sending it spiraling to the other side of the office. I had to get rid of her. Now. It was stupid of me to get attached. She'd messed with my head too much. I sniffed myself, and her damn scent, still lingering on me, was enough to make me hard again.

When she'd asked for help, I thought, for a moment, she saw me as a man she could trust. One who could protect her.

But when I'd realized the truth... I'd hoped that at least fucking her would clear my mind, and help me forget about her. Instead, I craved her more than ever.

She had been unbelievable, the best sex of my life. My cock throbbed at the memory of her moaning beneath me, of her cunt squeezing me, milking my dick like she was made for it.

All I'd wanted was to keep her a little more in my arms, to feel her snuggling into me and maybe whispering my name.

I poured a glass of whiskey and downed it in one swallow.

I hate her and everything she makes me feel.

"Boss," Sergei said, hurrying into the room with my clothes.

I grabbed them and started dressing, cursing the moment I'd decided to kidnap her. I should have destroyed Chernov from the start, instead of trying to force him to make amends.

Then I wouldn't have met her, wouldn't have fucked her, wouldn't have fallen in love with her.

Fuck!

The second the thought hit me I knew it was true. I fucking loved this crazy kitten. All those emotions that had been clawing at me since we'd met, they finally made sense.

I have to get rid of her. For both her and me.

"Boss, I got news from Chernov. He accepted the meeting, but he wants it on his territory."

I half-listened to Sergei's words, something tearing inside me as I realized it was time. If Chernov wanted to meet, he was ready to do what it took to get her back. He'd probably finally realized how important Katya was.

And now he was going to take her from me. Because he was her fucking husband.

I hurled the glass against the wall, making Sergei flinch. The sharp smell of whiskey filled the room, but it wasn't enough to drown out her sweet mix of vanilla and jasmine.

"Tell him I accept."

"He asked for it to be tomorrow, but I'll tell him to wait. We need to check the place, make sure —"

"No," I cut him off. "Tomorrow's fine. The sooner we end this, the better."

I couldn't trust myself to think rationally anymore. I had to give Katya back to her husband before I did something truly stupid. I wasn't a man who fell in love. I couldn't be.

And she saw me as a monster, anyway. She hated me, and more than sure wanted me dead.

It's better for both of us this way.

Chapter Eleven
Katherine

I hugged his pillow and buried my face into it, taking a deep breath. His scent soothed me, and I let out a soft sigh as I filled my lungs with it.

This is stupid!

Since Dimitry had left the room, he'd been avoiding me. I didn't see him at breakfast, lunch, or dinner, and he hadn't returned to the bedroom at night. I couldn't understand his behavior. But him treating me like this, ignoring and avoiding me ... it hurt.

Funny how I'd never gave a fuck when Ivan had done the same.

This was so frustrating. I should be grateful he was staying away from me. Damn him! I had no idea why or how he messed with my head so much.

I caressed the pillow, taking another deep breath, and as I closed my eyes, I could feel his touch on my skin, making my entire body tingle.

Fuck this. He can't avoid me forever! I'm not a toy he can throw away whenever he wants!

I jumped off the bed and sauntered out of the bedroom. He had to be somewhere in the villa. If I had to, I'd go room to room until I found him. And then...

Then what?

I had no idea. But I needed to see him.

"Are you going somewhere, Katherine?"

The voice made me flinch. I turned around to face the man who had spoken. He was jacked and strong, so I assumed he was one of Dimitry's guards. Had Dimitry ordered him to follow me? What, was he scared I'd try to escape again?

Well, maybe I should do that.

Fuck, I should be using the fact that he was avoiding me to work on my plan to get out of here, not to search for him. And yet, here I was, in the middle of the night, wearing only my nightdress, roaming the hallways and looking for him.

At least the man seemed to appreciate the view, judging by the way his eyes traveled over my body. He swallowed hard, shook his head, and finally focused his attention on my face.

"I'm looking for Dimitry," I said.

"He's not here. He went to talk to your husband."

My stomach clenched.

What?

Ivan accepted a meeting? That was unexpected. Maybe Dad had talked some sense into him and kicked his ass into action. And Dimitry ... he was ready to get rid of me. I should be happy about this. It meant I'd be free soon.

So why wasn't I?

Because I'd probably never see him again.

That thought should have thrilled me, but instead, it hurt. I hugged myself, but the coldness spread through me anyway. Why couldn't I be happy about this? I should be.

"Do you know when he'll be back?" I asked.

The man shrugged.

"No idea. Your husband requested the meeting on his territory, at some old warehouse. He should be back by morning, though."

Old warehouse?

I knew only one place like that. It was an abandoned storage facility, but Ivan always refused to go anywhere near it. The place was stocked with enough firepower to level half a city. My husband was too much of a coward to risk being near an explosion. He'd never call for a meeting there. Unless...

He's not going to be there.

"Call Dimitry! Please, call him and tell him not to go. It's a trap!"

"What?"

"Please!"

The fear in my voice and the panic on my face must have been convincing enough because the guard ordered me back to the bedroom before running down the hallway.

My heart pounded wildly as I obeyed. I closed the door to my room — my room? Since when had I started thinking of it that way? — and leaned against it. The realization of what I'd just done hit me like a cold shower.

I shouldn't have...

Ivan's plan might actually have worked. He would've killed Dimitry. I wanted to believe I'd done this to save myself. After all, if Dimitry's men learned their boss was dead, they'd have killed me too. Or worse.

But that thought hadn't even crossed my mind.

I did it for him.

Why? How the hell had he become so important to me?

My heart thumped in my ears as I crawled back onto the bed and hugged his pillow again. God, I hoped they stopped Dimitry in time. I curled into a ball and squeezed the pillow tighter. I wanted him to be safe. I wanted him back.

I needed him.

What am I doing? Feeling? Thinking? I can no longer understand myself ... God, am I falling in love with him?

Chapter Twelve
Dimitry

"Where's the doctor?"

"I'm here, boss!"

He and Sergei helped me get Victor inside. The other men followed, supporting each other. That fucking blast had almost killed all of us.

"Katherine?"

"I told her to wait in your bedroom," Sergei said.

I ordered him to take care of the group together with the doctor and darted toward my room. I needed to see her. Katya flinched as I stormed in, and before she could say anything, I was on top of her, crushing my lips against hers.

My kitten.

I'd thought I was going to die back there. That talking shit hadn't even shown up, only some of his men were there. We'd barely made it to the location when Sergei called to warn me about the trap. I'd ordered everyone to get the fuck out, but then the explosion hit.

In those moments, convinced I was about to die, all I could think about had been her. About how fucking stupid I'd been not to make her mine. Not to tell her how I felt. Not to keep her with me.

I wasn't sure why she'd warned me. Maybe because she was smart enough to know the danger she'd face. Sergei was my successor, and he knew to keep her safe if anything happened to me. But shit could have gone south fast anyway.

Maybe she'd done it for herself. After all, she hated me.

And yet, here she was, her arms and legs wrapped tightly around me, desperately responding to my kiss, deepening it as if her life depended on it.

This didn't feel like hate.

Maybe I was deluding myself. Maybe it was just wishful thinking.

But fuck it, that didn't mean I couldn't savor the moment, this fleeting, desperate illusion that she wanted me. Craved me.

Loved me.

She cupped my face as we broke apart for air. I wanted to believe the concern in her gaze was real as she studied me.

"You're hurt," she whispered, her soft fingers trailing over the cut on my cheek.

"I'm fine, kitten. It'll heal."

She melted into me as I kissed her again. Feeling her warmth against me sent a jolt of pleasure through my body. Katya stirred in my arms, trembling beneath me, and the way her body responded to mine had my cock straining painfully against my pants.

"I want you," I murmured as we parted for air.

I shouldn't have said that. I shouldn't have put myself in such a vulnerable position in front of her. Yet, I didn't regret it. Her eyes were glazed with mixed emotions as she looked at me. I didn't dare to try to decipher them.

Katya wrapped herself tighter around me, pulling me closer. A shiver rushed down my back as she tugged at my ripped shirt, undressing me. I allowed her to do it. I helped her get out of her nightdress, and I quickly unfastened my belt and removed my pants and boxers.

"Dimitry..."

Her voice broke as she took me in. Katya moved her fingers so gently along my chest and shoulders that it felt as if they were made of feathers. I realized she was tracing the scars and bruises that covered my skin. I didn't even notice them after the blast.

"I'm fine," I assured her again.

I froze as she pressed her lips to mine, clawing at my back in her attempt to pull me closer. I allowed myself to believe, for a fucking second, that she actually wanted me. Needed me.

She was so sweet, and more of her unique taste flooded my mouth as our tongues entwined. Katya squirmed under me, and she let out a tiny mewl as my cock jerked against her thigh.

"Please, make love to me," she breathed against my lips.

Those words ruined me. She sounded so vulnerable and innocent. Maybe she was trying to manipulate me, but I didn't care. I craved nothing more than to have her. My dick was so hard that it hurt and all I wanted was to hear Katya moaning my name.

Her eyes were so soft as they met mine. I moved on top of her, placing tiny kisses on her smooth skin. She writhed and stretched as I took my time to worship every inch of her beautiful body.

I cupped her large tits, massaging them while sucking on her nipples in turns. My pulse quickened as Katya moaned and thrust her chest forward, pushing herself more into me. As if she needed me as much as I needed her.

I felt her palms roaming over my back, pressing me into her. It made me feel as if I belonged to her. As if she owned me. I loved that feeling, and a shiver of fear zinged through me at the realization.

"Dimitry," she whimpered and thrashed, her lips curling into a gorgeous, sweet smile.

I didn't remember ever seeing her smiling like that before. Maybe when I'd told her about helping her father, but that one had been different. This one was content and passionate, and with a mix of lust and blissfulness I couldn't exactly describe. And pure. So fucking pure.

Fuck!

The desire to take care of her, to claim her and keep her as mine, to make sure she always had a reason to smile, was overwhelming.

Katya let out more tiny mewls as I crawled down her body, trailing my mouth along every part of her. I wanted to give her pleasure, and watching her so delighted by my touches pulled at something inside me I didn't know existed before.

I wanted to please her. To protect and care for her, to see her happy. Fuck, I really was in love with this wild kitten.

She's going to be the death of me.

Her breath grew labored as I moved closer and closer to her pussy. She trembled and let out more soft moans as I spread her long legs and caressed them.

I watched her quivering and panting as I placed little kisses on her inner thighs. God, she was gorgeous, and the way her body responded to any of my touches was like a drug. Intoxicating. Addictive. I wanted nothing more than to claim her and keep her as mine.

"Dimitry!"

She arched and lifted her hips as I buried my face between her legs. She tasted so sweet, and I couldn't hold back my hungry growl as I swirled my tongue between her soaked folds.

Katya was drenched. For me. My balls tingled with need, but I wanted to see her coming first. She was fucking delicious, and I knew I could feast on her all day long.

"Oh, God! Yes!" she whimpered, and her hand shot to my hair, pushing me more into her pussy.

My greedy kitten. Mine.

I groaned as I doubled down on my efforts, eating her out with gusto. I could have died right then and there and been the happiest man alive.

I focused on her clit, watching her reactions. She was like an open book, so easy to read, and I made sure I repeatedly teased the spots that made her shudder and let out those sweet little mewls.

"Yes! Yes! That's so good! Yes!"

Her words drove me wild and I dug my fingers into her hips,

pinning her wide open for me. I felt like a starved beast that finally found the perfect feast. Katya trembled and whimpered, and I could tell she was teetering toward the edge.

I glanced at her, and my cock jerked as I found her watching me with what I could describe only as raw, primal desire. Katya threw her head backward as I plunged two fingers inside her pussy while licking and sucking on her clit.

"You taste amazing," I groaned while devouring her.

She clenched around my fingers and let out another storm of moans that made my cock spasm. A wonderful tension spread through me, and seeing her so close to her release spurred me on.

I wanted her to come for me. Because of me.

And to scream my name.

Her body vibrated with need, and I growled as she desperately clutched at my hair, pressing my face into her pussy. I curbed my fingers, massaging her G-spot as I repeatedly thrust them inside her channel, and the lewd, hot noises she let out told me she enjoyed it.

"Fuck, Dimitry! Fuck! Yes! Dimitry! Yes!"

I thought I was going to come undone once with her as she surrendered to her climax while chanting my name. She came all over my face, and I greedily ate her up and fingered her faster and harder, heightening her pleasure as much as possible.

I glanced at her as she rode out the aftershocks, and God, that was the most beautiful image I'd ever seen. To watch her with all that pleasure glazing her eyes while she moaned and murmured my name switched so many buttons inside me that I thought I was in heaven.

She was my heaven.

Crawling up along her body, I kissed her, murmuring, "Mine," and my heart exploded as she whimpered, "Yours."

Chapter Thirteen
Dimitry

A few weeks later

Silence fell as I stepped into the room. I nodded a greeting to the men gathered, but my focus remained fixed on Chernov. The clown wore a stupid grin, radiating so much arrogance it made me want to vomit.

How the fuck had this pathetic excuse for a man ended up as Katherine's husband? Worse, he had no idea how to appreciate her. I had to admit, knowing I'd just fucked her mere minutes ago while he sat here, oblivious, gave me a certain satisfaction.

I'd invited all the bratva leaders to this meeting, except for Katya's father. I knew the kitten didn't want him involved.

I took my seat at the head of the table. The other leaders lined either side, with Chernov positioned right next to me.

He smirked, still unaware of the tension simmering in the room, or the fact that his wife was just in the next room, watching us. I couldn't see Katya through the one-way glass, but knowing she was there added a special thrill.

"So, you finally decided to make amends," Chernov said, puffing out his chest. "How much of Romanov's territory did he offer you in exchange for Katherine?"

Hearing her name in his mouth made my blood boil. It sounded vulgar coming from him, and the way he spoke of her, as if she were a possession rather than his wife, disgusted me. This was the woman he had vowed to love, protect, and cherish, and he had failed in every way.

"I'm not interested in making amends," I said calmly, leaning back in my chair. "I had Katherine lie to you because I knew you'd be too much of a coward to show up otherwise."

The color drained from his face, and a spark of satisfaction flickered in me. Chernov shot to his feet, darting glances around the room like a cornered animal. For the first time, he seemed to notice my men stationed along the walls, ready to carry out my orders.

The other pachans shifted uneasily in their chairs, exchanging glances. I could see their discomfort.

I'd bent the truth with them, too, telling them this meeting was a final peace talk. But they knew me well enough to trust that I'd keep my word. I'd guaranteed their safety on my territory, and they knew I wasn't Chernov. If I wanted someone dead, I didn't rely on cowardly explosions from afar. I'd do the job myself.

"Boris! Igor! Oleg!" Chernov barked, desperation seeping into his voice.

I smiled. He still thought his men were waiting outside, ready to protect him.

"They're already dead," I said.

The room grew deathly quiet as the truth sank in. Chernov froze, his face turning ghostly pale. For a moment, I let the silence stretch, enjoying the way he squirmed and trembled, making an even bigger fool of himself in front of everyone.

"Sit," I ordered coolly, nodding at his chair.

His apple bobbed as he reluctantly obeyed. I scanned the other pachans. Tension rippled through them, but I caught glimpses of amusement in their eyes, especially Maxim's.

Katya had told me he loathed Chernov, and knowing I had an ally before walking into this room had only bolstered my confidence.

"Look, you can keep my wife and the territory," Chernov stammered. "I'll stay out of your business, I swear."

Spineless idiot.

His sudden change in tone and pathetic attempt at negotiation only deepened my contempt.

"Katherine isn't an object you can hand over," I said.

Chernov flinched at the coldness in my tone, his visible panic intensifying. Even so, he had the audacity to roll his eyes.

"Whatever. The point is, I don't want to escalate this. If keeping her is what you want, fine. I won't set foot in your territory again."

"I'm sure you won't," I said, a smirk curling my lips. "But as for Katherine, that's neither your decision nor mine. It's hers. Why don't we let her decide?"

I knew the risk in putting this choice in her hands, especially here and now, in front of everyone. One of us, either Chernov or me, would end up completely humiliated.

She could still betray me, still choose him. But I trusted her. I loved her. And I believed her when she had told me she felt the same.

"Katherine," I called, my gaze fixed on the window, "come here, please."

Chapter Fourteen
Katherine

The look on my husband's face as I walked into the room? Priceless.

During his talk with Dimitry, I had wanted to kick him in the balls, not just for the way he spoke about me but for the blatant disrespect he showed my lover. When Dimitry had put him in his place, I couldn't help but grin.

I supposed that wasn't exactly loyal wife behavior, but I'd long since stopped considering loyalty as something he deserved from me.

I smiled and greeted the men at the table. I was grateful Dimitry didn't invite my father to the meeting. He needed all the rest after the procedure, and I didn't want him involved in this.

The leaders' gazes lingered on me, and despite the tension hanging in the room, I could see amusement in their eyes.

I glanced at Dimitry. He lounged in his chair like a king, his eyes tracking my every movement.

I knew what he wanted. He hoped to humiliate my husband in front of everyone by showing I belonged to him. But I also knew he would let me decide what to do. He trusted me, placing himself in a vulnerable position just to give me that choice.

I fell doubly hard in love with him for that.

A wicked smile tugged at my lips as I walked toward the table, swaying my hips. Instead of stopping, I climbed up onto it, slowly and deliberately. The leaders shifted in their seats, clearly entertained.

Part of me wanted to humiliate Ivan, but the truth, I would've done the same even if he weren't here. Punishing him was just a bonus, a petty one I couldn't deny enjoying.

Crawling on my hands and knees, I made my way toward Dimitry, undulating my body with every move. I could feel every pair of eyes on me. Ivan looked like he'd just swallowed a mouthful of acid, his discomfort fueling my excitement.

"Katherine!" he hissed as I neared Dimitry. "What the fuck are you doing?"

I shot him a cold, disdainful glance and kept moving. My deliberate disobedience seemed to push him over the edge, enough for him to forget how precarious his position was.

"You fucking traitorous whore," he growled, extending a hand to grab me.

I raised mine to defend myself, but Dimitry's cold voice sliced through the air, freezing us both mid-motion.

"Touch her, and I swear to God, I'll cut off your hand and fuck you with it."

Ivan shrank back into his seat. I smirked at him before crawling the last few inches to Dimitry, dropping myself into his lap like a spoiled kitten.

He laughed softly, steadying me as I settled in. I nuzzled him, pressing a kiss to his lips. Around us, I heard sharp intakes of breath, and I imagined one of them belonged to Ivan. Dimitry deepened the kiss, his hand splayed on my back, pulling me closer until I melted against him.

"Did you call me, love?" I asked sweetly.

"Yes," he replied. "As you heard, your husband proposed to hand you over to me."

I giggled, my gaze shifting to Ivan. The mix of disgust, fear, anger, and hatred painted on his face gave me a wicked thrill. Around the table, the other men watched us with a blend of amusement and shock, likely unused to seeing Dimitry act this way or tolerate such behavior from a woman in front of them.

"As if I ever belonged to him," I said, letting my disdain drip from every word. "He failed as a husband in every way. He was never truly there for me, didn't care about me, and, God, he definitely didn't satisfy me."

Ivan's face turned an alarming shade of red, a vein pulsing dangerously at his temple. I shifted in Dimitry's lap, draping my legs over the table and spreading them just enough to make the men at the table visibly react.

Except Ivan. He looked like he was about to have an aneurysm.

"Do you see this?" I asked him, tracing a finger between my folds. "Do you see how well he fucked me? His cum is still inside my pussy. In only a few days, Dimitry's given me more pleasure than you managed in our entire marriage. With him I didn't need to fake it. And more than that. He showed me love, care, and respect. Something you never bothered with."

Laughter rippled through the room, and my husband's face turned crimson.

Dimitry's arm wrapped around my waist, pulling me closer as he kissed my neck. I squirmed slightly, a jolt of heat running through me as I felt his erection pressing against my ass.

I dipped my fingers lower, coating them in the evidence of our earlier illicit moment. I brought them to my lips, sucking them clean with a satisfied moan.

"He's delicious," I said with a smirk. "And guess what? My pussy isn't the only hole he claimed. He claimed my mouth, too. And you know what? I actually love giving him head. Do you remember how many times I turned you down when you begged for it? I think I sucked you off only twice during our entire marriage. But Dimitry ... I've lost count of how many times I've eagerly done it for him. And swallowed every time."

"You filthy sl—"

"I would choose my words very carefully if I were you," Dimitry cut in coldly, holding me tighter.

Ivan clamped his mouth shut, trembling with barely contained rage. And now, it was time for the finishing blow. Not just to humiliate my husband but because I wanted it.

I fantasized about this in the last few days, but I still didn't ask Dimitry if he would want us to try it. But this seemed to be the perfect moment.

"He claimed two of my holes, but I want more," I purred. "I want him to claim the one you begged me to let you have, the one I always refused."

Dimitry tensed beneath me, his cock jerking violently. I turned to face him, letting him see the raw, unfiltered lust in my eyes.

"Please, love, claim my ass. Here. Now. In front of everyone. I need you. I beg you, fuck me."

Dimitry's pupils dilated, his eyes darkening with feral, primal desire. His fingers dug into my flesh as he studied me. I licked a slow line along his jaw, savoring the shiver that ran through his body.

I let out an aroused whimper as he stood up and roughly bent me over the table. Oh, yes! I wiggled my ass at him and moaned as he hitched my dress and caressed my cheeks. I was already drenched, and hearing the zipper of his pants made me quiver in anticipation.

"Are you sure this is what you want, Katya? To show your husband and everyone here what a perfect slut you are for me?"

I smiled and pushed back, teasing him, purring, "Yes. Fuck me! Please!"

The group of men watched us, visibly shocked, amused, curious, and aroused at the same time. Given that I caught sight of a few of them adjusting themselves, I assumed seeing me acting like a little whore was pushing their buttons.

I could feel their eyes on me, traveling along my body, and it surprised me how thrilling this was. It made me feel like the star of a porn movie. Ivan's strangled gasp cut through the silence, but I completely ignored him, his pain only fueling my pleasure.

Electricity pricked my hair as I felt Dimitry's cock touching my legs. Spasms of excitement floated through my core as my lover used my pussy juices to prepare my ass. My muscles tensed as he slowly pushed his fingers inside my tight hole.

"Relax, Katya," he murmured.

His voice was soothing and calm, and I tried my best to obey. I trusted him. Looking back, that had been another reason I had always refused Ivan, aside from his being completely unable to satisfy me in bed. I didn't trust him.

I moaned and squirmed as Dimitry repeatedly pushed his fingers inside my virgin hole, forcing my ring of muscles to stretch. I glanced at Ivan. He was petrified, clutching the armrests of his chair so hard that I was impressed the wood hadn't broken yet. He looked at me as if he wanted to throttle me, and I couldn't hold myself from smirking.

Well, since he so easily called me a whore, I find it perfectly fair to act like one. Just not for him.

"Are you thinking about all the moments when you begged me to let you fuck my ass?" I taunted him. "When you whined and pouted because I always refused to let you put that tiny dick you didn't even know how to use inside me?"

"Listen here, you fucking wh-" he growled, but I assumed Dimitry gave him a harsh glance because Ivan swallowed hard while looking at my lover and bit his lips shut while his face turned completely red.

"It doesn't even matter what he thinks about," Dimitry laughed, pulling his fingers out of my hole. "I bet this is an image he will never forget."

I tensed as I felt his cock probing at my entrance. My heart thumped. I tried to focus on my breath and relax when my lover whispered "Easy, kitten. Calm down, trust me." I did. I fucking did, more than I ever believed anyone else.

Pain shot through me as he pushed inside, inch by inch. Every cell in my body vibrated, and I cried out and squirmed as he stuffed me.

"You feel amazing, Katya," he groaned. "So fucking tight!"

I dug my nails into the back of my palms and closed my eyes as he continued to advance. I gasped and whimpered as he forced the last inches inside, but once completely nestled, the discomfort vanished.

Dimitry allowed me to get accustomed to the sensation of fullness, the throbbing of his cock sending gentle ripples of pleasure. This was new and different, but also so good. I moaned as he caressed and stroked my body, and my mind turned mushy as he whispered, "Good girl."

My lover grabbed my hips and started to thrust slowly. Given how fucking huge he was, I expected a new wave of pain, but it didn't happen. My muscles were still pulsing, and it definitely felt different, but it was good. I could tell Dimitry was holding back, his movements careful and calculated.

Blinking my eyes open, I glanced around the room, and a thrill of arousing embarrassment ran down my spine as I noticed some of the men were stroking themselves. What the fuck? I didn't expect that, but this was so naughty that it turned me on like crazy.

Ivan looked as if he was dead inside. If until then his ego had been at least bruised, now I bet it had been completely destroyed. I assumed now I clearly was a ruined slut, as he'd called me. Well, he wasn't going to be married to me for too long.

"Fuck, Katya," Dimitry groaned, slowly increasing the pace. "This pretty, tight hole of yours is amazing. And so fucking mine."

I moaned, pushing back and mirroring his rhythm. His words sent flutters of excitement through me, and my core pulsed as he started to hammer into my ass. My body jostled forward at every thrust, my nipples so hard that they grazed the wooden surface through the thin fabric of my dress.

"Yes! Yes! Yes!" I whimpered, meeting each one of his movements with one of my own.

Everything around blurred and ceased to exist. All that my brain cells could focus on at the moment were the amazing sensations of having that pole claiming my once virgin hole. His thrusts turned shorter and quicker with every passing second, tides of ecstasy rushing through me at every penetration.

"You're so fucking good," Dimitry groaned.

Stars played in front of my eyes as he snaked his hand between my legs and attacked my clit. My screams of pleasure increased in volume, and every cell of my body pulsed in arousal. Tension coiled in my core, and I could feel my orgasm building fast, in layers.

"Are you going to come for me, little slut? Right here, right now? In front of your husband?"

All my muscles tensed, his dirty words making my head spin. All I could do was moan and beg him to not stop while he railed me like there was no tomorrow. I could hear groans and grunts from around, so I assumed the other men loved the lewd view. The scent of sex was intoxicating, and my body purred as I spiraled toward my release.

"Look at him, Katherine," Dimitry growled, tugging at my hair and making me face my husband. "Keep your eyes on him while you come. Let him watch you having a real orgasm, not a fake one."

Ivan looked as if he had just been kicked in the balls. Dimitry used his hold on my hair to balance himself while fucking me rougher. With his other hand, he continued to torment my clit while he shoved that glorious cock hard and deep inside my ass.

"Show him how you look having the pleasure he never could give it to you," he grunted.

God, everything he was doing to me threw me over the edge. I clawed at the table as wildfire engulfed my entire being. I looked into Ivan's eyes while chanting Dimitry's name, the disgust, humiliation, and anger so visibly painted on my husband's face making everything hotter.

I could feel Dimitry's cock swelling and pulsing, and my mind shut off as he growled and filled me up. The warmth of his cum rushed through me, crashing against the aftershocks of my orgasm and making every cell of my body buzz.

"Oh, fuck!" I whimpered. "God, this was the best sex of my life," I mewled.

My legs trembled, and I went limp. Dimitry pulled out, but I didn't move, remaining draped over the table, barely able to breathe. Damn, I knew Dimitry was amazing, but I was more exhausted than I'd ever been. Moans and groans echoed in the room, so I assumed the other men reached their climaxes.

I looked at Ivan. I didn't think I'd ever seen him in such a ruined state, and I couldn't hold back my grin. The fucking asshole deserved everything. At least now he had reasons to call me a whore.

There was only one thing I needed to do.

Divorce him.

Chapter Fifteen
Dimitry

Tension coiled tight inside me, twisting in ways I hadn't felt before. Fuck, this was the hottest thing I'd ever done. She had been unbelievable. And watching the lust in the other pachans' eyes while knowing none of them would ever get to touch her—touch what was mine—sent a raw thrill coursing through me.

The bastard she'd married looked like he'd been fucked in the ass without lube. I didn't even bother hiding my disdain when our eyes met for the briefest moment.

Katherine moaned and squirmed against me, and I quickly helped her to her feet. My heart raced as she instinctively clung to me, melting into my arms. I couldn't resist pulling her closer, kissing her.

Maybe it wasn't smart to show everyone just how dear she was to me, but the damage was already done. They weren't stupid. They could see it. She wasn't a plaything or some temporary indulgence. The shock on their faces earlier when she'd plopped herself in my lap and kissed me had made that much obvious.

And that's fine. Let them know she's mine.

Katherine leaned into me, her eyes locking onto Ivan. Her voice was ice as she told him, "I want a divorce."

I fought the urge to grin like an idiot. I'd thought making her a widow would be faster, but since she'd made it clear she didn't want him dead, not yet, anyway, I'd shelved that idea. For now.

Chernov frowned, his gaze darting between us. It wasn't lust I saw in his eyes when he looked at Katya, but fuck, I still wanted to kick his teeth in for letting his filthy gaze linger on her at all.

"No," Ivan said, leaning back arrogantly in his chair.

My brow shot up. This fucking idiot was begging to die. What did he think he'd gain by refusing? Some scrap of self-respect?

Katya snorted, her whole demeanor shifting. The kitten was pissed.

"You will, Ivan," she said sharply. "It doesn't even benefit you for us to stay married."

I glanced at her as she straightened, reminding me of the moment we'd first met. Except now, her voice dripped with a hint of anger and hate I'd never heard from her before.

"No, Katherine," he sneered. "I'm not signing shit. And it does benefit me. How long do you think your father will last? The fossil's already in his late fifties. As your husband, I have rights to the Romanov bratva. I get it, you're Zaytsev's pet now, so you're untouchable. But your father isn't. And neither is your bratva. I'll make them suffer for your actions."

Before I could react, Katherine launched herself at him, cursing and throwing threats. I caught her, holding her back. I didn't want her to put herself in any kind of danger. That idiot knew that if he so much as laid a finger on her, he wouldn't leave here alive, but I still didn't want to take the risk.

"Dimitry!" she hissed, glaring up at me.

She didn't claw my face off, so I took that as a small win. But I'd never seen her this furious, and it made the air crackle with electricity. The other pachans glanced between us and Ivan, their interest piqued.

I knew what I should do—act like I didn't care, like this little spat over a divorce wasn't worth my attention. But I couldn't. Not when she looked at me like that.

Ivan stood up, grinning smugly.

"Well, I think this is over. I've got the message, Zaytsev. She's your plaything now, so keep her. I don't give a shit. I'm never going to mess with you or your territory again. But I'll be expanding into Romanov's. Your old man won't last five minutes under pressure, and we both know it, Katherine. That's why he arranged this marriage in the first place, isn't it? Your money, my muscle."

My grip on Katherine tightened as she struggled against me. Her emotions played out so clearly on her face that even a blind man could've read them. She was pleading with me. But I shouldn't let them know she was my weak spot.

Like it happened to my father.

Ivan smirked like he'd already won. I weighed my options. I could fix this without anyone realizing how important she was to me. Hell, I could even have Aleksei poison him as soon as he got home. Clean. Efficient.

But then she whispered my name.

"Dimitry."

Her voice was soft but laced with an urgent beg. I was a fucking idiot for doing this, but I couldn't ignore her. If showing everyone how much she meant to me was the cost, then so be it. I'd burn the whole world to ash for her, if needed.

"Romanov bratva isn't as powerless as you think, Chernov," I said. "From now on, they're under my protection. Katherine is the woman I love, and she's going to be my wife. Neither she, her family, nor her people will ever be touched."

Katya's eyes widened in shock, and I could feel the others' stares burning into me. I didn't care. Let them see. Let them know just how untouchable my kitten was.

"And don't worry about the divorce," I added, pulling a knife from its hidden spot under the table. "I have a quicker solution."

Ivan's face went ghostly pale as he stared at the blade. I wanted to throw it right at him, but I remembered Katya's wishes. Taking a steadying breath, I offered her the weapon.

"It's your choice, kitten."

Chapter Sixteen
Katherine

Wife!?

I stopped struggling against his hold and stared at Dimitry as if he'd lost his mind. Had he really just said that? I never expected him to get involved like this, especially not in front of the other bratva leaders. I knew it would put him in a vulnerable position.

All I'd wanted was for him to let me go so I could claw the life out of my husband. That bastard had no right to threaten my father or my people.

But Dimitry's words had completely derailed me. Wife. Was he serious? Could he really want this?

I knew he loved me as much as I loved him. I could feel it in every glance, every touch, but this? Declaring it in front of everyone?

My heart was doing wild leaps in my chest, and I didn't know whether I wanted to scream or melt. I wanted to throw myself into his arms, kiss him senseless, and never let him go.

I followed him with my gaze as he reached under the table and pulled out a knife.

"It's your choice, kitten."

I froze, staring at the weapon he was offering me. Our fingers brushed as I took the knife. I could feel the other bratva bosses' eyes on us, but I didn't glance at them. I channeled my attention on Ivan.

My husband had been frozen since Dimitry pulled the blade, but the moment I took it, he seemed to relax. Idiot.

"Put it down, Katherine," he said, his tone sharp and commanding.

It wasn't a request, it was an order. As if he still thought he had any authority over me. As if he had ever had.

Arrogance radiated off him as he glanced at Dimitry, expecting some kind of intervention. But Dimitry didn't even spare him a glance. His gaze stayed locked on me.

"Look," Ivan tried again, his voice oily and smug. "I'm willing to compromise. I'll sign the divorce. Consider it a gift for Zaytsev."

I tightened my grip on the knife, my knuckles turning white. Fucking fool. I studied him, searching for anything I might've still felt. Respect? None. Love? It had never been. Care or at least a little glimmer of affection? Not anymore.

He'd threatened my father. My people. Disrespected the man I loved. And then there was the way he'd talked about me, the way he'd treated me. No, there was nothing left for him.

"No need," I said. "I'll embrace being a widow."

The color drained from his face, his arrogance cracking in the blink of an eye. He managed to choke out my name, a pitiful plea, before I let the knife fly.

And just like that, I closed the chapter on him, and on my old life, once and for all.

Epilogue
Katherine

A few years later

"You've been amazing," I said, leaning toward my husband and brushing my lips against his. "They agreed to the new terms immediately. This expansion and new deal will double the wealth of our bratva."

Damn, almost eight years had passed since we'd married, and it still gave me a special thrill to call him my husband. Before marrying Dimitry, the word had no importance to me, but now, it made me smile every time.

"I couldn't have done it without you, kitten. You made them eat from your hand."

I giggled when he grabbed my waist and pulled me onto his lap. Straddling his body, I traveled my palms along his broad shoulders and chiseled chest. His muscles jumped under my touch, and my inner slut perked up as I felt his cock twitching.

Damn, I loved knowing I still had this effect on him, even after so many years. With every passing day, I thought I'd fallen doubly hard for him, and I'd already been smitten with Dimitry even before our wedding.

After I'd ended Ivan, with Dimitry's help, I'd secured my claim over Chernov bratva. A few months later, after my wedding, my father had decided to name me the head of Romanov bratva. Together with my husband, we'd brought our territories together, merging them into one.

Some of the other leaders hadn't been exactly happy about that, considering it meant Zaytsev brava becoming too strong, but Dimitry had crushed them even before they could move. If he had been ruthless before, I could swear after our wedding he'd become even more vicious, making sure to always be two steps ahead of everyone.

He smiled as our gazes locked. I was sure he could see the love and admiration in my eyes, also reflected in his. I ran my fingers through his hair and pressed my lips against his, making out slowly.

Not once in my life, had I felt as loved, safe, and cherished as when I was with him. My body purred as he freely roamed his hands over me. My pussy hummed as Dimitry cupped my ass and gave it a squeeze.

"What do you say if tonight we go out for a date and celebrate the new deal, love?" he asked.

"That sounds amazing. But why wait until tonight? I think I might want to celebrate with my husband right now," I teased.

Rolling my hips, I dry-humped him, his raspy groan sending shooting electricity along my entire being. Dimitry grabbed my hips and made me grind against him rougher. His cock throbbed, the sensation making my body zing to life.

"Whatever my wife wants, she gets," he said with a laugh. "As if I could ever refuse such a sexy, wild kitten. Especially since she's mine."

My pussy clenched as he said the word, "Mine." Fuck, I loved that about him, and knowing how much he desired me, even after so many years, was the biggest turn on ever. I teased him with another hump, winning myself a husky groan.

"Then what are you waiting for?"

About the Author

Evie Dawn is an author of extra spicy romance with a soft spot for forbidden love and

slutty women who aren't afraid to explore their desires outside the confines of marriage. In every

book, you'll find cheating wives discovering that true love sometimes lies in the arms of their

affair partners and that a HEA can come in the most unexpected ways.

https://books.eviedawnauthor.com/

Ava Kade is a passionate writer of sweet and spicy age gap stories, centered around

mature, dominant older men and naughty younger women. A lot of them contain a touch

of the forbidden and taboo, everything laced together with lots of romance.

https://books.ava-kade.com/

Fateful Vengeance

By: Marla York

Fateful Vengeance

Control, pain, and sorrow are all I've ever known. When something inside me snaps one night after too many cracks in my soul, I take matters into my own hands.

Freedom was supposed to taste sweet, not leave a sour pit in my stomach. When a nightmare from my past resurfaces. My deceased boyfriend's father helps remove the root of all my problems.

Let the scars serve as a testament—my vengeance will be absolute, and my abusers will pay.

Content Note:

This story has Domestic violence, abuse, murder, mutilation of bodies, torture, anal non con with object (not main characters), past mention of child abuse, questionable uses of kitchen utensils. Explicit sexual content, language, and violence.

Chapter One
Clara

The sun is out of sight as a layer of fresh dew envelops everything, as if the night wept. I cross my arm over my stomach, wincing at the pain from hours ago. Before heading back to the kitchen, to prepare him a perfect lunch.

"Clara, you okay?" Burke's deep voice makes me jump.

A forced smile replaces the tears welling in my eyes, the sweet facade I maintain for everyone near me.

"Good morning. Hope you have a great day," I whisper. Glancing up at his friendly face, his icy blue gaze locks with mine for a moment before I stare down at the cement slab outside our patio doors.

"I should be back in a few days. Tell Ryan he's gotta pay his rent. Just because I'm his father doesn't mean he gets to slack off about his responsibilities."

I nod and wave as I head inside.

Like I'm the one who will ask Ryan to pay the rent. Slipping off my slides, I make my way through the living room to get back to preparing his food, but I run into him instead.

"You couldn't have made my lunch any better? I work all fucking day and the best you could do was a ham sandwich. What the fuck, Clara?"

"Ryan, I'm sorry. There are more containers." I brush past him and attempt to open the fridge. Anxiety fills me as my muscles tense.

He clutches my ponytail, jerking me back, and my scalp screams in pain. When Ryan slams me against the wall, I stare into his hazel eyes and bite the inside of my lip. He grips my throat, squeezing until black spots cloud my vision.

"You are such a worthless fucking piece of shit. Can't even serve me the way I deserve." Ryan spits in my face and drops me before grabbing his lunch bag and heading out the door.

I crumple to the grey marble tile floor, using the bottom of my shirt to wipe my cheeks. Tears fall, and I feel as broken now as I did as a child. Useless, except for what I can provide. Memories flood my mind from the past with my stepfather matching what happened today, and pain seeps through my veins.

With no friends and a family who abandoned me long ago, my thoughts drift to Ryan's father, though I'm unsure of what to say. *"Hey Burke, your son has been hurting me for a couple of years, but I'm trapped in your basement pretending to live the perfect life to keep up appearances."*

This wasn't supposed to be my life. I dreamed for years of escaping abuse and growing up to be free. Except I'm under someone else's thumb and grasping at straws to keep myself from the death that seems better than what life is now.

Pulling myself off the ground, I run my fingers through my hair, checking for blood before I wander to the bedroom. I put on a pair of jeans and exchange my sleep shirt for a hoodie. I've been covering for Ryan for so long that I'm concerned no one will believe me anymore, and the bruises from his touch are spreading like wildfire.

With my phone in hand, I decide I need to at least try. Using the non-emergency number, I wait to connect with someone.

"Hello, how can I help you?"

"Hi, I'm calling to report my boyfriend. He's um... abusive."

"Are you in immediate danger, ma'am?" her voice is gruff.

"No, but I might be when he gets home. It's been happening for a while."

The lady on the other end of the phone sighs. "Ma'am, you are free to go if you aren't being held. Make the right decision. As for him, we can't do anything until something happens."

The phone is like a lead weight. Tears trickle down. "Thanks," I say before hanging up.

This was my last resort, that the police would help me. That they would take this seriously and take Ryan away from me. Darkness surrounds my vision, and tears fall until I can't cry anymore.

Wiping my face with the sleeve of the hoodie, I get up. If the apartment isn't clean when he gets home, there will be hell to pay. It's hard to believe how that woman could be so cold, making it seem easy to walk away when he would never allow me to leave.

Hours pass, and as I finish scrubbing the sink clean, and the door slams. I flinch, inhaling a deep breath to get ready for the night. I've made his favourite dinner, beef stew, and hope for an evening with the nice guy I once fell for.

"Wanna know something interesting, Clara?" His irritated voice coats my nerves with tension.

I turn to him and smile, waiting for his news.

"A police officer called me at work today. I had to take a break. Boss-man wasn't so fucking happy about that. The police informed me they got a call from you. Apparently, I'm hurting you and you want to leave, but I'm keeping you here?"

I grit my teeth, swallowing the lump in my throat.

"Not so fucking chatty now, are you?" He throws his lunch bag at me and opens the fridge to grab two beers before heading out to the patio.

No, no, no. The police did nothing, but they weren't supposed to put me in the bullseye. I can't move. Dread courses through me. I can never do anything right. Maybe I am the worthless whore they said I'd always be. My lungs feel empty, and I wish I could just fucking disappear.

With a deep breath, I turn to the counter and wipe the spotless space. I don't know how to smooth this over. There isn't a word that can soothe the cracks I've caused.

"Clara, beer!" His voice flows through the apartment from the patio.

I hesitate before reaching for another two glass bottles. Each filled with the poison that gives him the extra courage to rip me to shreds.

As I walk out to give it to him, I tread over the soft carpet, but each step feels like broken eggshells tearing at my soul. Fear is at least half of my blood type, and bile rises in the back of my throat with the unknown that lies ahead.

It wasn't always this way. He was kind when I met him. Red flags popped up in the controlling winds that fluttered through our relationship. In hindsight, I missed crucial exits. The first time he struck me, I should have left. Many breakups have sprinkled through our years together, but he always brings me back. It's like I'm tied to him, and I'll never be able to break free from the hold he has on me.

"Sit."

His jaw clenches as he chugs the beer. Opening the other, he sips it and glances over at the backyard. I settle into the wooden chair beside him. Nerves erode any armour I might have, and my heart is raw from the wait.

"You know, I always loved you. No one could hold a flame to you, not even the other bitches who blew me from time to time. But you don't fucking quit, do you? Always with the theatrics—running away, and now this fun petty act of calling the pigs on me."

"I'm sorry." I pick at the peeling wood on the armrests of the chair like he always does to my shattered soul.

"You're not. You thought those coppers would help you? Clara, I'm never leaving. You can never get away from me. I will always find you. I'll take everything you love and destroy it. Mark my words, I'll strip the flesh from your bones and dispose of you." His voice is chillingly quiet, each word dripping with promise and malice. "What did you make me for dinner?" he asks. The words slurred. He's been drinking more than beer tonight.

"Beef stew."

"Let's go eat dinner, shall we?" he grins, and rises unsteadily from his seat.

When I stand, he grasps my wrist and walks beside me to the sliding door. His hand tightens around my skin and his other slams me forcefully against the house. "You'll never fucking escape me. I own you, cunt."

Ryan grips my hair and pulls me away from the house before rearing his fist to connect with my cheek. As I fall against the bricks, he grips the base of my skull and presses me harder against the rough texture. "I own you," he whispers in my ear before he pushes me to the ground and walks into the house.

The physical pain is a fleeting bandage over the bleeding of my soul. A temporary distraction from the drowning feeling that overwhelms the inside of my body. With small movements, I push myself up off the cement, open the door, and go in.

Dishes crash in the kitchen, and I slip down the hall to the bathroom. A woman I don't even recognize anymore is before me in the mirror. The sunken eyes reflect the fear and exhaustion that runs through me. The tears I want to let go harbour in my chest, waiting for the gate to open.

With damp tissues, I clean the blood from my chin. My lip will heal. It's been worse than this before. The goose egg growing from my eyebrow isn't going anywhere soon. It'll be stuck, just like me. An aching pulse radiates through my face with its own heartbeat. It syncs with mine, and I open the medicine cabinet to take a couple of pain relievers.

"Clara!"

I jump at his voice, and panic chews at my muscles. I swallow the pills dry and wash my hands before heading to the kitchen.

"This tastes like shit. Why are you fucking terrible at everything you do?" He slams the bowl on the counter, and it shatters. He staggers to the fridge and pulls another beer out of the side before sitting at the kitchen table. Bottles must be lined up out on the patio. I'll have to remember to clean them up.

"It's your favourite. I make it the same way every time," I whisper.

I walk across the room, gathering the shattered pieces of the bowl and cleaning the brown liquid that spilled down the cupboard.

"All you do is fuck up. Today you were the stupidest you've ever been. I'm going to teach you tonight how much I own you. Betcha won't be calling the fucking pigs again."

The thought of his hands on me chills my blood. Every time he's angry, it's like a monster possesses him, and I end up black and blue the next day. "I promise I won't call them again," I tell him.

Wiping the counter, I damn well know I'm never going to phone them again. They will not assist me. Apparently, they put women in danger. Can't help until he kills me.

When I glance at Ryan, his head leans against his shoulder. The alcohol has dimmed him to the point of passing out. A quick look at the clock shows it isn't yet past eight. Which means I'd have enough time to get to the bus station and leave town before he wakes up. I nudge his leg with my foot, but he doesn't wake up.

Heart pounding, I rush to the bedroom, tossing clothes into my bag. I don't have any fucking money. I know he is holding everything in his back pocket. Ever since I bought some makeup, he's taken away my allowance, and I realize how fucked up that is.

I can never escape abuse. It's going to follow me for the rest of my existence. Every man in my life has shown that I am only seen as a servant, never amounting to anything more.

Something cracks deep within, and I whip open the closet to grab his belts. I can't leave because he will always find me, but if he's dead, he won't ever be able to touch me again. His tongue will never lash me with wicked words, and I'll be free. My dream of reaching freedom is the only thing I need to focus on.

Returning to the kitchen, I secure the belts around his wrists and the wooden chair armrests. I fasten his legs to the bottom rungs and move everything away from the table. I open the drawers and pull out our old set of knives and utensils.

Tonight will be the last time he will ever *fucking* hurt me again. Dead men can't own women.

Chapter Two
Burke

Business meetings being cancelled last minute is always a thorn in my side. I dislike it when nobody bothers to email. Gritting my teeth, I drive my Lexus around the bend to the house. I hadn't planned on coming home for a few days, and I know Ryan won't have the rent.

That kid has tested the limits of my patience. He's like his fucking mother, a drunk. I've wanted to kick him out of my house for months, but I hesitate because of Clara. God, she's so above the trash that he is. She could do so much better.

I've desired to take her away from him for years. Something about her drives me wild, and her sweet tone always sets me at ease like we've met in another life. I'd do anything for her. She never asks, but I'd love nothing more than to show her the good the world offers.

Clara came to live with us a couple of years ago, after her worthless father kicked her out over something fucking stupid. He's been in the back of my mind to take care of, but I can't go around killing people because they piss me off.

Although I have connections, I don't use them for personal

reasons. When the job calls for someone to be put down, we use them, but otherwise I don't want to bring work home.

After I pull into the driveway, I walk to the side of the house and beer bottles come into view. Fucking hell, I've asked him time and time again to not leave them by the side of the house. Jogging over to their patio, I pick them up and notice something red drying on the grey brick of the house.

My stomach twists when I stare through the glass. Clara is standing with her hands on her hips, looking around the kitchen. Her dark hair is pinned up in a high ponytail, but the black shadow across her face tells me all I need to know.

Although I suspected abuse, I didn't realize it was physical. I believed I'd raised him better. I watch for a few more minutes. She seems frustrated as she waves her hands and sifts through things on the counter.

Clenching my jaw, I stomp away from the door and head to the garage. I pace, wondering what I should do. I'd love nothing more than to be her knight and save her from everything bad in her world, but that's not what a woman like her wants. Clara is so fucking strong. The armour she wraps herself in is there for a reason, and I won't minimize her strength.

Setting the bottles down into the recycling bin, I run up the stairs and into the house. After hanging up my suit jacket in the hall, I round the corner to the kitchen and grab my knife block. I don't want to take away her power, but like fuck, I'm going to let her struggle with whatever plans she has for him.

With one arm holding the block, I make my way to the door that connects our apartments. Anger boils in my stomach. Ryan should have never laid a hand on her. My mind holds me back for a minute. If nothing else, at least she will be prepared. Unlocking the doors, I creep down the steps.

"You fucking cunt, untie me. The fuck you think you're gonna do?"

"Ryan, you've hurt me for long enough. I might be the dumb bitch who stayed, but you will not run my life anymore."

Her voice is strong, and I inhale before getting to the bottom of the steps and easing the door open.

"Stupid bitch is right. You think you can run your own life? You can't even shit without medication. What are you going to do out there in the big, scary world by yourself?" His words drip with venom, and I hate that he hurts her and pulls at something that sounds out of her control.

The door creaks as I open it, and Ryan strains against the belts tying him to the chair as Clara whirls around.

"Burke!"

"Dad, she's fucking crazy. You need to get her out of here and untie me." Ryan's face is red as he struggles under the restraints. Spittle flies out of his mouth, and his eyes are bloodshot and glassy.

"Clara, I brought you these. Thought you'd have better luck with something sharper." I leave the block on the counter next to her dull knife. I step forward, dropping a kiss on her head and squeezing her shoulder. "You got this," I whisper.

"Some father you are. Don't fucking touch her." Ryan growls at me.

"You ain't no son of mine, laying your hands on a woman? Enjoy what's coming."

I tear my gaze away from him and look at Clara once more before nodding to her and walking back upstairs.

Chapter Three
Clara

Burke's handsome face, with his salt-and-pepper beard, burns in my mind. My thoughts roam over the help that has been offered, the rare reassurance that I've always needed in a situation where I finally have control.

"Clara, baby, you don't really want to do this." Ryan's voice is coated in fake sugar. He always gives me emotional whiplash, and I'm tired of wearing a neck brace to appease him.

As my fingers brush the utensils, I pause at the pizza cutter. It's not sharp enough to cause deep damage, but it's adequate for what I need.

"Baby, you know my dad is gonna come back. He's trying to teach me a lesson."

I ignore him as I step closer and tighten my grip on his hand. Pressing it against the hard chair rest until his fingers splay open. Letting out a determined breath, I run the blade under his fingernails.

"Fucking cunt, you want to go there with me? Untie me and fight like a real person. You think you're so fucking tough, but you're a little wimp."

Ryan knows the right words to wound me, to make my nervous system snap to survival mode, but I've been here so fucking long that there's nowhere else for me to go.

"Save your breath, my darling. We have a lot of kitchen tools to go through," I whisper.

He struggles against the belts but can't seem to break free. I pull away from his right hand and slits of blood drip down from his fingers. I recall the night he bit every single fake nail off my hands because he didn't want me to be pretty for everyone else.

"Clara, you don't have the stomach to do this. You can't handle what you're going to do. You are too weak of a fucking little girl."

I grit my jaw, his words echoing my fathers for years.

Oh, sweet Clara can't do anything right. She can't handle the pain or do the work.

If only they knew they killed that girl a long time ago, stripped the soul out of her shell, and threw away any pieces that tied her to the woman who needed anyone to help her.

I spin around, throwing the pizza cutter in the sink. Glancing over the counter, I grab the scissors. Approaching Ryan, I cut off his shirt, tearing the pieces off around his strapped limbs, removing his clothing until he's naked. I want him to experience humiliation, but the alcohol in his system dulls any sensation except for the pain.

"Wanna final round, baby?" he bucks his hips, and I hold back from cutting his dick off right away. It seems like something too easy, and I can't have him bleeding out on me before the fun begins.

Leaning against the counter, I grab the carrot shaped peeler, and his eyes widen as I bring it toward him. With the sharp edge facing him, I spread my thumb and forefinger on either side of my target, then forcefully run it across his chest. Soon his nipples slide off, and as I continue, I enjoy the sight of blood flowing from him.

"Fucking bitch." Ryan spits, and I turn on the burner to heat a butter knife to stop the blood flow from his chest. Once hot enough, I press it to his skin, and the smell of burnt hair fills the area.

Ryan leans his head forward and tries to bite me. I jump back, snatch the frying pan used for preparing the beef stew, and hit him on the side of his skull lightly. The thud lingers in my mind as his head lands on his shoulder again.

Fuck.

I want him to feel everything. I leave the kitchen and walk to our bedroom. Piles of his clothes line the floor, like I'm a personal maid, and I groan, kicking through them, searching for another belt. With no luck, I pull the cord from the television and out of the wall.

Striding back to the kitchen, I take it and wrap it under his nose to the back of the chair, pressing him in place.

"Try to bite me now, fucker." Running my fingers over his buzz cut, he jerks his gaze up and his venomous hazel stare burns into mine. "So, you were saying I couldn't handle this, right? That I couldn't cause you the same pain that you've done to me for years?"

"Clara, you don't want to do this. What happens when you're done, and my dad kicks you out of here? Where are you going to go? Your own father doesn't even fucking want you."

I bite my lip, gripping the cheese grater as I bring it to his face. Shaving off the flesh while he screams proves to be very therapeutic. The blood beads and trickles down his cheek. I tilt my head as I drag the metal against the skin harder, then shift my position to the other side so they match.

Red drips from his jawline, its splatter making a pretty pattern on his upper body.

He can't move forward, but it doesn't stop him from wiggling around like a fish out of water. I grab my long charging cable and use it to secure his hips to the chair like a seatbelt.

"What? Don't you like it? The big tough man you think you are." I grin, knowing that he's a little bitch wrapped in a scary package.

"Fuck you, cunt," he bites out, and I've had enough of his words.

I throw the bloody grater into the sink and stare at my handiwork. It's a rough-looking job, but his skin hangs in small peels on his lap and across his broad chest. Crimson stains the floor, each drop a testament to the evil unleashed upon me. The metallic tang of blood fills the air, a sickeningly sweet scent. With the kabob sticks in hand, I turn and move back to him.

"You stole so much of my fucking life. You sucked the happiness from my veins for years. I knew better. I should have never listened to the words that you crooned to me because I fell for your stupid games."

Strength runs through my blood, and with an inhale, I feel like a different person. With a kabob stick in my hand, I grab his dick and pull until there's no more skin to stretch.

Which isn't much. Can't believe I was going to lose my life to a mediocre man with a pathetic cock. I spear the end to the wooden chair with force.

He howls, and I'm enjoying being on the other end of that sound. Ryan has taken so much from me, and as I look at him, I can't help but smile, knowing I'm about to give him more, even if he didn't ask for it.

"Fuck you. Bitch, when I get out of these ties, I'm going to beat you black and blue. You think you've had it bad before? I'll break every bone in your body and then fuck you to death."

"Ryan, when I'm done with this, you won't be able to fuck anything." I smile before grabbing the lemon zester. Dragging the sharp metal edge over his shaft, small cuts appear and blood beads. His face drips sweat as pained screams fill my ears.

"What's wrong, baby? Does it hurt? Just close your eyes. You're going to love what I have for you." My voice doesn't sound like mine anymore. I stand up from leaning over his shoulder, lukewarm wetness distracts me momentarily. *Did he fucking piss himself?*

"All you ever do is create messes for me to clean up," I hiss.

Remembering the many nights that he forced me against the mattress and took whatever he wanted against my cries, I continue to shred his cock, this time with more enthusiasm.

Once his junk is a mangled mess, I toss the zester in the sink to join its bloody friends. Ryan is covered in red, and part of me is surprised. My heart thought he'd bleed black because of the way he treated me for so long. He's only been a monster that takes and burns out my light for too many fucking years. Yanking the kabob stick out of his pecker, I jam it into his ear.

"Can you hear me now? The word is no. It's a full ass fucking sentence."

Ryan's eyes roll back in his head, and his mutilated body shakes in front of me. But I know he's not dead yet. His darkened soul will cling onto this life with its talons.

"How many nights did I beg, Ry? Hundreds? Thousands? You would laugh and make me bleed, but now, baby, it's your turn, isn't it?"

A maniacal sound escapes my throat, and laughter bubbles in my stomach. The kabob stick clatters to the floor, and as his cries lower into whimpers and shallow breaths, I know my time is running out.

I swirl around and check out the knives in the block that Burke brought. Choosing a utility and a chef's knife, I walk over to Ryan. Two more things to do to him burn in my belly.

"Remember how much you yelled at me? The ribs you broke because I wasn't smiling enough. Recall the work party we attended where my appearance disappointed you? When we got home, you hit me until I couldn't breathe, until I could not stand up, and you fucked me until I bled? Remember that night, Ryan?"

The memories run through my mind like a bad movie that I can't turn off, and bile rises in my throat as tears form behind my eyes. Gripping the smaller of the two, I hold the back of his head with my other hand and carve a smile into his cheeks.

"Joker style, baby, you'll always be able to smile now. Even in death, you'll look so pretty for the king of hell."

Crimson pours from his face, and as his chest falters, I drop the knife and slide the other into his neck. The floor no longer scuffed grey marble. Instead, brown and red mix in a swirl of bad memories, pouring out of the monster that kept me under his thumb for too long.

Once the silence envelopes me, I'm shaking. Glancing down, I'm covered in blood and fear; I'm no better than the fucker in front of me.

When the first sob escapes me, there's nothing I can do from holding them back. Freedom was supposed to taste sweet, and not like a heavier burden to carry. I slip in the blood and slide down the wall until the ground catches me.

Chapter Four
Burke

My muscles are filled with agitation from pacing the wooden floor for so long. When I saw the damage Ryan had done to her face, a desire to harm him surged through me. I should have paid attention sooner. I could have saved her long ago.

Walking past the door to the basement, her powerful voice is gone and has been replaced with gut wrenching sobs. I've held back, letting her have the time she needed, but now it's my turn to take care of her. Heading down the stairs, I beeline for Clara.

Ryan's eyes are no longer blood-shot, instead, they are vacant. He's been mangled, and various body fluids cover the floor. He's a problem I'll take care of later. Clara sits with her knees pulled up to her chest, gore splattered around her. I carefully walk around the mess, doing my best not to slip, and I pick her up. She's a lot lighter than I thought she'd be. I can feel her bones through her clothes.

"Burke?" she whispers and clings to my shirt.

"You did real good. I got you now," I whisper.

When I bring her to the living room, I nuzzle her hair before putting her down. Lifting the shirt off her body, I undo the buttons to her jeans and slip the blood-stained denim off her legs. Kneeling before Clara to help. Her nails dig into my shoulders, and I stare up at her as I remove her socks.

"I thought freedom would feel good, but I'm no better than him."

Her eyes are bloodshot, and I wish I could take the pain for her. Standing, I run my fingers over her jaw. Angling her face to stare at me, when our eyes meet, I fight the urge to kiss her. Something I've been battling against for a while, not touching her.

"You've been through enough with that abusive asshole. Freedom will take time. I'm so sorry I didn't see the signs sooner. You deserve all the good in the world, not the hellish scraps he threw at you. It's okay to lay your armour down for a minute."

Clara wraps her arms around my neck, and I pick her up again before heading upstairs. I don't put her down until we've reached my ensuite bathroom. With a twist of the knob, the water flows into the tub, and I add Epsom salts, their lavender scent filling the air.

After a few minutes, it's filled halfway, and she strips her panties before getting in. "I'm a wreck," she mumbles, and I sit on the edge of the large built-in tub.

"You survived for how long?"

"Too fucking long. I'm so tired. I'm exhausted to a level I can't even describe. Burke, I killed your son. Why are you taking care of me?"

"Because you deserved better, just because he's blood doesn't make him family. The moment he raised his hand to you, he cut anything we had." I turn off the tap and lean forward to wet her hair before grabbing the shampoo and washing the memories of tonight from her.

"I'm so fucking tired of fighting. The cops did nothing."

"Sorry, they should have done something for you," I mutter.

Anger courses through me, knowing that the system failed her like I did. I can't believe living under the same roof. I let this slip through my fingers. Even though she always stuck up for him and did such a good job at hiding everything. I should have picked up on something. If she hadn't already killed him, I'd be doing it myself. I can't let it consume me. I need to focus on helping her in any way I can. Clara is the person I've wanted for so damn long, and I must prove to her she is worth everything to me.

"It's not just Ryan. I've been fighting since I was little. Maybe there isn't a point of me even living anymore when I can't even escape the cycle of abuse. I was euphoric while I was torturing him, but now I feel like a broken shell."

"Bodies are a funny thing. They react in ways we don't want them to. I can't speak to your past, but your future is whatever you want it to be. You need rest. Do you want ice for your eye?" I finish rinsing her hair and stand to get her towels for when she's ready to leave the bath.

"No, it's fine. Can you help me out?"

I glance over my shoulder and swallow the lump in my throat. She's so fucking strong, gorgeous, and forbidden to me. With the towel around her, I pull her close and envelop her in a hug. I want nothing more than to put her broken pieces back together with my hands but know that will not work.

"Let's get you into bed," I whisper and press my hand on her lower back. Guiding her to the bedroom.

"My clothes are downstairs, but I can't go back down there."

Spinning around, I open my closet and pull out a gym t-shirt. I hand it to her, and she slips it on. She's stunning in my shirt; need bubbles within me but I ignore it. "I've got to go make some calls and clean up, but I want you to rest."

Once she's under the covers, I lower to kiss her head. "It's gonna be alright, Clara. I got you."

She grips the front of my shirt, and her green eyes stare at me. "Can you stay? At least until I fall asleep?" She glances away, like the question is too much to ask for.

"Of course, move over."

She scooches, making room for me, and I slide under the covers and wrap my arm around her shoulders.

"I'm sorry, Burke, I'll try to figure something out in the next couple of days to get out of your hair."

The crack in her voice breaks a part of me. I aim to protect her from her own thoughts and the shards of past trauma that rip her up.

"Don't worry about it. I wasn't lying when I said I'm here. My word stands." I pull her closer and kiss the top of her head. I stroke her hair until she falls asleep before I convince myself to ease out of the bed.

Once I get to the kitchen, walking over the wooden floor, I pull out a burner phone from a drawer and call my guy. "I know it's late, but we never call early."

His light laugh is forced. "Be there in fifteen. Clean-up crew?" Curt asks.

"Yeah, it's a pretty gruesome sight. I'll be waiting." I glance at the dark grey kitchen walls, end the call, and put away the phone before walking out to the garage to wait for Curt.

Chapter Five
Clara

It's been three months since the night with Ryan. I've been able to get my life in some sort of order, and working at this diner is the next step to becoming financially independent.

Having control over my life has been hard, and I worry constantly that I'm going to fail. Burke has been there every step of the way, and although I ache for him, he only cuddles me every night. Nothing else has happened. It's like he's afraid I'll shatter like glass if we take it any further. I wish he'd make a first move.

"Clara, funny seeing you here. I thought that boyfriend of yours didn't let you work?" The nasal voice that haunts my nightmares is alive and well behind me. Exhaling, I spin around and grab a menu.

"Andrew, isn't this far of a distance for you to travel?" With the black plastic menu in hand, I glance over his head, but he's here alone. The dirty flannel jacket he's had since I was young stares back at me, and I refuse to make eye-contact with him.

"It's not every day that you hear your little stepdaughter is allowed out into the open. Had to see it for myself. I didn't believe the guys down at the bar. Here you are in the flesh, though."

I grit my teeth and plaster my customer service smile on as I push the menu across the counter. "The special of the day is—"

"I'm not here to eat, Kitty Cat. I'm here to collect the debts you owe me." Tearing my gaze from the stark white countertop, I look into his deep brown eyes, noticing the fine lines etched by time. The sneer on his face fills me with unease.

"I don't owe you anything. I left in good standing when you kicked me out. Don't you remember?" I bite the words out, and he leans against the counter.

The scent of his greasy, thinning hair coming closer, along with the same soap that's haunted me most of my life.

"Oh, she's gotten a spark back. Can't wait to extinguish that." He winks at me before turning on his heels and leaving the diner.

"It's pretty quiet. You can clock out love," Debbie says from behind me. I bite hard on my lip, fighting back the tears that threaten to fall. "You okay?"

I shake my head no, and her arm circles around me, and she hugs me fiercely.

She's the motherly figure I've needed and wanted my entire life. No one has ever known the truth about my biological mother. She was just a whore who skipped out with the newest dick in town and left me with that monster.

"I'm okay."

"Nope. I'll call Burke. Sit in the back, girly-pop. Was it that old fucker that was in here?" I nod as she leads me to the back. "Alright, he's not allowed to come back. Let's wait for your ride."

* * *

"I told you I'd be back to steal everything good in your life. Mark my words, Kitty Cat. I wasn't lying when I said I'd collect." Andrew's voice wakes me from my sleep, and when I glance at the end of the bed, he's standing there as clear as day. "Scream and I'll kill the knight in shining armour next to you. Come on down here, show daddy how much you missed him."

Bile rises in my throat, and I scramble back on the mattress toward the headboard. I swear his sharp nails are digging into the skin on my ankle. A shriek escapes me as his hand circles my calf. I kick out.

"Clara, wake up. Come on, it's a dream." Burke's strong voice breaks through the haze and when I open my eyes again, no one is in the bedroom except the two of us. Light creates shadows on the wall as he turns on the lamp. My heart pounds against my ribs, and I burrow myself into his arms. "It's okay, Dragonfly, I got you."

He's been calling me the name for weeks, but it still makes me stare up at him like he has two heads. "Dragonflies, spiritually, mean change, transformation, and strength, and if that isn't exactly fucking you, I don't know what is." He strokes my hair as I clench onto his shirt.

"It's kinda dumb." I laugh, breaking the tension in the room. My jaw hurts from clenching my teeth, and I do my best to breathe past the nightmare that rocked through me.

"What happened tonight?"

"Don't worry about it. I'm sorry for waking you." I pull away from him, but he doesn't let go of my hair. The soft glow of his nightstand lamp covers his face, and his icy blue eyes gaze down at me.

"Clara."

"Same nightmare as the last few. It's so fucking real, though. I can feel the way he grabs me, and it's not fair. I never asked for the things he did to me, the things he stole from me. None of this is fair, and it's not reasonable to make you deal with it." I glance down at the black duvet, playing with a string poking out.

"You are mine, and I won't let anything happen to you."

We've been dancing to the same tune for over a month. He's so certain that he desires someone as broken as me, and I keep waiting for the music to stop and him to give up on me. Despite my fears,

Burke has been my rock, and I want him as much as he wants me. But I need him to show me how much he claims I'm his.

"Claim me. Replace their hurtful touches with yours."

Burke's hand twists in my hair and pulls my face to stare up into his eyes. I'm not sure what he's looking for, but I don't have time to question it. His lips crush mine, and I melt into his arms. My heart races, and butterflies explode in my stomach.

I kiss back fiercely until we pull away, gasping for air. He releases my hair, ripping the covers back as he turns toward me. Burke's naked muscular body greets me, and he cups my jaw, turning my head as his lips trail down my sensitive neck.

My nerves go wild, his touch igniting the fire within. As his head moves down to my nipples, he sucks before his teeth run over the tender tips. Moaning, I slide my fingers through his short salt-and-pepper hair. His hand slips down and grips my neck harder, and spots dance across my vision before he releases me. The loving dominance is something I crave.

Burke's tongue lingers on my sensitive flesh before he lowers down my torso and rips off the shorts I'm wearing. "So fucking perfect."

His caress has me arching my hips, needing his tongue on me lower. He teases me as his kisses feather over my thighs until he puts my legs over his shoulders. Burke stills, and my body trembles, waiting.

"You are my needy girl, right?" I don't answer him, and his grip on my thighs tightens. "This is my pussy?" he asks again.

"Yes, take me." I can't handle his breath on me. I'm going to burst as soon as he touches me.

Burke's hands spread me open, and as his tongue explores my wetness, my body responds eagerly. "Stay put," his gravelly voice fills my ears, and he pushes me down.

Chapter Six
Burke

I've waited for this for a long fucking time. With Clara sprawled before me, I'm captivated by the delightful view. Anyone who would be dumb enough to hurt this precious soul is a fucking idiot.

She whimpers as I take my time. Sliding my tongue around her clit, I swipe it down to her opening and back up. Slipping a finger into her tight cunt makes my eyes roll back. Clara's legs tremble against my shoulders. I smile and pull away from her perfect pussy. "Shaking already for me?"

Her nails claw at the sheets beside her, and she smiles wickedly at me. I dip between her legs and continue swirling my tongue through her folds, fucking her with my fingers. My dick throbs as Clara's whimpers fill the room.

"Please," she whispers.

"Such good manners." I latch onto her clit and suck as she clamps down on my fingers. "Fucking perfect," I tell her.

Rising from between her legs, I place my wet fingers on her lips and arch my eyebrow.

Without saying a word, she takes them and sucks my digits clean.

I lie back and stroke my cock with her spit. "Be a good girl and claim me."

Clara flips onto all fours and closes the space between us. I wrap my hand in her dark hair as she lies between my legs and slides her tongue over my shaft. Her green eyes meet mine, but her touch is too gentle. I pull her closer by her hair and push her down on my cock.

"You can take it. You are doing such a good fucking job," I tell her and release her as she continues the pace. "Fuck yes, don't stop."

She proceeds and uses her hand to stroke my base and play with my balls. Pleasure courses through my body, and I arch my hips as the coil unravels deep inside. As much as I want to let go, I need to claim her and show her how much I need her.

"Lie back for me," I tell her, and she pulls off my cock. Drool covering her chin, her hair all mussed up, as she does what I asked. "Fucking gorgeous."

I get up and kneel on the bed, pressing kisses along her legs, until I reach her thighs. Positioning myself at her entrance, I glance up at her face.

"Please."

I grin, and she wraps herself around my back as I sink into her. It's fucking incredible, and I know I won't last very long. Bending forward, I brace my hands beside her head and brush my lips against her jaw. Clara's nails run down my arms, and it sends shockwaves through me. I nip her neck before leaning back and pressing her legs against her chest.

"You take my cock so well," I growl.

Between us, I rub her clit with my thumb, and soon she clenches around me while moaning. I thrust into her hard until I can't hold back anymore. I pull out and scramble to her head.

"Open your mouth," I demand as I jerk off. My come covers her face. "Damn, Dragonfly, you look hot like this." I smirk and lie beside her until my legs don't feel jelly like. As I stroke her hair, its familiar scent fills my senses. This seals the deal for me. Clara is mine, and I'll fight to keep this feeling of hope for us.

I walk to the ensuite and wet a washcloth before returning to clean her up. Kissing her forehead, I tuck her back in my embrace.

"I told you that you're mine. I'll find out where he lives and end this. No one is going to fuck with you ever again." Clara tenses in my arms and twists to gaze up at me.

"Thank you. I don't know what I ever did to deserve this. I only have one request."

"Clara, you deserve the world. No man alive should have ever laid a finger on you. Love doesn't come with terms; it's not something you go into debt for. It's supposed to be given freely. You are such a strong woman. I intend to take out the trash because while trauma will live inside you, I can fix the outside world."

She nuzzles against me. There is nothing more I need to do but protect her. I'd take her memories to live with for the rest of my life if it meant she could always feel safe.

"I want to help. I need to be a part of this." Her voice is so muted.

"Deal, but his final breath? It's mine." I bring the covers up and wrap them around us before flicking off the nightstand light. "Goodnight, Dragonfly."

I've talked to all my contacts and ran her waste of space stepfather through our security system database. Finding he still lives in her childhood home makes bile rise in my throat. He's been waiting for her for years, just around the corner.

Pushing away from the desk, I wander out of my office to the sound of the door opening. Clara walks in from work, her jeans covered in flour, and her dark hair pinned in a messy bun. I don't want to handle her as if she might break. It's not fair to treat her like she is so fragile. A fire burns in her soul, and once we're done taking out the trash, I intend to prove to her I'm different. That I'll go to the ends of the earth for her.

"Hey," she says sheepishly. Wiping her palms on her jeans, before hanging her coat up.

"I have news, good or bad. What do you want first?" Slipping my hands into my pockets, I lean against the counter.

"Bad first I guess." She sighs and pads down the hall to stand next to me.

I drop a kiss on her forehead and grab a bottle of water, knowing that Debbie can only push so much food and fluids on my Dragonfly before she refuses. "Well, they're linked, so you get both this way. One, I found him, and he still lives in your childhood home."

Clara shivers, taking a drink of water before twisting her lips in disgust. "It always felt someone was around. I thought I was just paranoid from Ryan." A fist of anxiety squeezes my heart. I should have stepped in and protected her sooner. "When will we go?"

I wrap my hands around her waist and bring her closer to me. "Soon."

She traces my jawline. "Tonight," Clara states and grins. I bend to catch her lips with mine. When her fingers run over my neck, I'm a goner and know that I will do whatever it takes to be hers.

Clara grinds against my leg and, as much as I want to bend her over the kitchen counter, I have arrangements to make. "Let me make a call and we'll be on our way."

Pulling out my phone, I let go of her, and she sinks to her knees. Undoing my pants, I tilt my head and stare into her eyes. Without a word, she caresses me until I'm hard. Raising an eyebrow, Clara licks the length of my shaft, and I growl.

"Make your call."

I press the button for my cleanup guy as she takes me down her throat. I bite back the groans and let out a sigh as her hand strokes me.

"Early for ya, bud." Curt says.

"Making a reservation," I bite out.

Clara doesn't stop sucking my dick, and I grip the phone so tightly I fear I might break it. With my other hand in her bun, I shove her down the length.

"Tonight? I'm open for the night."

"Mhmm," I grunt out.

"Sounds good. Send the address when you're ready." Curt clicks off, and I've never been so thankful that he's not a small talk person.

"Clara, you take me so fucking well."

She pulls away from me with a suctioning pop and bounces up onto her feet. "I'll go get ready."

I grab her by the neck and pin her against the wall, running my lips over hers. "You better finish this," I growl.

"In time, I don't want to be late."

I hold her in place and slip my fingers into her panties. Wetness coats them, and I slide over her clit until she whimpers.

"Burke, please."

"Don't want to be late." I smirk and pull away from her before shoving my digits into her mouth.

She sucks them, and I groan before tucking myself away.

After we get ready, I notice a determined expression on her face. I have to walk faster to keep up with her as she strides to the car. Once we're on our way there, Clara doesn't say much. "You don't have to do this," I tell her.

"Stop trying to give me an out. I need to do this. More than I've ever had to do anything."

I grin and turn up the radio until we reach the neighbourhood, turning down the volume. I park alongside the other block.

"Home sweet home, I guess." She fiddles with her seatbelt and runs her fingers through her hair before putting it up.

"Clara—" I start talking, but she cuts me off.

"I got this."

Chapter Seven
Clara

As I walk along the sidewalk to the house alone, my stomach twists and turns, and bile rises in my throat. Nerves threaten to destroy my digestion system, but I inhale through my nose and exhale, trying to soothe them.

Once I reach the decrepit bungalow, I straighten my shoulders and hold my head high. Paint is peeling after years of neglect, and as much as I'd rather run away and hide in Burke's arms, I know this is what I need to do. The yard is overgrown, and the cement squares that part the grass are cracked in different spots. Memories flash before my eyes, spinning like a film reel, but I am certain I can't simmer in the pot of the past if I want my revenge.

Andrew took everything from me, my innocence, my family, and showed me that love was only something used to control people. It's his time to pay his debts for taking so much from a child.

The creak brings me out of the past, and the door opens. I walk up the cement steps and swallow all the sorrow and conjure the pain that has followed me for years. "Who knew I didn't have to go out looking for my Kitty Cat? She came crawling home for me, just like I knew she would." The gleeful tone of his voice raises the hairs on the nape of my neck, and tension wraps around my chest like a vice grip.

"Andrew. You need to leave me alone." I know the words are futile. He won't ever leave me be and will hide in every shadow until I can fix the holes he left in my soul.

"Ah, where would the fun in that be? I've been watching you. I'm the only one who knows you best."

The stale smell of alcohol circles him, and once I'm inside the entrance, the scent of stale air and rancid food attacks me. My gaze falls upon the threadbare carpet, its stains deep like old wounds, and then to the sagging couch.

"You don't know me anymore." My heart races as he slams the door. The house is closing in on me as I lean against the wall.

"Kitty Cat, I've explored every inch of you, inside and out. You can't say I don't know you when I was the first one to learn everything about you." Yellow teeth stretch into a smile, and he advances, reaching for me.

Before his tainted fingers touch my shoulder, I kick out and hit his bad knee. He stumbles back into the wooden cupboard that contains years of dust and sentimental ornaments from a time that has since died.

"Oh, you want to play? I can do all the games you want. In the end, you are always going to be mine and belong to me." Spittle files out of his mouth, his face turning a shade of red as he staggers to stand.

A quick glance shows me his hoarding has worsened over the years, making it easier for me to decide what to do next.

When he limps toward me, I bring my knee up to connect with his testicles, but he covers them. I push a kick into his bad knee again, and he falls to the ground.

I walk past the many stacks of newspapers and grab the bundles of cords, tying his feet together. As his hand snakes around my ankle like my nightmares, I stomp my other heel into his wrist.

He grabs his arm and wiggles on the floor, spitting at me, he yells. "Fucking bitch, you can't do this."

A giggle escapes me before I can stop it. I jump away from his form on the carpet and glance around the room before I observe his old chair.

The memories embedded in the fabric should be burned down like the rest of the house, but I focus on the task at hand. He won't stay down long, and I step around the piles for something else to tie him with.

A creaking noise steals my attention and as Burke walks into the house, he seems so out of place. My future mixing with my past isn't a feeling I thought I'd ever face.

"Want me to move him closer to the living room?"

"Yes," I say, before weaving through the maze of boxes filled with junk until I reach the kitchen. I collect scissors, a knife, and the rolling pin that has been hanging on the wall for so long that the paint underneath is now a different colour.

When I return to the living room, he's tied to the foot of his chair and Burke is standing back.

"Who the fuck is that? Kitty Cat, you won't get away with this. People will notice I'm missing and then you'll be locked up in a cell, and then I'll always know where you are."

His words give me pause until I remember the years he spent tearing me apart and how he never served a day of time for the little girl he killed within me. I use the scissors to cut off his pants. The stench hits me first. The sour smell of unwashed skin wafts up and hovers in the air. Forcing me to breathe out of my mouth.

"Wanna give your new boyfriend a show? Because I'm sure I can get it nice and hard like you loved," Andrew laughs.

I use the knife to stab him under the ribs. A stain blossoms on his plaid shirt as his blood seeps through, and a low groan escapes his lips. With each twist of the knife, I can feel the resistance as the muscle and fat separate beneath the skin. I apply more force with each strike, hacking away until his organs are laid bare, almost as if they are staring back at me.

Thick, crimson pools beneath my fingers, slick and warm against my skin. Rolling him onto his stomach takes me more effort, but I refuse Burke's help.

With the knife, I cut open the back of his shirt and carve along his flesh. His screams echo through the living room, like a song I've been craving for the entirety of my life.

Picking up the rolling pin he used to hit me countless times, I slide it through the blood on his back and between his cheeks. I think about telling him it won't hurt like he did for me, but why lie? I get the handle in, but I can't fit anymore. No matter how hard I push, it won't go in.

Frustration runs through my veins. I've had problems with my stomach my entire life because of what he did to me, and I refuse to leave without having this exact revenge.

I use the knife to cut his hole bigger and jam the rolling pin as far as it'll go. The rough wood texture should cause an agony like the nights he shoved into me. Andrew's guttural screams and groans fill the space over the squelching sound the rolling pin is making in him.

I let go, and fall back on my heels, glancing down at the well-deserved desecration of his body. For once in my life, I can finally take a full breath.

Burke steps forward and kicks him onto his back. He then steps over the body and kisses my forehead, wiping the sweaty hair from my face. "You did good, Dragonfly."

Andrew turns his head, blood pouring over his teeth and down his chin. He grins like this is a game he's in control of and wheezes out, "Dragonfly eh? Didn't you know she's a Kitty Cat, but not just any kinda feline, a fucking scaredy cat."

"I believe Clara is quite brave. She survived you *and* served up revenge. That, in itself, is more courage than you could muster up your entire life," Burke says.

Andrew directs his glassy gaze from Burke to me. "I took your innocence, everything I could, I stole it from you. I gave you enough scar tissue that you'll never be able to forget me."

His words hit me like a sack of bricks, as if I could escape his actions from the past and move forward in a world without my history following me.

"Scar tissue tells a story. A woman who's overcome so much and now never has to worry again. She can stand on her own two feet to fight the demons in the real world and the ones in her own head. Not only will she never have to worry about pieces of shit like you again, because I will never leave her side, but I will also show her what true love looks like and how she should have always been treated."

"Blah blah blah, I had her first, and you can never erase those memories," Andrew gasps.

I get up and step forward, but Burke stops me. He takes the knife from my hand and lowers his head to kiss me. "He's mine now."

Chapter Eight

Burke

Witnessing Clara perform her revenge was sweeter than I thought it would be. Now she gazes at me curiously. Even covered in blood, Clara and her radiant smile make my dick throb. Rage and lust swirl inside of me like a hurricane.

I shift my attention from her to my work. Lowering the knife to his neck, her voice gives me pause before I slice open his artery.

"What if we fucked right now? Would that be the ultimate send off?"

"Is that what you want?" I turn to gaze up at her, my mouth dries and I arch an eyebrow.

"It's wrong though, right? I mean, I know what I did to him, but doing this seems fucked up, and I don't know why I want it." She fidgets with the button on her jeans, and I stand, bringing the knife with me.

"Don't think so. If that's what you want, who am I to deny you?" I place the knife on the chair and rip her clothes off, tearing the fabric of her shirt and shucking off her jeans. I unzip the large hoodie I'm wearing, and as I pull the shirt over my head, her cool touch makes me jump. "God, you drive me crazy," I whisper.

Undoing my belt, she kneels in front of me. Her dark hair pulled back in a slick ponytail, letting me see those green orbs I can get lost in. She rips my jeans down and wraps her hand around the base of my cock.

When she pulls me closer to wrap her lips around my length, the room fills with the sound of her suction, and Andrews grunts. I should have sliced him wide open when I had the chance. He's ruining the moment.

Gripping her ponytail, I fuck her mouth and hold her to the base of my shaft, her throat milking me until I pull away and let her breathe. Wrapping my hand around her neck, I tug gently, and she stands in front of me waiting for direction. "You are such a good slut, you know that, right?"

She nods, and I bend her over the arm of the recliner. When she recoils, I release her, and Clara immediately stands.

"I can't... not there." She looks down at the floor, twisting her fingers.

I'm not about to press her for details. The memories crusted within these dirty walls are enough to make my skin crawl without needing details.

I lie down beside the crimson mess and pull her down onto my face. Gripping her thighs, I explore her folds and lick her sweet juices as she grinds her clit against me. As she tenses, I roll her over and Andrew's vacant gaze is locked on us. She sent him straight to hell.

"You'll rot somewhere. I win, not you. You could never fucking win," Clara spits out at him. I hold on to her, pulling her into the position I want, and slide into her wet pussy. She lets out a primal groan. "Fuck! Make me come all over your hard cock, Burke."

She's putting on a performance, and if that's what she needs, I'm happy to be here to deliver. I grab her ponytail, jerking her upright, and slam into her. The way she squeezes around my shaft is almost too much to bear. I let go of her hair and grip her hips as I pound into her.

Clara grips the carpet in front of her, thrusting back on my dick as she screams out and tightens around me. "Fuck, Burke, I've never come like you make me do."

"You belong to me, that's why." I growl and lift my leg to steady myself before pulling out and spreading her open to watch my cock disappear. "Dragonfly, you take me so fucking well," I grit out before slamming in to the hilt.

Clara lurches forward until her hands rest on Andrew's naked flesh. Blood seeps through her fingers, and it's undeniably hot as fuck.

"Don't stop, I'm going to come again."

I never intended to stop slamming into her and reach beneath us to swipe my fingertips over her clit. When she squeezes down again, I can't stop and fill her with my come.

"Just like that, such a good job," I whisper. As much as I want to give her another round, I am aware Curt will be here soon, and I pull out. "What do you want, Clara?"

"Make me come again, please," she begs.

Leaning back on my heels, I slide two fingers into our combined juices within her and rub her clit, and as she humps my hand, my dick throbs for more. Adding another finger, I fuck her until she clamps down on my digits.

"Fuck yes," she screams.

"Perfect, let's get out of here, Dragonfly."

"I don't have any clothes, you ripped them. What are we going to do? My prints are all over him now! Fuck, I'm stupid." Clara's face drains of colour.

"Nope, I know a guy. He's scheduled to be here within an hour. I got this covered. No one will ever tie you to this piece of shit. Not like this." I get up and pull my jeans on before doing them up.

"My clothes are still fucked."

I hand her my hoodie and slip on my shirt. Clara drowns in the fabric, but it covers everything it needs to. I grab her blood-covered hand and leave the knife next to his body.

"Any parting words?"

"I've said everything I need to," she whispers. Her gait wobbles, and I know the adrenaline is going to run out.

On our way home, Clara is silent, and I worry about her. I run my fingers over her bare leg, trying to keep her in the present, but she doesn't respond. When we get to the front door, she stumbles over the first step, and I pick her up and cradle her against my chest. Walking up to the bathroom, I set her on the counter before drawing a warm bath.

"You did so good," I tell her.

After I shed my clothes, I turn to her and watch the tears fall down her cheeks.

"Why does it feel bad, then?"

"Sometimes, it doesn't live up to the image you had in your head, but you were and are so fucking strong. I wouldn't want to get on your bad side. Clara, you are fucking powerful, and no one can take that away from you. Not Andrew, Ryan, or even me."

I unzip the hoodie she is wearing and place it, along with her bra, on the pile of clothes next to the door.

"I'm exhausted."

I pick her up and bring her to the bath. Laying her into the water, I get in behind her and rub the cloth through the bubbles before trailing it over her skin.

"It's tiring being a complete badass. We'll get you cleaned up and fed, and then we deserve a good night's sleep." I kiss her shoulder and continue to wash the blood off of her. She's so fucking exquisite, and I can't express the feelings that bubble in my heart. "You have a power over me. Have for years. I don't know how to control it, but I'd walk to the ends of the earth if that's what you wanted."

Clara relaxes against my chest, and for the first time in my life, it's like the puzzle pieces fit right. That even though I waited for her, it all came together when it needed to and not a moment before.

Chapter Nine
Clara

2 months later

"Clara, you are a godsend. I told you that you didn't have to come in today. I know it might've been a tough morning." Debbie smiles, crossing her arms before leaning against the counter.

"Therapy wasn't as bad as it usually is. We paused this week to focus on the present. Plus, you deserve a vacation more than anyone." I grin at her before turning back to stock behind the counter.

The new girl I've been training all week is doing great. Now that I have keyholder responsibilities, I've been opening and closing for Debbie, so she can relax without any worries about her business.

Debbie and I work together to close for the night, and soon Burke's slate grey Lexus pulls into the parking lot. He doesn't get out, and I know he understands I need to soak up all the time I can with Debbie. We've built a great relationship, and she's become more than just my boss.

"He's a lucky guy. You always think you're the one who is, but Clara, you are the best catch he could have found."

My cheeks heat. I covered this topic in therapy, but I still find it hard to believe anyone. I've finally almost come to terms with the fact that I couldn't control anything that happened to me when I was a child, and although I could have left Ryan, it also was a tough situation, especially with my history. "Yeah," I say quietly.

Closing up the box of jams, I shift it back to where it belongs and take off my blue apron. "I'm going to miss you." The admission is a big step for me. Being vulnerable isn't something I'm comfortable exposing yet. As if you can show your heart and let people break the valves inside.

"I'll be back before you know it, with presents," Debbie says and quickly envelops me in a hug. "When I return, we should check into the new girl."

"What do you mean?" I retreat, gazing into her blue eyes.

"Bailey is in some sort of situation. I just don't know how deep it runs, or if she wants our help. You know you can't help someone if they don't want it."

The last couple of weeks pass through my mind, and I think of the signs I've missed or brushed off. I freeze in place, my throat dries as the tears threaten to well up. I should have been more vigilant. Having lived through so much, the signs usually would hit me in the face.

"Clara, you aren't to blame, and you won't take this on alone. We have a wonderful support system here. You are healing and really, she's very good at hiding that anything is wrong." I lower my shoulders but mentally kick myself. I understand what it's like to be trapped in a situation you feel you can't control.

"We'll work together when you get back," I whisper.

Letting her go and exhaling a deep breath. Together, we lock up and exit through the backdoor to set the alarm and take out the trash. Once Debbie has made it to her truck, I turn to walk to the car and Burke is striding toward me.

"Have a wonderful vacation. Make sure you call if you have any troubles," he says to Debbie. Nodding her a goodbye, he links his fingers with mine.

Walking to the car, he opens my door, then circles around to the driver's side. "Alright, want to drive?"

"Nah, I'll focus on my license when she gets back." I look out the window, and Burke grips my chin to turn me to him.

"Hungry?"

"No, we had dinner together tonight. How was work?"

"It was good. What's wrong, Dragonfly?" He strokes my face.

"I missed signs. Debbie told me the new girl might be in a situation. I should have picked up quickly, and now I feel dumb." I try to turn my head away from him, but he doesn't loosen his grip.

"Clara, you know you can't save everyone. But let me check into it before you go in swinging, alright? We'll take care of this like we do. Let's get you home."

On the drive, his hand doesn't leave my thigh, and I revel in the comfort. Knowing I have people in my corner makes all the difference in the world. Not enough time has passed to undo the damage from the past, and I'm not sure it ever will, but the support has been appreciated in a way that they'll never know.

"Date night this week? We can do a lunch or breakfast since you've taken on Debbie's shifts, but I think it's needed." I smile and wrap my fingers around his hand.

"Of course, you spoil me too much."

Burke's deep laughter fills the car. "I've held back. I could lavish you with material things, but that isn't your style. Physical touch and quality time are the things you crave, and I'll provide whatever you need."

"Wanna show me how much you can spoil me, then?"

He parks the car in the garage and turns it off before leaning over the console. Burke kisses me passionately, butterflies or nerves zip through my body, and I ache for his touch.

"I'll never deny you." His gruff voice makes my core clench. It's been a few days since our schedules allowed time together, and I've missed it.

Burke wastes no time in circling the car and opening my door. He bends to sweep me off my feet, but I move out of his reach. "I have legs!"

"Keep it up, Clara, because I know exactly what buttons to push to have you begging."

I can't help but hide my grin and skirt past him to walk into the house. He is hot on my heels as I run up the stairs to the bedroom.

Before I can strip my clothes off to get in the shower, Burke grips the back of my sweater and pulls me to him. I melt against his chest as his fingers move to remove my outfit.

Trying to turn is futile. He will never control anything outside the bedroom, but when we play, he always makes me feel the safest, even if he calls all the shots.

"That's my girl," he growls into my neck.

Burke wraps his hand around my throat and leads me to the bed. I become a puddle of need under his icy blue stare. When the mattress hits the back of my legs, I fall back, and he shucks his clothes off.

He grips my sides, lifting me and scooting me back before he lowers between my legs, propping them up over his shoulders.

"Already wet, my favourite." His breath traces over my clit, and I clench around nothing.

"Please," I beg.

Burke doesn't pay attention to me as he runs his fingers through my wetness and teases me while ignoring my clit. His digits slide into me, curling against the spot inside that makes my hips thrust. The teasing drives me insane, and my body feels like it's on fire under the skin. I need him more than anything.

When his tongue slips over my clit, it's everything, and I tremble under him. I arch, and he continues to lick me as his fingers fuck me. The edge of my orgasm is just out of reach, and he soon pulls away.

"Roll over." I do as he says. "You listen so well," he growls.

His hands open me before he thrusts into me. Burke slips his fingers under us to play with my clit. I'm so fucking close, and as he slams into me, I explode. Pleasure courses through my body, and as I try to move away from him, he grips my hair. "Don't run from me."

Burke's rough voice makes my body tingle, and as he continues to thrust into me and play with my clit, I shake under him as another orgasm rips through me. It's too much, but the closeness of his breath on my neck, and the growls that fill the room are everything I need.

"Use your words."

"Please, make me come all over your cock again."

He slows but doesn't stop. His dick throbs inside of me, and his fingers rub over my clit until I'm milking his cock for the final time. I scream out, our guttural moans mixing in a symphony only made for us.

Burke pulls out, and I turn over. He kneels on the bed and jerks his cock, staring down into my eyes. I open my mouth, and he groans.

"I love when you look at me like this. See how hard I am for you? How much you are going to make me come?"

He fills my mouth, and I swallow while maintaining eye contact. He kneels forward, kissing me before wrapping himself around my body.

"I love you," I whisper.

"Forever, Dragonfly."

He's the person I've been searching for, the man who will help me clean up any mess I make, who never judges when I need to end a life. Burke is the home I've spent my entire life trying to find.

Marla York is the much darker alter ego of Tanya Lynn. She wanted to explore stories that don't have to end with a happy ever after, and have a pen name just to release the darkness from her mind. Stay Wicked.

https://tanyalynn100.ca/marla-york.html

Trust Me Not

By: K. Rose

About Trust Me Not

He's the danger I never saw coming—and the temptation I can't resist.

Uncovering secrets is what I do best, and Zenith Corp is hiding a big one—a groundbreaking contraceptive with no side effects at all, and they're desperate to keep it buried. Every clue pulls me deeper into their shadowy world and right into the path of Romello Reid. He's infuriating, impossibly attractive, and everywhere I turn.

I know I shouldn't get involved. He's the enemy, or at least he should be. But there's something about how he looks at me that makes my heart skip and something in his eyes that tells me he's hiding secrets of his own.

As the stakes get higher, the lines between right and wrong start to blur. Trusting him could be a mistake that costs me everything— including my heart. But with women's lives hanging in the balance, I can't back down now.

When love and danger collide, all bets are off.

CONTENT NOTE:

Mature Content intended for those of an appropriate age only. Please be mindful of your mental health and know this story has darker themes. There are mentions of death, attempted murder, espionage, and graphic on page sexual encounters.

Relationship type: M/F

This story is for the fearless women who refuse to be silenced, who channel their rage into uncovering the truth, and who find power in their voice even when the odds are stacked against them.
To the ones who believe that every secret deserves a reckoning and that love—true love—can be as liberating as it is unexpected, this book is yours.

Chapter One

The city pulses around me, a living, breathing entity of concrete and glass. Neon lights flicker to life as dusk settles, casting a kaleidoscope of colors onto the wet pavement. The scent of rain hangs in the air, mingling with the aroma of street food and the distant hum of traffic. I stand across from the towering monolith that is Zenith Corp's headquarters, its mirrored surface reflecting the chaotic beauty of the city.

My fingers tighten around the strap of my messenger bag, and the weight of my recorder and notes presses against my side. The cool breeze carries a hint of autumn, rustling the leaves of the sparse trees lining the sidewalk. I take a deep breath, the crisp air filling my lungs, grounding me.

"Truth is the most potent weapon we have," I whisper to myself, the mantra steadying my nerves. As an investigative journalist, uncovering the hidden injustices that plague society is more than a job—it's a calling.

My phone buzzes in my pocket. Pulling it out, I see a message from my best friend, Mia:

Dinner tomorrow? Got news to share!

A small smile tugs at my lips. Mia's been my rock since college, her optimism a beacon in the often murky waters of my work. I type back:

Count me in, around six...I'll bring the prosecco!

Turning my gaze back to Zenith Corp, a shiver runs down my spine—not from the cold, but from the enormity of the task ahead. Rumors have been swirling about a new contraceptive they've developed—a breakthrough with no side effects—that they've allegedly decided to bury. The implications are staggering, especially for women like Mia, who suffer from the adverse effects of current options.

Last year, she nearly died from a blood clot that traveled to her lungs, and now she can't take any of the traditional hormonal contraceptives. That leaves little by way of protection against pregnancy—that a woman has full control of with a high success rate. Implants, rings, patches, most IUDs, and pills are all hormone-based and the best options for the prevention of unplanned pregnancy. Diaphragms can be placed incorrectly and cause more problems than they're worth, and are really only good with spermicide gel, and that stuff comes with its own side effects too. For a woman who hasn't had a child yet, getting her tubes tied isn't an option either. The state's laws suggest that since it's irreversible, they won't allow it regardless of the patient's wishes. Insert eye roll.

I want this for her. I want this for all women. Sure, it makes this investigation, this story, personal, but that is what's going to make it the best piece I have ever done.

My editor's warnings echo in my mind. "You're treading on dangerous ground, Wynter. Zenith isn't just another corporation; they're a powerhouse with friends in high places."

I shake off the doubt, my resolve hardening. "If not me, then who?" I murmur, stepping forward as the crosswalk signals it's safe to proceed. The cacophony of revving car engines pulling away from where the red light held them at bay and chattering pedestrians surrounds me, but I feel strangely isolated, focused.

As I near the entrance, a sleek black car pulls up, drawing my attention. The door opens, and out steps Romello Reid. Even in the dim light, his presence is commanding. Tall, with sharp features softened by a hint of stubble, he exudes a mix of charisma and something else, something darker. He's the man every woman wants, and every man wants to become.

Our eyes meet briefly as he adjusts his tailored suit jacket. The silk fabric hugs perfectly to his muscular body like a second skin. For a moment, I swear a flicker of curiosity crosses his gaze, but then he's swept away by a group of associates, their laughter punctuating the night air. I assume they're having some sort of meeting.

I exhale, realizing I've been holding my breath. Romello Reid, the recluse executive rumored to be Zenith's rising star. His reputation precedes him, a man both admired and feared within the industry. He's been the most sought-after CEO in the last decade. He makes every company he graces with his presence a fortune in the first year...every...single...time.

I have done my research, and I know more about him than I should. I might have a photo or four of him on a super yacht that was leaked last summer when he was being recruited to this position with Zenith stuck to my storyboard at home. And I may or may not have pulled out a rose a time or two too many, while staring intently into those piercing dark eyes. Ignoring the fact that he is old enough to be my father, I still wouldn't mind playing out my fantasy.

"Focus, Wynter," I chastise myself, pushing aside the unsettling distraction. I have work to do. I quicken my pace and walk to the ground-level coffee shop in the next tower. The familiar green and white mermaid sign illuminated in the window promises a safe haven for me to get some work done.

Entering the nearby café, the warmth envelops me, and the rich scent of coffee beans provides comfort. I walk to the counter and place my order for my favorite chilled franken-beverage. It's better to have a cold coffee that stays relatively drinkable over time than to have a hot coffee that gets cold and undrinkable after a while.

I find a corner table and pull out my laptop. The hum of conversation creates a soothing backdrop as I delve into my research, fingers flying over the keys.

"Winter! Trenta Vanilla Frap extra shot caramel drizzle with whipped cream and sugar sprinkles."

I personally hate it when they call out the order at the pickup counter. I always get this sense of embarrassment that's wholly unfounded, but it's there nonetheless.

Hours slip by unnoticed until the barista's gentle tap on my table brings me back. "We're closing up, miss."

I blink, rubbing my tired eyes. "Oh, sorry. Lost track of time."

She smiles kindly. "Happens to the best of us."

Gathering my things, I step outside and into the night. The city's vibrancy has dimmed, leaving a quiet stillness. I hope the contact I have is right about the meeting tomorrow. This could be the big break I need to get the scoop on this story.

Chapter Two

The morning sun filters through my curtains, casting golden stripes across my hardwood floor. The aroma of freshly brewed coffee wafts from the kitchen, beckoning me. I wrap a robe around myself; the soft fabric brushes against my skin as I pad barefoot to the source.

Mia stands by the stove, her dark curls piled messily atop her head. She hums softly, swaying to an unheard melody as she flips pancakes.

"You're up early," I remark, sliding onto a stool at the counter.

She turns, her eyes sparkling. "Couldn't sleep. Thought I'd surprise you."

I smile gratefully. "Best surprise I've had in a while."

She sets a plate before me, the pancakes perfectly golden. "So, what's the latest scoop? Still chasing after the big bad wolf of Zenith Corp?"

I drizzle syrup over the stack, the sweet scent mingling with the coffee. "You know me too well. I got a tip about a meeting they're having tonight. High-level executives discussing something they'd rather keep under wraps."

Mia arches an eyebrow. "And you're planning to crash it?" She walks over with a cup of liquid life and my favorite caramel creamer, which I pour until it's immediately cool enough to drink.

I shrug, take a giant gulp of coffee, and stuff a big bite of pancake into my cheek. "That's the idea." It comes out a bit muffled, but the buttery syrup-covered goodness is totally worth it.

She places a hand over mine, her expression turning serious. "Just...be careful, okay? These aren't the kind of people who play nice."

I squeeze her hand reassuringly. "I will. Promise."

"So, I take it that means we no longer have dinner plans?" she asks.

"Well, shit. I'm sorry, Mia. I forgot...but you're here now." I hope she understands that this is so important to my story, and I am not just ditching her willy-nilly.

"Yeah, don't worry about it." She starts to pick at her chipped nail polish.

She seems sad now. "You know I didn't mean to hurt your feelings or anything, right? You're my bestie." I walk around the countertop and give her a half hug while she plates off the last of the pancakes.

"What did you want to tell me?" I ask. I remember the text said she had news to share.

"Nothing, no big deal."

"Oh, c'mon. Don't do that."

"It's really nothing. I, uh...just wanted to spend some time out. Have a girl's night." She bumps one shoulder in the air.

"All right. Raincheck?"

"Of course."

Mia walks over to the sink with the frying pan and wipes the little crumbs with the washrag I left draped over the little center divider. I make a mental note to rewash that pan later with a fresh rag and some actual soap. She's my bestie, so I forgive her.

The day passes in a blur of preparations. I dig through my closet, pulling out an outfit that could pass for corporate chic—sleek black slacks, a crisp starched linen blouse, and sensible heels. My heart pounds as I apply subtle makeup, the mirror reflecting a composed exterior that belies the nerves beneath.

I barely recognize the woman in the mirror. I rarely dress this fancy for anything.

"I guess I do clean up nice." I do a little half-turn in the mirror and check out my butt in these pants. I knew there was a reason I bought these; it looks like I got a BBL.

As dusk approaches, I make my way to Zenith Corp's auxiliary building—a less conspicuous venue for their clandestine meeting. The air is thick with anticipation, the cool evening breeze rustling the leaves overhead. I wish I had chosen ballet flats instead of heels; I can feel a little blister forming already.

I slip inside amid a group of employees, the security guard barely glancing up from his phone as they scan their badges. I hold my breath, offering a confident nod as I pass. Nobody bats an eyelash at me at all. Surprising myself at how easy that really was to sneak in, my heart races with a new shot of adrenaline.

The sterile corridors stretch ahead, illuminated by fluorescent lights that cast a harsh glow. My heels click lightly on the flooring as I walk aimlessly away from the crowd I came in with.

Voices drift from a room down the hall with its door open. I position myself near the slight gap to the room, the hushed tones becoming clearer.

"...cannot risk this getting out," a stern voice asserts. "The financial repercussions alone—"

"Agreed," another interjects. "We need to ensure all data is secured and any leaks are plugged immediately."

My pulse quickens. This is it—the proof I need. I rummage through my cross-body bag for my recorder but fumble with the zipper as it gets snagged on itself.

"Excuse me, can I help you?"

I whirl around to find Romello Reid standing before me, his gaze piercing. Up close, the intensity of his gunmetal-gray eyes is almost unnerving. His scent carries over to me on the slight breeze of his approach. Intoxicating and expensive is the best way I can describe it, and it makes my mouth water. I realize I am staring at his lips now.

"I, uh..." My mind races for a plausible excuse. "I was just looking for the restrooms."

He studies me for a moment, a hint of amusement curling at the corners of his mouth. "Romello Ried. Pleasure to meet you."

He extends a hand, and I wipe my sweaty palms on my thighs—before offering it in return. Somehow, I manage to click my heels together like Dorothy while my arm moves up and down in an over-exaggerated handshake.

"The restrooms are on the other side of the building." He hitches a thumb over his shoulder.

Heat rises to my cheeks. "Must have taken a wrong turn."

He tilts his head slightly, a lock of dark hair falling across his forehead. "You're new here, aren't you?"

"First week," I lie, forcing a smile.

"Welcome aboard," he says smoothly. "Perhaps I can escort you to your destination."

"That's not necessary," I begin, but he gestures down the hall.

"I insist."

As we walk, the silence stretches. I can feel his gaze flickering toward me, assessing.

"So, which department did you say you're in?" he asks casually.

"Research and Development," I lie again, hoping it's vague enough.

"Interesting. I thought I knew everyone in R&D."

My palms start to sweat. "Well, it's a big department." I hope it's big. I have no idea what I was thinking when I snuck in here. How am I ever going to get away with this?

He stops in front of a door, the universal symbol for restrooms displayed prominently. "Here we are."

"Thank you," I murmur, stepping past him.

He lingers for a moment. "Be careful not to wander too much. This building can be...worse than a prison."

I nod, slipping inside the restroom. Once the door closes behind me, I exhale shakily. That was too close. I can't believe I just met Romello in the flesh.

My mind wants to climb him like a tree and see if he can hit that spot like my little toy does, but lucky for me, my logical mind kept it cool and professional. I might've blown my one chance with him, though.

Oh wow, do I want a chance with him?

Waiting a few minutes to ensure he's gone; I peek back into the corridor. It's empty. Deciding not to push my luck further tonight, I make my way back to the exit. The same security guard is still staring intently at his phone. I can hear a referee whistle and a bunch of booing coming from the small device. He must be watching some kind of sports match game thing. I never really got into sports, but I know the sounds of a game.

As I step into the night air, relief washes over me. I may not have gathered concrete evidence, but at least I've confirmed that something is definitely amiss.

I now know one thing is certain, Romello Reid is even hotter in person. Not only that, but he might well be a part of the conspiracy to cover up the new drug. What else would he have been doing heading to that very room?

My mind races with theory after theory while I make my way home, eager to take down notes and get these forsaken heels off.

Chapter Three

Back at my apartment, the familiar surroundings offer little comfort. The soft glow of my desk lamp casts elongated shadows across scattered notes and files. I sit, staring at the blinking cursor on my laptop screen, the events of the evening replaying in my mind.

"Was I reckless?" I whisper to the empty room. The silence offers no answers.

My phone buzzes, startling me. It's a call from my editor, Mark.

"Hey, Wynter. Got a minute?" His voice is gruff, tinged with concern.

"Sure, what's up?"

"I heard you were snooping around Zenith Corp tonight."

"How? There's no way. I didn't even talk to anyone!"

"I have my sources," he says with a serious tone.

Word travels fast, I guess. "Just following a lead," I admit.

He sighs heavily. "Listen, I admire your dedication, but you need to be careful. Zenith isn't a small-time operation. They've got resources, connections."

"I can't just ignore this, Mark. They're hiding something that could impact countless women, maybe even the world as we know it."

"I get it, but I don't want to see you get in over your head. Promise me you'll tread lightly."

"I'll be careful," I assure him, though my resolve remains unshaken. Someone needs to get to the truth; why not me?

After we hang up, doubt creeps in. Is this worth the risk? A memory of Mia's hopeful face flashes before me. She's suffered so much due to the side effects of her medication—the migraines, the mood swings. Not to mention the life-altering near-death experience. If there's a chance to bring about change, I have to take it.

I pour over my research again. I need to find the missing link, the piece that connects everything together. Why would they want to suppress millions of dollars in research and a new product if there really isn't anything wrong with it?

I get lost in rereading my notes until my eyes close of their own accord.

The next morning, I decide to dig deeper from a safer distance. I head to the public records office, the musty scent of old paper greeting me as I enter. The dim lighting and rows of filing cabinets create a labyrinth of information.

Hours pass as I sift through documents, my fingers tracing over financial statements and patent filings. Patterns begin to emerge— shell companies, redirected funds, suspicious gaps in reporting.

"Find anything interesting?" a familiar voice asks.

I look up to see Romello leaning casually against a nearby shelf, a curious glint in his eyes.

My heart skips a beat. "Wh-what are you doing here?"

He smiles faintly. "I could ask you the same question."

I close the file slowly. "Research."

"Ah, the relentless pursuit of knowledge." He steps closer, and the scent of his cologne—a subtle mix of cedar and something distinctly masculine—envelopes me.

"Isn't that what drives us all?" I reply evenly.

He chuckles softly. "Some more than others."

An uncomfortable silence settles between us. His gaze holds mine, and for a moment, the air feels charged.

"Well, I won't keep you from your work," he finally says, turning to leave. "Just remember—curiosity killed the cat."

He winks, then turns. I can't help but watch as his toned, muscular body walks away from me with that very sure-of-himself swagger. His almost too-tight suit pants hug his firm body in all the right places.

"Oh, and kitten. Don't sneak into my building without being invited."

As he walks away, a mixture of frustration and intrigue swirls within me. There's more to Romello Reid than meets the eye.

I chastise myself for getting caught by him yet again. How does he do that?

Chapter Four

That evening, Mia and I meet at our favorite rooftop bar for that raincheck. The city sprawls below us, a tapestry of lights stretching into the horizon. The air is warmer than usual for this time of year; the gentle breeze carries the sounds of music and laughter.

"To good news," Mia toasts, clinking her glass against mine.

"Good news?" I raise an eyebrow. "Do tell."

She grins widely. "I got accepted into the clinical trial for this new drug. My doctor thought I'd be the perfect candidate for it, being as I can't take any of the currently offered meds."

My glass hovers mid-air. "Wait, what? How did you—"

"Dr. Patel mentioned it during my last appointment. It's supposed to be a game-changer."

Alarm bells ring in my mind. "Mia, I don't think that's a good idea."

Her expression falters. "Why not? This could be the solution I've been waiting for. I want to stop being such a prude all the time. I mean, I like my toys and all, but you gotta have the real thing once in a while."

I hesitate, choosing my words carefully. "I have reasons to believe that Zenith Corp might be involved in some unethical practices regarding that drug specifically."

She frowns. "Wynter, are you sure? This could really help me."

"I'm working on getting the full picture. Just...promise me you'll hold off until I know more."

She sighs, swirling the last of her cocktail in her glass. "All right, but don't take too long; the trial is supposed to start soon and I don't want to miss the opportunity. You know insurance sucks about giving coverage to new drugs, they only want to pay for generics, and it takes at least ten years to wait for that to happen."

Changing the subject, I tell her about my encounters with Romello. She listens intently, a mischievous glint appearing in her eyes.

"Sounds like someone's caught your attention," she teases.

I scoff lightly. "Hardly. He's infuriating and cryptic."

"Not to mention rich and uber attractive," she adds with a wink.

I feel a blush creep up my neck. "That's beside the point."

She laughs. "Maybe, but don't let your guard down. Men like that can be trouble."

"Trust me, I know."

* * *

Later that night, I find myself replaying every interaction with Romello. There's a magnetic pull I can't quite explain, a dance of curiosity and caution.

That still doesn't stop me from feeling a flush when my mind wanders to him. To that strong physique hidden underneath those designer suits. The subtle, nonchalant way he flirts without flirting.

My hands drift down and slip below the waistline of my panties. My fingertips gently caress my throbbing clit, already moist with desire.

My mind is filled with images of Romello. His strong body on mine, his plump, kissable lips with that defined cupid's bow, and his large hands gripping my hair as he pulls me in closer to deepen that kiss.

The soft moan that leaves me almost breaks my concentration, just long enough for me to redouble my efforts and slip two fingers inside my aching core.

My imagination runs rampant with the thoughts of his fingers... his hard cock. I wonder if he has a big dick to go with all that big dick energy he gives off. The booze lends itself to my letting go and embracing the sensations.

"Yes...yes...Romello...fuck yes."

A small yet satisfying orgasm courses through my body. Just enough to curb the lust that was building over a man I likely have no chance with anywhere but my imagination.

As I drift off to sleep, I can't shake the feeling that our paths are entwined in ways I never anticipated.

Chapter Five

The next few days are a whirlwind of covert meetings—mostly online—and late-night research. During one of the dark web chatroom meetings, I managed to secure an invitation to a charity gala hosted by Zenith Corp—a perfect opportunity to gather more intel. They have a hacker for just about anything now. Kids as early as ten are learning to write professional code, and it's a dangerous world when you can just ask an AI to write code for you, too. The computer is supposed to have guidelines and standards, but they are bypassed just as easily with—you guessed it—another piece of code. At least I am comfortable in my abilities as an investigative journalist that no piece of technology would ever be able to take my place or do my job as well, at least not with the current tech. We aren't at that level of consciousness just yet with computers; no Matrix or Skynet is coming to kill off all of humanity just yet.

* * *

I woke up late after pulling another all-nighter. The charity gala is in about an hour, so I should have just enough time to get dressed and gussied up enough to fit in and schmooze with the crowd of hoity-toity creme-de-la-creme of high society. I am sure that should all be red carpet worthy themselves. The donors for the charity gala always make a show of themselves, probably to make sure the world still knows they're rich assholes who have exorbitant amounts of expendable cash.

My rideshare driver has a black Lincoln with blacked-out everything, and it's actually perfect to show up at the doors of the event. I couldn't have asked for anything better unless I sprung for a limo driver to take me there.

Dressed in an elegant navy gown that hugs my curves, I step into the grand ballroom. Crystal chandeliers cast a warm glow over the opulent décor, the scent of expensive perfume and hors d'oeuvres fill the air. Laughter and clinking glasses create a symphony of affluence. I had never imagined that this story would bring me here, but I am damn sure going to enjoy it.

I weave through the crowd, subtly eavesdropping on conversations. Snippets of information float by—mentions of offshore accounts and hush-hush projects. I regret not wearing my wire, just so I can take notes on everything without having to actually take notes. I have a great memory, but this is just information overload.

"Wynter Morgan, isn't it?" Romello's voice sends a shiver down my spine.

I turn to find him beside me, impeccably dressed in a tailored tuxedo. His eyes trail over me appreciatively.

"You clean up nicely," he remarks.

I offer a polite smile. "You too."

He extends a hand. "Care to dance?"

I glance around, weighing my options. "Why not?"

He leads me to the dance floor, his hand resting lightly on the small of my back. As we move to the soft sounds of the orchestra, I can't help but notice the warmth of his touch, the way his gaze seems to see straight through me.

"Enjoying the evening?" he asks.

"It's enlightening," I reply.

He chuckles. "Have you learned something I should know about?"

His question takes me by surprise.

"You're in R and D, right?"

I giggle nervously. "Yes, yes, I am. But I regret to inform you that I haven't found anything I would need to run that far up the flagpole just yet."

"Always such a good *employee,* aren't you?" He squints down at me.

"And you, always the enigmatic executive."

He leans in slightly, his breath warm against my ear. "Perhaps we both wear masks."

"Perhaps," I concede. I do my best to ignore the sensation that his whisper sent down my spine. I can't help the reaction to his proximity. My body wants him.

The song ends, but neither of us steps away immediately. The air between us is thick with unspoken words.

"Would you like to get some fresh air?" he suggests.

I nod, allowing him to guide me toward the terrace. The cool night air is a welcome contrast to the heat of the ballroom. The heat is building within me for this man. The city lights shimmer below, a sea of stars mirroring the sky above.

"Beautiful, isn't it?" he muses.

"Yes," I agree, though my attention is more on him than the view.

He turns to face me, his expression unreadable. "I have a feeling you're not here just to enjoy the party."

I meet his gaze steadily. "And what makes you say that?"

"Call it intuition." He pauses, his eyes searching mine. "Be careful where you tread, Wynter."

"Is that a warning?"

"Consider it friendly advice."

I step closer, the distance between us shrinking. "Why do you care?"

His jaw tightens ever so slightly. "Maybe I don't want to see you get hurt."

"Or maybe you're trying to protect your own interests."

He smiles faintly. "Believe what you will."

Without thinking, I reach out and place a hand on his arm. The contact sends a jolt through me. "What aren't you telling me?"

For a moment, vulnerability flashes across his features. "Some truths are more dangerous than lies."

Before I can respond, he leans in, his lips brushing softly against mine. The world seems to halt, and the only sensation is the warmth and softness of his kiss. It's brief but filled with an intensity that leaves me breathless.

My hand is mid-air and reared back, ready to strike, when he grips my arm around the wrist. He pulls me closer to him while turning my arm so it's behind me along with his. My fist bunches and pounds into his chest. His very hard, muscular chest.

He leans down to my height and takes my lips again, this time much more forcibly. His tongue prods at my lips for entrance, and I grant him that. I taste expensive champagne on his tongue as he twirls his around mine with expert precision. He grips my ass in one of his large hands after releasing his hold on my wrist. While pulling me closer, he lifts me off the ground enough that even in the heels I'm wearing, I can barely touch it with my toes.

He pulls back, his eyes reflecting a mix of regret and longing. "Goodnight, Wynter."

Before I can process what's happened, he's gone, disappearing through the terrace doors and back into the crowd.

My fingertips touch my lips, still tingling from the unexpected kiss. Confusion and desire swirl within me, complicating everything.

What does he know?

Chapter Six

I wake the next morning to a flood of emotions. Last night's encounter with Romello has thrown me off balance. Part of me wants to believe there's more to him—that perhaps he's not the villain I imagine. The other part of me thinks he's trying to distract me from getting the information I want.

Determined to find answers, I dive back into my investigation. At a local café, the aroma of freshly baked pastries mingles with the rich scent of coffee. I spread out my notes, and the soft murmur of patrons provides a comforting backdrop.

As I sift through the documents, a particular file catches my eye—an internal memo with Romello's signature. My eyes scan the lines, each word sinking like a stone in my stomach.

"Initiate Project Eclipse. All research and prototypes related to the contraceptive drug are to be terminated effective immediately. Ensure all data is secured and personnel are reassigned."

Staring at the page, I feel a sense of disbelief giving way to a crushing sense of betrayal. He's been orchestrating the suppression all along.

The café suddenly feels stifling. I gather my things hastily, needing fresh air. I shove everything into my messenger bag haphazardly, with crumpled pages and all. Outside, the city buzzes around me, oblivious to my turmoil. My world is spinning with rage. I want to turn green and smash everything within sight.

My phone rings—it's Mia. I know it before looking because I have our favorite song set as her ringtone. This month it's "Rain" by that masked man that has the world guessing his real identity. I wait until the beat drops then answer the call.

"Hey, are we still on for lunch?" she asks brightly.

I swallow hard. "Actually, something's come up. Can we raincheck?"

"Everything okay?"

"Yeah, just work stuff."

"All right, but don't overwork yourself," she chides gently.

"Talk soon."

I end the call, leaning against a lamppost. The weight of my discovery presses down on me. How could I have been so blind?

I grip my bag tighter against my chest and decide to walk back to my apartment rather than take a ride share. The brisk air does nothing to clear my head of all the racing thoughts. Even less to check the feeling that had crept in for Romello. How could I be so stupid to think there was actually an option there?

Once back in my apartment, I stare blankly at my laptop screen. The spark that fueled my investigation feels dimmed by personal hurt. I type up my findings, the clacking of keys echoing in the quiet room.

I have plenty of tabs open to the internet and dark web pages. Everything adding to the puzzle of why they would want to suppress this groundbreaking new drug. Nothing is giving a clear-cut answer though. There doesn't seem to be anything that screams cover-up.

Seemingly, the math isn't math-ing here. Zenith Corp and their big wigs are set to make billions of dollars in the first year alone. Billions from just the projections that don't include cash patients without insurance coverage, too. Why would they give all that up after years of pouring cash into the product to get it through to this last round of human trials?

I need to scream, throw something, or smash something. I am so frustrated with this whole scenario. I really am a peaceful person, so having all this internal rage bubbling to the surface is taking its toll on me.

A notification pops up—a message from an anonymous sender:

Stop digging or face the consequences.

A chill runs through me. Quickly, I check my apartment's locks, paranoia creeping in. The shadows seem darker, every sound amplified. How did they get through my security protocols?

I try to type back but the moment I click on the messenger—that looked suspiciously like an old version of AOL—it closed and shut power to my laptop completely.

"Fuck!"

I press the power button and luckily the screen fired right back up. I click on the menu and restore all my previous browser history. Moving as quickly as my fingers can I back up all of the data onto a removable drive and start sending zip files to my cloud.

Just as I am finishing with the last file of my research my heart sinks. A grainy picture of Romello and I kissing on the veranda flashes across my screen.

I am not normally an overly paranoid person. This...this makes me pause.

My brain is running a marathon right now with how fast the thoughts are careening by. How long have I been watched? Who is following me?

Am I just collateral damage, and this is just more ammo against Romello? Surely, it has to be someone out to smear him. He's a top executive in a Fortune 500 company.

"Who are you people?"

I have the distinct feeling that I am in some kind of danger. My gut is rarely ever wrong, but I have been distracted by my hormones and that man.

Romello is my kryptonite. I am the Superman in this story, Zenith the Lex, and Romello the only thing poised to derail every-thing I have done to stop this villain from winning. My daydreams and playtime featuring him are my fault, true. But that kiss...

Fuck this. I will not be silenced.

I decide to send my findings to Mark. At least if something happens, the truth won't die with me.

"Try and stop me now, mother-fucker!"

Chapter Seven

The following days are a blur of jump scares, nail-biting, and tension. I notice unfamiliar faces lingering near my building, cars that seem to follow me. Every small noise has my nerves frayed. My apartment feels like a prison, the walls closing in.

Mark calls with bad news. "Zenith's legal team is threatening to sue if we publish. The board is pulling the story."

"What? They can't do that!"

"Money talks, Wynter. I'm sorry."

Frustration and helplessness wash over me. "So that's it? They get away with it?"

"Maybe there's another way," he suggests gently. "But you need to lay low for now."

I hang up, seething. Just then, a knock sounds at my door. Peering through the peephole, I see Mia's worried face.

I open the door, pulling her inside. "What are you doing here?"

"I've been trying to reach you. Are you avoiding me?" she asks, concern etched on her features.

"I've just been...dealing with some things."

She notices the scattered papers and my disheveled state. "Wynter, what's going on?"

I hesitate, then decide she deserves to know. I explain everything —the investigation, the threats, Romello's involvement.

Her eyes widen. "This is serious. You need to go to the authorities."

"I don't have enough solid evidence. And besides, they might be in Zenith's pocket."

She grips my hands tightly. "Then we need to find a way to expose them."

A surge of gratitude fills me. "Thank you."

"Always," she replies softly.

Just then, her phone buzzes. She glances at it, her face paling. "It's the clinic. They said there are complications with the trial."

"What? I thought you agreed to hold off."

She looks away guiltily. "I didn't want to wait. I'm sorry."

"What kind of complications? Are you okay? Do you feel sick... pain...where does it hurt?" I rapidly fire questions at her in hopes of an answer to each one.

"I don't think so. I just haven't been very hungry."

Fear knots in my stomach. "We need to get you to the hospital."

"It's not like that, I'll be fine. They just need to see me up at the clinic."

"You had better be all right, if they did anything to hurt you...so help me."

I knew that they were suppressing this new drug, but now to have rushed another trial; someone had to be bought off. They better not be putting women's lives in danger because they need to hide this drug! There is no way that I have all of the information yet.

"I'll be all right. They wouldn't have put these meds out to trials if they were seriously hurting people."

"Mia, that's exactly what they would do. They gave you a list of possible side effects before you signed off, right?"

"Well yeah, but...I didn't actually read the whole packet, I basically skimmed it."

Everything inside of me wants to scream at her for being so careless. But I don't, I just hold out my hands and wait for her to come closer. I really need a hug right now.

"If anything ever happened to you I'd be beside myself. Please go to the hospital right away, and you'd better call me when you leave."

"I will, Wynter. I love you too."

We held that hug a beat longer than usual. Something inside me was still so scared that she wouldn't be okay. That this new mystery drug was far worse than anyone was letting on, I can feel it in my bones.

"I'll be fine, I just need to go to the clinic, not the hospital. I'm sure it's nothing but paperwork or something silly."

"You call me the minute you're done."

Chapter Eight

I find myself at the hospital, the sterile scent of disinfectant is overpowering. Machines beep rhythmically, a stark contrast to the chaos in my mind.

Mia lies in the bed, her skin pale, eyes closed. When she didn't call me by midnight I used the find my phone feature we added for each other, and found her at Mercy General.

A doctor approaches, his expression grave. "She's stable for now, but there were adverse reactions. We'll need to monitor her closely."

"What do you mean *adverse* reactions?" I asked with gritted teeth.

"I am not at liberty to discuss the patient's healthcare due to HIPPA law, I could lose my license to practice medicine."

I watch him type a few more notes into the laptop on the cart that he wheeled in with him. His eyes going back and forth between the screen and the monitors that beep with a rhythm matching Mia's heart.

I nod numbly. "Can I stay with her?"

"Of course."

Sitting by her bedside, I feel the weight of failure. "I'm so sorry," I whisper, tears blurring my vision.

Guilt and despair envelop me. Everything I've done feels meaningless. The system is too powerful, the obstacles insurmountable.

As the morning sun shines through the thin window on the far wall of the hospital room, I rest my head beside Mia, exhaustion pulling me under.

Chapter Nine

A gentle touch on my shoulder wakes me. I look up to see Romello standing beside me, concern in his eyes.

"What are you doing here?" I ask coldly.

"I heard about your friend. I wanted to help."

I stand abruptly. "Help? I think you've *helped* enough already?"

He sighs. "It's not that simple."

"Then explain it to me," I demand, anger boiling over.

He glances around. "Not here. Can we talk somewhere private?"

I hesitate, then nod curtly. We move to an empty corridor.

"I'm undercover," he begins quietly. "I'm working with a government agency to gather evidence against Zenith."

I laugh bitterly. "Do you expect me to believe that?"

He pulls out a badge, showing me credentials that seem official. "The agency recruited me after the company hired me. I was told they'd make sure I had a golden parachute, so no matter what I would come out of this unscathed. I couldn't risk blowing my cover, even when you started digging."

"How did you know I was digging into the company?" I crossed my arms and gave my best side-eye death stare.

"I knew from that first day in that hallway when you said you were R and D, yet you didn't know where the bathroom was. My team had a dossier delivered later that night on who you really are."

I sheepishly looked away. I knew I was caught, but I was stupid enough to believe that I had gotten away with it.

"Why didn't you tell me? You let me keep fumbling every time we crossed paths?"

"It was too dangerous—for both of us."

I search his eyes, looking for deceit, but find none. "Then why interfere with my investigation?"

"To protect you. Zenith is onto you. They won't hesitate to eliminate threats."

The weight of his words sinks in. "Mia." I feel sick.

He places a hand on my arm. "I know, and I'm sorry I couldn't stop that without blowing my cover. The real threat is still out there, Wynter. With what we have now, we should be able to stop the counterfeit drugs from being disbursed to the general public."

"What do you mean, counterfeit?" My eyebrows knit together. This is new.

"Zenith is a shell corporation and has been stealing patents and reproducing formulas from other pharma companies. The real tragedy is what they do to shut down the companies they steal from."

I pull away slightly. "Why should I trust you?"

"Because the truth matters to me as much as it does to you."

Romello puts his hands on my arms, squeezing gently. He looks me square in the eyes, probably searching for the same thing I am.

Trust.

Chapter Ten

U nder the cover of night, we work together to compile all our evidence. The seedy motel room on the outskirts of town seemed so cliche to meet him at but now seems so fitting. The air is thick with tension and unspoken feelings. The soft glow of computer screens illuminates our faces as we cross-reference files, piece together timelines, and prepare to send everything to a contact Romello trusts within the agency that recruited him, who just happens to have a massive reach with the media outlets.

"Once this goes out, there's no turning back," he warns.

"I'm ready," I affirm.

"They'll know it was your work; your name is all over this research." He tries again to stall.

"They can come after me all they like, it'll be too late. The world will know what pieces of shit they really are, and the rightful owners of all those patents will get them back." I argue.

"Here goes nothing." He hovers his finger over the mouse pad to send the files.

I press my finger on top of his as we hit send; the files are encrypted and dispatched to multiple agencies and news outlets. A sense of relief washes over me.

Romello turns to me, his expression a mix of exhaustion and affection. "You were incredible. The entire time, you never quit."

"Couldn't have done this part without you," I admit.

He steps closer, brushing a strand of hair from my face. "I'm sorry for everything—for deceiving you."

I look up at him, emotions swirling. "I understand why you did it," I say, even though I am not sure I truly do.

His gaze drops to my lips, and this time, I don't hesitate. I close the gap between us, our lips meeting in a tender yet passionate kiss. The world fades away, leaving only the warmth of his embrace and the steady beat of our hearts.

"I've wanted you since the first day we met. Your scent lingered in that hallway for days. Teasing...no, tormenting me."

His hand tangles in my hair and directs me to where he wants me. Our lips press together with such force they're likely to be bruised. My tongue slips out to taste him, and it's everything I needed it to be. Sweet, slightly lingering bitterness of the gas station coffee and something uniquely him.

When he pulls back again, he looks directly into my eyes. Staring so deeply, he might steal my soul.

"I watched you... in your room. I heard you call out my name...I want to hear you moan it again for me," he growled the words into my ear.

I'm shocked that he confessed his voyeuristic activity. Also, not too sure how I feel about the blatant invasion of privacy.

He moved forward, his growing erection pressing into my stomach. The table that held our notes and laptops is cleared in one large swipe of his arm. Lifting me by my ass as though I weigh nothing, he sets me down on the table just a moment later.

My head spins with lust. The oxytocin and dopamine being released is all I crave and they make my whole body buzz.

Did I actually like that he watched me?

"I want you so badly. Let me taste you." He hooks his fingers into the waistband of my leggings and starts to tug them down my thighs. I have to place my palms on the table and lift my ass up a little for him to gain any purchase with the tugging. It's my way of giving him permission before the words would actually form.

"I want you too." I cringed internally. I've never been good at pillow talk.

He either accepted my awkwardness or ignored it, which lightened the weight on my shoulders. Romello left my leggings around my calves and pressed my thighs open.

"So fucking pretty." He leans in and runs his lips lightly against my inner thigh until they meet my weeping core. His wide flat tongue runs one swipe across, then one vertically, splitting the center and easily finding my clit. A shudder burns through me.

After all those nights with my imagination, the real thing is so much better than I imagined. His hands roam across my skin, leaving it heated in his wake.

I throw my head back and enjoy every lick, suck, and tickle of his tongue. He grabs me around both thighs and tugs me to the edge of the table. One arm remains banded across me, pressing down on my lower abdomen, while the other finds and parts my lower lips before inserting one finger.

Slowly in time, with his tongue and the added pressure from his arm banded over me, that finger finds my spot, releasing a slow build shudder that falls into an orgasm.

"Romello, please don't stop."

He doubles his efforts and adds another finger while increasing his tempo. Massaging that same spot through the still-blossoming orgasm until I feel my body ready for another.

I brace myself by grabbing the edges of the table, my back arched off the flat surface completely, placing my clit directly where I need it most. Just as he hooks his fingers up and sucks a bit too hard, I feel my legs tremble.

He stops.

I sit up and look at his cat-ate-the-canary smile glistening with my juices.

"I think we should save that one for when my cock is deep inside you. The only choice you need to make is if you want to watch it slip inside or feel it as I press inside you from behind."

"Both. I need both."

He chuckled lightly. "I have a condom in my briefcase. One sec."

"Actually, I'm allergic to latex. I have an IUD, and I'm clean. If that's okay?"

When he turns to look back at me, the look of a deadly predator spreads across his face. The hunter has found his prey and is going feral with the scent of blood in the air.

"You have no idea how hard that just made me. It's more than okay. I absolutely love the idea of fucking you raw."

He walks back to me, pulling his belt from the loops and unbuttoning his slacks. His cock emerges from his pants, revealing that he was commando this whole time. I can feel my jaw drop, but I do nothing to hide it.

"Like what you see, kitten?"

My mouth waters, so I swallow hard and manage only to make an appreciative hum.

"How about we put this bed to good use?" He picks me up with his hard cock bobbing between my legs and tosses me onto the bed. I bounce up once before landing somewhere near the middle. His hands clamp around my ankles, and they are held above his head while he lines himself up.

"Are you ready for this?"

"Yes."

My one-word answer is barely finished when the "es" noise turns into a hiss as his large dick stretches me until he is fully sheathed inside me. I watch as every inch glides straight into my already sensitive and slightly swollen core. The tremors of the orgasm he stole from me are pulsing around his veiny cock.

He sits there inside of me for a moment while he peppers kisses all over my chest and nipples. When he starts to move, I almost feel that orgasm again, ready to explode.

Almost.

He stops his motion as soon as I clamp down.

"Ah, ah. Not yet. You said both," he chides.

He draws out of me, and with a swift motion, he flips me on all fours on the bed and presses down on my lower back with his large hand, creating a larger arch from me and an easier entry for him.

I can feel his fist between us, along with his thick head pressing at my entrance. When I press back into him, he lets out a noise somewhere between a growl and a moan. The sound has my already wet core grow impossibly more slick for him.

Slap.

I'm surely going to have a mark in the shape of his hand after that crack to my ass. Then, he soothes the sting away with small circles that are in time with his slow, steady strokes.

"You feel so fucking good, Wynter."

"Harder. Please, Romello. Make me cum, please?" My voice is bordering on a whine with how much I am begging him to let me cum. I want to hit that cliff and explode with the orgasm he has denied me.

"You have no idea what that does to me. Fuck, it's so fucking hot."

He's not even winded. I'm not sure that I can even keep up with him and he's nearly twice my age. He keeps a punishing pace, his thighs slapping against my own. His dick is so deep inside me that I can hardly tell where I end and he begins. When I arch even further so that I can peer over my shoulder at him, he finally hits that tender spot inside of me. I don't dare move. I want this, need this.

"Say it again, baby. Say my name again," he says through gritted teeth. His tempo is still set to rabbit rather than the turtle he started with. A bead of sweat rolling down his forehead grabs my attention, and I lick my lips.

"Fuck me, Romello-oh-oh-ohhhhh!"

His grip on my ass cheeks spreads them wider, and he gains that much more purchase entering me to the point his pubic bone is pushing into my skin. He reaches his climax just as I see white stars flashing in front of my eyes. I'm holding my breath but can't seem to tell my body to stop and breathe.

My legs shake, and I can't hold myself up any longer. Before I fall to the duvet, his arms band around me, holding me to him while he fills me with hot pulses. The sensation is so much more than I ever could have imagined. His hand around my throat holds me close to his chest while he sucks on the sensitive skin behind my ear.

He slips out of me and taps the head of his dick on the top of my ass cheek before smearing that last vestige of cum across the surface.

"Fuck, kitten," he says with a sideways grin on his face. "Let me go get a washcloth, don't move."

I watch while he hops up and walks with his still semi-hard cock bobbing in front of him toward the bathroom. His round ass is perfect and on full display, like two perfect scoops of ice cream, and the cones are his delicious thighs. Proof that this man has never skipped leg day.

A moment later he's walking out of the small bathroom with a hand towel and a washrag.

"I made a bit of a mess." He actually seems sheepish for a split second before his uber-confidence returns.

Ever the gentleman, he watches me watch him as he cleans up our combined mess and dries me off. He then lies down next to me and pitches the soiled linens toward the bathroom door.

His arms wrap around me, one between my breasts and the other around my belly. Holding me close in the big spoon, little spoon position. His cock resting perfectly between my thighs.

I twist in his arms and inhale his scent, feeling his heart thud against mine.

I look deeply into his eyes and kiss him gently on his lower lip.

He returns the gesture and deepens the kiss, then places a gentle little kiss to the tip of my nose.

We part slowly, foreheads still resting against each other.

"What happens now?" I whisper.

"For us...or them?"

"Both."

"We wait and see."

Chapter Eleven

In the days that follow, the scandal breaks wide open. News outlets explode with coverage of Zenith's corruption. Arrests are made, and policies begin to change, favoring transparency and women's health rights. The drug trials are halted for all of Zenith's products. The paperwork for all drugs that have passed trials is temporarily restricted until the rightful owners can be reinstated.

We found out that Mia's drug during the trial was actually not the same one they were suppressing. When the information was originally leaked that there was a contraceptive with no side effects, there was one small detail that didn't make it out with the rumor itself. Mia's doctor had been paid off to put her in a trial that didn't exist just as a means to an end. To get to me.

The trials that I was investigating were for a new contraceptive, true, but the one they had been suppressing was for men. With the FDA approval for that drug already completed and no side effects whatsoever, they would have lost millions, if not billions, on the hefty list of women's contraceptives already on the market. Or so they thought.

They quickly pushed up another drug to take its place, which is why I assume Mia got the appetite suppressant side effect. They skipped weeks of pre-trials and proper documentation requirements. I would never have known as much as I do now if Romello hadn't allowed me to join in with his covert operation.

The real reason she was in the hospital, though, was still me. They had "slipped a mickey" in her trial pack that was an extremely high dose of estrogen, which caused another blood clot to form in her lung; she nearly died because of me. They were using her as leverage, to get to me. To silence me.

The sad part of all of this is that the drug approved by the FDA as a contraceptive for men will likely sit in litigation for years before it ever sees the light of day. Men could take a pill every day, much like women do, but with no hormones interfering and no side effects whatsoever. The trials said that people with a placebo complained of headache, dry mouth, and other things, while those on the drug reported none. None at all.

Nobody knows that Romello isn't just another rich CEO. He hid his involvement well, and with me as the "fall guy" for the exposure and the story leak, nobody will ever know. Yeah, he needs to find another job, but his multi-million dollar pension says that he has plenty of time to look around.

This news from Zenith won't tarnish his record because, of course, he had no knowledge of the misdeeds—not publicly. He was brought on to run the business, not any of the criminal activity.

Mia still needs some time until her strength fully returns. We visit the park together, the scent of blooming flowers and fresh-cut grass revitalizing our spirits. I walk next to her slowly until we get to the nearest bench. She has to take blood thinners and has a portable oxygen device until the blood clot in her lung dissolves.

"I'm proud of you," she says, squeezing my hand.

"Couldn't have done it without you," I reply with a smile.

Romello joins us, bringing coffee and pastries. There's a lightness to him now, a freedom.

"Ladies." He nods his head at Mia and winks at me.

As we sit together, I feel a sense of peace. The future is uncertain, but for now, there's hope.

Epilogue

S tanding outside the now-abandoned Zenith Corp building, I take a deep breath. There is a small white sign taped to the inside of the glass that says:

PROTECTED BY LIVE SECURITY SURVEILLANCE

I have to laugh at the absurdity of a huge skyscraper with dozens of floors fully occupied last week, and now only a few security guards remain on the premises.

The air is crisp, carrying the scent of possibility. Romello joins me, slipping his hand into mine. A forehead kiss follows.

"Ready for the next adventure?" he asks.

I glance at him, a smile tugging at my lips. "Always."

He opens the door of the sleek black car. "Your chariot awaits, m'lady."

With Zenith taken down, this battle had been won, but the war is never over. Women will always have to fight for their rights until there is true equality.

I will carry this RAGE inside of me, the embers of a fire burning eternally. A Woman's work is never done.

THE END

Did this story make you feel something? Don't let the connection end here. Visit https://linktr.ee/k.roseauthor now to explore more stories, exclusive updates, and ways to stay in touch. I'd love to hear what you think!

About the Author

K. Rose has been a part of the Indie Author Community for years. Getting her start as a reader, her keen eye led to a wonderful career in Beta and ARC (Advance Reader Copy) reading. As a joke to her fellow Beta colleagues, she created a spoofed blurb and cover for a story, and the feedback was so positive that it sparked her to run with it.

SOCIAL MEDIA:

Website – http://www.kroseauthor.net

Newsletter – https://geni.us/KRoseNewsletter

Link Tree – https://linktr.ee/k.roseauthor

Facebook Group – https://www.facebook.com/groups/krosesgardenofmischief

Savage Heirs

By: Maisie Kane

About Savage Heirs

My brother's best friends are powerful men, but I'm a secret weapon.

Trying on the bridesmaid dress for my brother's wedding should be simple. Instead, I'm kidnapped and locked in a trunk with two oversized strangers.

Only, it turns out they aren't strangers at all: Liam and Xander haunt my childhood memories, future heirs to their families' criminal empires.

They have no idea why I'm trapped here with them.

I do. Despite the gown, I'm no princess locked in a tower—I'm a goddamn warrior queen.

And in this story, I'm the one doing the rescuing.

Content Notes:

This is a violent story meant for readers 18+. Specific concerns include, but are not limited to: alcohol consumption/abuse, assault, attempted murder, blood, cancer, captivity/confinement, car accident, child soldiers, cheating (not any of our leads), death, fisticuffs, gang violence, group sex, gun violence, kidnapping, knife violence, mafia/mob/cartel/triad/bratva/organized crime, murder, and violence–just in general...a lot of violence.

In short, there will be blood, there will be dirt, and the bad guys take down the worse guys. There is an excellent sexy celebration to cap it off and a HFN ending for our leading lady and her two men.

Relationship type: MFM

Chapter One
Cece

Being locked in a trunk should probably upset me more than it does.

The thing is, the third time you've been kidnapped, it's more annoying than scary.

Should I be terrified? Yeah. That'd be smart. Instead, I'm pissed at myself. I mean, it's my own damn fault for being distracted by the hideous bridesmaid dress my brother Eddie's fiancée had picked out. I know better than to get distracted in public. But seriously. The damn thing is peach. And poofy.

I'm barely five feet tall. Poofy is not for me. I look like I'm a seven-year-old playing princess instead of the future head of a criminal empire.

Which might be why Nat picked it out, now that I think about it. She was a little salty to find out that my brother wasn't the heir we want the world to think he is. Luckily, he's on my side, so I don't have to worry about getting stabbed in the back in my own home. Or, at least, not by Eduardo. The jury's still out on Natalia.

The car hits a bump and I slam into the top of the cargo space, cursing. "I never thought I'd complain that a trunk was too big, but I'm flying around back here."

The driver doesn't answer, just continues belting along with middling success to Pink's "So What?" on repeat. We've been driving long enough for me to know exactly when his voice is going to crack. And...yup. There it is.

As if the gods of kidnapping victims hear me, the car takes a sharp right, throwing me to the side as I try my best to brace myself with my bound hands and feet, then slams to a halt, my head cracking against the wheel well. The music, thankfully, stops as the car turns off, the creak of the door telling me the driver is out of the vehicle. I wait to be pulled from my dark box, but nothing happens.

Nothing happens for so long that I debate a nap. At least they took me on a nice night—not too hot or cold. It's downright comfortable in this trunk.

Sleep's whispering when the trunk opens, the bright light of headlights blinding me, preventing me from taking a well-aimed swing. I'm jammed into the tiny part at the back, and before I can scramble to the front for a shot at freedom, two more loads are tossed in, the trunk clicking shut to the sounds of masculine cursing.

An elbow gets me in the sternum, and I yelp. "Careful, bony."

"Shit, there's somebody else in here," a male voice murmurs.

"No wonder it's so damn tight," another man says, this guy's voice lower and gruffer than the first.

"Are you telling me they just shoved not one, not two, but three people into the same trunk? Who the fuck are these idiots?" I mutter.

The car turns on, Pink belting out the same bop, the driver joining with his unpracticed yodels. "What the fuck is that?" the gruffer voice asks.

"Pinky will serenade us for however long we're shoved in here," I reply.

This time, when we hit a bump, I don't fly around, but I do get that elbow again, this time into my cheek. "Ow," I whine. "Can we shift around so I don't end up losing an eye every time we hit a pothole?"

The bony guy answers, his tone light. "I'm wedged in here pretty damn tight, but I'll see what I can do. Make sure you're tucked in before I move."

I press my back against the seats behind me. "Your turn."

"My head is opposite yours and we're back-to-back," the deeper voice says. "We should try to kneel on our sides, so our legs have space. Tuck our heads into the backs of each other's knees."

"On it," the other guy says, and after a whole lot of wiggling and cursing, they must get set up in a way that works for them. Unfortunately, what works for them has the guy closest to me wedging his face into my boobs.

"Is this okay?" he asks, his breath tickling my chest.

"It's better than losing an eye, so I can't complain. You comfy?" I ask.

"Very," he answers, the grin in his voice evident, even over the painful sing-shouts about fighting coming from the front of the vehicle.

"So, first time?" I ask, not sure how to pass time in a trunk with two men, one of them getting very up close and personal with a sensitive part of my anatomy. His proximity is making my nipples hard, and if I didn't know how weird bodies can be under stress, I'd be more concerned about how turned on I'm getting.

"You say that like this is just an ordinary Tuesday," gruff voice says.

"I mean, I wouldn't say this is an ordinary Tuesday, but this sort of thing happens." *Especially when you're the secret heir to a criminal empire.*

Bony laughs, and it vibrates through me like electricity. "I like you. Chill under pressure."

"Or delusional," the other voice adds from somewhere down by my knees.

I'd shrug if I could. Instead, I click my tongue. "I'm in complete control of my faculties."

"I take it this isn't your first kidnapping?" happy guy says.

"Nope. Third."

"Maybe you need to do better keeping yourself safe," Grumps says.

"I was a kid the first two times. This one was a bit of a fuckup, though, I'll admit. How'd you two get nabbed?"

"Car accident. They dragged us out while we were stunned. You?" Happy asks.

"I was trying on a hideous dress for my brother's wedding. Stole me right out the back door before my security even noticed."

"Is that why there's all this extra fluff down here?" Happy asks, tugging on the tulle of the ridiculous gown with his bound hands, the backs of my knuckles registering the movement of his forearms, our skin burning where it touches. I try my best to ignore it. Not the time. Not the place.

"Yup. I'm embarrassingly princessy right now."

"Could use a little less fabric and a little more leg room," gripes the other guy.

"I think we could all stand for a little more leg room. No need for the attitude," I say.

He scoffs, and Happy pipes in with a stage whisper. "He's six four. This trunk situation is pretty dire for him, I imagine."

"Damn. I've only known one guy that tall. He was a bit of an asshole, too," I mock whisper back, thinking about one of my brother's friends and a major crush of my preteen years.

"I can hear you. And who isn't an asshole when they've been in a head on collision then stuffed into a trunk with a chatty debutante?"

"I'm no debutante! I'm a grown-ass woman, I'll have you know."

"Sure feels like it," Happy says, nuzzling the crevice between my boobs.

"Buy a girl dinner first," I tease, liking what he's doing, wishing this were an entirely different encounter.

"I'm a little tied up right now, but I promise I'll take you for a fun night out as soon as we're free. Deal?" His hands find my knee under the tulle and give it a surprisingly comforting squeeze.

"Deal," pops out of my mouth before I can fully vet my response, but really, his hands against my skin feel like they were made for getting me all riled up. A date might be nice. At least I know we have chemistry.

Grump scoffs. "Only you would find a date locked in a trunk, Liu." Liu? *Funny. My brother's playboy best friend's last name is Liu.*

Liu laughs. "You're just jealous you didn't get tossed in first, O'Connell. Then you could have your face pressed into the sweetest smelling set of tits I've ever been blessed to know."

O'Connell? No, no, no. Not Liam, "I had a crush on him when I was eleven and he was seventeen," O'Connell. Not possible.

"Liam O'Connell? Xander Liu?" I squeak out.

"I see my reputation precedes me," Xander says, but my ears are buzzing as the panic I wasn't feeling earlier hits me all at once.

"Who's asking," Liam demands.

It takes all my courage to respond. "Cece. Cecilia Rodriguez. Eddie's little sister."

"Oh fuck," Xander breathes out, my nipples not getting the memo that this is dire.

But if that statement doesn't sum this situation up, nothing does.

Chapter Two
Xander

My face is jammed into Eddie's sister's tits, and if that doesn't guarantee my death on the lucky day all three of us get out of this alive, I'm not sure what else would.

And because I'm sometimes an idiot when it comes to nice tits, I burrow in farther. "Eddie can't kill me twice," I mumble, liking the way her breath catches when I press a careful kiss to the side of one swell.

"Maybe not, but, um, maybe we should talk about this?" Cece says, panic lacing her tone. So getting kidnapped has her cool as a cucumber, but her brother's best friend nuzzling her tits has her freaking out? That means she likes what I'm doing. I can work with that.

"What's there to talk about? Nothing's changed. We're all still locked in a trunk together," I say, trying to shove aside more of the fabric pinned around her legs.

"Yeah, but you're the heir to the triad, right?"

This stalls my attempt to get more of her skin under my fingers. "What of it?"

"And Liam, you're the Irish mob heir, right?"

Liam grunts, not wasting words when an animal sound would suffice.

"This isn't good."

"If they'd caught Eddie, we'd be a full set," I say, figuring out what she's getting at.

"If they'd caught Eddie, we'd be dealing with an outsider," she says instead of agreeing with me.

"How so?" Liam demands.

"It's not important," she says, her breath tickling the hairs on the top of my head. "What's important is that we're dealing with somebody who has knowledge about not one family, but all the families. They must have known you two were on your way to Eddie's bachelor party."

"Whoever it is, they'll die for this," Liam says, and I try to nod, forgetting that the movement just has my face rubbing against Cece's soft skin. Which, all things considered, isn't such a bad fuck up. She smells like something heady and deep, a scent that would cling to my sheets and make me hard every time I caught a whiff.

The thought alone makes me hard. Which is pretty damn awkward, as I'm locked in a trunk with my best friend's baby sister and my other best friend's bony ass digging into my spine.

Cece doesn't notice, what with all the fluff between the two of us. And something about a hard on rubbing against her shins is epically unsexy, so I guess it's a blessing in disguise.

Unknowing of my internal struggle, Cece responds to Liam. "Obviously they're going to die. Even so, this isn't your run-of-the-mill kidnapping. This is serious."

"So, what do we do about it?" I ask, the car jostling us all, my shoulders and elbows smacking the top and bottom of the car as it levels out again. The pain reduces my hard on. Some. "I mean, besides hunt the bastards down once we're free."

"Get me a gun and put me at the front of the line," Cece says, and I'm even more intrigued. Not freaked out by the unknown and ready to jump into the bloodshed? With one hell of a pair of tits? If I imagine my dream woman, those traits would be right at the top of my list.

Liam scoffs again, and I can almost hear Cece rolling her eyes at him. "I'll bet you a grand I'm a better shot than you are," she says.

Liam laughs this time. "Fine, princess. I'll take your money if you're so willing to throw it away."

"I'm not a goddamn princess. And when we get out of here, I'd be happy to prove it to you," she responds.

"And I'll watch the show," I say, taking another whiff of the woman like a creep. What is it about her?

I try to remember what Eddie's baby sister looked like, and all I've got is a tiny spitfire with eyes ready to kill. Which was probably weird on an elementary schooler, but hey, our world fucks up the best of us. When Eddie's big brother disappeared in the middle of the night, nobody in that family took it well. They lost their heir and the heart of the next generation of Rodriguez cartel kids in one fell swoop. Add a dead mom, and yeah. Of course she was ready to do some damage to the world. It's not like it was on her side.

What I never would have guessed, though, is that the same angry girl would end up stuffed in a trunk with me. And I sure as shit shouldn't be sniffing her cleavage like an addict.

Eddie's as loyal as they come. I don't want to fuck that up, no matter how sweet his sister smells. Or the way she's oscillating between cool and furious while locked in a trunk. Girl's got steel ovaries, that's for sure.

I guess that hasn't changed.

Liam shifts, his leg twitching and smacking my head. "From what I remember, I'm twice your size, Rodriguez. You don't stand a chance."

"Size isn't everything," she says.

I try not to say anything. I really do. But I've got a fucking hard on while stuffed in a trunk. I can't let that go. "Size ain't a problem for me, sweet thing," I mock whisper.

Liam's elbow gets me on the hip, but I can't stop laughing at my joke. And after a second, Cece joins me. "You're absurd," she says.

"But plenty big, if you want to give it a go."

"Damn it, stop hitting on Eddie's baby sister, Xander," Liam barks as the car bounces and bobbles over something that is not a paved road.

"We've got to pass the time somehow," I say. "Might as well enjoy ourselves." And I give another little kiss to the side of her other boob, once again enjoying the way her breath hitches.

"My brother warned me about you, Xander," she says, her breath a little reedy. She's definitely into what I have to offer.

"Warnings are just intriguing advertisements," I say.

This startles a laugh out of her, and before I can see how willing she is to play, the car comes to a halt. Well, that sucks. Hopefully, we're not one step closer to death.

One never knows about these things.

At least I know I can take down a few of these assholes on my way out.

Liam shifts behind me. "Game face, Liu."

"Don't need to tell me twice, O'Connell."

And we wait.

Chapter Three
Cece

I'm starting to get the hype around Xander Liu. The combination of charm and consideration, matched with a giant dose of humor and soft lips that make my heart stutter, well, I'm already half sold. I'd assumed it was his devil may care attitude and Hollywood good looks that gave him his fan club. I may have underestimated his appeal.

Then again, I was team Liam O'Connell for more years than I care to admit. It's a damn shame he's grown into an antisocial asshole. I don't need that kind of attitude while I'm jammed in a trunk and heading toward a kidnapper who has somehow figured out my family's closest guarded secret: me.

So, he'd better get his act together soon. One good deed shouldn't gift him an eternity of my lenience.

But still.

As we wait for the kidnappers to do whatever they plan to do next, the car blessedly silent after hours of Pink on repeat, I can't help but remember the moment he earned my childish devotion.

Me, so lost after my brother Oz left, then Mama leaving, too. Not that she had a choice. That cancer ate her up from the inside out before anybody even realized she was sick. Eleven years old and I'd lost the two people I'd loved the most. It would make anybody act crazy. It's the only thing that makes sense.

Late one night, my skin tight and my mind a mess, I snuck out to the pool, diving in wearing my pink and neon green tie-dye pajamas I'd made at summer camp. I left the pool lights off, not wanting to draw attention to myself, and I sank to the bottom, needing the weight of the water against my skin.

Wanting a hug from my mom so badly that I was seeking it from the deep end of the swimming pool. I stayed down there long enough that my chest ached. When arms wrapped around me from behind, I panicked, my imagination conjuring electric eels instead of help.

I fought against them until the heat of a body at my back registered. It took longer than it would have if I'd just rocketed myself up, and by the time we broke the surface, I was dizzy from holding my breath for so long.

Liam, seventeen, lanky and long-haired, swam us to the edge and tossed me onto the concrete like I weighed nothing.

"What the hell were you doing?" he hissed, hauling himself out beside me, his submerged tennis shoes wobbly blobs of white under the waves in the faint light from the landscaping lamps.

"Swimming."

He gazed down at me, his eyes covered in shadows. "Bullshit, Rodriguez."

Nobody had called me on my shit in months. It had been almost a year since Oz disappeared, and the reminder of my oldest brother's take no shit attitude was just too much.

I broke down, the first time I'd cried since Mama's funeral, and after a while, Liam wrapped one arm awkwardly around my shoulders. It wasn't a hug, but it was more than I'd had in what felt like an eternity to my eleven-year-old self.

He said nothing else, and I was okay with that. I don't know if I would have fallen in love with him so completely if he had.

Instead, I wiped my tears, slipped from under his arm, whispered, "Thank you," and sprinted back to my room, likely leaving wet footprints the whole damn way.

From then on, I was smitten. Every time Liam came around, I'd spy on him, never where he could catch me, but always watching. The way he only laughed when it was really earned, usually at some crazy thing Xander said or did. The way his eyes would cloud every time he looked at the pool or when Eddie brought up his dad. And his routine of sneaking out back with a bottle of something expensive, needing a break from even his best friends.

Eventually, the boys graduated high school, and Liam came around less. Eddie moved out after college, I got my first boyfriend at sixteen, and that was that. Crush gone.

It's been six years since I last saw Liam O'Connell and Xander Liu. A lot can change in that time.

I know I did. At twenty-two, I'm nothing like the girl they remember.

I'm tougher. I can take care of myself in ways they couldn't guess, and there's a good chance I've got as much blood on my hands as they do, if not more.

Now when I go for a swim, I do it like a normal person, stroking across the top of the water or lounging on floaties in a bikini with a drink and my friends.

The trunk flies open, snapping me out of my memories. Not surprising me at all, the lumpy shadow of Liam flings himself at whoever is waiting. The unmistakable sound of a scuffle makes it into the trunk as Xander twists and wiggles to the edge, making space for me to follow.

Then, the crack of gunfire rings out, and Xander freezes, his bound hands raised in awkward supplication, half out of the trunk.

"Is Liam down?" I yelp, terror whooshing to my toes.

I might not like what I've heard from him so far, but I have zero desire for the guy to die.

"Shot, not fatally," Xander answers, all business, his feet trying to push me farther back into the trunk to safety. "Let me tend to him," he says to whoever is out there.

"Out, but no helping him," the familiar voice of Pinky directs, and moving slowly, not spooking the gun toting bad guy, Xander rolls out of the trunk, landing without much grace on the ground. "Cartel, you tend to him," Pinky says.

I've never been straight up called by my family's business before, and the casual drop verifies what I've feared. They know *exactly* who I am.

I scoot to the edge, taking a moment to evaluate my surroundings. Gray scrubby plants and rocks descending into nothingness as the mountain falls away from the plateau we're parked on. The lights of LA are not visible on the horizon.

Nowhere near home.

Xander squirms over to Liam and presses on the bullet hole, despite the guard's orders. Liam glares at Pinky, begging for a fight even as blood soaks through his designer jeans below his knee.

Not fatal, but he's not making his escape by foot anytime soon.

Choosing expediency over grace, I fling myself from the trunk, landing with a grunt, then drag myself by my elbows to Liam's damaged leg. "Any first aid supplies?" I ask Pinky. He doesn't even swing the gun toward me, focused on the guys instead.

I work best when I'm underestimated, so I'm not going to complain about the lack of respect.

The guard nods at my dress. "You've got more than enough bandages there."

"Have you ever tried to tear silk? It's the strongest fabric out there."

He just glares, so I flip up the ridiculous skirt and start yanking the underskirt loose. It's tulle-free where it touches my thighs—some silky synthetic that stands a better chance of removal. Not that it'll do much to absorb the blood. Luckily, Xander figures that out without me saying anything and strips off his burgundy T-shirt, tearing it apart so he can jam it against the wound.

If we were in a less dire situation, I'd take more than a moment to admire the grown-up version of Xander Liu that's across from me.

Because, yum.

A gunshot wound takes precedence, though, so I force myself to focus.

It takes long enough for me to yank the tulle off that I'm wondering if they'd prefer Liam bleed out over my helping him, but eventually, I get the dang thing free. Xander works with me to tie it tight, his dark eyes serious, each of us one-half of a functioning set of arms as we squeeze the fabric between Liam's bound legs. Damn zipties.

The way his muscles bunch and flex even while doing this small task is distracting, though.

Business first, Cece, I chide myself. Twisting to survey what's on the other side of the car, my heart plummets. Because what's there is something no kidnapped criminal ever wants to see: the iron gates of a cemetery.

Chapter Four

Cece

Shit.

A cemetery doesn't bode well for us.

"You, get him to the gate," the guard says, motioning for Xander to drag Liam to the entrance of the cemetery.

"How? I don't have much in the way of hands or feet here, man."

"I don't care. Just do it."

I hate to say it, but I preferred it when this guy was singing.

"I'll help," I volunteer, partially to not leave Xander in a lurch, but also to gauge what the guard will do. He doesn't seem to mind, so I wiggle alongside Liam. "Put your arms above your head. Xander and I can slide our arms through and drag you along."

Liam's typically pale skin is a sickly paper white, his now shorter, barely brown hair soaked with sweat, a trickle tracing over the handful of freckles that I assumed would have faded with adulthood. He nods, then Xander and I loop our arms through, the three of us making painful, awkward progress across the gravel parking lot.

Once we reach the gate, the guard motions for Xander to wiggle into the graveyard. Then, keeping the gun on Xander, the guard leans down and zip ties Liam and me to the gate by our bound wrists.

Now that Liam and I are contained, he points the gun at me as he latches Xander's hands against one leg with a zip tie under his knee. Xander effectively hobbled, he cuts his ankles free. "Up. Walk," he barks.

Xander gets to his feet and starts a slow, half-bent shuffle into the graveyard, a spotlight in the distance signaling the destination, the shadow of a backhoe shouting that this is the end.

The fact that there are two other cars in the lot doesn't help me figure out how to get out of this mess. More people, likely more guns, and what must be three pre-dug graves waiting for us. Mob, Triad, and Cartel, all cut loose without heirs, a power vacuum created in a single night under the sliver of a new-ish moon.

I'd appreciate how well planned this was if I wasn't going to die tonight.

Xander must be thinking along the same lines. "Say Cece?" he calls.

"Yeah?"

"You owe me a date, this life or the next, got it?"

On an impulse, I shimmy to standing, then lean forward and loop my thumbs in the top of the obnoxious strapless dress and yank down, my boobs falling free. "I can't guarantee this package in the next life, so aim for this one," I call out, not liking that he's already accepted there's probably no way out of this.

He whistles, winking as he shuffles past the first line of headstones. "I'll keep that in mind, sweet thing."

Liam makes a choked sound, drawing my attention, only to find he's transfixed by the boobage that's now dangling over his face. Not that it's super clear, what with my arms zip tied to an iron bar, but still. It's a pretty enough picture, I suppose. "This isn't for you, O'Connell," I say.

"Even if I'm a dying man?"

"We're all dying. It's just a matter of when." I go to shimmy the fabric back up, but his hand on my ankle stalls the motion.

"Don't."

"You really think you're dying?"

"It took a hell of a long time to get that bandage on."

"I warned the guy. He didn't listen. I can't say I'd choose this monstrosity of a dress for my next kidnapping." I flop down on my butt beside Liam's arms.

"Planning on another trip in a trunk?"

"If it means I made it through this one, then yeah."

He goes quiet. I can't blame him. We're all crime kids—we learned how to calculate odds before we learned long division, and it's easy to see the odds aren't in our favor tonight.

The chattering howls of coyotes in the distance have a shiver running down my spine, but I opt to keep my boobs out for the time being. Just in case they *are* his last pair.

The dress was strangling them, anyway.

"Can I ask a question?" Liam asks, his voice quiet and deep, a comfort that I wish I had more time to enjoy.

"Shoot."

"Why'd you do it?"

"Flash Xander? Because he needs something to fight for, even if this situation is hopeless."

"Not that. Not now. Why'd you try to drown yourself when you were a little kid?"

"Oh. That." I scoot forward, resting my chin on my knees, the silk pooling around my waist, the dress fluid against my skin now that I've lost the annoying fluff. "I wasn't trying to drown myself."

"What else could it have been?"

"Honestly?"

"Please. It's bugged me for years."

I sigh. "I just really missed being hugged. And the bottom of the pool was as close as I could get."

The silence lets murmured conversation from the other side of the graveyard reach my ears, something about one voice tickling my memory, but not enough for me to place it.

Liam's thumb brushes the inside of my wrist, and the gentleness has tears pooling in my eyes. I blink them away, staring over the canyon between this mountain and the next.

"I should have given you a real hug that night. Not that half-assed thing I did."

"It was more than I'd had in forever. It helped enough for me to make it through the worst of the grief."

"Still. Maybe if I'd given you a real hug, you wouldn't have been such a creeper, Rodriguez."

"Creeper? Me? How so?"

"You thought you were so good at hiding from us, but Xander always picked you out. He teased me for years about your little girl crush on me."

Thank god it's night, or I'd be roughly the same color as the dress I'm not really wearing right now. "I refuse to believe that either of you ever saw me. Otherwise, I will have to go back in time and remove myself from literally years of my memories."

He laughs, and because it's Liam, I know it's earned. "It was kind of cute, at least when Xander wasn't giving me shit about it."

"You're not helping."

"I'm just saying, in the interest of honesty, before we meet our maker, that you were a cute little creeper."

"Thanks, I guess."

"But Cece?"

"Yeah?" I glance down at him.

"From where I'm lying, you grew up into one hell of a beautiful woman."

Chapter Five
Liam

Even in the half-light, zip-tied to a post and leaking more blood than is healthy, I can see Cece's dark eyes get big with the compliment.

But it's true.

The scrawny, angry kid I remember has turned into something no less vicious, but clad in curves that any reasonable man would be happy to have his hands on.

Always willing to stand up to the men in her life, her three big brothers, and fuck, even her dad, swore she would fight to the death for what she wanted, for what she thought was right. Eddie warned us not to get on her bad side. And somehow, I'd ended up on the other end of the spectrum with her.

For the first time, I'm grateful I'm not on her shit list. Because if anybody is going to get out of this shit-show, it's Cece Rodriguez. If I'm lucky, she'll get Xander out of this, too.

And that's the best-case scenario. There's no way I can run right now.

So, knowing that I have no right to ask, no right to risk Eddie's wrath, I voice what I've been thinking about since I'd been shoved into a goddamn trunk with an unreasonably brave, chatty woman. "A kiss from a beautiful woman for a dying man ought to be a no-brainer. Want to give it a go?"

I'm not as suave as Xander. Never have been. Never will be. But that doesn't mean I don't go for what I want.

And Cece Rodriguez is exactly what I want.

Instead of bending over, giving me a better view of those beautiful tits Xander was lucky enough to be burrowed into, and pressing those pillowy lips to mine, she throws her head back, her laughter loud and unexpected.

"You're not dying, O'Connell. Not on my watch."

Well, if I doubted that her crush was good and gone, that doubt's been put to rest. And now I'm the one pining. "Maybe not from the bullet wound in my leg, but you and I both know there are pre-dug graves waiting for us."

She tilts her head, a heavy hank of hair sliding over her shoulder, brushing the tops of those swells in a way that makes my fingertips itch. "True."

She shrugs, then in careful, tiny movements, she half drapes herself across my chest, her breasts heating my skin through my shirt as her face hovers above me. "I always wondered what it would be like to kiss you."

With no preamble, she lowers her head, and at the first press of her lips to mine, she's captured me completely. My arms yank against my restraints, trying to get my hands on her. Instead, I drag us both closer to the gate, gravel digging deeper into my back. The burn hardly registers as I run my tongue along the seam of her lips, wanting to taste her. Wanting so much more than to just carefully kiss her like a virgin at junior prom.

And with a hum that has me half hard, she lets me in.

It's just a kiss, just lips and tongue, the angle slightly off kilter. It should be an awkward, half-assed thing. Instead, it's everything.

Every soft press of her lips against mine, every sweep and dance of our tongues, her feathery breaths against my cheeks, it's a magic spell cast over me.

When she eventually pulls away, I chase her, nipping at her bottom lip for daring to end the enchantment.

She smirks, a little less dread in her gaze. "That was unexpected."

"How so?"

"How often does a kiss with a childhood crush end up better than you imagined?"

I bark out a laugh, wishing this were any other situation. That I'd re-met Cece at Eddie's wedding, asked her to dance, stolen her out into the night and ravaged her mouth in some wholly inappropriate locale, while a part of me worried Eddie would find us and kill me.

Even that anxiety laden dream would have been so much better than tonight.

"I guess we all have something to live for now."

She scoots back, leaning against the iron bars with one shoulder. I already miss the warmth of her pressed against me. Even if I still have a perfect view of her boobs, the piles of peach fabric pooled at the top of her soft-looking thighs.

"Any chance you have a knife hidden somewhere on you?" she asks, ignoring my comment.

"They stripped me of all my weapons before they threw us in the trunk."

She sighs. "Of course I'd get nabbed while dressed like a cartoon princess and totally unarmed. Any sharp rocks digging into your back?"

"None more than the others. And my back is probably closer to ground beef than flesh after being dragged over here."

"Gross."

I chuckle. "Kiss it better?"

The crack of a gun has my grin falling, my chest immediately tight with fear.

And a shock of fury and grief.

Xander has been the only salvation in my godforsaken life. I've needed his brand of lightness to survive the years of darkness in my father's house. If that shot took him out, well, you don't need a functioning leg to shoot a man in the head.

Chapter Six
Cece

The gunshot isn't unexpected, but damn, does it hurt.

Straining to listen, I make out shouting in the distance, masculine, and surprisingly, feminine joined in angry, panicked sounds drifting over the gravestones. The floodlight in the distance wobbles before righting itself.

Not a death sentence, then. Probably. It looks more like a scuffle where a gun went off.

Xander had better be okay. I've spent half my life listening to the exploits of one Alexander Liu, and I want in. The older sisters of a few classmates dated him, and based on the rumor mill, he's worth it.

To prepare for whatever happens next, I plaster myself against the bar I'm attached to and get my boobs contained. I don't want them flopping around if I have to prove why I'm next in line to lead the cartel. And if the dress has one saving grace, it's that it's tight enough to act like a sports bra.

Then I double down on looking for a way free from this post. Liam is mumbling something furious about retribution and death, and I'm right there with him. Although, I'm not sure what he's going to do with a bloody leg, mangled back, and a likely concussion, based on his griping in the trunk. He's got size on his side, but besides that, if anybody is going to exact vengeance, it's more likely me than him.

Looking down at my dress, I have an idea. A crazy one, but better than just sitting here hoping that we live.

"Liam, I'm going to ask you to do something really weird."

"Will it let me get out of here and fuck shit up?"

"Hopefully. I think there's steel boning in this corset. Can you chew a piece free? I can use it to break the zip ties."

"You want me to chew through your dress?"

"Hopefully?"

"Didn't you say that silk is the toughest fabric?"

"Yup. But I'm hoping your teeth are sharp. Once there's a hole, we should be able to wiggle the wire out."

He huffs, then lifts his chin. "Okay then. Get down here."

I flop myself over him, and as his teeth dig into the fabric, I can't help the way my breath gets tight. Because it's all too easy to imagine him doing something similar, only without a few layers of silk between us. The fabric gets wet, and I'm embarrassed when I do, too.

I want to say something to break the tension humming between us, but it's not like he can say anything back. Instead, I watch him, like the creep he accused me of being. His hair is dark with sweat from the pain he's feeling, but not acknowledging. Those freckles are begging for tiny kisses, his blue eyes earnest as he gnaws at my dress.

I shift my lower half, trying to get in a less painful position, and my thigh brushes against his obvious erection. "Shit," I mutter, even more turned on knowing he isn't unaffected.

His eyes flick to mine, and the longer we stare at each other, the hotter I get, my breath ragged just from the force of his gaze.

Then his tongue slips from between his lips, circling the peak of my nipple once, before his teeth latch onto the newly freed boning, tugging it half an inch out of the hole he created.

"Thanks," I say, my voice high and breathy, like we're alone in bed instead of zip-tied to the gate guarding our graves.

He swallows as I move myself off him, inching the boning free. "My pleasure."

I smirk, even though this isn't the moment. With careful fingers, I pull the boning out and weave it around the zip tie. Then I twist, and twist again, the moment stretching now that I'm so close to being free, the light in the distance wobbling again, the voices raised as more shots are fired, before the light tumbles down, rays cutting through the even lines of stones like a searchlight through blinds.

The plastic digs into my wrists the tighter I twist the wire, but cut wrists are nothing compared to dead, so I grit my teeth and keep going.

And with my nerves screaming and my fingers slippery with blood and sweat, finally, the plastic snaps.

One down, three to go.

Chapter Seven
Xander

amn, that stings. Blood trickles into my eyes, and I wipe them as best as I can with my bare shoulder, wishing I hadn't given my shirt to Liam.

No, scratch that. I wish that I'd worn more than one shirt to Eddie's bachelor party. One for me and one for Liam.

Not that I knew we'd both be shot by the end of the night, but stranger things have happened. I've got a couple of scars to prove it.

Although, stumbling between gravestones and mausoleums while a fucking elementary-school-aged kid with a semiautomatic tries to take my head off as his father screams at him to do better? Well, it'll be one for the books.

If the kid didn't have such good aim, I'd be safer, but I've got a graze on my skull and a solid shot into my left arm. I'm a lefty, so that's not a lucky break in the slightest.

Apparently, the Bratva gets their babies killing young.

I recognized Mikhail Morozov, Bratva legend, the second I hobbled into the spotlight, but the rest of the welcome committee was a surprise. While they were debating whether having Liam and I watch as they killed Cece would be more impactful than the slow winnowing down of our numbers with shots in the distance, the scrawny blond kid took it upon himself to just take his shot.

And fuck. It was not what I was expecting.

At least I didn't fall into my grave when he first hit me—I'd be dead for sure. I mean, my goddamn hands are tied to one of my knees. Me still being alive at all is a miracle.

I've got to assume I'm only still alive because I'm destined to take Cecelia Rodriguez on a date. As she so clearly showed, the package that goes with the irreverent spitfire is one that I'd like to spend hours, no fucking days, exploring. But first, I have to survive long enough to make that happen.

Another shot cracks into the side of the fucking crypt I'm crouched behind, and if I don't free my hands from the zip ties, I'm dead. I duck around the other side and nearly lose an eye on a scrubby bush. Thinking quickly, I tuck myself into an alcove between two columns, mostly hidden by the bush, and wait.

The crunch of footsteps has my heart slowing to match the cadence of my enemy's movements over the gravel. I drop into the headspace I've trained in since I was a kid. Nobody grows up in this world without learning how to protect themselves. And an heir apparent must be sharper than most. I might be the life of the party, but that doesn't mean I'm not deadly as fuck.

When the Pink loving grunt swings around the side of the building, I'm already flying headfirst at his junk, slamming us both onto the ground. I've only got a second to win this—I'm down two hands and one leg. So channeling Liam's favorite move, I slam my forehead into his while kneeing him in the junk. Then, while he's wheezing and crying, I lock my knee around his neck, choking him out with my only free limb.

It's awkward as fuck, and I'm not winning any points for technique or grace, but once again, somebody out there is looking out for me, and Pinky stays locked down long enough for me to win the fight mostly uncontested. Thank fuck.

It takes longer than I'd like to find where he keeps his knife, but eventually, my wrists are blessedly free. Checking for a pulse, I slit his throat when I find it, not wanting any extra muscle on the playing field with Cece here and Liam shot. I clean it on his slacks, then slide it into my belt.

Next, I take off his shirt, cut it in half, and tie part of it around my head to keep the blood out of my eyes and the other around my arm to keep me from losing more blood. I'm already a little lightheaded. Liam can't be doing much better. Hopefully Cece's got some secret skills, otherwise this mess doesn't look too promising.

I grab his sidearm, but a shot nearby has me sprinting away before I can check for more mags, my head spinning as I duck and dodge around the outskirts of the cemetery. I've got to save my friend and my future date.

My future date with a grave beside my own.

Why not take Eddie? Eduardo Rodriguez is the other heir apparent, and with his pending marriage to Natalia Morozova, he's all but underground royalty. So why take out his baby sister instead of him? We would have all been at the same place tonight, and likely drunk off our asses to boot. Easy picking.

Something about this doesn't add up. And from what I saw of the peanut gallery, Eddie's in for a bloody breakup.

Chapter Eight

Cece

Liam insists on trailing me through the shadowy graveyard, even though he can hardly put weight on his damaged leg. The scent of wet blood screams that this is a bad idea. But there's no way he's leaving until he knows Xander is okay, so here we are, crouched behind a weeping angel, peering toward the light.

Shouts from across the space tell me that, at least for now, Xander is free. "I'm going to get close to the light. Stay here. Xander's probably looking for us, and they're looking for him, so now's our best shot to see what they had planned."

Liam squeezes my bare ankle, and my breath hitches. "Just run while you can. You can get out of here. I'll worry about Xander."

Anger flares. "Why? Why should I run instead of staying and fighting?"

"Because you're Eddie's baby sister. He'd kill me if I got you killed."

I keep my scoff quiet. "You have no idea what Eddie would think of that. If I don't get out of here with both you and Xander in one piece, I can guarantee my brother will never forgive me."

"You're worth more than we are. If you knew the amount of blood we each had on our hands..."

"If you knew the amount I had on *my* hands, you wouldn't bother saying such stupid things," I mutter, and taking my opportunity, I slip away, slinking between stones, ears pricked, only hearing Liam's soft curse as I vanish from his line of sight.

The fallen floodlight is set to rights, and concern that they've caught Xander has me rushing from stone to stone with less caution than I should use. So, all I can do is curse my impatience when I trip over a small figure crouched beside a stone cross and go flying across the dirt and headfirst into a grave.

Is it mine? No idea. But I'm six feet deep and five feet tall, so this isn't ideal. The lump I tripped over comes to the edge, and I'm staring up at a little kid with big blue eyes and a steady hand on his Sig-Sauer.

"Hello," I call up, trying to figure out what this kid is going to do with that gun.

"Name," he barks, his voice high and gruff. Poor thing. At least I was a teen before I was doing similar shit.

"Not important. You going to shoot me?"

"Depends. Are you Cecelia Rodriguez?"

"What do you think?" I ask, motioning at my semi-destroyed, mud-and-blood-spattered formal gown.

The kid looks me over, squinting, so I take my chance, racing toward him and bounding up, kicking off to hook one knee on the edge while I grip both his ankles and tug. He goes flying over me, the gun firing off a few rounds before he hits the bottom with a grunt.

Scrambling the rest of the way out, I look down at the poor bugger. "Sorry, kid. But I've got some boys to rescue."

He sits up, pointing the gun at me again, mud smeared across his childish features. "I'll kill you," he says.

"Not today. Who should I watch out for in the future?" I ask, hoping his pride will give me the answers I need.

"Gregor Morozov," he says, his finger sliding to the trigger as I hit the deck. Rolling away from the grave as another shot rings out, I dodge behind the backhoe they used to dig those holes.

Shit. Morozov. Eddie's going to be pissed. He invited Nat into our family's biggest secret, and now she's trying to kill me. I hope those wedding deposits are refundable.

But that's tomorrow's problem. Right now, I need to find Xander.

* * *

Following his trail is child's play after the training I got from my abuelo over the years. Which makes it even funnier that Morozov's guys haven't caught him yet. At least the dead body of Pinky tells me Xander is well enough to take on a henchman and win.

Either way, it's obvious the Bratva don't send their people to the jungle for live fire training against la Chota for their eighteenth birthdays. I'd asked for a convertible, but it turns out that tracking and guerilla warfare tactics *are* more useful in my line of work, so maybe Abuelo was onto something.

Xander figured out that Liam and I were free, but apparently, he knows Liam has a hero complex, so instead of making a run for it, he turned back into the graveyard, a smear of blood here and there leading me right back in the direction I started.

I never thought loyalty could be annoying.

His trail disappears near an ancient-looking mausoleum, so I climb up to the roof, the rock scraping off the fresh scabs on my wrists and ankles. Once I'm up there, I pose like a gargoyle and scan. Halfway between the gate and the graves, three figures crowd together, likely trying to decide if we made a run for it or not. If it weren't for Morozov junior stuck in a grave, they'd assume we're long gone.

Sadly, I wasn't as stealthy as I'd hoped, so we're still mildly fucked. Less fucked than we were an hour ago, but still, they've got weapons and nobody with major blood-loss. I can't say the same for our side.

Motion catches my eye, and with quiet feet I patter to the other side of the mausoleum just in time for Xander to reach it, his steps light as he slips from shadow to shadow. Wishing I could watch him longer, I flop my top half over the edge and tap him on the shoulder.

The muzzle of a Glock finds me before Xander's eyes, but when he sees me, he stows his purloined gun immediately. Then he pulls me off the roof and drags me against his hard body. "Tell me I can kiss you," he says, his face pressed to my crown.

Is this a good time for a kiss? No. But is it exactly what I want to do after worrying that he was dead? Yes. Yes, it is.

"You can kiss me," I whisper, suddenly shy.

Because this is Xander Liu. He might not have been *my* childhood crush, but he was pretty much everybody else's. And when his dark eyes meet mine, his charisma captures me. I'm lost in his full attention.

He kisses me like I'm the center of his entire world. The energy that coils around him and drags people into his orbit instead shatters into individual tendrils, each of them wrapping around just me. The sheer inevitability of our attraction has me plastering myself against him, opening for him, wanting him in ways I shouldn't. Especially not in the dark of a cemetery with enemies in the distance. Especially not with his best friend, who I also recently kissed, not so far away.

I can't fight it, too caught up by the magnetism of the man, by the violence in this kiss that echoes my own. One of his hands digs into my hair, tilting me the way he wants, the other gripping my elbow like he's afraid I'm going to run away. But I'm not. There's no way. Instead, I drop one hand lower, the weight of him heavy against my palm, a nearly inaudible groan falling from his lips.

"Damn," he whispers, kissing my cheek, my neck, the top of my collarbone while I stroke him through his jeans.

"Xander," I mutter, wanting more, needing more, but knowing we need to get the hell out of here first.

"I know, sweet thing. But damn, I don't want to stop," he says, his tongue lining the top of the bodice, my head thrown back against the stones to give him access.

"Xander," I croak, this time with a touch more force, and he stops his exploration of my skin, instead pulling me flush against him, his cock heavy against my belly.

"I know, I know. Give me a minute."

We pant, and I can't help but strain to hear where our Bratva friends might be, a whistle sounding, followed by the yips of those distant coyotes again. "I kissed Liam, too," I whisper when it quiets.

Instead of anger, I just get a soft groan. "He's going to lord that over me."

"Huh?"

"That he got to taste you first. He'll never let me live that down."

"You're not mad?"

"Nah. Your body, your choice. Just be honest with a guy. You're doing exactly that."

"And if I wanted to kiss Liam again?"

"Then I'd ask if I could watch."

I barely stifle my laughter. Yet somehow, despite all the dark and deadly nonsense tonight, this conversation almost makes it worth it.

"I'd let you join in, you know."

He loosens his hold, letting me see his crooked grin. "Thank god for that. Let's go find the grouchy bastard and see if he's game."

"I'll lead the way." Taking a few steps, my skirt snags on one of the stones. "Fuck. Next time I'm kidnapped, can it be while I'm wearing tactical gear?" I ask the heavens.

A knife appears in answer to my prayer, Xander grinning. "Not quite the same thing," he says as I take it from him. Away from the shadows of the mausoleum, I can see both his head and his arm are bandaged, and I add those to our growing list of injuries. But he seems in better condition than Liam, so a half-win.

Using the knife, and perhaps too much glee, I chop at the dress until it's well above my knees. Then I tie the bits into a parcel, because you never know when a length of good silk will come in handy, and continue toward where I left Liam.

I'm calling it, though. This version of the dress is much, much better.

Chapter Nine
Liam

Resting my eyes was a bad choice. I knew it as I did it. But Cece ran away, there were gunshots, and when I tried to follow, my leg gave out. I'm pretty sure I hit my head on the way down. Hence, resting my eyes.

But opening them to a dirt covered child with a semiautomatic has me convinced I'm dreaming.

Or that I'd hit my head harder than I'd thought.

"Up, O'Connell," the kid says, and I laugh.

Then the tot pistol whips my already tender scalp, and my hands catch one of his bony wrists before I can stop myself. And that tiny, weaponless wrist is real enough for me to freeze. "Do not fucking hit me, kid. I'm having a shit night."

"Same. Which is why I'm bringing your busted ass to my dad." He twists his wrist, his other hand far enough away that I can't quite reach the gun without risking my leg again. I consider tugging the kid into my lap and wrestling him for it, but he's a kid. I can't guarantee that he won't shoot me by accident if I spook him.

This whole thing is fucked up. So, I hold on to his wrist long enough for the kid to know that I'm *letting* him free.

I might be a bit battle-worn, but I've got two decades and two feet on the pipsqueak. Even if the Sig evens things out considerably.

"If you can find a way for me to walk successfully, I'd be all ears," I reply, motioning at my blood-dark, tulle covered leg.

The kid wipes his mouth with his shirt sleeve, smearing more dirt than he's clearing. "They left you to die. Some friends you've got, old man."

I can't say I've ever been called old before. First time for everything. But at least I know that the last time this kid saw Cece and Xander, they were both still alive. Good news, based on all the shooting that's been going on. "I sure can pick them," I say, wondering if I can win over this gun wielding preschooler. "Where were you hoping to bring me?"

"To your grave," he answers, dropping his tone like he isn't a soprano, like my destination is a surprise. I can see the backhoe if I peer around the tombstone I'm leaning against.

"Alright kid. Let's get this over with," I say, hoisting myself upright on one foot, the chunk of stone beside me the only thing keeping me vertical.

Then, because I'm an asshole at heart, I take my chance and dive at the kid, twisting the gun from his spindly fingers and pointing the damn thing right back at him.

Before I can figure out how to get the kid to lay off, though, a voice cuts from behind me. "Think about your next step, O'Connell. That's my son you have there."

I turn in place, pretending like I'm not using a gravestone to keep myself upright, and meet Mikhail Morozov's pale gaze. "Starting him a little young, aren't you?"

"Worked alright for your father," he replies, motioning with his gun for me to toss him the Sig.

"Or maybe not, because here I am, not even thirty, and looking forward to a shallow grave." I take apart the weapon and toss each piece into the darkness behind me.

"But you did plenty before now. Enough for your grandfather to name you heir apparent."

"True. Ahead of even my father."

His lips twist at that, before he motions for his kid to come to him, and the little guy does, trotting over like the well-trained mini mobster he must be. "Enough talk. Let's get you lined up for a clean shot."

"That's going to be a problem."

"How so? You walk, or I shoot."

"When was the last time you hauled two hundred and sixty-five pounds of dead weight a quarter mile, Morozov? Because if the rumor mill is right, I'm not sure you've ever stooped to that level of grunt work."

"I'll wing you. You'll be fine."

"Your man already did one better. My leg's been leaking for probably an hour. I'm not sure I can handle too much more blood loss. Where is ol' Pinky anyways?"

Morozov huffs and whistles. A moment later, a different grunt jogs up beside him. "Go nowhere without help. You could learn from my example, O'Connell. If you were going to live past tonight, that is."

With that, I'm 'helped' to my grave by this new minion, my leg numb and my head spinning.

I thought I was ready to die. Figured I have been since I first killed a man at twelve. Take a life, give a life, some sort of cosmic balance shit that's been aching under my skin for years, only soothed at the bottom of a bottle.

I've spent most of my life surviving, not really living. I've got Xander and Eddie, that's it. Not even a houseplant to worry about if I don't make it home. As soon as I took that shot, I figured I'd sacrifice myself to get Xander out of here. Cece, too.

But there was something about that kiss.

An instant connection that screams I have something to live for. Something that sings, lights up, makes little hearts bobble around in my eyes, all that stupid poetic shit that I figured the lousy saps of the world made up. But maybe it's not all idiot poets with nothing better to do. Maybe people really do change when they meet the right person.

The dream shatters as I approach my grave, even knowing that Cece could be that person for me.

At least she'll have Xander. I hope they bond over my death, become some unstoppable duo, Eddie and Nat by their sides.

That thought has a few more falling into place. If Morozov is out here killing us, Nat must be in on it—and poor loyal-to-the-core Eddie is in for one shit awakening.

Why Cece's caught up in this still makes no sense, though. Could it be jealousy? Cece's gorgeous and powerful, but so is Nat. Nat's old-fashioned, but that's a virtue in our world. Tradition matters when you're ruling an empire like a king over his country.

Confirming my suspicions, Nat steps out of the shadows, the excitement on her face telling me she's hoping for some reaction from me.

"Hi there, Liam. Long time, no see," she whispers in that annoying way she always does, so that people have to lean in to hear her, making her words feel important because you have to work to understand them. "I'm so glad you could make it. This is going to be such a fun night. All three of you, taken out at once? That power vacuum is exactly what my brother needs to climb to the top, and with me there by Eddie's side, that family will have no choice but to give my poor, mourning husband the position he always should have had."

Two heirs taken out at once would be a scramble, but I can't figure out what else she's yammering on about. Nat always loves to speak and make powerful people listen. "Hello, Natalia. It took you long enough to get here," I reply instead of addressing her villain monologue.

Her brow crumples, frustrated that her revelation didn't amount to much. "How'd you guess I'd be here?"

"He's your brother, Nat. I might be morose and a borderline alcoholic, but I'm not an idiot."

Morozov's kid chuckles, then dodges out of reach of his father. The guard behind me also stifles a laugh, and while that wasn't the goal, striking my best friend's viper of a fiancée with a few choice words feels like a win here at the end.

"Well, I'd ask if you have any last words, but I think those were honest enough for an epitaph," Morozov says, taking a few steps away from his son for a clean shot, Nat covering her ears with an eerie grin on her face.

Then shit gets weird.

A windy whistle sounds right as the grip of the henchman on my body slackens. I assume that I'm hearing the whoosh of the bullet before I die, instead of the bang. It makes as much sense as anything else. Only both the kid and Nat's eyes get big, and instead of falling into my grave, the weight of the guard falls on top of me, with my bad leg getting the brunt of it, and we both go down in a mess of limbs and blood. Blood that isn't mine.

Stranger than even that, though, is the vision of one Cece Rodriguez, covered in mud and a strapless minidress, swinging down from the bucket of the backhoe like Tarzan, and kicking Morozov in the chest.

That last bit was mostly a glancing blow, but the woman lands in a roll, grabs the kid, and hauls him up as a body shield.

That's all I see before the handle of a knife, which just happens to be attached to the eye of the guard who used to have a hold of me, bashes me in the cheekbone.

It might be a mess, but a knife is a gift that won't go unused.

Chapter Ten
Cece

Ten Minutes Earlier

Xander lifts his fingers to his nose, sniffing for the metallic scent of fresh blood to verify that we're stalled out at the correct gravestone. I'm not offended. In fact, I'd be worried if he trusted me blindly. For all his playfulness, you don't get named heir without the skills to back it up. Caution is probably the most important of those skills.

It was one reason Abuelo didn't choose Eddie after Oz left. My brother sees the best in others, even when he shouldn't. While it brought Xander and Liam into our lives, it also brought Nat. Statistically, he's still batting above average, but average odds are a dangerous place for a crime lord to sit.

"Morozov probably found him," I say, recalling the whistle I heard not too long ago.

"Yeah," Xander says. "How do we get him back?"

"We've got a knife and a gun. Anything extra I should know about?"

"Nope."

"How are your knife throwing skills?"

"I'm more of a hand-to-hand expert." I might imagine the hint of a double meaning as he answers me, but as he's Xander Liu, I can't tell one way or another.

"Then give it here."

He raises his brows but slaps the handle into my palm. "You sure about that, sweet thing?"

I play with it, getting a feel for the weight of it. "This isn't a throwing knife, so no. But it'll have to do. What about your arm?"

"It hurts like a bitch."

"Will it affect your aim? You're a southpaw, right?"

He glares at me, but I wait him out.

"You think you can out-shoot me?" he finally asks, more curious than combative. I'll take it.

"Any other day, I'd challenge you to a competition for bragging rights. But not tonight. All I know is I've got two good arms and excellent aim while you only have one."

He checks the mag. "Only one bullet left."

"Can you promise it'll end up where it needs to be with a bum arm?"

"Can you?"

"Yup."

He shakes his head, but hands me the gun, and I hook it into the monstrous bow that has somehow stayed tight around my waist. This thing is ugly, but it's proven it's sturdy. I pick up the bundle of silk, keeping the knife in hand, in case we're ambushed.

I turn to Xander, and before I can say anything, he taps my nose, the contact familiar while still making my heart race. "You're just full of surprises," he says.

"You've got no idea."

His grin is bright in the dark. "Maybe not, but I've got a feeling I'm figuring them out. And I'm liking them all."

My cheeks flush as I lead the way through the slabs, ignoring his flirting as both of us step silently across the gravel. We crouch just past the backhoe, out of the circle of light. A guard holds a pale Liam next to his grave, while Nat pontificates nearby, too quietly for us to hear her.

I tap Xander's shoulder, and he inches closer, my bare knee brushing the seam of his jeans. And once again, my damn heart races. "I'll take out the guard behind Liam," I whisper. "Will you be able to get him out of here?"

"What about Morozov?"

"The kid's his. I guess it's my turn to be the kidnapper. Or at least a hostage taker. Sucks that it has to be a kid, though."

"That's savage." He looks me over, then shrugs. "Sounds like a good plan, though. How are you going to get a drop on them? This place is lit up like an airport tarmac."

Drop. Huh. Haven't done anything this crazy since I last visited Abuelo's jungle. "From there," I say, pointing at the backhoe.

Xander blinks at me in the dark, a grin stealing across his face before his lips are on mine. This kiss is brutal, a flash of lips, tongue, and teeth. It's over so fast that I half-tumble toward him. "More of that later, my sweet little savage," he whispers, and slinks into the dark.

Later. I can do more later.

Turning to our targets, I note I don't have much time. Morozov's impatience with Nat pontificating is written in the tightness of his shoulders. So, I clamber up the backhoe, for once grateful that I'm small. Yeah, one of them might still see me climbing this thing like a jungle gym, but I'm a lot less noticeable than a six-foot-tall man.

And at this point, my peach dress has enough blood and mud on it, I should consider it a ghillie suit.

I'm in the bucket, tying the silk as quickly as I can into a shitty, black-tie appropriate rope, when Morozov announces that it's time for him to take out Liam.

Nope. Not going to happen. That one's mine.

Hopefully.

I yank the last knot tight, pop up, and with a flick of my wrist and a prayer, I fling the knife at the guard holding Liam.

For a second, I'm sure I've accidentally hit Liam, but I have no time to worry about my possibly terrible aim. Instead, I throw myself from the basket, the silk slippery in my hands as I careen down, kicking out at Morozov on my way past. The angle's wrong, so it does nothing but force him to take a step back, but it still feels good.

Not as badass as I'd hoped, but I roll with my landing, my left wrist slamming into the gravel hard, then I'm up, grabbing Morozov junior and getting my gun in position before Morozov senior gets gun happy himself. "Freeze, or you're out your only son," I bark.

Morozov puts his hands up, his gun loose in his fingers. Xander slips up next to Liam in the corner of my eye. I want to make sure he's okay, but I can't risk shifting my focus right now. I've got the whole of the Morozov family to deal with on my own.

Morozov gives me a slow clap, his firearm dangling from one finger, his lips a mockery of a smile. "So what Natalia said is true, then? A little girl outclassed her scads of brothers and cousins. I never figured your grandfather would be the first to embrace such a modern mindset. A woman as an heir."

The soft, surprised curses from the direction of the guys would distract me if I wasn't wrestling with a squirmy and competently trained kid trying to break free of my grip, my wrist aching the longer I hold him.

"Hence the secret," I say. "The old guard would put me under before I could prove myself. And look, here we are, with that exact problem. Thanks for that, Nat."

"You stole my crown," she murmurs, always whispering when somebody else would yell.

My anger flares. "It was never yours."

"It should have been. We were brought up in this world together. Women are supposed to be the prize, not the soldier. We use our looks, our mystique, our connections to get to a place of power, of security. Eddie was perfect—soon to be a king with hordes of family ready to fight his battles for him. He adores me, and I'd want for nothing. Only you took what your brother should have had. You ruined everything we stand for."

"There's more to a woman than her connections and looks. And our traditions have to catch up with the rest of the world sometime. Why not now?"

"I thought I was marrying into a good family, but it turns out you're nothing but a bunch of classless progressives. Misha, where's Vlad? I want to get out of here. I feel dirty just talking to this tacky creature."

Morozov spares his sister a glance. "Nat, I have no idea where your lover is. Go find him on your own time. Can't you see I'm busy keeping my son alive?"

Every muscle in my body stills as what Morozov said registered. I whip my gaze to the serpent across from me. "Did you seriously cheat on my brother? Eddie would kill for you. He'd die for you. And you cheated on him?"

Nat waves me off, picking her way around the pile of dirt beside the three graves. "Like your brother knows how to treat a woman like me. I chose him because he was the heir to a fortune and endless connections. Although, it *is* a bonus that he is so very loyal. I'll never have to worry about a wandering eye." She sighs, looking skyward. "But Vlad? Vlad is the man of my heart. He was so happy to pick you up personally. The bridal shop really needs better security. I only wish he'd grabbed you once you were back in your street clothes. You've thoroughly ruined a beautiful gown." She pauses for the drama of it as my mind clicks it all together. "Now you'll be buried in rags, like the classless little girl you are. It's tragically poetic, if you ask me."

"Say, Nat," I call as she takes a few more steps away. "Vlad's dead. And now you are too." I pull the trigger as she turns to me with big, tear-filled eyes, and all I feel is a sense of pride when I hit her right between her perfectly arched brows.

Good riddance.

Chapter Eleven
Xander

I've dragged Liam over a few rows, despite his insistence that he should battle it out alongside Cece. The cartel heir. Damn. I should have figured that out. One hell of a reveal for one hell of a woman.

"Listen, man, you heard Cece. She's the heir, not Eddie. She beat out not just her brothers, but all of her cousins, too. I don't think she needs your one-legged ass getting in her way."

He slams the blood drenched knife in my hand, retrieved in the chaos of my girl swinging in like a silver screen commando wearing a destroyed prom dress and a manic grin. "Heir or not, I need her to be okay. Go. Keep her safe. It's three against one, if you count the kid. Even the odds."

I take the blade, looking down at one of my oldest friends. "I really like her."

"Now's not the time, Liu. Get your ass in gear."

"She likes me too. Stranger still, she likes your grumpy ass."

He drops his head back against the gravestone. "Once again, not the time."

"I'm just saying, if you're willing to share, I sure as shit am."

His half-hooded eyes snap open, meeting mine where I'm crouched beside him. "Share?"

"I mean, yeah? I don't know. But she's into both of us, we're both into her, so why not try and see what happens?"

He blinks at me, then closes his eyes. "I must have hit my head harder than I thought."

"Nope. But I'll go play watchdog. Thought I should clear the air, though, as we've both kissed her senseless tonight. And I'm not letting her go without shooting my best shot."

"Same. But Liu..."

"I'm going, I'm going. Don't get your panties in a bunch."

I slip back through the gravestones, picking my way over until I have a clear, short jump at Morozov. If I could get closer without fucking everything up, I would just pop out and end this stand-off. It's not like Nat is the kind of woman to carry a gun.

Oh no, all the big, strong men around her are supposed to keep her safe. The woman must have a brain in there somewhere, but it defaults to men taking charge in a way that diminishes women everywhere. That she found out a secret like the one the Rodriguez family is keeping and immediately tattled to her brother says everything I needed to know about her I hadn't already figured out myself.

She's a dinosaur in designer dresses.

Cece will just be the first of many female leaders, and a damn fine one at that. These stuffy old families are due for some shake-ups, and Cece can't be the only girl raised in this world to want more than to look pretty and pop out piles of criminal children. I know my mom wanted more, even if she never got it.

No, Nat's views belong dead and buried, left in those unmarked graves.

A shot has me bounding forward, my mind working furiously to figure out where I'm most needed.

Across the way stands Cece, gun arm steady, Morozov's kid shaking as she clutches him against her front. Morozov, meanwhile, turns, his gun arm wavering, as a single shout of "Nat!" forces my attention to the last guest at the party.

And there, closer to me than Cece, close enough that little details lodge in my mind, I watch my best friend's fiancée tumble sideways into a pre-dug grave, her eyes blank, a dribble of blood barely trickling from the bullet wound in her skull before she disappears from view, a soft thud sounding when she hits the bottom.

Turns out that Cece's not just good at throwing knives. She's one hell of a shot, as well. Makes me wonder if there's such a thing as strip shooting. Because I'm suddenly game to give it a go.

Ears ringing, knowing that was Cece's one and only bullet, I use my surprise attack as best I can—by throwing the knife at Mikhail Morozov's heart before he can get his gun hand steady again and risk a headshot at Cece around his son.

Only the bullet wound in my arm has my aim wonky, and the knife lands with a *thunk* in his left arm. Whoops. No going back now, though. "Give up, Morozov. You're outnumbered and outgunned," I say, stepping toward Cece, wondering if I'm going to have to be a human shield.

I sure hope not. There's one hell of a woman here that I can't wait to get to know better, and that'd be impossible if one of us is dead.

He glares at his injured arm, but leaves the knife in like a smart man. "Give me my son and I'll leave," he says, more emotion in his voice than I would have expected for the underdog currently scrambling his way to the top of his organization.

Cece pushes the kid forward, and he sprints to his dad like the scared kid he should be. This shit isn't for kids. I don't know what the fuck Morozov was thinking, bringing an elementary schooler with him.

Morozov backs away, his kid in hand, his head bowing for a moment as he passes his sister's grave, but his gun hand never straying from Cece.

And she keeps her empty weapon trained on him as well, her gaze intent to kill. Lack of bullets be damned.

She doesn't relax until the rumble of an engine descends the mountain. "Well, that was messy," she says, tucking the empty gun into the sash of her dress.

I inspect the graves, the dirt, the backhoe, and the woman now lining the bottom of one of them. "Why'd you kill Nat?"

"She cheated on Eddie. With Pinky, of all people."

I spit into the hole. "Good riddance. That woman was an archaic toxin."

She walks over to the unnamed guard and rolls him toward another unoccupied grave. I rush to help her, not because she can't do this alone, but because she doesn't need to.

"So, you're heir, not Eddie."

"Yeah. I am. What of it?" The fight in her voice has my cock twitching.

"It's surprising, but after tonight, I'm all for it. You're one hell of a woman, Cece Rodriguez. Your family will be lucky to have you as a leader."

She dips her chin as we push the grunt into the hole, her cheeks pink in the spotlight. "Thanks."

We drag Pinky to the last grave, tossing his tone-deaf ass in as well. "And Cece?"

"Yeah?"

"I'd be lucky to have you in my life, too."

Leaving her to sort through my confession, I hop into Nat's grave, rummaging until I find her phone and unlock it before tossing it up to Cece. "Why don't you go check on Liam? Give Eddie a call and see if we can hitch a ride out of here. I'll finish cleaning up."

A barely audible shout from Liam cuts through the darkness. "There's another piece dismantled by the weeping angel."

"On it," I shout back, before pressing a quick kiss on Cece's lips, her warmth plastered against me like she needs a release from this adrenaline the same as I do. But business first. Fun, second. "Go. Kiss him better," I say, pushing her toward my friend.

"We'll see about that," she says with a smirk, before sauntering away, muddy, bloodthirsty, and gorgeous.

Just the way I never knew I wanted. But I've gotten a taste, and I'm not letting that girl go.

She'll have to kill me to get rid of me. Which wouldn't be a problem for her, it seems.

Best point that energy at our enemies. She'll have them if she's planning on changing this old boys' club. And I'm thrilled I might get to help her dispose of each and every one of them.

Chapter Twelve
Cece

Liam's eyes shine in the dark as I pick my way to him. "What happened?" he asks as soon as I'm close enough to not shout.

Instead of answering, I look him over, frustrated to find that his leg is drenched and black, even the tulle blood dark. "I might need to improve my field medicine skills."

"We all probably should."

"Let's call Eddie and get Doc out here for you."

"And you? Are you hurt?"

I shrug. "I jammed my wrist earlier, and I have some cuts from getting the zip ties off, but I'm perfect, all things considered. Especially compared to you and Xander getting shot."

He lifts his arm up in a half circle beside him, something hopeful about his face, waiting for me to crawl next to him. After a moment of hesitation, I tuck myself against him, the weight of his arm around me soothing. "You're heir," he says.

"Yup."

"Your family made the right choice. All this would be too much for Eddie."

"I killed Nat. It's going to break his heart."

"But it was necessary. Unfortunately. Call him," he says.

Using a dead woman's phone should probably cause some remorse to bubble up, but I don't feel much about the woman besides fury that I have to break my brother's heart.

Eddie picks up after a few rings, the background oddly silent for a man who's supposed to be living it up for his bachelor's party. "Nat?"

The panic in his voice has my fury burning hotter. "No, it's me," I say.

"Cece? Is Nat with you? I can't get a hold of her, and Liam and Xander are missing."

"I'm with Liam and Xander," I say, not sure how to break it to him that I killed his fiancée not thirty minutes ago. "Can you come get us? Bring Doc."

"Wait, but you're calling from Nat's phone."

"Yeah, about that..." Liam tugs me closer against him, the warmth of his body giving me strength. "Nat wasn't who you thought she was."

The stillness in his voice when he answers makes my chest tight. "What did she do?"

"She took our secret to her brother, and they conspired to take out three heirs to create a power vacuum."

He says nothing for a painful minute. "How quickly do I need to get Doc to your location?"

I turn to the most damaged of us. "How bad are you, Liam?"

He takes the phone from me, then he and my brother talk medical stuff, regrets, and all kinds of things that best friends talk about, while I work to not eavesdrop on their conversation. Instead, I focus on the steady beat of Liam's heart beneath my ear.

If tonight had gone differently, I might never have heard its even rhythm. I might never have discovered my childhood crush on the man beside me could be anything besides an embarrassing memory. Or that Xander Liu has a temperament to match my own and a kiss that's more dangerous than any weapon he could wield against me.

One or all of us could be dead right now. We should be.

Liam hangs up on my brother, setting the phone aside before tilting my chin to him, his fingers hot against my skin. "He's going to kill me when he finds out about this," he whispers.

"I'd like to see him try."

"Are you sure you want to take on both me and Liu? We'll be a hell of a lot for you to handle."

"I've always been partial to a challenge."

His lips twist into a smile before they brush against mine, a question more than a kiss.

And I answer it, clambering onto his lap, the shredded dress offering no barrier as I settle against him, taking his mouth like it's another challenge, one I plan to come out on top of.

The patient dance of tongues lulls me while we both explore the planes and valleys of each other's bodies. Then he tugs my bodice down, his rough fingers circling each nipple in turn, and I groan, rocking against the hardness that's rubbing me in all the right ways, even with layers of cloth between us. "Liam," I mutter a moment before his mouth joins his fingers, hot and wet, lighting me up from the inside out.

I stop him for a moment to yank off his shirt, and once I do, I'm greeted by an expanse of muscles and scars, evidence of the same upbringing I had. "God, you're handsome," I say, and the same twist of lips is all the response I get before his mouth is back at it, coaxing me higher with every swipe of his tongue against my chest. Every exploratory tweak and caress makes me eager for release, for an outlet for all the adrenaline left in my system.

A celebration of survival, of a beginning with two men I've always known, but never really got to know.

From here on out, we're fixing that.

My fingers sweep over his chest, learning the planes of it, as the hum of the backhoe revs in the distance, Xander filling our unmarked graves, now housing the bodies of our enemies. But I don't pay it much mind. I'm too invested in finding the points where Liam's breath stutters against my skin, his hum of pleasure so deep that I can barely hear it. Then I find a spot on his side that has him twitching away from me.

I stifle a laugh. "Is Liam O'Connell ticklish?"

"Terribly. Don't tell anybody." His eyes are bright as they meet mine. "Is this really happening? I'm not passed out somewhere, am I?"

I dig my fingers into his hair, the texture fine and silky smooth. "Feels pretty real to me."

His hands come to rest on my waist, the breadth of his palms making me feel delicate instead of simply short. "Yeah. I guess it does."

He doesn't kiss me again, like I figured he would. Instead, he opens his arms, that same small twist of his lips hinting at a smile. "Hug?"

A well of emotion, of vulnerability that I wasn't sure I still had washes through me, and I tuck my head into the crux of his neck so he can't see how much the simple offer means to me. His big arms wrap around me so tight it hurts, but it's good pain, like he's trying to hug the tiny me in tie dye pajamas more than a decade ago, too.

We stay locked together. Whatever passion we'd been working off is set aside as he holds me, his breath even while mine grows ragged. It's sweet, caring, and absolutely everything to the angry little girl I used to be.

A few tears end up rubbed into his skin, cleansing the last of the grief I'd been clinging to for years. Tears that had been trying to fall for much too long, even if I wouldn't let them.

As the emotion subsides, I'm no longer wallowing in the grief of a child, but rather inching back into the arousal of a half-naked woman pressed against a half-naked man who I really want to get to know better.

A low whistle has me pulling away from Liam's chest, but not far, his grip keeping me close. Xander stands outlined by the floodlights behind us, the strip of fabric from his head lost, but his arm still bandaged. "This wasn't what I was expecting to see when I finished cleaning up."

"What, like you didn't say you were fine with both of us being involved with her," Liam huffs.

"Oh no, that I was expecting. I was preparing myself to see your naked ass, O'Connell, not cuddles. And unless you're risking the bite of your zipper there, they don't even look like post-coital cuddles."

"Fuck off, Liu. It's just a hug. You should try it sometime."

The glint in his eye is all the warning I get before I'm squeezed from behind, Xander's chest warm against my bare back, his arms just as tight around me as Liam's, his nose pressed to my neck. I let out a sigh, relaxed between the two of them, even as my nipples grow harder, Liam's dick rock solid beneath me, and Xander's pressing with increasing urgency against my ass.

"Damn, you smell nice," Xander mutters. "But as great as this is, my little savage princess, my adrenaline won't let me just cuddle. If I should go take care of myself, let me know."

Instead of answering, I twist in the nest of their arms and drag him forward to kiss me. He does, the kiss coated with suppressed violence, and I meet it beat for beat. After too short of a moment, he opens his eyes, his breath catching when he finds what the shadows had hidden from him. He hisses, then takes my naked breast in his palm with a groan.

"God, these are perfect," he says. "No, fuck it. I'm not saying enough. You're perfect, Cecelia Rodriguez. And I'd be happy to fight alongside you whenever and wherever you'll have me."

Liam runs his tongue along the shell of my ear, and I shiver. "I'm happy to take you up on that offer," I say. "I don't think Morozov is going to let the Rodriguez heir stay secret much longer."

"I get first blood," Liam whispers against my neck. "Since I had to miss out on this fight."

"Heal up first, and we'll see who gets to take out who," I say, turning to him and kissing him as well, this kiss slower, deeper than Xander's, but no less amazing.

One to start the fire, one to stoke it. And I'm left to burn in it.

A girl could grow to love this.

Chapter Thirteen
Cece

With a nip at the back of my neck, Xander rolls away from us, his grin bright in the spotlight as he stands. "I'm glad I went fishing in the pockets of the dead."

"How so?" Liam asks, his lips working across my chest, my skin tingling with each press.

Two condoms fall into the dirt beside us before he pulls out a packet of baby wipes he must have found somewhere. "Because now there's no waiting. If that's what you want?" he asks, his face suddenly concerned that he's read the situation wrong, his hands pausing mid-clean.

"No, you got that right. I want you. Both of you." A wave of uncertainty flares. "If that's what you want?"

Liam chuckles beneath me. "Cece, I could be half dead in a hospital, and I'd want you. Fuck, I should probably be in a hospital right now, and still..." he hitches up his hips, his cock solid beneath me.

A tiny moan escapes me as it hits me just right, and their voices join my own. "Sweet savage, you keep making those noises, and I won't be gentle with you," Xander says.

I flutter my eyes open, gazing up at the guy my brother always warned me away from, the guy whose brand of trouble I never guessed matched my own. "Then get naked and do something about it," I challenge.

He throws his head back, laughter echoing off the old stones around us, before stripping off the last of his clothes, the sight of him leaving me aching and wanting. Liam's fingers slide between us, dipping under the hem of my underwear, making it worse.

"You keep looking at me like that, and I for sure won't be gentle," Xander says, the teasing in his voice notably absent.

"All talk and no action, Alexander Liu. Don't disappoint me."

Liam chuckles, then without warning, I'm lifted from his lap and half tossed at Xander. "Show her you're good for it, Liu."

He catches me like I'm a precious vase, and my skin burns everywhere it touches. Flicking me free from the last of my dress, it falls from my hips. With a muttered curse, Xander drops to his knees, his hands sliding down my body like he needs to savor the feel of me, before dragging my underwear down as well.

Then I've got no choice but to grip his muscled shoulders as he devours me, the same brutal mixture of tongue and teeth leaving me rocking against his mouth. Pleasure zaps through me, each nip soothed by a kiss, each thrust of his tongue accompanied with a twist that makes my toes tingle.

"God, please, more," I mutter, one hand sliding up and gripping the back of his hair, the black strands barely long enough to keep myself steady as I try to get impossibly closer.

His chuckle against me vibrates, and I squirm. Then, he scoops first one of my knees, then the other over his shoulders, leaving me to tumble backwards with a shout.

I'm ready to murder the bastard when two other hands catch me. Liam lowers me, the angle strange and vulnerable. Blinking open my eyes, I'm left in awe as the light slices between the graves, highlighting exactly what Xander is doing to me, an erotic show for Liam and me. With Liam's fingers roaming over my skin, the show isn't just visual. It's a decadent mess of pleasure from the tip of my ears to my pinky toes.

Aggression and passion highlighted between my legs; slow, sensual teasing hidden in the shadows across my chest.

I sink into the juxtaposition, reveling in my worship, the moments long between breaths, the point where I catapult over the edge, inching closer with every caress.

With a hum that's more vibration than sound, Xander spears two fingers into me. After all the lead up, the simple move leaves me teetering, every nerve aching for release. Then he pulls my clit into his mouth and sucks, his tongue lashing against the sensitive nub.

I explode from the inside out, my limbs and mind no longer my own, instead captives locked to my pleasure. "Holy fuck," I whisper, my mind silent as my orgasm continues to rocket through me, wave after wave, Xander wringing every ounce of pleasure from my body like it's his one purpose on earth.

It takes what feels like forever for my spirit to return to my body, every inch of my skin sensitive to their joint touches. "Okay, challenge won," I mumble, and Liam shakes with laughter beneath me.

"Nope. You're not getting out of your challenge that easily," Xander says.

"You call that easy?" I gasp. Instead of answering, Liam turns me so I'm plastered against his mostly naked body, kissing me with an intensity I could easily bathe in forever. Xander passes him a condom and, using what little muscle control I have after that explogasm, I slowly lower myself onto him.

I ride the excruciatingly delicious stretch of him entering me, throwing my head back as if it'll make more room for the beast I'm trying to fit inside of me.

When I finally take him all the way, I sigh, my body still half limp.

"Oh god, so tight," Liam mutters, his palms on my hips like a barely held back demand.

Xander takes my bonelessness and adds to it, nipping at my neck, kissing down my spine, his hands slipping around me and rolling my nipples between his fingers, every motion turning me to jelly between the two of them.

Liam starts to move, and I let the two of them manhandle me as I run my palms over the expanse of muscle before me, and the thrill of him filling me nudges my mind back toward blank. Each time we come together better than the last as we learn each other's rhythms, learn each other's bodies. It's simply exquisite.

The sharp crinkle of the second condom wrapper tearing has my eyes snapping open, and I twist to find Xander's brows raised in question. "Game for taking us both?"

My breath halts at the thought. And my clit throbs. "More than game," I whisper, my voice hard to find as excitement skitters through my system.

Xander grins, and Liam slides one of his big hands between us, running slow circles around my clit, easing me into a strange sex trance where all I've got is sensation, four hands working to bring me more pleasure than I should have, especially considering this night started with graves dug for each of us.

"You're cheating," I manage after who knows how much teasing.

"How so?" Xander asks, as he continues to twist and pinch my nipples gently.

"You promised me two dicks, and right now, I've only got one. One very nice dick, but still."

Liam's chuckle has my insides lighting up once again, but his deep voice by my ear has me getting improbably wetter. "We're making sure you're ready to take us both. Without lube, we're not going to risk your ass."

"Oh. Fun," I breathe out, surprise and arousal mingling in the sound, as first one finger, then a second slip in alongside Liam inside of me.

"Lean forward, my sweet savage," Xander whispers before nipping at my earlobe.

I follow the directions, eager to find out if this will feel as good as

I imagine. The shift allows Xander to push even deeper, the stretch nearly overwhelming. But still, they make me wait as I grind myself against Liam's fingers, wanting more. So much more. I'm ready to demand it when Liam gently presses against my clit, stalling out my words as my body leaps even higher.

The guys must have some unspoken communication, because the fingers disappear, and one of Liam's big hands presses me closer to him, while one of Xander's hands spans my back.

"Ready?" he asks.

"God yes. Please just fuck me," I groan, the anticipation nearly killing me.

They both huff out strained laughs, then Xander slowly eases in, the stretch impossible, the sensation decadent. Some strange, high pitched mewing noise escapes me, and I don't even care. This is so much—my brain is short circuiting from the intensity. Liam kisses me, coaxing me, begging my body to relax and let Xander in with slow circles of his fingers around my clit. And with a groan, Xander bottoms out, all of us frozen and vibrating from the enormity of it.

I'm so goddamn full. I couldn't move if I wanted to, plastered between them both. All I know is that I don't want this to end. I don't want this to be a onetime thing, a memory built on adrenaline and danger.

I want this always. This level of care, of compassion, of challenge and excitement. I want it all. And I want it with the two of them.

Before I can voice my realization, Xander does as he'd promised, pulling out and slamming back in. Liam and I both shout, then he does it again, and again, my ears buzzing, my fingers clenched against Liam's chest. All I can do is just take it. I'm a prisoner to my pleasure.

My lips tingle, my toes clench, and my heart thunders some-where in my throat. Tears gather in the corners of my eyes, all of it so much that I'm desperate for the last bit of something to push me over the edge. The need for my demand of "more" like the tremor a moment before the true earthquake strikes.

Liam curses, and with a frustrated sound, he presses on my clit, hard, and I shatter. The world blanks, my body nothing but white-hot pleasure and motion. Hardly a moment later, first Liam, then Xander come too, all of us a shuddering mass of limbs, heat, weight, sweat, and blood. Liam's chest rises and falls in an uneven rhythm, and Xander's heart pounds hard enough for me to feel it through my back.

I fade into the unending pleasure, unable to form words, or even thoughts, just drifting in a space outside my body, but fully kept in a circle of strong arms.

Eventually, I'm coaxed out of the clouds by long, soothing caresses on my back and kisses feathered across my front like so many raindrops, each touch precious in its newness.

"Okay. You win this round," I mumble, my face pressed against a freckled pec.

"Damn right I do," Xander mumbles against my back.

"I'm fairly certain we all just won," Liam says, one palm sliding from my shoulder to where my hand presses against his thundering heart.

"Meanwhile, I'm fairly certain I'm going to have to kill someone," a voice says from a short distance away.

I don't need to move to see who's speaking. None of us do.

"Hey Eddie," I say from the middle of my man sandwich.

A shirt lands over my head, blocking out the brightening sky. "Get your asses dressed. I don't need to see anybody's shit right now."

"Or you could fuck off for another twenty minutes, boogerhead. You're ruining my afterglow," I reply.

"I swear to god, I will shoot my best friends right now, snotnose."

I pluck off the shirt and twist to glare at him. "You shoot them, I shoot you."

This gets me a kiss against the back of my neck from Xander and an exasperated groan from my brother.

"I'll give you a single minute. Doc's getting his supplies out of the car. He doesn't need to see your hairy ass, Liu. Or my baby sister's tits. And who knows what all you're showing under that pile, O'Connell, but that leg looks like shit, even if it is wearing a tutu."

"Feels like shit, too," he mumbles, taking my palm and kissing it. "But it can wait just another minute."

Another minute. Or a lifetime. We'll have to see what they agree to.

But another minute is a good start.

Chapter Fourteen
Liam

Doc patches me up the best he can, but he still recommends I head to a hospital and get my leg looked at. There's a good chance there's nerve damage, which is fucked up, but still better than dead.

As Xander tries to talk Doc out of dragging him away from Cece, who's perched on top of the trunk we were all jammed in just a few hours ago, I can't say I regret much about tonight.

Getting shot? Yeah. I should have had a better plan than just throwing my superior mass blindly out of the trunk, but all I could think about was Eddie's anger if I let his kid sister get hurt.

And as Eddie hangs up from one of his various damage control calls and strides to me, I have to admit that I'm still in for it with him.

Even if his kid sister ended up being the one doing the protecting.

Sure enough, when the fist flies at my jaw, I brace for it, but don't dodge. It's deserved, especially with the way he found us.

"Seriously, O'Connell? I expect this kind of shit from Liu, but you should know better. She's my sister."

"And a grown-ass adult," I say, rubbing my jaw, remembering her annoyance when I suggested otherwise. Before I knew who I was dealing with. If nothing else, it will help sell the "I was mugged" story I plan to use at the hospital.

Eddie glances down at my leg, then motions for me to get into his hand-me-down GTX. Once I'm in the passenger seat with my leg on the dash, he turns to me, his eyes flicking to Cece and Xander. Doc's treating him while Cece's curled up in his lap like a cat, Eddie's shirt not covering nearly as much of his sister as he likely hoped it would.

"She's more than just a notch in Xander's bedpost," I say, guessing where his head is at.

He taps a finger against the wheel. "And you know that how?"

"You weren't out here tonight. It...listen, we've all been in shitty situations. Dangerous ones. Deadly ones. Only there's something about standing in front of your grave, waiting for death, only to have a SoCal princess, complete in a prom dress, swoop in and save you. I'm just saying it changes a man."

"So, you're a changed man, O'Connell?"

Xander says something, and Cece throws her head back, laughing as a kick of wind tugs at her hair. And all I want to do is to drag myself across the gravel to be with them. To catch that lock of hair, tuck it behind her ear, wrap my arms around her, and give her all the hugs she's missed out on over the years. To be by her side as she shows the world exactly what kind of woman hides behind those shining eyes and mischievous grin.

One who will fight to the death to protect the people she cares about; a woman who will fight for what she wants. While she hasn't said it, not yet, I'm pretty sure she wants me.

I might be morose, and I might have to work on being less of an alcoholic, but I'm not an idiot.

And tonight was just the beginning.

"Yeah, Eddie. I'm a changed man. And no big brother bluster you could throw my way would keep me from Cece if that's what she wants."

He slumps back against his seat. "But all three of you? How's that going to work? Three heirs can't all play happy family. That's not how this world works."

"This world doesn't allow female heirs. So, what's another change? We'll figure it out. Either that, or we'll kill anybody who disagrees with the way we conduct our business. But we'll make it work. We both know that if it's what Cece wants..."

"Then she'll fight to the death to get it." Eddie sighs, snapping his head to me when Xander drags Cece's mouth to his, the kiss hot enough that even my already spent, injured ass gets turned on. I have a feeling this is going to be a constant state for me going forward. I can't say I hate it.

"In that case, O'Connell. Welcome to the family. And if you hurt my sister..."

"You'll kill me. I know the deal."

"No, you idiot. If you hurt her, I'll hunt you down and drag you back to her, where she can exact whatever vengeance she's due. And trust me, what you saw tonight is just a taste of the violence hidden in Cecelia Rodriguez."

A smile twitches at the corner of my mouth as Doc finishes up, freeing Xander to pin Cece against the back windshield of the old Honda Accord. The newly risen sun coating them in shades of pink and orange as they toy with each other. This leg had better heal fast. Because I want in on that shit. "Understood. It'd be one hell of a way to go, you've got to admit."

Eddie snorts. "If you say so, man."

He honks the horn, and Cece and Xander both throw up their middle fingers in response. He rolls down the window, something between exasperation and contentment on his face. "Knock it off, you two. You're acting like teenagers. And your third little lover needs to get to a hospital. So, unless you want O'Connell to lose a leg, get your asses in gear so we can get the hell out of here."

This gets their attention, but before they slide into the back, Cece throws open the passenger door, one hand on the swell of her hip as she looks down at me. Then she's wrapping her hands around my neck, directing my mouth to hers. This kiss is better suited for the cover of night, but Eddie's mortification gets drowned out by the feel of her thighs under my fingers and the taste of her against my tongue.

"I didn't want you to feel left out. Because I choose you, too," she whispers as she draws back. But for just a second, I hold on too tight, and she sighs, relaxing against me.

"Same," I rasp, words tough to gather as peace and hope, so unfamiliar I hardly recognize them, flood through me with her claiming.

Once we're on the way, driving toward the sunrise and hospital, away from the lingering night beyond the graveyard, it's obvious that this is my chance to start again. A new life for my battered old soul.

One that centers around a tiny, lethal woman and a world that needs to be changed. If it takes a bit of blood to get there, well, I'm more than familiar with the stuff.

Maybe this time, *I'll* get to save *her*.

Although, somehow, I have a feeling it will always be the other way around for us.

It's a future I could look forward to, as strange as the realization is. The stroke of her fingers against the back of my neck as she and Eddie bicker, Xander taking her side with a smirk, is more perfect than a fuck-up like me deserves.

If it takes being less of a fuck-up to keep it? Then I better get my head on straight. Because if I'm going to spend my life standing beside the amazing woman currently running her nails over my scalp, I've got to be the best.

I catch Xander's eye, and I see the same steel that's just cooled in my spine reflected at me. His clenched fist and the tick in his jaw greet my silent question. We'll be her armor, freeing her to fight the battles she needs to without the worry of taking damage.

We're hers.

Forever.

About the Author

Maisie Kane is a writer of spicy polyamorous romances, risk-loving criminals, and fearless love that shatters expectations.

When she isn't reading or writing, you can find her wandering the woods near her house with a ceramic mug of coffee in hand.

Yes it spills, and no, she doesn't give a damn.

If you want **more of Cece, Liam, and Xander**, as well as other fun bonuses and updates, follow the link below to find out how that game of strip shooting went. Wanna bet who won? (Spoiler alert: they all did...eventually.)

https://tinyurl.com/mkshbonus

The Viper and Chef

By: Kenya Goree-Bell

About The Viper and Chef

Scooch in for a Takeda suprise

Content Note:

As promised this book is all Dark Vibes and hunching. This story has on page meanness from the hero. There is light BDSM. There are also elements of intimidation and harsh language by the villain. If you are uneasy with any of that I ask that you pass on this book. My writing is not for you and that is okay.

Relationship type: Male, Female, cis, het

The Viper and Chef

Krie

"The fuck is your problem, wife?"

Dragging my gaze away from the landscape of the countryside just north of Osaka, I look at my mean-ass husband in utter disbelief.

"Nothing," I mumble, swallowing the lump in my throat. Turning from back to the landscape we're racing by in the sleek Rolls-Royce Phantom, flying like we're on a cloud. A queasy cloud. With every sleek turn or swerve we take up the countryside my stomach heaves.

Silence drops between us so heavy and hurtful. I try to swallow it down, but it may as well be a huge wad of cotton clogging my throat.

How can someone who has a genius-level intellect be so fucking dense? I guess he'd have to care first. Which he doesn't, as I am starting to realize more and more — at least not about me. His business, his connections to the vast Yakuza syndicate he's forging with his brother and cousins, and whoever he keeps running back here to Japan to fuck is what he cares about, but it ain't me. Definitely not me.

"You will look at me, Krie-chan." The words are uttered with so much wrath that I do, in fact, find myself looking at him aghast. He hasn't called me that in months. Try as I might, I can't pinpoint what I could have done or rather what he could have found out that has left him acting this way. The truth is, it's probably something to do with my family. The proverbial thorn in our sides or rather our marriage.

His gaze rakes me from my Uggs up the lines of my elegant jumpsuit to the high, loose, messy bun I'm wearing. The way his gaze flicks over me, you'd think I had on a dirty sack. No my couture YSL jumpsuit is not to his exacting standards. Not that I care. I'm tired — in fact, I'm exhausted. I'm bloated, and I worked my tail off at my restaurant, The Camellia, before entrusting it to my capable but still young sous chefs for the holiday season.

Coming to Japan to spend this precious time with my husband's ruthless family was not on my list of things to do and definitely not a preferred activity during such a sacred time.

Yet when Flower extended her invitation, the first since she and Akchiro reconciled last year, Kiyoshi felt an obligation to accept for both of us. I love my cousin by marriage, I do, but I'd rather be caught in a Sun Down Town after dark than come back here. I'd probably fare better.

I face him still not believing he brought me back here.

"What?" Immediately, I realize my mistake snapping at him. His face grows colder if that is even possible.

"The fuck, you say?" Steely hands are snatching me into his lap, making my tender breasts smash into his hard chest. Eyes narrowing at my gasp and the wince I give from the contact, he assesses me silently for a long moment.

"You will not demand my face. Your behavior is unacceptable. We won't even talk about your actions, your lies." He bites at me through gritted teeth.

"I-I haven't done anything." I look him straight in the eye. The truth is I haven't. I may have helped my cousins with various enterprises and escapes from their unhinged men, but I haven't done anything to him. I'd never hurt him.

The cruelty of the smile he gives me wretches my heart. The tinge of sadness behind it, the disappointment is nearly unbearable.

I push down thoughts of my secret project. He couldn't have possibly figured it out otherwise this trip would have been canceled.

Suddenly my chest heaves. I can't bear that look. Acid eats up the back of my throat.

"Stop," I gasp, lunging forward. "Make him stop the car." I manage to get out, holding back the gorge rising as best I can.

Kiyoshi gives the command, and the car swerves, stopping seconds later.

I'm out of the car and on the side of the road, heaving up the meager contents of my tummy like a drunk sorority girl after a game night party.

After what feels like a lifetime and I've birthed a lung out of my mouth later, I rise weakly to stand to my full five-foot-two height.

I notice his huge shadow looming over my shoulder seconds before a monogrammed handkerchief comes to rest there. The scent of it reminds me of him and is soothes me despite us being at odds.

"Arigato," I mumble, taking his offering.

More stony silence as he passes me a mini bottle of water to rinse my mouth.

I don't say anything this time. Words are useless to a man like my husband. Action is all he knows and respects. It's enough that I gave my thanks. Anything else is seen as weakness in a man who deals with sycophants on a daily basis. The last thing he wants from his wife is obsequiousness.

Silently, we make our way to the car. He helps me inside.

As soon as he settles, he pulls me into his arms almost as if he's cuddling me.

I know better. He's going to punish me. Tenderness always precedes his punishments, and aftercare always follows.

"You will tell me why you are sick," he quietly demands after we have gotten back to the road leading to Takeda Manse.

My mind spirals. "Eating hastily yesterday as I was getting ready for the trip," I shrug mumbling into the tendons of his neck. I can feel his gaze peeling the skin of my skull back in an attempt to figure me out. To see if I'm lying to him. I'm not. Everything has been so hectic. My nerves frayed from the tension that plagues our marriage these last couple of months.

Taking a chance, I snuggle closer. By the way his stiffens, I expect him to pitch me over to the other side of the car. Eventually, he relaxes. Probably in a far shorter time than my harried brain realizes. Still why is he stiffening? Holding himself rigid as if he can't stand to touch me?

Strong arms circle me. I sigh. The cramps from the retching have subsided enough for me to relax.

I let exhaustion pull me under and dream about sweeter times...

Months earlier...

* * *

"Wake up, sleepyhead," I murmur, smiling when my husband's eyes peek at me through the thick fringe of his lashes.

"You beat me awake. Impossible," he scoffs, rising to ease back against the headboard, letting the sheet fall to his waist. His wiry form is a mass of lean muscle, not an ounce of fat to spare. It takes everything in me not to fall into the invitation I see in his singularly focused gaze.

"I set my timer. I have something special for you," I tell him.

His brow quirks, and a skeptical smile plays across his face. "For me?"

"Yes, silly." I lean in, taking his mouth. Long, taper fingers spear into the curls at my nape.

Our tongues tangle. He never has morning breath, so I'm more than eager to let him linger on my lips, drawing out sighs that make my coochie clench with promise his mouth is making.

It takes everything in me not to lean in more when he tries to draw me down. "Uh-uh, babe. Come on." I pull back with a cajoling smile, gently tugging on his arm.

"Are you serious?" he grumbles, looking meaningfully down at the tenting cover.

"Later, I promise." Backing up because I know if he presses the issue, I will put my hands on him and he won't stop until I'm ruined with no energy. Today is too special to let him distract me.

"I'm going to hold you to that, wife." He growls, throwing off the covers, standing nude before me with a ragingly hard dick. The glistening tipped, heavy-veined appendage has my mouth watering.

"Go ahead and take care of your business. I'll be right here." Shooing him away, I pull my robe a little tighter to reduce some of the tension that kiss caused in my now-sensitive body.

"Ready?" I ask when he emerges moments later in the black silk loungewear he prefers. Per his tradition, not an inch of his body is revealed. I'm the only person who has ever seen him fully naked. Seems fair since he is the same for me. My first, my last, my everything.

"Sure." He deadpans the obvious with a dry smirk on his face.

Rolling my eyes, I grab his hands, pulling him behind me.

My heart trips over itself as I take him through the grand expanse of the samurai mansion my husband had built in my small hometown of Shelby-Love, Alabama, when he was installed as the CEO of the Creative Chaos factory by his cousin, Akchiro, as punishment for trying to usurp his position.

The fact that he survived that and managed to marry me is a miracle, which is why I feel no small amount of trepidation about what I've done. Kiyoshi is not a man who likes secrets, and he also doesn't like surprises, but if I can't surprise him today of all days, then what are we doing?

"What's this?" he asks when we step onto the garden terrace.

"Just a little something I threw together for your birthday. Happy birthday, babe." I can feel how tremulous my smile is. I see him track it.

I see the confusion on his face then as the realization dawns. My heart aches as I come to a realization as well. He forgot his own birthday.

I watch as his onyx gaze falls on all his favorite dishes from home. Some he's probably never had in the years he's been the CEO of Creative Chaos, some he's not indulged in since childhood.

Almost as if he's afraid the food is going to attack him, he makes his way over to the spread and picks up a hanami dango. His eyes raise and meet mine in wonder. I give him a slight shake of my head.

"I made them all myself," I say softly. "Sit, sit, eat while they are still warm."I tell him in Japanese, knowing I rushed back to our bedroom as soon as I had everything ready. Waving for him to take the seat centered among the various treats.

I hold my breath watching as he does. As soon as his bottom touches the chair, I hurry over to serve him. Patiently, I wait, nerves frayed as hell, as he samples every dish from sweet to savory.

"Come sit with me, kirei." He says with a solemnness that I've come to expect. Still, I preen just as I do every time he calls me beautiful.

When I sit, I more than feel his quiet appreciation. Smooth, firm lips press a kiss on the hollow of my neck.

"Taste," he rumbles near my ear. My mind can't help going back to a few years ago when he was my ultimate nemesis, making me taste all the food I served him before he'd dare touch it.

I meet his gaze just as I did back then when my lips close over the sweet rice ball of the hanami dango. His gaze fires, smolders, and consumes me, watching as I take the ball from the skewer. The flavor is light and delicate, with just a hint of sweetness.

"Good?" A small smile plays across his mouth, and he watches me.

"Um-hum," I smile back. Cupping the nape of my neck, he draws me into the sweetest kiss.

"Not as good as you," he says when he leaves me panting.

"Arigato, little chef."

* * *

"Okay," I say, looking over my shoulder to make sure he's not peeking. "You can open your eyes.

Stepping out of his way so he can view his gift, I move to stand at his side.

I watch, and he looks at the portrait of his father I had commissioned.

"How?" He asks, stunned awe packed into the word. Quickly, he looks at me, then back at the portrait. I see him visibly swallow as he takes in the painting of his father standing out against what looks to be a matte black background, but as he steps closer, it becomes clear that there is a myriad of colors inlaid within. Closer still, you see messages inlaid in kanji with the portrait.

We uncovered many of his father's writings after the death of his mother. Kiyoshi treasures them more than anything.

"Kana and Hisashi helped me pick the best ones," I tell him in answer to his question about his gift. My Japanese is good but not that good to determine which of his father's writings were the best to use. So, I enlisted his siblings for help. They were so excited, though Hisashi seemed to be in an intense debate with his Guardian, who wanted to be a little more bloodthirsty. Acquiescing to the fact that his father was not all sunshine and roses; they eventually came to family, art and beauty from Kana. Hisashi chose loyalty, work and sacrifice.

Taking his time to read them all, he moves gracefully from end to end of the portrait?"

"Who did the portrait?" He asks, never taking his eyes off the piece.

"Mai's brother, Tsuyoshi. I saw one of his paintings when she had me over for lunch, and it was amazing. When I saw it, I knew he would be perfect... and discreet." I add that last part knowing more than anyone how private my husband is about family matters.

His visible stiffness at the mention of his once-fiancée and my association with her eases when I go into more detail about the process of having the piece made for him. The Yakuza Prince, as he is known, is famous for his discretion as he is for his ruthlessness. What many don't know about him is his virtuoso artistic talent.

Turning fully to me the first time since seeing the painting, he looks down with all the love he never believed he could have for me. "It's perfect. Just like you."

Tugging me into his strong arms. He whispers against my curls, "I don't need gifts when I have you, but thank you. Thank you, Aishiteru yo."

* * *

Now...

* * *

I look how I feel. Like a corpse. I could dead-ass be an extra on The Walking Dead with the way I'm looking. My messy bun is totally flopped to the side, hanging in a limp ponytail with a clip looking like it decided against jumping at the last minute and is hanging on by its fingernails.

My eyes are hollow, my cheeks sallow, and my lips look dry with the gloss chewed away by nerves. I'm starting to feel as frazzled as I did when I first got involved with Kiyoshi.

That time was maybe the most fraught time of my life aside from losing my parents a few years prior.

I nearly lost everything. The whole town and some of my family seemed so against me. At the time, I didn't know Kiyoshi worked quietly in the shadows to support me — not until the very end. Somehow, we made it through. I hope that he stops icing me out and tells me what his deal is.

The urge to use the restroom interrupts my critical assessment of my current dishevelment screaming at me from the mirror.

At least I was given the small mercy of having no one but the most minimal of the Takeda staff present when we arrived. I still kind of miffed that Kiyoshi didn't bother waking me until the car came to a stop at the entrance. Though it is only mid-afternoon, we were told Akchiro and Flower were indisposed at and could not personally greet us. Like I said, small mercies. It would not be good for the de facto head of the family to see me in such a state, and Flower would certainly have been worried. So much so that she'd reached out to Delightful, my cousin, and her sister-in-law, not to mention my other cousins in Shelby-Love. Then all hell would break loose if Oz thought for a moment that Kiyoshi was mistreating me. Knowing how intense my family is, I cringe at the thought. No, things are not that bad. And I know how to deal with Kiyoshi. He's mine, and I know who I married.

Pushing the door of the water closet open, I hobble over to the toilet. I'm all but starting to tinkle when the door is shoved open.

"Here," he snaps with a damning look, whipping out a pregnancy test strip, causing me to jump with a high-pitched "eep".

Startled, I touch the place over my heart he made gallop with his popping up like a weirdo super villain out of nowhere to attack me with a pregnancy test.

Fuck.

"Stop and take the test, Krie," he bites out.

Obeying his demand, I try — I really do, but now that I think of it on the plane I drank a lot of water and wine.

Heart racing, I finally manage to Kegel enough to stop the flow.

My hand trembles as I take the stick he's holding out like an indictment.

Dropping his arm, he steps back and watches very much like the vipers he tattooed on his body.

His gaze is lasered between my legs as I let the stream flow. Just as I finish, he steps forward, grabbing a tissue.

"Open," he grounds out.

Splaying my legs wider, I try to bite back the strangled squeak as he reaches between my thighs, brushing the tissue against my pussy before letting it drop.

"Give it to me." Handing him the stick, I watch as he wraps it in another tissue before stepping out, leaving me there staring after him.

My heart is beating out of my chest.

Scrambling, I take more tissue to do a better job — because what was that little swipe going to do; and hurry after him.

He is staring at the stick when I reach his side. His breath is sawing in and out like he's run a marathon.

It's like slow motion when he turns his wrath-filled gaze on me. His jaw works like he's grinding glass. His nostrils flare. He closes his eyes and shakes his head before allowing his gaze to rest on me again.

Pressing his lips closed in a hard line, he flings the test on the counter, making it clatter against the marble then stalks out of the bathroom.

My tummy is in knots like my period is starting while I stand watching after him for a few moments.

Picking up the test, I know that is an impossibility when I see the double lines.

* * *

Kiyoshi

This little motherfucker, I swear. I could ring her neck. I needed to leave before I did or said something that would further solidify me as the monster she likes to make me out to be.

We have been through this. She has been adamant about not having a child, especially mine, anytime soon. And now when I am in the midst of restructuring part of our organization to work with the Tatsumoto, Cruz, Love, and Savelle syndicates, she decides without any consultation to bring an innocent into the midst.

Rage pours through me like a gasoline fire. Having no place to put it. I go to my family's dojo.

I waste no time stripping and getting work going, going through the motions to loosen my body.

Sufficiently warmed, I take my sword from its scabbard clearing my mind as I take my first kujutsu form.

Slowly building my momentum until I'm making smooth slashes and sharp, precise lunges, I lose myself to time, totally immersed in the graceful fluidity of movements drilled into me with more than three decades of training. Takedas begin training at the age of three formally, but really basic instruction starts as soon as we can stand and follow basic commands. This is all I've ever known, and for a long time before a certain little curvy chef came into my life, all I have ever felt comfortable with. Training, strategic thinking, and working to increase the vast holdings of the Takeda has been drilled into me from the time I was a child. The Takeda Legacy is all I have ever been taught to want — it wasn't until my brothers' misfortunes and later loving Krie that those dreams turned to ash. Our legacy, though storied in Japan's history, is rife with psychotics, carnage, and despair, the bequeathment of the Takeda. I can't allow it to continue. The devastation when Krie chose not to allow my seed to take root almost broke me, only then to discover it was helped along by my mother's machinations. Knowing we would have no children resulting from our union gave way to relief, knowing the probability of creating a monster like my mother.

Those lines on that fucking stick — fuck. Her deception is even worse. All this bullshit about communication when she went behind my back and had her IUD removed.

Fluid movements slide into more. Ferocity holds me in its

embrace as I practice one kill after another. We don't battle our enemies like this anymore. My demons are my only adversary in the moment. I can't allow the rage eating at me to further push Krie away. I didn't miss her confusion and hurt at my reaction. Did she really not think I wouldn't find out? Did she think I wanted this after everything we've been through?

"Do you want a real fight, cousin, or would you rather keep punching the air?" Words like ice draw my attention to Akchiro, lounging against the entrance of the dojo.

Narrowing my eyes as he moves gracefully into the room going over to the wall laden with weapons, I say nothing, only nod when he pulls a kanabō from the wall, swinging the bat-like spike mace. His eyes glint with malice as he regards me.

"Family issues?" His mouth hitches up in a cruel smirk.

"Whenever is there not with the women we've chosen?" I ask, reminding him none too gently about his own recent circumstances.

"Hai," the motherfucker has the nerve to chuckle, not at all bothered. "Shall we?" He bows, and I return the salutation.

We clash in a stinging blow. Neither the katana nor the kanabō are blunted, so when he glances my shoulder with a particular devious move, I wince as the sharp spikes rip my skin.

"For her sympathy, old man." Akchiro winks in a particularly mischievous way.

Dropping low, I swirl in a rapid circle, taking one leg beneath him. He flips, using the kanabō as a counterbalance.

I grunt in approval. My cousin's moves have always been superlative.

Still, the rage purging through my veins gives me the advantage. Attack after relentless attack finally leaves a nick opening at the base of his throat. In a move that, if I held any real intention behind it, would have separated his head from his body, I slice into the divot right beside his jugular.

"Enough," he grounds out, acquiescing to my win with a bow. Nodding grudgingly because I could've gone a couple more rounds.

"Good session." I say, taking my sword to clean before retiring it to its place on the wall.

"So what is all this about?" Ripping off a square of muslin to stanch his wound, he eyes me shrewdly.

"Krie's pregnant." I tell him, not bothering to meet his gaze as I perform my cool-down routine. The sparring session has done nothing to relieve the tension in my body.

"I assume congratulations are not in order," he murmurs, eyes steady but holding no judgement.

"We'd agreed to wait." Sighing, I move into another position.

"I too thought Flower and I were aligned on the issue of more children." He tells me, going through his own exercises. "Quite the opposite of what you seem to be going through, though. I wanted more kids, and she wanted to wait — indefinitely."

I don't miss the frown that attests to one of the core reasons he almost lost his wife a year ago.

"I'm in that same space. For many of the same reasons, probably." I tell him, using none of the tatemae we are known for, no. I'm laying it out, plainly for him. Full honne. "Insanity runs deep in this family. Who knows what kind of monster we are going to bring into the world?"

"You mentioned monster brother?" The low drawl of amusement has me meeting the clear gaze of my brother.

Stopping the cringe before it registers, I face my brother, Hisashi, as he moves into the room dressed for exercise with a smooth, casualness that would mislead some to think he's not the ruthless killer that he is. He did what I could never bring myself to do, and for that, he's my hero.

"Brother, I misspoke." Bowing to him in apology is wasted. He's already waving it away like it doesn't matter.

"I am who I am." He comes to stand opposite me alongside Akchiro. "I assume congratulations are in order?" He pauses, taking me in. "Or rather, lamentations?" Chuckling, he shakes his head. "I felt the same until my little wife assured me. That when we are ready

— which I can assure you would be any day if she were to have her way. Diluting the bloodline with fresh stock will probably offset some of the madness that we've been plagued with. Also, Kiyoshi," he muses, his eyes flashing with the momentarily with the other entity that lies within. "Your brother was nurtured to become what we are. Your father did his best, but Hisashi nursed at the breast of a viper. You did as well." The cold chill of my brother's Monster-Guardian doesn't negate the truth of his words.

"Your children will have you and Krie to safeguard them." Akchiro agrees, giving me a sliver of hope.

"Now who'd like to spar with us?" Hisashi asks, pulling a spear down. Never to be called a coward, my cousin and I both pull down new weapons, knowing it will take both our prowess to tame my brother and the monster who lives in his mind.

Krie

Kiyoshi is angry with me, and I can't even blame him. Hell, I'm mad at myself. It was never my intention to get pregnant, just as my restaurant is taking back off after the fire destroyed it a little over a year ago. Now is not the time to be a new mom.

Still, I want this baby. As much as I know I wasn't ready last time. I know with everything in my being I am now.

I look up to the slide of the door as Kiyoshi enters. Very much like the last time we were here when his mother feigned her illness, he's incensed. Color is riding high on his cheekbones, and I don't for one moment delude myself into thinking it is because he's just finished working out. Which is evident by the way the linen of this keikogi is clinging to him.

His gaze is like ice as he looks at me like I've betrayed him. Lost as to what to do, I simply look at him, not sure if I should start talking double-time or remain silent because there is nothing I can say at this point to get him to believe me.

I was the one to insist on taking charge of contraception once the mishap on the plane occurred, and I had to take the Plan B as a result. We only found out later what his mother had done, slipping herbs into my food so that I'd miscarry anyway.

The discomfort of the IUD became all too much, and in a fit of frustration, I had Mimi take it out while he was away. I got the birth control pills she gave me, and I really didn't think about anything other than the relief I felt from not being in excruciating pain every month when I got my period.

His nostrils flare, then exhaling, his gaze slides to the side, then back at us, spearing me with an intensity that should have me fleeing.

I gird myself for the vivisection of words he's about to unleash. His jaw works, shifting away from me, the heads toward the bathroom.

"You will attend me." The words drift to me after he's already passed out of the room.

My heart thuds while I remain rooted where I stand.

"Krie." The whiplash of my name makes me jump into the moment. No thought, only movement as I follow my visibly angry husband into the bathroom.

When I enter the shower area he's removed his belt. The top of the martial uniform hangs loose.

Stepping into his space, I take in the scents of sweet musk, nascent cologne, and him. I have to bite back the moan catching my lower lip between my teeth. My eyes dart up to his, and I immediately know he didn't miss my response.

"Oh, none of that little chef," he tsks, pulling my lip out of the cage I put it in. He rubs the indentation with his thumb, shaking his head at me.

Reaching inside the keikogi, I untie the innermost fastening. When it releases, lean muscle rippling with every breath captures my needy gaze. It's been so long since he last made love to me. I realize that moment it was a punishment. He withheld himself from me.

My fingers tremble as I move behind him. I get on my tiptoes. Reaching as high as I can, I grab the edge of the material, dragging it over his broad shoulders.

He does nothing to help. Holding his body as rigid as the thousand-year-old statues that populate the gardens here, his gaze simply flicks over me as I move to put the top away.

A hard hand just short of painful grabs my upper arm, halting me.

He snatches the shirt. Tossing it onto a nearby bench.

"Continue." He drags me to his front. His dick is pressed high against the pants. I pull the string, untying then loosening them. Dick springing up he steps free.

"Join me." His voice is a cruel seduction. I know better than to believe this is anything other than discipline.

My hair is already up, so it's nothing for me to pull off the chemise I'm wearing, letting it fall to the floor.

Moving in front of him, I lead the way into the shower that can more than accommodate five more people. The controls have already been set to my preference, and I don't bother to change them for him. He can suffer a little if he's so determined to be mean.

Smoothing my hair back more, I secure it as the spray cascades over our bodies.

Taking my net sponge, I begin to soap it. Facing away from the water, I face him and begin washing his torso.

"Did you think I didn't know?" He asks, looking down at me. Water clings to his onyx lashes. His obsidian eyes bore into me. There is a vulnerability there I hadn't seen before. His jaw works as he struggles not to let the vipers out to tear me asunder. But I can tell he wants to so bad.

"I didn't know." I dip my head down, feeling more than a little silly. "I should have thought to consider the possibility. I just assumed it was my body adjusting to the birth control pills. I guess they hadn't kicked in before we got pregnant."

"And you didn't think to tell me that you removed the IUD?" Tipping my chin up, he makes me meet his gaze. His eyes search mine, waiting. Doubting.

"I didn't think it would be a big deal—"

"Everything about you is a big deal to me, Krie," he scoffs, skewering me with the blaze of his regard. "You know this. So tell me fucking why?"

"You were busy, traveling—"

Canting his head to the side he blinks, ferreting through what I'm not saying. Slicking his hair back from the water, his gaze hardens.

Unable to take him looking at me like he's about to peel the flesh from my bones, in silence, I wash him, trying to find solace in the water hitting the tiles.

Smoothing circular strokes over his body, I make quick work of the task. Dropping low, I wash his lower half before standing again, taking his dick in my hands, thoroughly washing him the way he likes. I can't hide the smirk when I reach his ass, and he tenses like he always does. Switching so he can rinse, I don't bother telling him I already showered, knowing he won't care.

He takes the soapy sponge from my hands. He takes particular care in his handling of me. Soon the entire front of my body is covered in luscious bubbles of scented jasmine and musk. It marries well with my signature vanilla-rose. I turn so he can cover my back. Gentle swirls across my tummy make my eyes sting. He turns me away from him, doing my shoulders, back, and bottom. The sponge drops with a sloppy splat on the wet tiles.

Pulling me flush with his hard body, his hand circles my neck massaging the soapiness making his fingers play over the tendons there in a delightful dance.

"You thought I was fucking around." The surety of his words eats at me. I did.

He pushes my legs apart. My breath catches. I feel the head of his dick pressing into me. I couldn't move if I wanted to. His arm is a vise around my waist, holding me still for his loving.

"You kept coming back here for business," I scramble to answer. My words ring high as he pushes in — the last syllable almost on a scream. The heavy beat of the water hits my body as he arches me, making me take all of him in one ruthless drive.

"Fuccck this pussy's so tight. Gushy too, see how my baby got you?" Dipping down, he nips my ear, fucking into me.

"You thought I wouldn't immediately notice the difference in your body? Your nipples were the first sign." Running, swirling little circles over the tips of my breasts with one deft hand, he makes my pussy clench so hard it almost hurts.

Long drives into me my aching pussy as he cups my mound follow driving me to my toes. Trying and failing to find purchase on the slick wall in front of me, I have no choice but to hold on to the arm holding me in place.

He hisses when I leave little crescents on his forearms.

The steady slapping of our bodies is its own erotic beat. His hips drive into me, making my bottom bounce on his dick.

"Why would I ever want another when you were fucking made for me, Krie-chan?" he grounds out. Bending over me, not missing a second of the driving rhythm of our bodies, he sucks hard on my neck. "When I own every part of you — your pussy, your heart, your very soul — is mine. Why would I fuck that up, little one?" He bites. I shatter. He doesn't stop; only goes harder. Driving me to my toes so hard I have no choice but to hold on as he uses me like a toy.

"Never doubt my love for you." Harsh words couple his maniacal fucking.

"Ki—" the words cut off as he drives even harder, cupping and grazing my clit over and over with his long fingers. I'm gone. My body pulls taunt as another orgasm shatters me. I screams name as I come undone.

"Never." He all but shouts, following me over the precipice.

* * *

"Your pussy tastes sweeter, little wife. Open wider for me." I whimper, doing as he demands.

Looking down, watching his head move between my legs. My body arches. He's edging me. Punishing me. I should have known the shower earlier was only a precursor to what was to come. He's taken me so many times I have lost count.

And I folded every time. I can deny him nothing. He's fierce, unhinged, and mine.

"I should make your little ornery ass wait, but if you promise to be a good girl and take me down your throat, I'll let your punishment end — for now."

I'm already nodding like the good little sub he's made me.

His mouth covers me with such delicious heat it causes my eyes to roll back. "Kiyoshi, babe, please." I don't even know what I'm asking for at this point. More? To stop? The way he loves on me is its own excruciating pleasure.

"Be a good little wife and thank your husband." He growls, spearing his tongue along the edges of my pussy lips before delving inside with a decadent slide.

"Arigato, otto." I cry, arching into his mouth as he ruins me.

Dragging me up to my knees, he grips my curls in a strong grip, guiding me to his thick length jutting from the dark thatch of curls.

"Good girl," he groans, thrusting into my mouth as I cover him.

"So fucking good. Take me down your hot little throat, tsunami." His guttural demand makes me clench and work harder for his release. With steady thrusts, he fucks my mouth, guiding me with one hand and stroking my nape.

"Krie-chan," he groans, holding me tight as he floods my mouth. "Let me see." Pulling away, I open my mouth, careful not to spill. "That's my hot little wife. Now swallow for me."

Holding his gaze, I do as he bids.

He covers me, kissing me deeply, tasting himself on my lips.

Exhaustion nearly takes me under, but not before he pulls me into his arms. I hear him whisper, "Rest for now, beautiful, but I'm far from done with you."

* * *

Later...

"Why didn't you say just coming here bothered you?" I scoot over to make room for him in behind me the soaking tub.

Another bath should be ridiculous, but after all the festivities my sore, aching muscles need it.

Kiyoshi's long legs encase mine as he pulls me back to his chest.

"I didn't think. Not until Taylor mentioned it, and you agreed with her." He grumbles pressing against my ear.

Nodding, I let my fingers dance across the water. "I thought you should've known. It made me mad that you didn't think about how I felt."

His arms tighten around me. "Krie—" he stops, and I feel him shaking his head, carefully choosing his words. His body tenses with frustration. "We eliminated the threat, and I made the mistake of thinking we were past it. I would never allow danger to ever touch you, kirei." He strokes me across my shoulders, turning me to face him.

"I breathe because you exist. Thank you for our baby." He presses a kiss to my temple.

"You gave me a precious gift." Bending, I kiss his fisted hand. He relaxes it, lacing his fingers through mine.

"What changed?" I tense, knowing it was going to eventually come up.

"I-I forgot to use a barrier method while the pills kicked in. But I want this baby with all my heart, Kiyoshi." His hand slips to my tummy.

"I'm so fucking glad you said that. We have to be vigilant about their mental health." I nod, already knowing his worries, though it was the least of my mine.

"Is that why you were so angry?" Turning, I catch his quickly shuttering gaze. Reaching up, I cup his cheek.

"It's okay. Your feelings are valid." Searching his gaze, I see the truth.

"We're going to be okay, and our baby will be loved no matter what." Pulling him down, I take his firm lips. In seconds, he's consuming me like I'm air.

"Aishiteru, yo." Releasing me, he stands, water cascading down his magnificent body. Scooping me into his strong arms, he wraps us both in towels.

"I love you, too." I whisper into his neck as he takes me to bed.

About the Author

Kenya Goree-Bell lives in Alabama with her former warrior husband and three kids. She is the author of the Harem Diaries Series and the bestselling Mogul Series and Blood Legacy Series. When not writing she is a romance novel influencer, lifelong bibliophile and can be seen weekly on Instagram and Facebook Live interviewing other authors on her IG: TheKGB — The K's Grown and Sexy Book Club. She believes that Happy Ever After belongs to everyone and writes about worlds where everyone deserves love.

Follow me on all social media @kenyagoreebell

Sign-up for my newsletter to get more information

The Naughty List

Join My Patreon to read my current WIP as I write it!

Kenya's Patreon

Twisted Help

By: Lily Prince

About Twisted Help

After a date goes terribly wrong, I can only call one man: Declan West. Then I ask for one more favor. A night of passion to help me forget. I didn't count on the price of his help.

Content note:

This story features attempted sexual assault (not romantic lead), dismissive family members, murder, and a one-night stand with a favor attached. It's a happy for now.

Relationship type: Male, female, cis, het/bisexual

Chapter One
Alice

Someone pulled my hair back and whispered, "Looky looky, it's Alice from Wonderland."

Inwardly, I groaned. Only *one* person would call me that. I twisted my body in my chair and glared at the handsome face in my space. It was Declan West, the son of a family friend. He sat beside me and I glanced at my mom. She nodded like she planned this.

"I saw Declan the other day and invited him to dinner with us. He had mentioned he hadn't seen you in years."

I widened my eyes to prevent myself from rolling them. "Maybe that was on purpose, *mother*," I snapped. I closed my eyes as I realized that came out harsher than I meant and sucked in a quick breath. Declan spread his legs and my heart raced at the sudden touch. My eyes snapped open, and I glanced at him. "Sorry."

My mother cleared her throat. "Like I was saying, I wanted to get everyone together. It is my birthday dinner."

"Sorry, mama," I mumbled as Declan chuckled under his breath. What my mother didn't know was the reason I avoided Declan for the last few years. As an adult, you find out what people are truly like. I found out Declan's family was involved with the mafia. That was enough for me to steer clear of him. I wasn't sure if he was high up or anything. I tried to forget about Declan and my childhood crush on him, which was easy since he teased me mercilessly as a teen. "Declan's and my life diverged in ways we'd never be around each other normally. It's just how things are."

"That's so sad," she said with a hand over her heart. I don't think anyone in my family knew about his dealings. I didn't want to tell them; it wasn't my place. The server walked to our table and my mother started to ramble off her order. I turned towards Declan.

"Why'd you accept?" I hissed.

"I wanted to see you again, and I wanted a chance to ask the pretty Alice out."

"The answer is no. Anyway, I have a date tomorrow," I whispered.

"He's the wrong fella for you," he replied as he brushed a stray lock of his dark hair out of his eyes.

I rolled my eyes before turning towards the server. "What would you like, ma'am?" he said brightly.

I quickly rattled off my order before waiting to finish my conversation with Declan. Once the server left, my mother turned towards my brother and chided him over something he had done recently. Same shit different day. Declan grinned as I turned towards him. His hand darted to my thigh, and I shoved it off.

"You can't say that. He seems pretty perfect from the app we clicked on," I said.

"Oh, I know things like this."

"You're still a dick. Anyway, you should have refused my mom."

Declan's eyes locked onto mine, and my heart skipped a beat. "I wanted to see you."

"But I didn't want to see you," I said.

"Alice, are you and Declan catching up?" my mother said and my head swiveled towards her again.

"Yes, I was just telling him about my plans tomorrow. I have a date with a lawyer I met recently," I exclaimed.

My mother smiled. "That's good to hear. Maybe you'll settle down like your brother. How far is the wedding?" she asked.

My brother chuckled. "Dawna is busy planning the wedding. She can't wait to be a spring bride," he said. He turned towards Declan. "I'll have to talk to Dawna about an invitation for you. How's your business going?"

Declan leaned forward as he sipped his wine glass. "It's been good." His eyes drifted towards me before returning to my brother. "Been single for a while. Been focused at making a name for myself at work. Not all of us are as blessed as you to find the partner of our dreams. The person who completes us and makes us whole."

I stared at him over my glass. Was he hinting at something? My brother nodded. "Yeah, I'm lucky. What do you do?"

"Family business. Got in with my uncle when he moved to town," Declan replied. "Been moving up in the ranks. It's been good."

"Better than Alice. She's working at a bookshop."

He turned towards me. I waved my hand. "Not everyone aspires to be globetrotting girl bosses," I replied.

"You left a decent job a few years ago."

"Too much stress, *mother*. I'm not cut out for that sh—stuff," I said.

Declan laughed as he placed his hand on my thigh again. I smiled again and pushed it off again. My father and mother started to argue back and forth about wedding plans with my brother. I turned to Declan. "Stop touching me," I whispered.

"Fine. I thought you might still have that crush on me."

I shook my head. "Nope. I don't deal with criminals."

Declan grinned. "Oh, so you are the only non-idiot here, aren't you?"

"That's my family you're talking about."

He leaned in closer and whispered, "I know. They like to see the nice things in life, don't they? Everything is always so nice and cheery for them. But there's a darkness in you. Or you've seen the dark."

I pursed my lips, but before I could argue with him again, our

food came to the table. We muttered our thank you's. I pulled my
phone out and checked for any messages. I had a message from my
date tomorrow and I tried to respond when Declan grabbed my hand.
He pulled my phone from my hand and opened my phone book app.

"I want you to remember if you need *anything*—and I mean
anything—you need to call me."

"Oh, whoop de doo. I don't think there is anything that could ever
happen that would make me do that," I snapped.

"Just wait. The dark will come to get you again," he said with
confidence.

"Are you threatening me?"

"Absolutely not. Now enjoy your meal," he said. "Let's stop these
petty quibbles."

"Petty for you. Your trouble. Always have been," I replied as I
shoved a bite of pasta in my mouth.

"Didn't you date that Dillion at one point? He sold drugs. Bad
boy type."

"I didn't know at the time."

"But he was a 'bad boy', as you girls like to say," Declan argued.
"I'm just your type."

"Stop it," I hissed. "Be pleasant."

Declan chuckled. "I can be very pleasant. You just have to spread
your legs for it," he whispered. The fiery touch of his breath traced
down my neck and straight to my pussy.

I shook my head and grabbed my cup again to distract myself
from my feelings. This night was going awful and my family kept
getting wrapped up with my brother's wedding plans instead of
talking to me, which meant Declan could flirt with me all he wanted.
"I would never."

"Never say never. Life has a way of finding a way."

"Oh, are you quoting Jurassic Park?" I snapped.

"It's a good movie. Better than their wedding planning. What do
you want yours to look like?"

"Not like Dawna's, that's for sure."

"Well?"

"She wants a princess style fairytale wedding. I don't, but it doesn't matter. I'm not getting married anytime soon."

"What if..." He glanced at my phone sitting between us as the notifications lit up once more. He tapped the screen and grinned. "Harry here is the one?"

"He's not the one. But he'll be fun to be with for a while. Plus, it's only the first date. Can't be all weird and plan a wedding after a first date."

"Alice, why are you monopolizing Declan's conversation?" my father said.

I turned away with my cup covering my face to hide the sneer I made. "Sorry. I don't think he wants to talk about weddings and gowns," I replied. "I was giving him better conversation."

Declan winked. "Yes. Absolutely. I was telling her how much I missed her over the last few years and I was curious about how we all grew apart."

"That's the sad thing about growing up. We all grow apart."

"Our lives diverted. It's what always happens," I mumbled.

His hand lifted and ghosted my hair like he was touching me. I waited for his touch, but he never touched me. "How poetic."

The server walked back to our table and asked about the checks. Declan cleared his throat and offered to pay for everyone's meals. As soon as he passed the card to the server, I said bye to my family and stood up. Storming to my car, I enjoyed the chilly breeze hit my face, a hand gripped my shoulder, and I turned around. Of course, it was Declan.

"What are you doing?"

He glared. "You didn't say bye to me."

"Of course not."

Declan frowned. "Remember what I said," he said as he stepped back.

"More like a threat," I hissed. "I know what you do. And I want nothing to do with it."

He shrugged. "Well, I want you to remember that you always have a friend in me."

"You've said it. It's kinda creepy now."

He smirked, his eyes glittering with mirth. "Good luck on your date tomorrow. I feel like with some jerks around here, you'll need it."

"I'm a big girl, I can handle myself," I snapped as I opened my car door and flipped him off as I shoved my keys into the ignition.

Chapter Two
Alice

I tapped my foot as I waited for my date to arrive. My phone dinged, and I looked at it. Kevin's name appeared on the screen and I walked out of my apartment door. A tall man that matched his profile picture stood beside a black jeep. He stepped forward and held out his hand.

"Hey, I'm Kevin. Nice to meet you finally," he said. His eyes looked down my body and a shiver of unease slid through my spine. I brushed it off and grabbed his hand. "It's nice to finally meet you."

I brushed my brown hair out of my face and nodded. "Yeah, nice to meet you after all these weeks." He turned and opened the car door. I sat in the seat and he walked around to the driver's side of the car.

He drove to the movie theater and parked. Before I could open the door, he opened the door for me. "Ah, you're a gentleman," I muttered.

"Of course."

He wrapped his arm inside mine and led me to the ticket booth. He quickly paid for our tickets and we went to our theater. While we waited for the movie to start, he leaned in closer to me.

"You're really pretty," he said.

I fiddled with the edge of my skirt. "Thanks." I tucked my hair behind my ear as I dipped my head lower. Saved by the dimming of the lights. I hated first dates and nothing felt natural yet. Hopefully, after the movie it would. Through the movie, his fingers would skirt on my thighs and hands. My heart fluttered as he would touch me, but it wasn't like a connection sort of flutter. Instead of paying attention to the movie, my mind drifted back to Declan. Those were different flutters. I wished these were those types of flutters, but they weren't.

Once the movie was over, he grabbed my hand and led me out of the dark theater. "Do you want to go back to my house? We can grab pizza on our way?" I asked. Maybe I needed more time with him. Love at first sight doesn't happen.

"Sounds great," he replied. "Order it and I'll pick it up."

Within a few minutes, the pizza was ordered, and he drove towards the pizza place. Parking at the side of the curb, he jumped out and grabbed a pizza. While he was gone, I texted my best friend to tell her what I was planning to do.

Shauna

You're being stupid.

Alice

He seems fine. I'll be fine.

Shauna

Make sure you text me later to make sure you are fine.

Kevin slipped into the jeep, and we drove to my apartment. "Did you like the movie?" he asked as we walked to the door. I tossed the pizza box on my coffee table and sat down.

"The movie was okay. I was kinda distracted," I mumbled.

He sat beside me. "I was too. You're extremely beautiful."

My stomach lurched again, and I tucked another hair behind my ear. "Thanks." I leaned forward and grabbed a piece of pizza. "I hate first dates. Don't you?"

He nodded as he grabbed his slice. "Yeah, they suck. Hopefully, this will be the last first date after a while."

A flutter erupted in my stomach. "Yeah, hopefully." But as much as I said the words, I didn't believe it. Some people had that instant connection and spark. This wasn't us. I already knew. His hand touched my thigh, but I didn't move it yet. Maybe it was time to see if feelings would blossom. But nothing was happening, no matter how long he touched me.

This was a dud of a date.

Oh well.

I wiped my mouth with my napkin and wiped the grease off my hands as he launched himself at me. His tongue pushed into my mouth as I tried to push him off of me. He was much stronger than I thought. I bit his tongue, and he lurched back.

"What the fuck?!" he screamed.

"I don't want to kiss you right now!" I screamed.

"You shouldn't have invited me back if you didn't want to fuck!"

"It's not like that!" I screamed as I tried to push him away again.

Kevin slammed me on the edge of the hard couch, and stars dotted my vision. His hands reached around my throat and everything spun as the air left my lungs. I thrashed and reached behind the arm of the couch for my knitting needles. I grabbed one and stabbed at his throat and face wildly. His hands fell off me and I rolled out from under him. I stumbled to my feet and grabbed a knife from the kitchen.

Was he screaming? Was I screaming? Someone was. I couldn't hear it over the thudding of my heart and the fear inside my soul. The needle stuck out of the side of his throat as blood poured everywhere. He lurched for me and I stabbed him in the gut. He dropped to the ground, and I pulled the knife out and stabbed again. In a trance, it was like every creepy guy interacting with me passed through my mind. I wasn't just stabbing my date, but every damn asshole in the world. It took a few more minutes before I stopped. My biceps screamed in exhaustion as I realized I was covered in blood. My eyes widened as I scooted backwards.

There was a dead body in my kitchen.

What was I going to do now?

Chapter Three
Declan

I should be grateful for a quiet night, but I wasn't. I was itching to do *something*. Or it was the feeling that something was about to happen. I flipped through my texts, seeing if there was anything I would need to handle. Next was my emails. Nothing. As I stared at my computer screen begging something to happen, my phone rang.

A name didn't flash with the number. I slid the icon over and said, "Hello?"

"Hi. Hello? Is this Declan?" a familiar voice said.

My eyes narrowed. There was no way she was calling me, was there? "Alice?" I asked.

"You said I could call you if I needed anything, right?"

"Yes. What do you need?" I asked.

"Can you get rid of a body?" she asked meekly.

A wry smile crossed my face. "Well, yes, I have people that can fix that for you. I'll be there in a few minutes," I said.

"Don't you need my address?" she asked.

"No. I know where you live."

I stood up and grabbed my jacket. I started texting the men I used for cleaners and walked out of my condo. I turned to one of my bodyguards at the door. "We're going on a trip."

"What sort of trip, boss?" he asked.

"It seems that the woman I'm in love with has a dead body on her hands. We're going to save the day," I replied.

He chuckled as we went to the car. He slid into the front seat as I started my car. "Can you drive us back? She might be shaken."

"What do you think happened?" he asked.

"I didn't ask. I told her the other day that I would be there if she needed me."

He grunted and continued to text the other men. It didn't take us long to get there, and I didn't even bother to knock. Sure enough, the front door was unlocked. The smell of blood filled the air. "Alice? Are you in here?"

"I'm in the kitchen. You didn't call the cops, right?"

I followed the blood trail all the way to the kitchen. A stranger with a knife and a knitting needle in his throat lay in a pool of blood on the floor. Alice was covered in his blood as she held her knees to her chest. Drips of his blood splashed onto the tile. Alice could have just called the cops, but she didn't. She called *me*. She shook her head, and I reached out my hand.

"Can you come here and pack a bag? I'll have my men clean this up. You'll need to leave for the next little bit," I said. "Or we don't have to pack anything. I can get someone to get you more clothes and toiletries."

"I shouldn't have called you," she whispered. "I didn't know what else to do."

"You did the right thing. We'll take care of everything. Come here."

She didn't move. I sighed and picked her up in bridal style carry. On our way out of the door, my cleaners arrived. My bodyguard slid into the front seat and I buckled Alice in the backseat and sat beside her. I tried to wrap my head around the fact she called me. I'm assuming she was defending herself. Why?

"You know what people say," she whispered, as if she could hear my thoughts.

"What?"

"She was asking for it. It was implied consent. Whatever whatever whatever. I didn't want it. He was trying to force himself on me," Alice mumbled.

"You don't have to explain yourself," I said as I looked out the window.

"But I do. I'm still trying to figure out what happened."

"Okay."

She wrung her hands in her lap. "One of my exes hated it when I did that. Talk about something over and over again as I tried to figure out what happened. Like, was I in the wrong after all? I don't feel wrong."

"If he was touching you in a way you didn't like, then he was in the wrong. You didn't do anything wrong."

"I should have called the cops, but they won't believe me. The media would call me a whore. They'll probably say I wanted it. They—"

I pushed my fingers over her lips and pressed my forehead to hers. "Shh. Don't explain yourself to me. Don't work yourself up over it. I trust you, and I'm glad you called me."

She nodded. "Thank you."

"When we get to my condo, you're going to take a shower and get clean. Okay?"

"Yeah."

I grabbed her hand. Her shaking stopped as I rubbed the back of her hand in comforting circles with my thumb. Alice sighed and relaxed in the backseat until we arrived at the parking garage. I pulled her out of the backseat and carried her upstairs. She clung to me as I carried her to my bathroom. I sat her on the toilet and pulled off her blouse.

"I hope you weren't sentimental over this," I whispered.

"No. Burn it all."

"Perfect." I tried to avoid looking at her and stepped back. "I'll bring you a change of clothes. Get in the shower and wash off."

Alice nodded as I walked away.

Chapter Four
Alice

The blood was gone.

I stumbled out of the shower in a daze and wrapped a towel around me. I picked up the clothes he placed in the bathroom while I stood underneath the water. This all looked like stuff that would fit him. If my thigh would fit in it, it wouldn't go further. There was a fluffy robe, though. Robes were one size fit all, and I slipped that on. While I was in the shower, I decided on something.

I wanted to fuck Declan.

Opening the door, Declan looked up from his massive bed. "Feeling better?" he asked.

"Yeah, but you know I have a fatter ass than that, right?"

"I sent a man to get some clothes that will fit you. I'm sure it will be here soon."

"Thanks." I sat on the bed beside him. "At least the robe is one size fits all. Although I can't cuddle into it like I want." I waved towards ample cleavage spilling out of the edges of the robe.

Declan avoided looking at me and stared at his phone. "Do you feel better?"

"I already said yes. I need a favor from you."

"What else could you need from me?" he asked with a smirk on his face.

"Can we fuck?" I asked bluntly. "I know I'm not as pretty as the super models and stuff you can probably date. I just really need to forget what happened. And I want to choose it. I want to *feel*."

"You're asking me to have sex with you? After you just rejected a guy and killed him?"

I looked away from him and fiddled with the sash. "We can forget it happened afterwards. I just want to feel and I want it to be my choice. I know it's stupid. I just need control. Please? It sounds stupid."

"If we do this, you owe me."

"So cleaning up my mess is favor free, but this is a favor?" I asked.

"I told you the other night to call me if you were in danger. It wasn't an invitation for a booty call."

I sighed. "Fine. I'll owe you a favor."

His face shifted like he won something. Not sure what. I wasn't a supermodel like his last few exes. Yes, I googled him after the other night. All of his notable exes were gorgeous and whatever I wasn't. He'd be slumming with me. The flirting from the other night, I figured it was just for show. Maybe a way to show dominance and throw me off. That made sense to me with how he used to treat me as a teen. Or how many people treated me growing up. Another furl of nervousness bloomed within me. At least that was better than replaying what had happened a few hours earlier.

I sucked in a breath and pushed him into the bed. His phone clattered onto the floor. I straddled his body and crashed my lips into his. His fingers curled into my wet hair and he pulled me tighter against his body. Declan's tongue tapped at the seam of my mouth and I opened for him. Our tongues twisted and glided against each other as I rocked my hips on top of his pelvis. He moaned into the kiss as he pushed the robe off my shoulder. Fingertips traced down the nape of my neck before he broke the kiss. His lips dragged down my cheek and neck as he nipped and kissed my skin before he sucked on my skin. A larger spark of desire coursed through me, and I moaned in delight. He pushed the robe off my body and I pulled away as the fabric revealed every roll on my body to him. I swallowed. This was the moment he could reject me or call me ugly.

Declan's eyes darkened as he looked down at my body. His fingers glided down my shoulders towards my imperfect breasts. "Have you ever thought of me as you touched yourself?" he whispered.

My face grew warmer. There were a few times when I was a teen. "No," I lied.

He grinned. "You're lying." He reached up and caressed my cheek. "Your body's telling me the truth. You're so wet already, grinding all over me and your skin's red."

I pursed my lips but didn't respond. Declan rocked his hips upward and his bulge hit me in the best way. I moaned and my eyes rolled onto the back of my head. He pushed me into the bed and slid off. I propped myself on my elbows and watched Declan undress. He slowly unbuttoned his shirt as I watched every muscle reveal itself. Declan grinned as he threw off the shirt and it slipped to the floor. Every muscle in his body was well defined, and he had dark tattoos covering most of his chest. My fingers itched to touch them. The click of his belt filled the air as he pushed his slacks down his hips. He wrapped his hand around his cock and pumped it a few times. A drip of pre-cum welled at the tip. Declan was *thick* and pierced all the way down.

"I've never fucked a guy that was pierced," I whispered.

"I guess there is a first time for everything," he said huskily. "Spread your legs and show me how wet you are."

I swallowed again as my heart pounded. I scooted further in the bed and spread my legs. His eyes seemed to devour my body as my fingers skated down my stomach and between my legs. Hesitantly, I dipped one finger between my lips and slid up my seam. My legs quivered as I exposed everything to him.

"Are you scared?" he whispered as he kneeled between my legs.

"Nervous. It's not like it was a wild moment of passion that led to fucking," I whispered as my fingers swirled around my clit.

Declan's fingers traced up my calves and thighs. The missing zing of arousal earlier was there for Declan. My body wanted him and I wanted this with every fiber of my body. I sucked in a breath as he touched me and explored my thighs until he was at the vee. "Look how soft and fuckable you are," he whispered. He pushed my hand away and replaced his fingers on my mound. "So wet. Is this just for me?"

"Shut up and fuck me or something," I whispered.

Declan's fingers slipped into my pussy, and I gasped. "I don't know if you can fit my cock."

"It stretches," I hissed as I tried to hold back an eye roll.

He pushed another finger into my pussy, and I arched against him. "Oh, I know. That's what I'm working at." Declan pumped his fingers in and out of my pussy. His other hand gripped the bottom of my chin. "Do you have a bit of a brat inside you? I could hear the attitude in your voice."

"No."

His fingers gripped my chin harder. "Are you going to be a good girl for me?"

"I can be good," I gasped.

Declan's grin widened before he licked his teeth. He increased his speed and more arousal pummeled my body. I sucked in a breath through my nose as I tried not to moan. "Oh, fuck, I'm going to have so much fun with you." Declan's lips crashed into mine as he positioned himself above me. A moment later, Declan stopped the kiss and pulled his fingers out of my pussy. He slowly licked his fingers as he kept eye contact with me. Declan sat on his heels as he wrapped his hands around my hips.

"Are you ready? You said you wanted to feel something," he said.

"I've been waiting."

He rolled his eyes before flipping me over. His cock slid up and down my seam before he pushed into me. My fingers gripped into the satin sheets as he bottomed out inside. The piercings were unbelievable as they touched parts of me that had never been touched before and I moaned loudly. Declan grunted as he dug his fingers into my hips while he started to thrust. Every movement sent sparkles of more desire through me.

"Harder, Declan," I muttered into the bed.

Declan lifted a hand up and slapped my ass. The pain sliced through me and straight to my pussy. For the next few minutes, between thrusts, he slapped my ass until I was moaning and thrashing underneath him. "Did you feel that? I felt your cunt grip my cock hard with every touch."

"Yes, thank you, Declan. Thank you for everything," I moaned.

"Now, that's a good girl. Look at how well you're taking my cock." Declan wrapped his arm around me and his fingers skirted over my clit. The muscles in my stomach started to tighten as my orgasm rushed through my body.

"I'm about to come."

"Good. Come all over my cock," Declan groaned as he increased his movements. A moment later, everything broke inside me and I lost the feeling in my calves as I writhed underneath him. He pulled his hand off my clit and rocked into me even faster. His thrusts became more erratic before he stilled inside me. His hot seed splashed against my insides. When he pulled out of me, the hot liquid dripped down my thighs, but his fingers caught it. Declan pushed his come covered fingers back into my pussy before he pulled me into his arms.

"That was fun," Declan said.

I nodded and closed my eyes as I laid my head against his chest. All the adrenaline from earlier started to fade away, and I felt sore all over. Every muscle screamed inside my body as sleep threatened to take me.

Declan caressed my hair gently. "Get some sleep."

* * *

In the early morning hours, I climbed out of Declan's arms and found the clothes someone had brought for me. I got ready for work and was able to get to work on time. Everything was normal for a few hours. Customers came and went. I stocked the shelves with books and tried to forget the last twenty-four hours. Everything changed when I received a text from my mom: *What do you mean you're engaged to Declan?*

My face fell as I realized what that favor was. Declan was making me marry him. There could be worse things. Although why didn't Declan say it last night? I guess there were things we still needed to talk about. I should be mad about the situation, but I wasn't. Maybe I knew deep down something like this *could* happen with him. I made my bed and I would have to lie in it now.

About the Author

Lily Prince is a stay at home mom that loves to write stories featuring dominant men and kink. You can sign up for Lily's newsletter at http://www.lilyprincebooks.com

Shattered Silence

By: L.B. Martin

About Shattered Silence

Silence betrayed her, rage will define her.

In a world where shadows lurk and silence screams, Raine has lived under the suffocating thumb of her father, a man whose twisted desires have turned her life into a waking nightmare. When Cole "Huxley" Rhodes, an undercover special ops agent, enters her life, everything changes. Tasked with dismantling her father's dark empire, he is drawn to Raine—not just as a mission, but as a woman who ignites a fire within him that he never expected.

When a violent confrontation at their shared workplace spirals out of control, Cole is forced to take drastic measures, drugging and kidnapping Raine to protect her from the monster that is her father. As they find solace in each other's arms, the line between captor and captive blurs, and an undeniable passion ignites. But when Raine's father tracks them down, she must confront her past in a way she never imagined.

Armed with a bow and arrows—gifts from the man who tried to break her—Raine discovers her own strength and unleashes a storm of feminine rage. In a gripping tale of survival, love, and empowerment, Raine vows to shatter the silence that has haunted her for too long.

Join Raine on a journey of love, vengeance, and empowerment in this gripping dark romance that explores the depths of feminine rage and the light of newfound hope. *Will she find her voice, or will the darkness consume her?*

Content note:

This is a dark romance full of feminine rage toward her father that leads to his eventual gruesome death. Some scenes in this novel may be extremely upsetting, therefore, reader discretion is advised. This book contains references to an off-page sex trafficking ring, mention of off-page illegal abortions and suicide, on-page drugging, kidnapping and emotional and physical abuse. Also, sprinkle in a little murder... Some sexual scenes involve dubious consent, breath play, Dom/brat, arrow play, blood play, and spankings.

Relationship type: MF

Chapter One

Raine

The rain hammers against the grimy windows of Double Edged Bar & Grill, the dimly lit dive bar where I work. Each drop is a reminder of the darkness I can't escape. The place reeks of spilled beer and lost dreams, a fitting backdrop for my life. I wipe down the counter, my movements mechanical, my mind elsewhere, as Jason's words echo in my head—words that leave deeper scars than his fists.

The bell above the door jingles, and I look up to see a figure stepping in from the storm. He's tall and impossibly handsome, with chiseled features and a rugged, dangerous allure. *Huxley Rhodes. The bouncer and man everyone fears.* His presence is commanding, his broad shoulders and muscular frame effortlessly cutting through the haze of smoke and cheap alcohol. He brushes off the rain from his jacket and surveys the room with a predatory gaze. His dark hair falls in messy waves around his face, and his stormy gray eyes are filled with an intensity that's both captivating and terrifying.

There's a darkness that shrouds him, a sense of controlled violence that makes it clear he's not someone to be trifled with. But there's also something else—a protectiveness, a fierce determination that makes me wonder if maybe, just maybe, he's not the monster I thought he was.

His eyes lock onto mine for a moment, but I quickly look away, fearing he might see the marks Jason left on my arm. Huxley has only been here for about a month, and he never says more than a few words. But something about him—the way he carries himself, the intensity in his gaze—makes me believe that seeing these bruises would bring out a side of him I've never seen. It's irrational, really; I know next to nothing about him. Still, an instinctive need to hide away from him surfaces. I definitely don't need more trouble than I'm already in.

Huxley moves through the room with the grace of a panther, every step purposeful and controlled. He has an aura of danger that makes the usual drunks and lowlifes steer clear. I watch him out of the corner of my eye as he takes his spot at the end of the bar, scanning the patrons with a practiced vigilance.

"Another rough night, huh?" comes a voice beside me. I turn to see Bree, a fellow bartender and the closest thing I have to a confidante in this hellhole. Bree's gaze drops to the fresh bruises peeking out from under my sleeve, and her expression darkens.

"I'm fine," I lie, forcing a smile that doesn't reach my eyes. I pull my sleeve down, trying to hide the evidence of Jason's rage, but she isn't fooled. Bree opens her mouth to say something, but before she can a commotion erupts near the back of the bar.

The bar is alive with the sound of laughter and clinking glasses, but that all comes to a grinding halt the moment Jason's gruff voice pierces through the ambiance.

"Raine!" he bellows, staggering forward with that familiar swaying gait of his, eyes wild with anger. It feels like time slows as I realize Jason is drunk–*again*.

Fear clenches my stomach, my body freezes on the spot as the tiniest piece of glass shatters somewhere behind him, a sharp note of danger hanging in the air. My heart skips a beat, its rhythm erratic.

But before I can run, Huxley is already in motion, a silent

guardian stepping between Jason and me. His broad shoulders effectively block the view of my boss.

"Leave her alone," Huxley growls, his voice low and menacing,
each word a simple command.

Jason doesn't pay heed; his sneer drips with contempt as he tries
to push past Huxley, his drunken bravado seeming to make him think
he has the upper hand.

"This is my bar, Rhodes. You don't tell me what to do. Know your
fucking place and move aside!"

The crowd holds its breath, their gazes darting between the two
men like spectators at a boxing match. Huxley's grip tightens,
catching Jason's wrist in a vice-like hold.

"I said, leave her alone," he repeats, his tone so calm it's almost
chilling.

Jason struggles against the hold, rage visibly bubbling within him.

"I'll call the cops! You think they will believe a bouncer over the
owner? I'll ruin you!" His threats only thicken the tension, but
Huxley's demeanor remains fearlessly composed.

"Go ahead, Jason. Call them. I'm sure they'd love to hear that
you're threatening your employees. And while you're at it, maybe you
can explain those fresh bruises on Raine's arms." Huxley's words
pierce through Jason's drunken haze, eliciting shock from the crowd.

Jason's narrowed eyes dart between Huxley and me, and I can
feel the accusation lurking beneath his words.

"So that's it, huh? You're screwing him now? You little slut. Of
course you'd spread those fat thighs for this punk ass. Just wait until
your father hears."

Every word feels like a knife, but the cold grip of fear drowns out
any possibility of striking back. My heart races as Huxley's hand
tightens around Jason's wrist.

"Watch your fucking mouth," he warns, each syllable dripping
with barely contained fury.

Jason snarls, wild with rage and embarrassment. He swings his
free hand, a chaotic punch directed at Huxley. *That's definitely a*

wrong move. With an almost effortless twist of his body, Huxley disarms Jason, his other arm moving like lightning to bring Jason's arm behind his back, forcing him to his knees.

The bar erupts in whispers and gasps, patrons mesmerized by the escalating confrontation. Leaning down, Huxley brings his face close to Jason's, the words that follow make the air crackle with tension.

"If you lay a hand on her again, I'll make sure you regret it."

Jason's struggles are futile against Huxley's strength. Humiliated and furious, he manages to push Huxley off just enough to get back on his feet. In an impulsive fury, Jason lunges towards me. My instincts scream at me to jump away, but Huxley is faster. He dives in front of me, delivering a quick elbow strike that hits the bridge of Jason's nose.

The sickening sound of splintering cartilage echoes in the bar, mingling with Jason's wails as he clutches his face. Blood pours through his fingers, painting a glaring contrast against the dark wood floor—his anger bleeding out just as quickly as his pride.

"You mother fucker!" Jason howls, his voice raw, clinging desperately to what is left of his dignity.

Bree rushes over, her face pale as she assesses the situation. I'm sure she's deciding whether to call for help or if that would only escalate things further. I stand frozen, my breath caught in my throat.

"Call the cops!" Bree nods shakily then runs the other direction.

t"You're both f-fired!" he screams, his voice strained. "Pack your shit and get the hell out of here! And Raine, I'm going to tell everyone about your little secret. Let's see how you manage without me!"

Huxley wraps his arm around Jason's neck, pulling him into a chokehold. Jason thrashes about trying to regain his footing but it's a lost cause. His face turns red as he gasps for air, digging his slimy fingers into Huxley's arms.

I'm motionless, my heart pounding in my chest. Huxley tightens his hold for a moment longer before letting Jason go, watching as he collapses to the floor, unconscious.

"Everyone out!" Huxley shouts at the stunned patrons, but they don't hesitate to do as they're told. Everyone runs from the building without looking back.

Huxley turns to me, his eyes softening just a fraction as they meet mine. "Are you okay?" he asks, his voice gentler now, a stark contrast to the lethal force he just displayed.

Anger and fear bubble up inside me. "No, I'm not okay. And thanks to you, I'm in even more danger," I snap, turning away from him. I need to get the hell out of here *fast*. I try to think of all the possible places I can hide, but I'm in full panic mode and unable to concentrate. I grab my purse and round the bar toward the exit.

"Why did you do that?" I hiss, my voice trembling in rage. "You don't know what you've done. He's going to come after me now! You've made everything worse!"

Huxley dares to stand in my way, holding up his hands in a quiet gesture of peace. "Raine, let me help you."

I glare at him, my body shaking with fear and fury. "Help me? You've done enough."

Huxley's expression hardens, but his voice remains calm. "I won't let him hurt you. I promise."

I shake my head, feeling the panic rising. "Well, you've been here for a month and haven't stepped in until tonight. Why the hell would I trust you when you clearly knew what's been going on?"

He clenches his jaw, clearly unhappy with the way things are playing out. If he thought he could just come in here and play hero one night and then sweep me away like everything is right in the world, then he's sorely mistaken.

"You're right," Huxley says, his voice strained with frustration. "I should have done something sooner. But I had to be careful." I don't wait for him to finish his ominous statement as I push past him.

"Raine, wait!" Huxley calls out, but I ignore him, squeezing through the toppled tables and chairs that flew around as people made a fast exit.

As I reach the door, I hear the distant wail of sirens approaching.

My heart races, and I freeze. Huxley grabs my arm, his grip firm but not painful.

"What are you doing?" I shout, trying to pull away.

Huxley's eyes meet mine, filled with a mix of urgency and determination. "I'm not letting you go. It's not safe."

I open my mouth to argue, but Huxley is quick. He pulls a filled needle from his pocket and before I can react, he injects something into my neck. I struggle against him, my vision blurring as I try to push him away. My limbs feel heavy, and the room starts to spin.

"Huxley, what did you—" My words slur as the darkness creeps in, my body going limp in his arms.

The last thing I hear before the darkness takes over completely is the sound of the sirens growing louder and Huxley's voice, a soft whisper in my ear. "I'm sorry, Raine. I'll keep you safe."

Chapter Two
Huxley

The night air is cold and heavy with the weight of what just happened. As the sirens grow louder, I hold Raine's limp body close, her breathing shallow but steady. Guilt gnaws at me, but there was no other way. Jason's threats and the imminent arrival of the cops left me with no choice but to act quickly.

I scan the bar, now empty except for the shattered glass and overturned chairs. The patrons fled the moment I ordered them out, the fear in their eyes reflecting the chaos that erupted. My mind races, calculating the next move. I have to get Raine somewhere safe before the cops arrive and everything spirals further out of control.

I look down at her. She feels so small and fragile in my arms, the rise and fall of her chest barely perceptible. The moment I began working with her, I knew I wanted her. Unfortunately in my line of work, I'm not afforded such luxuries. However, tonight's fresh marks on her perfect skin snapped my final thread of resolve. She needed me and no fucker will ever touch her again.

Carrying her to the back door, I push it open with my shoulder, the rain immediately drenches us both. We need to move fast. My gunmetal Ford Mustang Mach 1 is parked in the alley, hidden from view. It would raise questions had I ever parked in the employee parking area. I lay Raine gently in the back seat, her head resting on a makeshift pillow I grab from the front. As I close the door, the sirens are almost on top of us, their flashing lights bouncing off the wet pavement.

I slide into the driver's seat and start the engine, my heart pounding. This isn't how I planned for things to go down. Raine's life is already complicated enough, and now I've dragged her into an even darker mess.

The car lurches forward and screeches around the corner, away from the bar. In the rear-view mirror, I see the police pull up to the curb and run inside, followed by an ambulance. They won't find any clues as to where we've gone.

I navigate the slick streets, my mind replaying the events of the night. Jason's accusations, his threats, and the way Raine looked at me with a mix of fear and anger. She doesn't trust me, and I can't blame her. Keeping my cover has come at a cost, and now I need to find a way to make it right. Drugging her definitely didn't help, but I was out of options and I wasn't letting Raine out of my sight.

Pulling into a secluded parking lot, I turn off the engine and take a moment to breathe. The rain drums against the roof, a steady reminder of the chaos outside. I check on Raine, her face pale and peaceful in the dim light. She'll be out for a couple hours, giving me some time to figure out our next move.

My mind shifts to the investigation. Jason's criminal activities run deep, and bringing him down requires more than just evidence—it requires careful planning and a lot of luck. I've been gathering information, slowly piecing together the puzzle, but tonight's events have accelerated the timeline.

We can't stay in the open. Too many eyes, too many risks. I need a safe house, a place where I can keep Raine protected while I sort this mess out. My contacts might have a location, but reaching out to them now could blow my cover entirely. Trust is a double-edged sword in this world, and I've learned to wield it carefully.

I pull back onto the highway, heading toward the outskirts of town and beyond, where the city lights fade and the wilderness takes over. I know exactly where we're going—a small cabin I own, tucked away in the mountains. It's remote, surrounded by a dense forest with thick snow. It's the perfect place to lay low and keep Raine safe, even if she may not see it that way.

The drive is long and treacherous, the snow growing thicker as we climb higher into the mountains. The darkness is complete, broken only by the car's headlights cutting through the swirling snowflakes. I keep a steady pace, careful not to lose control on the icy roads.

Finally, the cabin comes into view, a lone structure against the backdrop of towering pines and snow-covered ground. With a screech of tires on the icy driveway, I pull up to the front, and let out a breath. This is it—our safe haven, for now.

I put the car in park, the engine humming to a stop as I scan the quiet surroundings. The moonlight glistens on the fresh snow, making everything appear ethereal, yet I know the darkness lurking outside requires constant vigilance.

I step out into the biting cold, my breath fogging the air as I hurry back to the rear door to Raine. I carefully lift her out, cradling her against my chest like fragile glass, her body small against my large frame. I feel her stir slightly, her head resting on my shoulder, the warmth of her skin igniting a fierce protectiveness in me.

I carry her inside, the cabin's little heat still contrasts sharply with the freezing night outside. The familiar scent of cedar and the faint smell of woodsmoke greet me like an old friend. The cabin is small, but I've kept it well-equipped. Tucked away in the corners are enough supplies to last us a few weeks, and the fireplace promises warmth against the cold isolation.

I lay Raine gently on the couch, covering her with a thick blanket. She snuggles into the plush fabric, a soft moan escaping her lips, and my mind begins to spiral.

Fuck! Focus, Rhodes.

The sweet noise makes my cock stir to life, and I try to force my mind to think about anything other than her perfect, plump lips wrapped around me as I fuck her face hard and fast. I can picture her dark blue eyes watering as she looks up at me, glistening with pleasure, and my frustration peaks.

Get it together, Rhodes. This investigation has to take precedence over everything, especially the woman on the couch. Even if she's the most gorgeous creature I've ever seen.

I need to be smart about this—about Raine. Not just because of how she affects me, but because of the shadows that loom just beyond the veil of safety we've found.

An icy current flows through me as Jason's words echo in my mind. His threats, each like a throbbing nail. I have to protect her from him.

I press the button beside the mantle, and a fire roars to life, the flames crackling as they cast a soft glow over the rustic furniture.

Moving to the window, I peer out at the endless expanse of snow. There's no way she can escape from here, not in these conditions. For now, she's safe, and that's all that matters.

Turning slowly back to Raine, I sit beside her, watching the rise and fall of her chest. A sudden flash draws my attention—a phone dings, making my heart accelerate because mine always remains on silent.

The outline shines in her pocket, and I slide it out quickly. I know I need to destroy anything that could possibly lead threats here, but before I smash it, an odd text catches my eye. Curiosity outweighs precaution as I swipe open the message.

Sperm Donor: You fucking worthless bitch. I knew you couldn't keep your mouth shut. Go ahead and run. I'll find you and this time, the only thing you'll be begging for is death just like she did. Goodnight, *Rainebow*.

. . .

My blood runs cold, and my jaw tenses.

What the absolute fuck did I just read?

How long has this bastard been harassing her?

And why is she keeping this a secret?

Anger surges through me like a raging tide.

Scraps of the puzzle start connecting in my mind. The accomplice I've been searching for must be her father. He must be the one pulling all the strings, leaving Jason to do his dirty work.

I shatter the phone in my hands, pulling out the sim card, and with my heart pounding, I throw it into the fire.

This changes everything.

I look down at Raine's innocent sleeping form as an overwhelming need to save her washes over me. She looks so peaceful, unaware of the storm brewing just outside. Her long, dark lashes fan across her pale cheeks, and her bow-shaped lips are plump and pink. The rhythmic rise and fall of her chest is mesmerizing, pulling me in like a moth to a flame.

I vow to shield her from the shadows of the past and any harm that may come her way. The stakes are even higher now. I need to get to the bottom of this quickly and find a way to protect Raine from the fallout.

I'm done fighting it; this obsession with Raine has grown tenfold since the first day I saw her in that shithole. Tonight sealed her fate, whether she likes it or not. I've seen those baby blues looking at me with a similar heated desire coursing through me.

"Fuck it," I murmur, unable to contain the longing any longer. I lean down to capture her lips with mine. Raine tenses only for a moment, surprise hitting her, before her body melts against mine. The moment her lips part on a soft moan, I'm a goner. Our tongues dance, gliding and crashing against each other as I deepen the kiss.

My fingers feather through her silken strands while cupping the back of her head, losing myself completely in her warmth and sweetness. I want to explore every inch of her sexy mouth, until we are both panting messes. Our breaths mingle as heat radiates between us.

"Huxley," she breathes, pulling back to look at me, her eyes glazed with a mixture of confusion and desire.

"Yes, Raine?" I whisper, my voice rough with need. This is the first time I've said her name like that. It feels like a prayer, a promise, a half-formed destiny.

In that moment, under the soft glow of the fire, amidst the chaos of our realities, I realize I would do anything to keep her safe, and I'm willing to fight for her heart if I have to.

Raine is the missing piece I've needed all along—for this investigation and more importantly, myself. If someone wants Raine, they'll have to come through me. Protecting her just skyrocketed to my top priority because no one hurts what's mine. And Raine Evans is fucking *mine*.

She's my obsession, my salvation, and my destruction, all wrapped into one. And I'll do whatever it takes to keep her.

Dragging her into my world paints a target on her back, but I'm a selfish bastard who's never played fair. The stakes are higher now, and I'll face any hell that comes our way.

Chapter Three
Raine

Strong arms gently wrap around me, as I'm carried to a different room. The familiar spicy scent of bergamot, pepper and amberwood swirl through my senses making me intoxicated with lust. I'm laid gently on a plush bed with smooth satin sheets.

A fire flickers in the corner, casting elongated shadows across the small, rustic room. My heart pounds with each memory that surfaces, clawing its way through the haze of the afternoon. With every recollection, the world tilts precariously on its axis.

As I blink away the remnants of sleep, physical sensations return–the throbbing pain behind my temples, but also an ache between my legs that I've never experienced before.

"Where am I?" I whisper. The events from the bar flood my mind–Jason's threats, Huxley's intervention, the tension that ignited between us, and then—darkness.

"Easy, love." His familiar voice rings out through the room, easing some fear. His presence is both a comfort and a source of turmoil.

"What happened?" I manage, the words barely escaping my lips

as confusion colors my tone. The shadows shift, elongating the lines
of his face, revealing the worry etched in his brow.

"We're at a safe place. We had to leave town in a hurry," he
admits, his voice grave; the weight of his words hangs between us like
a thick fog.

"But... why?" I ask, my voice trembling. "I mean, we barely know
each other."

Huxley's eyes soften, and he runs his hand through my silky
blonde hair, tucking a stray strand behind my ear. "I couldn't stand
the thought of something happening to you, Raine. You're too damn
beautiful and pure for this cruel world. I had to keep you safe, even if
it meant breaking a few rules."

I survey the room closely—log walls embrace us, sturdy and
unyielding, while a stone fireplace flickers feebly in the corner,
attempting to keep the cold at bay. The atmosphere is heavily lined
with an unsettling intimacy, but it's the dawning realization of
betrayal that pierces my heart.

He drugged me.

"What the fuck? You knocked me out!" The accusation explodes
from me, fierce and unyielding. Rage swells in my chest, a wild beast
fueled by the confusion and fear gripping my mind. *How could he
betray my trust like this?* I try to pull away from his embrace, but his
muscular arms hold me captive.

"Raine, I'm not going to hurt you. Take a deep breath," he urges,
his tone calm and soothing, yet filled with a weight that reflects my
own turmoil. I inhale sharply, but the clenching of my heart lingers.

He runs a hand through his tousled, brown hair, brows knitted
together in regret.

"I'm sorry. I had to get you out of there. Things were about to
escalate, and you were in danger. It was the only way."

I can see the torment in his fierce gray eyes—the pulse of guilt
echoing in the space between us. My heart softens slightly, yet the
anger remains, like embers refusing to extinguish.

"You're the one who escalated things! I had it handled! You don't get to decide for me! And why the hell do you walk around with syringes filled with drugs?" I cry out, my mind racing with what this means for me. My father will come for me now; he's probably already on his way to wherever the hell we are.

"You have no idea what you were dealing with, Raine. I can protect you," he assures with a firm voice that leaves no room for argument.

I cross my arms defiantly, raising my chin as I glare at him with challenge. "How can I trust you, Huxley? You're basically a stranger, and you just drugged and kidnapped me. How do I know this isn't all part of your plan?"

His silence stretches, and for a moment, the air thickens between us. I can feel the pulse of tension as he searches for the right words, his chest rising and falling with each breath.

"I understand why you'd feel that way, I truly do. But you have to trust me when I say I would never hurt you... not intentionally. I care for you, Raine, more than I should."

"Trust? What does that even mean anymore?" I shoot back, recalling the shadows of betrayal that loom large from my past. My father's unorthodox teachings have ingrained a profound sense of caution in me, an armor that is now hard to peel away.

"Look, Huxley, whatever Jason's done, it doesn't mean you can just drug and kidnap me," I retort, my voice laced with an assertive annoyance that just poses against the uncertainty swirling within me.

He meets my gaze head-on, his jaw clenched tightly, a taut string ready to snap. "What Jason did? He threatened your life, and who knows what else, and you're worried about what I did?" His incredulity is mirrored in my heart, pounding with a mixture of fear and something else—curiosity, perhaps?

"You have no idea what you've gotten yourself into. I may be a stranger to you, but think about it, Raine. I'm the only one who seems to care enough to risk everything to protect you. I don't want to see you hurt, and I won't let that happen."

In that moment, the fire in his eyes softens, morphing into something vulnerable yet fierce. I feel it too, that tumultuous need to believe, the sheer desperation to latch onto whatever light he offers in the tempest of my confusion.

But trust is a hard currency, one I struggle to trade. "I don't understand why you care so much," I whisper, my frail resolve cracking under the weight of vulnerability. "You've barely even spoken to me before last night."

Huxley shifts closer, the heat radiating off him drawing me in like a moth to a flame. His fingers brush along my jawline, his touch gentle yet electric, igniting a shiver that ricochets through my body.

"I'm not your enemy, Raine. I promise. Let me prove it to you."

The pleading in his voice almost breaks me, and the walls I've built around myself sway, threatening to crumble into the warmth of his sincerity. The realization of how touch starved I've been hits me like a freight train. It's been so long since anyone has shown me genuine care, and the intensity of his gaze makes my heart ache with longing I didn't know I had. But I can't afford to let my guard down. Not now. *Not ever.*

"I can't trust you," I whisper, heart racing at the conflicting emotions raging within me.

"You don't have a choice, Raine," he replies, the firmness of his tone slicing through my confusion like a knife.

"Just let me go. Please." The desperation in my plea clashes violently with the undeniable chemistry crackling between us.

Huxley moves closer, his presence overwhelming. He leans in, ghosting his warm breath over my skin, making every nerve in my body tingle with anticipation.

"I can't. You'll have to trust me. I'll protect you, Raine." The way he says my name sends ripples of excitement coursing through me.

Closing my eyes, I take a shaky breath, the tension between us palpable.

Why does my heart scream that maybe he's the most dangerous of all when my body aches for his touch?

I shake myself out of the haze, desperately trying to regain my composure. My heart pounds in my chest, the rhythm chaotic and wild, a frantic scream that warns me of the danger lurking so close. *Is the danger Huxley or my father?*

"I don't have a choice, do I?" I whisper, the ghost of defiance lingering in my tone. The air thrums with electricity as Huxley, the mystery that both entices and terrifies me, leans even closer.

"No," he confesses, his voice low and dangerous, laced with an undertone of authority that sends shivers down my spine. He cups my cheek, warmth radiating from his hands as they caress my skin, momentarily shielding me from the storm brewing inside me.

My heart dares to dream of safety, yet the part of me that screams caution knows better. His eyes hold secrets that could shatter my world.

"I need you to trust me," he repeats as his lips tentatively press against mine.

Fear and desire wage a war within me, each battling for dominance. My mind screams to pull away, to protect myself from the unknown danger that Huxley represents. But my body betrays me, leaning into his touch, craving the warmth and safety he promises.

"You think you can just sweep in, mess with my life, and make everything alright? To protect me from what? Your demons?" I challenge, anger swirling with an undeniable allure that pulls me toward him.

"No, not my demons, dammit. Your demons—Jason, your father, the life you've been living. You may not see it, but you're in deeper than you realize. I won't stand by and watch you get hurt."

"Then maybe don't knock me out next time!" I snap back, trying to stifle the softer emotions stirring in me.

"I'm not the one you should be worried about, little girl, and you're starting to piss me off."

His words hang in the air, weighty with implication. The certainty in his voice is like a cold breeze on a warm summer night, sending shivers down my spine. I can't deny the way my body reacts to Huxley's presence, the way my heart races and my breath hitches every time he looks at me like he wants to eat me whole. Huxley's eyes bore into mine before he pounces on top of me, pressing me to the bed.

Chapter Four
Huxley

"What the hell–" I don't let her finish before I slam my lips over hers, effectively shutting her bratty mouth up before she says anything else to infuriate me. Her words, sharp and laced with sarcasm, have seeped under my skin, grating on my nerves. The way she challenged me, the way she jutted her chin and crossed her arms defiantly, today of all days—has my patience running dry.

For a fleeting moment, she is completely still, shocked by my sudden move. Then, as if on cue, her defenses crumble; her delicate fingers tangle in the fabric of my shirt, pulling me closer as I intensify the kiss, trying to drown out the mayhem around us.

Her soft, warm body presses against mine, and I can feel the fight slipping from her; the tension in her shoulders relaxes as she surrenders to the heat radiating between us. I pull her closer, desperate to bridge the wild chasm that has grown between us in the light of our argument.

"You're so fucking gorgeous, Raine," I whisper between kisses, my voice hoarse with desire. "I've wanted to do this since the moment I laid eyes on you."

"Wait! What are you doing?" she finally mumbles against my lips, breathless but caught in the moment, her body betraying her bewilderment.

"Shutting you up," I reply, teasingly, smirking against her mouth. Then I feel her smile, just a fraction, her annoyance replaced by a spark of mischief.

"You think this will make me quiet?" she challenges, her eyes shining with playful defiance even as she presses against me, seeking more of what we have stumbled into.

I chuckle softly, brushing a strand of hair behind her ear, bringing my forehead to hers, my gaze intense and commanding.

"You'll be anything but quiet, Raine," I growl, my voice deep and husky, "but you won't be saying a word I don't want to hear." I can feel her shiver against me, her breath hitching as I trace a path down her neck with my tongue, nipping at the sensitive skin there.

She swallows hard, her eyes widening slightly at the promise in my words. I can feel her heart racing against my chest, her breath hitching in her throat. I take advantage of her momentary stillness to scoot her up higher on the bed where I want her.

I press her down forcefully into the mattress, my body hovering over hers as I trail kisses down her jaw, her neck, her collarbone. She arches beneath me, her fingers tangling in my hair as she tries to pull me closer, her breath coming in soft, desperate moans. Raine lifts her hips from the bed, probably hoping I'll give her exactly what she wants. Too bad I'm in charge.

"Someone is needy," I taunt against her skin. I can feel her body trembling beneath me, her need for release growing stronger with every passing second. Pulling off my shirt, I throw it to the floor then tear Raine's over her head in one swift move, her eyes never leave my inked chest. Her perfect teeth sink into her bottom lip as she runs her nails along my torso. A smile plays across my lips at her unabashed stare. Her jeans are the next to go, not bothering with a verbal consent when I can already see it shining in her eyes.

I continue my deliberate assault on her senses, my lips and teeth and tongue teasing and tasting every inch of her bare skin. I can feel her body tensing, her breath hitching, as I near the apex of her thighs.

I look up at her, my gaze meeting hers, as I gently push her legs apart. She's wearing nothing but a thin pair of white lace panties, and I can see the damp spot where she's already soaking through the fabric. Her eyes are wide and pleading as she begs me to take her over the edge.

"Please," she whispers, her voice fueled by desperation. "Please, Huxley."

I smirk, my eyes shining with a blend of amusement and desire. "Please what, Firefly?" I tease. "Tell me what you want, and I might just give it to you."

Her jaw clenches, and I watch the battle play out behind those captivating eyes. She swallows hard, determination glimmering in her gaze. "Fuck you!" She hurls the words like a dagger.

A low laugh rumbles from my chest, the heat between us palpable. "Oh, little one, you will be soon enough, but I think that earned you a punishment."

Before she can retort, I flip her onto her stomach, a motion that sends a gasp escaping her lips. The sight before me is a masterpiece—the soft curve of her back leading to that perfect round ass, a tempting offering illuminated by the play of flickering flames.

Her breath catches, anticipation hanging heavy in the air. I lean down, planting teasing kisses along her spine, each touch relishing the way her body responds—how it shivers and arches at my ministrations.

"Raine," I murmur, my voice low and demanding, "you need to learn who's in charge."

With that declaration, I deliver a not so playful swat to her ass. A sharp gasp escapes her throat, but rather than retreat, she pushes her backside higher, challenging me.

"Admit it. Tell me what I already know. Who owns this sweet pussy?" She lets out an aggravated growl.

"It's mine, asshole," she quips, making me chuckle. I'm thoroughly amused by her fierce spirit. *Game on, my little Firefly.*

"I'll keep that in mind when I have you begging for the relief only I can give you. I'm sure you'll be singing a different tune when I've got your body so wound up that you're desperate for release," I promise.

I kneel behind her, my fingers tracing along the delicate lace of her panties, the heat radiating from her skin nearly intoxicating. I blow cool air on her dripping cunt, her reaction immediate and full of need. She sucks in a sharp breath, her back arching instinctively, driving her closer to me.

"So, this isn't what you wanted?" I tease, my fingers expertly working the fabric aside to reveal her glistening treasure. The response I receive is a soft, pleading moan that resonates deep within me, stirring an insatiable hunger.

"Are you all talk or—" Her words are cut off by the harsh slap of my palm meeting her ass once again—a reminder of her place. It seems Raine has more of a backbone than I thought or maybe I just bring out the beast in her.

"Shall I retrieve a ball gag? You'd be hot as fuck, lying there, taking everything I want to give you without that backtalk that seems to accompany everything you say," I suggest, letting my fingers skim the freshly reddened flesh.

She shivers under my touch, goosebumps erupting across her skin, and in a sudden burst of movement, I rip the lace of her underwear to shreds, tossing the remains behind me like confetti.

"Hey!" she screeches, her surprise fueling a rush of adrenaline through my veins. But before she can voice her frustration any further, I dive between her legs, tasting her sweetness. My tongue flicks expertly against her sensitive folds, each deliberate move eliciting gasps and moans from her that resonate in the air like a symphony of raw desire.

"You taste divine," I growl into her skin, tasting the essence of her eager arousal. My fingers dig into her hips, holding her steady as I drink her in. Her breaths grow more erratic, each gasp matching the rhythm of my movements, and I can sense her pulse quickening.

"Huxley, please..." Raine gasps, her voice thick with need, and the bravado she wore moments ago is stripped away, leaving her vulnerable and more enticing than ever.

I can't help but chuckle, the sound rich and deep, vibrating through her core. "Not yet, Firefly. Let's play a little longer."

"Huxley!" she cries, a mix of annoyance and longing lacing her words, and the desperation in her voice urges me on. Each cry drives me to explore her further, to guide her closer to the edge where I know the real magic happens.

Each flick of my tongue, each deliberate kiss and caress, stokes the flames of desire between us. I want to make her feel every bit of the wild hunger I've awakened in her. Tonight, the fire will burn hotter than before, and when all is said and done, I'll have her begging for more.

"Do you want to fly, my sweet Firefly?" I murmur against her skin, my voice thick with desire, watching as she nods fervently, the fight long gone. I have her right where I want her.

"Beg me," I command, my voice low and dangerous as I pull back slightly, teasing her soaked cunt with my fingertips.

"Please, Huxley," she whimpers, the need evident as she looks over her shoulder at me, her eyes pleading.

"Good girl," I praise softly, allowing my desire to mix with pride as I finally relent, pinching her clit. She yelps, then screams into the pillow, her voice a perfect melody to my ears as I thrust my fingers in and out, licking and devouring her delicious honey.

"Fuck yourself on my fingers, Raine. Swallow every inch until you're coming all over me," I demand, the words leaving my mouth like a growl.

She arches her back, each thrust of my fingers drawing her closer to the precipice, our bodies entwined in a dance as raw and primal as the two flames that we are.

"Let go for me," I whisper, feeling the tension building in her body. She grabs handfuls of the sheets, desperation coating every inch of her skin. Raine's body responds with a fury, her muscles contracting as she succumbs to the crescendo of pleasure I've orchestrated.

"Now, Raine!" I command, and her cries envelop me, her body quaking with the force of her orgasm, spilling warmth all over my fingers.

As she rides the waves of ecstasy, I lean down beside her, my breath mingling with hers, gasps and moans slowly fading to silence, leaving us tethered by the intimacy of that shared moment.

Raine, still recovering from the aftershocks, turns to me, a mischievous glint in her eyes. "Is that all you've got?"

I chuckle, knowing that this was only the beginning of our night. "Oh, you have no idea, Firefly. This is just the warm-up, and I plan to take you higher than ever before."

Chapter Five

Raine

Huxley's hands roam across my body with a deliberate slowness, igniting a craving that I had never previously acknowledged was simmering beneath the surface. Each brush of his fingers feels like a feather-light touch that ignites my nerve endings, awakening a wildfire of sensations in me.

With a sudden, overwhelming surge of need, I pull him closer, my heart racing like a stampede. My fingers thread through the luxurious dark strands of his hair, pulling him into me hungrily, as if I could consume him entirely. His hand trails down the curve of my side, stopping just above my breast, causing me to gasp as his thumb grazes my nipple.

A soft moan slips from my lips, involuntarily escaping as I feel the heat pool between my thighs. "God, Raine," Huxley groans, his breath warm against my neck, sending shivers racing through me. I arch into his touch, craving more, desperate for the feeling of his body against mine.

"What are you doing to me?" I breathe, and the thrill of my own voice surprises me. His eyes darken, an ocean of burning need that threatens to drown us both.

"Fuck, Raine, you're stunning," he growls fervently, almost feral in his desire. A moment of hesitation grips me, my instincts trying to force my arms to cover myself, the cruel echoes of my father's words flooding my mind.

"Don't hide from me, Firefly," he commands, his voice low and demanding, igniting something within me that screams to let go. There's something about the way he looks at me, as if deciphering a puzzle only he can solve, that makes me want to slowly uncover every curve, every secret.

His mouth descends on my chest, nipping at my skin, hot and teasing as he travels down, licking and drawing soft moans from deep within me. The mixture of pleasure and anticipation wraps around my mind like vines in a dense forest, drawing me deeper into this moment.

"Huxley," I gasp, surrendering to this reckless abandonment of desire. I'm teetering on the edge, no longer caring about the world outside; only he exists now, his heat wrapping around me like a blanket.

"I'm going to fuck you so hard, Raine. I'm going to make you come until you can't think straight. And then I'm going to do it again and again," he promises, each word a brewing storm of intensity that tightens my resolve. I cling to this pleasure, letting it drown out every rational thought that comes crashing in, each wave pulling me deeper towards him.

"Please, Huxley," I plead, desperation spilling from my voice. I feel my body responding, bowing to his every command, the thrill of submission consuming me whole.

"Tell me who made this pussy so wet? Do you like being at my mercy? Does fucking an older, experienced man turn you on, Firefly?"

His words send shockwaves through me, and despite the embarrassment, I reply without hesitation, "Yes." I bite my lip, holding back the moan threatening to escape as he pushes his fingers deep inside me. He pumps them slowly, unleashing waves of pleasure that crash over my defenses, unraveling me completely.

"Do you like that, Firefly? Tell me," he demands, his voice thick with lust, and I nod without hesitation.

"Good girl," he purrs, satisfaction dripping from his voice like honey, stoking the inferno building within me. He yanks off my jeans with a possessiveness that sends a bolt of electricity through my core.

"Such a perfect little cunt. This is mine now, do you understand? Every fucking inch of this," he growls, his voice deep with lust.

As his fingers delve deeper into my slick warmth, he traces circles around my clit, teasingly slow, driving me to the brink of madness. My breath hitches as I writhe beneath him, desperate for more.

"Please, Huxley, I need more," I beg, my voice thick with yearning, echoing the primal desire surging through me.

"Such a beautiful response," he murmurs, his fingers moving agonizingly slow, sending me over the edge into ecstasy. I twitch and shudder, my climax washing over me like a wave crashing onto the shore.

"You're going to come again for me, Raine. Then you're going to take this fat cock inside your tight little cunt," he promises, and his words send me spiraling anew. I tumble over the edge, my climax washing over me, waves of ecstasy crashing against my senses. I cry out, my body shuddering as Huxley's fingers continue to pump inside me, mercilessly drawing out my orgasm until I'm gasping and spent.

Huxley leans down to capture my lips, feeling the softness transform into something deeper—an urgent, primal need that wraps around us like a consuming fire, burning away my hesitation. He moves with a possessive urgency, a promise of what's to come.

"Such a good little girl," he praises against my lips, and I can't help but melt under the heat of his voice, a shiver racing up and down my spine. I never imagined I would crave such words, and yet here I am, consumed by my desire for this sexy man hovering above me.

With deliberate precision, Huxley coats himself in my slickness, and I can't help but gulp at the sight in fascination. My mind wrestles the reality of it all; there's no way that he's going to fit inside me. *Abso-fucking-lutely not.*

"I've never wanted anyone more than I do you," he murmurs, his voice heavy with desire, a low growl that makes my insides clench in anticipation. I watch as he grips his thick shaft, his movements deliberate and slow, causing my breath to hitch in a mix of awe and trepidation. "This is what you do to me, Raine. This is what you make me feel."

I bite my lip, humiliation rising as a blush creeps up my cheeks when the truth of my inexperience flashes through my mind. I don't want to reveal that I'm a virgin; it's a declaration I can't bear to make. He lifts my chin with his long, calloused finger, forcing me to meet the intensity of his smoldering gaze.

"Raine," he warns, his voice thick with authority and need, "keep those sexy eyes on me, baby." I don't form a response before he dives in, his cock sliding into my wetness with a ferocity that pushes me backward. My body shudders as I let out a strangled cry, tears gathering at the corners of my eyes as I feel like I'm being torn apart.

"Oh, f-uck!" I whimper, my legs trembling in protest as I attempt to adjust to him filling every inch of me while I try to hold back the despair of my own weakness. *Never show your weakness, Rainebow.* Why my father's haunting words would choose this time to present themselves, I'll never know.

"You were a—" his voice falters, eyes flickering to the satin sheets beneath me, stained bright with crimson. A wave of embarrassment crashes through me, a sea swelling inside my throat wanting to reject whatever he's thinking.

I can't bear to see the disgust I'm sure will mar his face, but a part of me craves him too much to care at this moment.

His hands cup my face as his thumbs wipe away the fallen tears. "Hey, look at me, baby," he whispers, his tone more gentle than I've ever heard it.

In that moment, all my fears melt under the warmth of his tenderness, my heart pounding with reckless abandon.

"I'm here," he whispers, and I feel a rush of safety emanate from him, the soothing balm to my burning soul.

Huxley holds my gaze, his confidence igniting something fierce within me. "We'll take it slow. Just breathe for me. Allow yourself to feel."

I nod, not trusting myself to speak as the initial pain quickly gives way to a wave of pleasure that washes over me. Huxley holds still, allowing me to adjust, to adapt to the overwhelming sensations flooding my body.

"You saved this sweet little pussy for me?" he asks, his voice teasing, a playful edge sharpening his words. It is as if he is challenging me, his dark eyes shimmering with raw mischief and insatiable hunger.

I nod, my throat dry, my thoughts swirling as I succumb to the heated moment. Huxley is a force of nature, pulling me in closer with nothing but the gravity of his presence. I can feel the heat radiating from his body, beckoning me to surrender.

"Good girl," he rumbles, the words coating me in warmth and a sense of security I didn't expect. His hands, warm and exploring, roam my body as I lean against him. The softness of his touch ignites every inch of my skin, setting me ablaze with longing.

"You're so fucking tight, Firefly," he growls, his voice strained with barely concealed need. "Please tell me I can move, baby," he begs, as my body begins craving more, the ache inside me igniting into flames. I nod, giving him all the assurance he needs.

With a primal growl, he begins to thrust, starting slowly but quickly losing himself in our rhythm. Each thrust sends shockwaves of pleasure through me, igniting my senses completely.

With each thrust, he fills me completely, claiming me as he promised. I can't hold back the cries of pleasure spilling from my lips, each sound culminating in pure ecstasy.

"You feel so fucking good," he grunts, sweat glistening on his forehead as he watches me writhe beneath him, arching into him, matching him thrust for thrust.

"Yes, Huxley, please," I cry out, the building pleasure becoming a crescendo, threatening to consume me whole. He trails his hand between us to pinch my clit, eliciting a sharp gasp from me.

"I'm going to claim this perfect cunt as mine," he vows between gritted teeth, gripping my hips and driving into me harder, the intensity rising dramatically with each thrust. The pain from his fingers mixes beautifully with the pleasure to create this electric current within me.

"Trust me," he demands as he wraps his hand around my throat tightly. Fear quickly morphs into something else entirely. I should be fucking terrified but for some reason I trust the bastard. Seeing the sincerity in his eyes is my undoing.

"Come for me, Firefly. Come all over my cock," he commands, and my body obeys, shattering into a million exquisite pieces.

A silent scream falls from my lips, as my muscles spasm around him, washing over me in waves of pure ecstasy.

His mouth finds mine in a fervent kiss, capturing my gasps and turning them into whispers of need. He cradles my face, fingers dancing against my skin as he deepens the kiss, adding a gentle urgency that pulls me deeper into him.

"You're perfect, Raine," he murmurs against my lips, a promise laced with the heavy weight of desire.

Huxley thrusts a few more times, his cock pulsing inside me, filling me completely with his seed. He collapses on top of me as if the sheer force of our passion has driven the breath from his body.

As we lay tangled together, gasping for air, a sense of serenity fills the air around us. My heart races, but this time it is from joy, as Huxley presses a gentle kiss against my temple, whispering softly, "You're mine now, Firefly."

"Yes," I agree as he nuzzles into my neck.

"You took me so well, baby," he purrs, licking along my neck.

The world outside fades, drowned in the intensity of my desire for Huxley, the intoxicating mix of danger and pleasure that promises to consume me whole. I surrender to the fire within, letting it scorch our boundaries, leaving only ashes of caution in its wake.

Chapter Six
Huxley

Sunlight streams through the curtains, waking me from the best sleep I've had in a long time. My gaze drifts down to the figure beside me, and a smile breaks across my face.

Raine lies on her side, her bare skin glowing in the morning light. The way her body cuddles against mine sends rivulets of heat coursing through me, my already hardening cock pressing against her backside. Damn, this little vixen is going to be the death of me. We spent most of the night marking every surface in this cabin, indulging in our desires as though the world outside had crumbled away.

I remember the moment I broke through her defenses, the way she surrendered to me, insatiable and wild. The memory sends a stir of longing through my body, and I can't help but watch her as she sleeps, her blonde hair fanning out around the pillows like a halo. Everything about Raine is pure and sweet, making me wonder, not for the first time, how she got pulled into her father's illegal activity. I need to know everything, even if she's scared to tell me. I'm the only one who can protect her from him.

Gently, I pull the blanket over her bare shoulder, feeling the softness of her skin against my fingertips. She stirs slightly but doesn't wake. With a sigh, I slide out of bed, careful not to disturb her. The chill in the air raises goosebumps on my skin, so I make my way to the fireplace, wanting to tend to the flames that had lulled us to sleep.

The wood crackles as I add more logs, the heat brushing against my face as the flame reignites. I step back, letting the warmth envelop me while I take a moment to gather my thoughts. This place, a sanctuary away from the prying eyes of the world, feels like our secret. The cabin, nestled deep in the woods, is a perfect getaway from the chaos that always seems to follow us.

Heading to the bathroom, I turn on the shower and let the hot water cascade over my body, the steam enveloping me like a comforting shroud. As I lather shampoo into my hair, I think about Raine—her laugh, the way her eyes light up when she's excited, the sound of her voice as she whispers my name. In contrast to those sweet moments is the darkness surrounding her, the shadows cast by her father's activities. It's a burden she carries alone, and I can't help but feel the weight of that responsibility as I stand beneath the water, it mingles with my own thoughts.

After rinsing off, I towel-dry my hair and throw on a pair of jeans, opting to go bare-chested for now. I step back into the main room, where the fire casts flickering shadows against the walls, reigniting the passion from last night. Glancing at the bed, I see Raine has shifted. Her back is to me, and even in sleep, she radiates an aura of innocence mixed with an untamed spirit.

"Morning, Firefly," I call softly, watching her wake. She stretches luxuriously, the blankets slipping down her body before she turns to face me, that sleepy smile lighting up her face.

"Morning," she replies, her voice still husky from slumber. "What time is it?"

"Early enough that we can make the most of the day," I say, stepping closer. Raine's gaze wanders down to my bare torso, a smirk tugging at her lips.

"I can think of a few ways to spend the morning," she teases, her eyes twinkling with mischief.

I step closer, the heat between us palpable. "We could pick up where we left off last night," I suggest, leaning down to capture her lips with mine. She responds instantly, melting against me, her fingers tangling in my hair.

In that moment, everything outside the cabin fades away—the worries, the danger lurking in the shadows, the threat of her father. All that exists is the warmth of her body against mine, the fire crackling in the background, and the quiet promise of what lies ahead.

As I pull back, I look into her eyes, searching for answers. "Raine," I begin, my voice serious but soft, "we need to talk about your father and Jason. You need to tell me everything."

Her expression shifts, a shadow crossing her features as she avoids my gaze. "I...I don't know where to start, or even what to say," she stammers, looking down.

"Just tell me what you can," I urge, my heart aching for her. "I want to keep you safe. I can't do that if I don't understand the situation."

She takes a deep breath, steadying herself before meeting my eyes again. "Okay...I'm going to need some coffee."

I nod, letting her gather her thoughts as I step into the kitchen nook, feeling a mixture of hope and concern. As I prepare the coffee, I glance back at her, determined to peel back the layers of her past, ready to fight for her future.

"Here. This is the closest thing I have to a caramel macchiato," I shrug, passing the piping hot drink to her. She looks at me curiously before she takes a tentative sip and her eyes widen.

"How did you know?" she asks, surprise lighting her features.

"I pay attention." She doesn't need to know the amount of things I've gathered about her while I was working at Double Edged. That's a discussion for another time.

She looks at me, her brows knitting together in thought. Finally, she speaks. "How do you know my dad and Jason work together?"

I lean back against the wall, trying to maintain my composure. "You just confirmed it," I reply, my tone even, while her confused expression morphs into something darker—anger, and maybe a touch of betrayal.

"How dare you set me up like that? Is all this," she gestures between us, "Was this all to get information?"

The question stings more than I want to admit. "No, it's not that. I care about you, Raine. But your father—"

"Don't!" Her voice rings sharp, slicing through the layers of tension enveloping us. It's a mix of anticipation and fury, and I can hardly keep up. "I'm not a child who needs saving. I can handle everything myself. I've been doing it most of my life anyways. At least ever since—" Her hand flies to her mouth, and she sets down her coffee as if it's turned to poison.

The silence stretches, heavy and pregnant with unspoken pain. "Ever since what?" I prompt gently, my desire to understand overriding my instinct to tread carefully.

Raine meets my gaze, a storm brewing behind her deep blue eyes. Her perfect, plump lip is caught between her teeth, a habit that betrays her distress. "He did it," she whispers so low I barely catch it.

Rage floods my senses, primal and raw, forcing my vision to turn a shade closer to red. "What did he do, Firefly?" My voice snaps as desperation claws at my throat, not meaning to frighten her further.

She slumps, defeated. "He's going to kill me too, Huxley. Oh, God. He probably knows I'm here." Her fear is palpable, wrapping around me, and I know I can't stay passive any longer.

"Raine, tell me," I plead, urgency imbuing my tone. As she tenses and tries to jump from the bed, panic driving her every move, she gets her foot tangled in the sheets. Time slows as she tumbles headfirst into my outstretched arms.

Her warmth ignites a storm of emotions within me, fierce and protective. "Raine..." I murmur softly, securing my grip as her rapid breaths mingle with my own. I feel every frantic beat of her heart thundering against my chest. "You're safe. I won't ever let anything happen to you."

Her wide eyes search mine for truth, and I hope she sees the sincerity etched in my soul. "Tell me, baby," I urge, my grip softening as she relaxes against me despite the quaking of her body.

"He and Jason run this illegal underground sex trade society. He made Skye take part even through her insistent protests," she confesses, her voice cracking like shattered glass. "I heard them arguing one night, and the next thing I knew—she was being taken away in handcuffs by Jason. I only knew him because my dad had forced me to get a job at his bar, Double Edged. I never saw her again, alive at least." Her words break, weighted with haunting grief.

A cold flame of anger ignites in my gut, pushing against the boundaries of my resolve. My fingers tighten around Raine, squeezing gently. I can't imagine the horrors she witnessed, the pain she holds, and it only fuels my determination to protect her. "Raine, I need you to be strong. We have to come up with a plan. There has to be a way to take them down. I won't let your father hurt you."

Tears spill over her lashes, and she looks up at me, vulnerability laid bare across her features, undeniable and stark. "I've fought for so long, Huxley. I—I'm so tired."

I brush a thumb under her eye, catching a stray tear before it can drop. "You don't have to fight alone any longer. I'm here, and I care too damn much to let you slip away right now. I've been undercover investigating Jason Hayes and I knew he had a partner but I didn't know until last night that it was your father. What is the secret he's threatening you with?"

Her shoulders quiver, and I can feel the tension radiating from her like heat off asphalt. "He said if I ever told the cops about Skye or his abortion practices then he would plant evidence to make me take the fall for everything." She's shaking in my arms and it takes every-thing in me not to hunt the bastard down right now. "I hear their screams in my head sometimes and there's never anything I can do."

"Look at me. I've got to make some calls and hand over this infor-mation so we wipe our hands of them. Go take a shower and I'll set some clothes out for you to put on." She nods, her eyes reflecting a mix of relief and exhaustion. As she heads towards the bathroom, I feel a surge of determination. This ends now, and no one will hurt her again.

As I hang up the phone, I finally feel a sense of grim satisfaction. Finally, some action. But then, the silent alarm—buried beneath layers of snow—triggers, and I realize we're no longer alone. Someone has breached the perimeter.

A cold wave of adrenaline rushes through me as I move quickly but silently towards the small panel hidden in the wall. I glance at the screen and see the three flashing red dots moving steadily towards the cabin. Whoever it is, they're getting closer.

I hear the water shutting off in the bathroom and know Raine is just finishing her shower. There's no time to lose. I grab my gun from the drawer and head towards the bathroom door, knocking softly, but urgently.

"Raine," I call out, my voice low and steady despite the tension. "We've got company. Get dressed quickly and stay close."

Chapter Seven
Raine

The bathroom is still steamy from the hot shower as I wrap myself in a towel, relishing the brief moment of warmth and calm. But this fleeting peace is shattered by a soft, urgent knock on the door, followed by Huxley's low, steady voice.

"Raine, we've got company. Get dressed quickly and stay close."

Fear and adrenaline spike through me, and I rush to pull on the clothes Huxley set out. My hands tremble slightly as I fumble with the buttons. The events of the last day replay in my mind; a rush of chaos, betrayal, and the gnawing sense that danger is closing in on us.

When I step out of the bathroom, I find Huxley standing there—a sentinel, gun at the ready, his eyes alert and intense. The sight of him, so determined and protective, sends a shiver down my spine. He motions for me to stay close, and we move together silently through the cabin.

My heart pounds in my chest, each creak of the floorboards amplifying the tension. I have to trust him—our survival depends on it.

The soft glow of the room's ambient lighting contrasts sharply with the reality that was beginning to unfold.

He makes his way to a place on the wall where a picture hangs. I gaze at the ornate picture that hangs on the wall, a masterfully painted landscape that did nothing to reveal the secrets behind its frame. Confusion swirls within me as I feel a mixture of intrigue and fear. With a quick hand, he pulls the picture aside, revealing a sleek keypad hidden behind it. Huxley's fingers dance across the buttons as he types in a code with the ease of someone who has done it a thousand times before. The wall behind it clicks, and the whole panel slid open to unveil a hidden James Bond type weapons cache.

"Who the hell are you?" I question, my breath hitching as I take in the sight before me: sleek guns line up like trophies, each one more menacing than the last. Without looking up, he reaches for a small handgun and hands it to me. The cool metal feels foreign in my hands, alien even, as I cradle it awkwardly.

"I'm a Black Ops Shadow Agent," Huxley admits nonchalantly, as if we are merely discussing the weather on a sunny day. My brows shoot up in shock, my heart racing in my chest. The thrilling, terrifying news leaves a chasm of confusion and a sinking darkness within me.

"What the—" My words stumble as I try to find footing. "Is Huxley even your name?" I whisper, my voice a shaky breath tinged with apprehension.

He pauses, his steel-gray eyes locking onto mine with an intensity that sends shivers down my spine. "Now's not the time, Firefly, but no, my name isn't Huxley." He returns to stowing weapons, his movements efficient and practiced, but the sharp beep of his watch slices through the air, snapping my focus back to the reality of our situation.

"Dammit," he curses under his breath. There is urgency in his movements as he shoves more weapons into a tactical backpack, strapping guns onto himself until he seems more soldier than man, but even that isn't enough to calm the rising tension.

"They're getting closer. Take this and go to the basement. Lock the door from the inside. Don't let anyone in. I have a key, so I won't ask you to open it. Do you understand? Do not open that door for any reason." His voice is steady but edged with urgency; his stare bores into me, causing adrenaline to surge through my veins.

I nod, my limbs feeling heavy, yet compliant. It is as if an unseen force had taken control of my body, guiding me toward the stairs.

"Wait! What if something happens to you? I don't even know your name..." My voice trembles as his features harden, and I fall silent, struck by the weight of my helplessness.

In response, he slams his mouth over mine with a sudden intensity, crashing against me like a powerful wave. His arms encircle my waist, and I surrender to the onslaught of emotions that dances between us. Warm, expert lips move against mine, sending waves of passion through my body, igniting every nerve ending until I feel as though I am drowning in our connection.

I open for him, and he takes the invitation, exploring deeper with a fervor that leaves my head spinning. The kiss feels like an eternity wrapped in moments, like time has slowed and the world outside melted away.

But too soon, the passionate maelstrom subsides, leaving us both gasping for air, our foreheads press together. I feel alive yet scared, heart racing in a way that is entirely new but entirely wrong.

"I'll be back for you, baby. Don't worry about me," he murmurs, pulling my chin up gently. His fingers are rough yet tender, and there's an unshakable bond that forms in that fleeting moment. He kisses my forehead softly, a promise simmering in the air between us. "And my name is Cole." With a wink that sparks a flicker of hope amidst the chaos, he turns away, heading into the fray of whatever danger lay outside.

As his silhouette disappears into the shadows beyond the door, I feel a surge of fear combined with a deep, undeniable longing. My heart clutches in my chest, a fierce determination igniting within me.

I can't let him go alone.

This is my fight too.

My determination hardens as I hasten back upstairs to the hidden arsenal I previously bypassed. I've always had a knack for numbers, and watching Huxley—Cole—enter the intricate passcode is ingrained in my mind like a mantra. I repeat the sequence, and the heavy doors slide open with a soft hiss.

I set down the gun that's suddenly too foreign in my hands and pull out a bow and quiver of arrows. An odd choice perhaps, but I know how to use it—something my father inadvertently gifted me when he forced me to learn the skills he hated. And how poetic it would be if I used it against him.

I hastily pull on some of Cole's warm clothes, the familiar scent surrounding me and providing a strange comfort amidst the chaos that erratically unfolds.

As I slip out of the cabin, the biting cold hits me instantly, crunching underfoot, the snow swirling like tiny shards of glass beneath my boots. My breath fogs in the air, but the chill does nothing to quell the inferno burning in my heart. It dawns on me too late that I'm heading in the opposite direction of Cole, the man who had unwittingly stolen my heart when he stepped into my world of darkness.

Suddenly, I come face-to-face with my father. Surprise flickers in his cruel eyes, but he's too caught off guard to notice the bow tucked behind my back. The air thickens with tension as I reach for the small recorder I'd discovered among Cole's belongings, pressing the button.

The harsh wind bites at my cheeks, but my voice comes out steady, unwavering. "I know what you've done. I'm not scared of you anymore. This ends now."

He laughs, a low, chilling sound that resonates, reminding me of countless nights spent hiding from his rage. "You think you can stop me? You're just like your sister—weak and pathetic."

The sting of his words fans the flames already roaring in my chest. "Skye was the strongest person I've known. She stood up to you, didn't she? But you couldn't handle someone not doing your dirty work. That's why she's dead, right?"

The words flow from my lips like molten lava, laced with truth that I had buried for too long. I can see the shock dawning on his face, quickly morphing into rage, yet I feel the power shift; his strength wanes while mine claws its way to the forefront.

"You're wrong; she was a mistake," he hisses, taking a menacing step toward me, but I stand firm, bow poised and ready, a defiant soldier in the war against my own blood.

"No, she was brave. And unlike you, I can overcome your tyranny. I will put an end to this today!" He laughs maniacally, always underestimating me. This sick son of a bitch should never have had kids. Maybe that's why my mother killed herself? She couldn't stand another day in his dreadful presence. We're the same on that front, but I won't be the one dying today. No, the infamous Dr. Wellington will.

His laughter echoes through the trees, a manic cackle that fills the air with dread. "Shut the fuck up and come with me. You knew the rules and you broke them. Perhaps two months will teach you where you belong—on your back for all the rich fucks that want a piece of that untouched pussy. I've been doing you a favor, Rainebow, but now it's time to cash in."

My heart races, a war drum pounding against the confines of my chest. "If you think I will be going anywhere near your whore house other than to save those poor girls, you're sorely mistaken."

A shot rings out through the woods, tearing the fabric of the tense moment and sending birds scattering in all directions. I have to believe that it was Cole's gun that went off, that he's safe, if I want to continue this conversation. The thought of him, the warmth he brings, pushes me forward, fueling my resolve.

"You're too late, Rainebow. You think that little toy could save you?"

"It's not just the recorder, Dad. It's everything. I'm going to expose you, bring all of this to light. You're done hiding behind your wealth and influence."

He narrows his eyes, the calculation rolling over his face. I can see his mind working furiously, plotting angles while I stand defiant, ready to take back the power he always wielded over my life.

Suddenly, the bustle of the forest fades as anger replaces fear in his eyes, "You'll never escape me. I will always find you."

"Not this time," I declare, tightening my grip on the bow. The icy world around us seems to hold its breath, but I know I can't waver now—not in the face of his darkness. I drop the recorder into the snow. "Thank you for that confession, father."

Without hesitation, I flex the bowstring, ready to unleash a storm of strength that has taken years to cultivate.

"Let's see if you can shoot me down, little girl," he taunts, taking another step towards me.

The challenge ignites a burning fury inside me. "I won't let you ruin another life. This ends here!"

My father's eyes widen in realization, but it's too late. "This is for Skye," I whisper, releasing the arrow. It strikes true, and he falls to the ground, the snow around him slowly turning crimson.

The trees stand sentinel as I draw back the arrow, feeling the rush of adrenaline coursing through my veins. I am ready. This time, the version of me that he crafted in shadows and fear is vanquished. I am the flame, the reckoning that rises against the darkness. With a swift, calculated breath, I release the arrow, time folding around the moment like a cocoon.

As it pierces the air, everything hinges on that single act of defiance. I realize in this instant, it's not merely about vengeance; it's about freedom and reclaiming the life that had been stolen from me and my sister. A blur of noise erupts, but in the core of it all, I hold onto knowledge that I was never weak; that I carry with me the unyielding spirit of Skye and all the girls like her.

In this frozen wilderness of shattered expectations, I am ready to fight, for love, for truth, and ultimately—for myself.

My father is in a crumpled heap, blanketed by crimson snow and I take my first real breath in years.

The sound of another shot echoes through the forest, and almost instantly, I hear Huxley's footsteps rushing towards me. He arrives just in time to see me standing over my father's body, the bow still in my hands.

"Raine, I told you to stay in the cabin," he says, his eyes filled with a mix of shock and admiration. "But I can see you didn't need my protection."

Huxley's eyes are filled with pride. He steps closer, his presence grounding me. "You did it," he says softly. "You're safe now."

I nod, but the weight of what I've done settles heavily on my shoulders. "I had to," I reply, my voice barely a whisper. "For Skye, and for me."

Chapter Eight
Cole

"Fuck, you look like a goddess wrapped in death," I confess into the shell of her ear, loving to see her breath catch in her throat. Raine stands in the snow, crimson splatters painting the pristine white around us—her father's blood against the backdrop of his lifeless body. The sharpness of the scene sends a thrill through me, and I feel my cock harden painfully in my pants. Memories of last night flash through my mind, the way she laughed despite the chaos, the way we both knew this was coming. I clear my throat.

"Wait here, I have a surprise for you, Firefly." I haul ass inside, my heart hammering with anticipation as I rifle through the wardrobe, my fingers finally gripping a wool blanket. The moment I step back outside, my breath catches. Raine looks ethereal against the backdrop of death—her pale skin juxtaposed with the red splattered around her.

My eyes roam over her as I approach, desire and reverence fighting for dominance within me. "You're so beautiful, Raine," I profess, my voice husky with raw emotion. "So fucking perfect."

A blush creeps up her cheeks, contrasting against the grim scene, and she turns to me, confusion flickering in her eyes as she takes in the blanket. My heart races—fueled by the adrenaline of what had just happened and the depths of what we both needed.

"Do you trust me, Raine?" I question, stepping closer, my fingers tracing a path down her arm. Her skin quivers under my touch, the warmth igniting a defiant spark in the cold air.

She nods, biting her bottom lip, and my breath hitches. It's incredible that after everything she's been through, she's entrusting me in this moment. I can't help but wonder if I even deserve a goddess like her, wrapped in shadows yet glowing with fierce life.

I open the blanket wide and spread it over the frozen ground, pushing Raine down gently to wait. I can still feel the intensity of her gaze on me, passion and fear woven together.

"Wait for me," I murmur, throwing a glance over my shoulder. The snow crunches under my feet as I walk over to her father. I pause for a moment, allowing the weight of what he's done to settle on my conscience. My foot rests solidly on his chest as I dig my fingers into his blood-soaked garment, pulling the arrow from his bloodied eye socket with a sickening squelch.

Once the dripping shaft is free, I kick the fucker as hard as I can. The body rolls over, face buried in the snow, he won't see what's mine. My voice is low and menacing as I growl, "Even dead, he won't see what's mine."

When I turn back to Raine, that Firefly light is strong in her eyes, illuminating the tumult swirling within me. It ignites something primal; a fire that pulses through my veins, fierce and relentless. I don't waste a second; I'm on her in an instant, my lips crashing against hers.

"Hux—er, Cole," she whimpers against my mouth, the sound making me groan with longing. I hold her close, feeling her warmth seep through the layers that separate us.

I need her to understand—it's not just lust. It's a promise, a commitment in this chaos we call our lives.

"I've killed for you, and I'd do it a million times over," I promise, my voice steady, imbued with an intensity that surprises even me. There is no hesitation in my tone, no second thoughts; it is a vow cast in blood and fire, one that echoes deep within my soul.

"The only danger you'll ever face is me." My declaration hangs heavy in the air, and I mean it. The world could go to hell, but I would lay waste to it to keep her safe.

It's a love borne from shadows and peril—a bond that feels indestructible and devastating all at once. I cradle her face in my hands, a gesture both possessive and tender.

"Firefly," I call her, the name rolling off my tongue like a clandestine secret, steeped in the warmth of my affection.

With palpable tension crackling in the air, I reach out, fingers brushing along her jawline, and she leans into my touch, craving my proximity.

In that moment, the remnants of our surroundings fade; the ticking clock of impending danger, the weight of bloodshed, all blur into a haze. All that exists is the magnetism pulling us together. Beneath it all lies a simmering passion, wild and untamed.

"You're mine," I whisper, my lips grazing her ear softly, igniting goosebumps across her skin.

"No one can take me from you," she breathes, her electric blue eyes locking onto mine, fierce resolve igniting a spark between us.

"I'll scorch the fucking earth to prove it," I vow, my grip tightening like a brand around her neck; a promise that can't be broken—a bond forged in fire, raw and fearsome. Every word is a spark, igniting a blaze that threatens to consume us both. Yet, here in the heart of chaos, I wouldn't have it any other way.

"Cole," she whispers, a blend of affection and awe dancing in her voice.

I pull back slightly, searching her eyes for any hint of fear; all I find is unyielding trust and a wild desire that mirrors my own.

"Take it all off, Raine. I need to see every inch of you," I demand, my voice growing hoarse with longing. My mind blanks, and all rational thought evaporates as the sight of my beautiful goddess begins to undress. She unzips my jacket that she is wearing revealing the milky flesh of her breasts and waist.

I'm enthralled, panting at the sight of her sheer beauty. Raine pushes down her jeans, kicking off her boots in the process. Her smooth skin, now uncovered, pebbles with chill bumps under my gaze. So fucking beautiful, soft and silken, and completely mine. I long to touch and taste, to imprint every moment forever.

Before she can react, I rip her shirt, letting it fall between us, leaving her utterly exposed. She sits there, breathless, her eyes wide and laced with shock but then delicious anticipation, and in response, she leans forward to undo my jacket, pulling it from my shoulders.

Her slender hands slip under the hem of my shirt, her fingertips igniting a trail of fire as they roam over my abs before helping to pull the fabric over my head.

She looks at me expectantly, and I can't resist the urge to touch her skin first. I want to memorize every dip, every curve, the essence of her.

With a desperate need, I lean in, ghosting my fingers across her sides, feeling her shiver beneath my touch. The way she bites her bottom lip urges me on, heightening the craving that simmers just beneath the surface.

"Every inch of you is perfection, Firefly," I murmur, the sincerity spilling into the air between us. My hands explore further, mapping her body as if it were the very terrain I'd fight for. My gaze drinks in her beauty, and I can hardly believe she's real.

"Cole..." she breathes my name, the sound like music, laced with longing.

My heart races in tandem with the primal urge outside of us. I want—need her in a way that transcends flesh, that digs deeper than mere desire. I want to consume her, envelop her until nothing remains but the echoes of our hearts, pounding against the tyranny of fate.

Raine pushes my pants away, leaving us both panting in the icy air surrounding us. I sink between her legs, holding the bloody arrow between us. I run the cool metal along her skin, marring the pale skin in blood.

Her mouth falls open, pupils dilating, but not with fear. Raine wants it as badly as I do, the wicked edge promising pain and ecstasy. I drag it higher, across her collarbone to her breast.

She wraps her arms around me and rolls her hips against me, her pussy growing wetter with every teasing movement. "C-cole, please. I need you," she whines, trying to bring her hot cunt to my aching cock.

I chuckle as I drag the tip of the weapon over the puckered nipple, watching it tighten. "Be careful what you wish for, little girl." My voice is threatening, yet soft. Raine tries to draw me closer, to bring our bodies together. Instead, I lean up, moving the tip of the now hot metal down her belly, then slam my fingers inside her.

"Don't you look like a dirty little slut."

Raine's breath hitches. Her body arches into mine, begging, pleading for that connection we both crave. The world outside fades, leaving only the two of us, tangled in a web of desire and urge.

I toss the arrow aside, and dip my head lower, capturing one nipple in my mouth. Her sharp hiss sends shivers down my spine, and with every tug, her fingers grip my hair, urging me on.

I finally let my fingers explore her most intimate depths, teasing along her sensitive folds, discovering just how ready she is for me. She's drenched, every moan echoing the flames of desire that envelop us. I expose her clit, swollen and yearning for attention.

"Please," she begs. There's a beautiful desperation in the way Raine grinds against me, seeking more, begging me silently not to stop.

"Look at you, Raine. Such a pretty little mess. You want to come, don't you?" I taunt, my voice thick with lust.

"Yes, please, I need it," she cries, her voice trembling as I continue to coax her towards her peak. As I slide three fingers deeper into her heat, I thumb her swollen clit, eliciting a desperate squeal that hangs in the air.

"Just like that," she whimpers, "don't stop."

"Never." Her stomach taut as pleasure coiled within her, ready to snap.

"That's it, baby, come for me," I growl, the sound raw and primal as I watch her fall apart.

"Oh, fuck!" she screams, shaking violently against the ground, her body succumbing to bliss. But before she can ride the wave of her high, before she can float back down to the reality around us, I slam home inside her. Her wet warmth envelops me, and I fight hard against the overwhelming tide of ecstasy threatening to pull me under.

"Look at me when I'm fucking you!" I command, my voice thick with desire as her thighs wrapped around my waist, pulling me deeper into her.

Raine's eyes widened, a mix of surprise and lust swirling together as I lost myself in the rhythm of our bodies, entwined in this reckless dance of unyielding passion. The world around us melted away, leaving only us—two souls ignited in fire, yearning to be consumed.

And consume, I would.

Epilogue
Raine

With the dirty inheritance from my piece of shit father, Cole and I set up a shelter for the battered women from the basement of the Double Edged bar. It's a sanctuary built on the rubble of his misdeeds, cloaked in shadows, but brimming with hope. Every woman that finds refuge in our haven bears the marks of trauma—some physical, most emotional. Watching them heal became my obsession, a purpose to latch onto when memories of my sister claws at my mind.

The bar's cool surface held secrets, hidden scars etched in the wood, just like the ones carried by the women we shelter. It could have broken me—his legacy—but instead, it brought me closer to Cole.

"Are you ready to go home, Firefly?" Cole's question pulls me out of my thoughts.

"Yes, just let me get something." He nods, dropping his hands as I make my way to my father's study upstairs. With each step, I feel the echoes of my past, the air thickening with resentment. In my heart, I know I have to confront it all.

Inside the dim room, dust particles dance in the slivers of dying light while memories cling to the walls. I stumbled upon a box hidden beneath the desk days earlier, and the desire for closure drives me to retrieve it. My fingers tremble as I open it, revealing Skye's jewelry—a memory that gleams brightly among the darkness. My mother used to wear that necklace, the diamond sparkling inside the infinity knot, signifying hope and everlasting love.

Sadness washes over me, but the determination to not let more people be victims outweighs everything else. This necklace isn't just a token; it's a promise I made to myself: I will prevent my father's cruelty from shadowing another life.

When I return to the bar, Cole is leaning against the bar counter-top, watching me with those deep-set eyes that understand the unspeakable parts of me.

"What's that?" He motions toward the box in my hands, his expression a mix of curiosity and caution.

"A reminder of who I'm fighting for," I reply, the weight of my words settling in the space between us.

"A beautiful reminder." He steps closer, his presence grounding me against the turmoil that swirled within. He kisses my forehead, then leads me out of the condemned bar, never to return.

As his fingers intertwine with mine, I feel strength coursing through me. Together, we are not just battling our pasts; we are crafting a new future—one where every woman will be heard, weaponized against the silence of their tormentors.

And as I lift Skye's necklace to the light, I know—my father's legacy is finally crumbling beneath the weight of the love and compassion we pour into each day. The shelter will become a sanctuary, and I will reclaim my voice with the fervor of a thousand storms.

Together, we will shatter the silence.

For every time I've been silenced, my fury will echo

louder. I won't just reclaim my voice; I'll shatter the silence that dared to suppress it.

If you enjoyed this dark and rage filled story, click here to read *Deadly Desires*, a dark and twisted Snow White retelling.

About the Author

L.B. Martin aspires not just to tell stories, but to change lives. Her words are a bridge, offering readers a passage from their own struggles to a place of understanding and hope. She believes in the transformative power of literature, the way a good book can make you feel seen, heard, and less alone. With every page, she invites readers to find solace and inspiration, reminding them that even in the darkest times, there is always a glimmer of light.
Find her on all social: https://linktr.ee/lb_martin_author

Devil in the Details

By: Amanda Cessor

About Devil in the Details

Briar wakes in a cave with eight other women and no memory of how she arrived there. When she learns that they were all abducted for their virginity, she knows only disaster can lie ahead.

Fear like nothing she has ever known seizes her when she is lain upon the sacrificial altar, but it is soothed by a voice–familiar, dark, and seductive. A voice that has been with her for a long time, though never has it been so clear.

It makes her an offer she would be mad to refuse.

Content Note:

Mature content. For readers 18 & older. This story makes references to sexual assault (off page,) sexually abusive family members (alluded to, non-graphic,) miscarriage (non-graphic), abortion (non-graphic.) References also to loss of a sibling/twin, loss of a parent, maltreatment of women, drugging, cult-like practices, kidnapping, captivity, misogyny, gambling, alcohol, and murder. There is quite a bit of on-page gore. There is a size difference between the main character and the love interest that comes into play during intimate scenes depicting PIV sex, fingering, oral sex. This is a monster-fucking story, and all on-page sex is consensual, though there are parts that are a little rougher than others. Please proceed with caution if any of the above would be triggering to you.

Relationship Type: M/F

Chapter One
Briar

I woke to a pounding head and the sounds of hitching sobs.

"Quiet, they're going to hear you," a voice hissed.

"Where are we?" the sobbing voice asked.

"What makes you think I know?"

The stone floor beneath me was hard and damp; moisture that only appeared in the wee hours before dawn—or beneath the ground in caverns or mine shafts. I drew in a deep breath through my nose, smelling urine, sweat, and the sour tang of stomach acid.

I tried to comb through my most recent memories, finding them obscured behind the shadow of pain and exhaustion. Agonizingly, I wrestled myself up onto one of my elbows, squinting in the dark. I could feel my eyes moving, but they saw nothing. Utter darkness stretched out around me, but the room was humid with body heat. How many of us were there?

Sobbing continued from the direction I'd heard it; the sound became deeper, each breath shattering and sawing through the poor girl's throat.

"You're going to get us all killed," the second voice said.

"I don't think you're helping," a third voice came. This one was close—only a few inches away from me.

I reached out and felt warm skin under my fingers, along with the jolt of a flinch. "Sorry," I croaked.

"I didn't even know you were there," she replied.

I continued combing through my memories as the sounds of other people waking around us wove together in a sort of indiscernible mess of noise. I pressed my fingertips to my now-sweating brow, as if I might reach into the confines of my skull and pull something out. Nothing became clearer. I had to go further back, thinking of the morning and my tasks for the day.

I'd had to mend my best dress—the one with the lace I'd kept from yellowing with a bit of lemon juice and some time in the sun. I was going to have to wear it in the evening...I was going to be meeting with someone. Someone important.

"Where are we?" the sobbing voice wailed again and the way her voice caught on the syllables, wet and miserable, made something stir in my chest.

"Shh," I said softly. "Shhhh. Calm down, love. Take a deep breath in. If you keep that up you're going to fall unconscious."

"She's not going to listen to you," the snippy voice said.

"Would you shut up and let the woman help," a new voice said, thickly accented. "It's not as if your methods have been doing much good."

"I–I–I'm terrified of the dark," the crying girl whimpered. "I sleep with a candle lit each night. The servants keep it lit."

So she was well-to-do. Poor thing. I wondered what got her on the wrong end of someone's notice.

"What's your name, love?" I asked, using my most disarming voice.

"C-C-Cassandre—my papa calls me C-Cassie," she said.

"Alright, Cassie," I said. "We're going to breathe together, alright? Let's calm you down so we can figure out what's going on and get you out of here. Take my hand. Reach out; I'll find you."

I heard the quiet hiss of satin on satin as she reached out. She must have been in her night shift. I stretched my arm ahead of me until I felt the stickiness of sweat and tears on fumbling fingers. We grasped blindly for each other for a bit before she caught my hand in a vice grip. I tugged on her arm, pulling her toward me and cradling her against my chest. My fingers caught in the tangled curls of her hair as I pet soothing lines down her head.

I heard her breathe in a shaky breath before she let it out in a long, shuddering exhale. Her sobbing quieted to small hitches. Her body was so small; twiggy. She must have been no older than eighteen.

Her body went limp in my arms as I soothed her. Her breathing slowed to a steady rhythm in the slow minutes that passed while I whispered soft comforts to her the way I did for my younger sister when we were small. I'd always been good at getting someone to calm down.

"Thank gods for that," the snippy voice said once she was asleep. "I was getting ready to strangle her myself."

My jaw tightened as I continued petting down Cassie's hair. Getting in an argument with the woman wasn't going to help any of us so I bit my tongue. All the same, if we'd run into each other under different circumstances, I would have gladly wrapped my own fingers around her throat.

Instead, I focused on what I could do.

"And what's your name?" I asked her.

"Yours first," she sneered.

"You must be fun at parties," I said.

"Wouldn't know; never been to one," she said. "Just know better than to give my name out freely to strangers. 'Specially ones that coo little niceties to comfort babes in swaddling. That's how you end up in a bargain you can't afford. I'm not stupid enough to fall for it when we all woke up in the dark."

So she was superstitious. Maybe she was one of the wise women that called the tent encampments outside of the city home. I'd only heard a few of their stories, usually chortled by the men at the gambling tables that complained about how the encampments were eyesores at best and slowed the flow of commerce at worst. I always hated how they sneered at the tales of the very people that staffed their factories at a fraction of the cost that would be paid to someone born and bred in town.

"My name is Briar," I said. "How many of us are there in here? Does anyone remember anything about how they wound up here?"

There was quiet for a while, broken only by the shifting of heels against the wet dirt beneath us. Details were slowly coming into focus; not so much through vision, but through sound. The floor was irregular and rough, covered in sand or dirt but not carpeted in it. So we were definitely in some kind of cave. As voices hesitantly chimed in, I formulated a rough idea of the size of the place we'd been thrown into; it was tiny. Perhaps the size of the patio outside of my tenement in the pleasure district.

Names were given, and by the time everyone quieted again, I'd counted nine of us. The wise woman, Atreya, was named for the goddess to which she devoted herself to as a high priestess; virgin goddess of the hunt and medicine.

The woman closest to me, Diana, called herself homebody and a bookworm. She wrote books under the *nom de plume* of D. T. Trenton, a name we all recognized.

Freya had only just arrived at the port from the warring country of Vidalgo. She hadn't even been here long enough to have an occupation.

Marguerite, an aptly named florist. A nurse named Bella. A young spinster by the name of Eugenia. And a recently emancipated orphaned girl called Lily.

None of us had anything in common as far as we could tell. We all hailed from different countries, all had different backgrounds of family, different levels of wealth. We did slowly begin to piece together memories, though. Each hand stitched more pieces of it to the quilt until a picture became clear.

"I was casting stones for a man. He asked about how his god regarded him," Atreya scoffed. "Arrogant thing to assume his god even looked his way. Even more so to think my mistress would act as his messenger."

"I was meeting with my publisher," Diana said. "We were toasting my most recent best seller."

"Wait, I was drinking, too!" Lily exclaimed. "Someone left a handle of whiskey outside the place I'm squatting in. I thought it was my lucky day."

"I don't drink," Marguerite warbled. "My pa always struggled with it so I never touched the stuff. I remember someone grabbing me, though–f-from behind. I didn't see his face but his hand smelled like the tobacco shop across the street from mine."

"It was the same for me," Bella said, her voice steady. "Someone injected something into my neck, too. I was only in the room with the doctor but...he's usually so kind to me."

None of my memories had returned as clearly as they had for the others. I did remember who I'd been meeting though. Richard Ganswell. We were meant to go to the gambling tables. The last thing I remembered was pinching my cheeks in the reflection of the carriage window he'd picked me up in.

"So safe to assume we've all been drugged," I said.

"They would have had to drug me," Atreya scoffed. "Never would have let an oaf drag me away."

I rolled my eyes and shook my head. "The bravado is getting tiresome," I griped.

"We can't all become a shrinking violet like dear, sweet *Cassandre,*" she sneered.

"Can't you just leave the poor girl alone?" I said. "It's not her fault she was captured. No more her fault than it was yours."

"Gullible thing like her probably let herself be carted away for the promise of candy," Atreya said.

"Shut it," I snapped.

"Or what?" Atreya said.

A familiar rage built in my chest–though it was the first time I could remember that feeling burning behind my sternum for anyone other than a man. I almost lost myself to it, but then Cassandre spoke.

"My brother brought me tea," she said sullenly. "I was feeling under the weather. Been....out of sorts since Papa died. He said it would balance my humors."

Silence fell like a wet blanket over a campfire. We'd all known our captors, or at least could place them. But she was the only one who had been drugged by a family member. Cassandre didn't seem to sense the heaviness in the room, for she continued, "Papa cast him out a long time ago. Called him shameful. He never told me why. He...seemed so nice until all of this."

Judging by the silence that still sat heavy in the room, we all knew exactly why her brother had been turned out.

I rested my cheek on the curve of Cassandre's head, squeezing her close.

I heard Diana wet her mouth, pause, then exhale. "A-Atreya," she said hesitantly.

"What?" she asked, her mood even more sour than it was before.

"Aren't...don't the high priestesses of Atreya take a vow of celibacy?" Diana asked.

"Yes, on the day of our first bleeding," she said, her tone becoming wary. "What of it?"

I heard Diana wring her sweat-damp hands. "Well...not to be impolite but... I'm a virgin myself. N-not because of any vow of celibacy, just because I'm...disinterested in copulation I suppose."

More silence. Then Bella, the nurse, spoke up. "I was–I *am* saving myself for marriage," she said. "Work has just been getting in the way."

"I'm intact," I said flatly, not feeling the need to explain myself.

My stomach twisted as each woman reluctantly confessed their virtue. They all spoke slowly, as if they hoped one of us would be the outlier. After all, what good could come from a group of entitled, arrogant men gathering a clutch of virgins?

Cassandre started to cry again, quiet and breathy.

But this time, Atreya did not bark an order for her to stop.

Chapter Two
Briar

"You are *cheating*," I teased Richard coquettishly.

"I *told* you, Briar. I don't *cheat*, I'm a *magician*," he said.

Richard was handsome. Charming. The kind of man who got away with murder. And rape. And cruelty. The most dangerous kind of man and one I'd worked my way into the circle of over the course of several months. He was like a venus fly trap, luring girls in with sweet words and presents and false promises before crushing them between his too-straight teeth.

"Oh, here we go again," I said with the tone of a long-suffering lover. "The only sorcery you have is the uncanny ability to talk yourself out of a beating from the bouncers."

"Oh, is that all? You really think so?" he asked.

"I *know* so," I said, pretending to sip from the brandy he'd bought me.

"What if I can prove to you that I have other powers?" he asked. "Will you concede?"

"Perhaps," I said.

"What do I get if I prove it?"

"Bragging rights, naturally," I said, not liking where the line of conversation was headed.

"Come, Briar," he said with a *tut* of his tongue. "You know that I prefer a game with stakes. That's why I hang on your every word–in the hopes that one day they will be an invitation to your bed."

Feeling grateful for my poker face, I threw two chips onto the pile at the center of the table. If I'd been as green as I was the first day, I'm sure my face would have contorted with disgust.

"You don't need an invitation, you've paid for my time, just like the rest of my clients," I told him. "Simply take what you paid for."

"And give up on the challenge of wooing you properly? No, the time I pay you for is like a buy-in for the greatest game I've ever played." He picked up a stack of his chips and set them firmly down in front of the dealer as if in demonstration. "Come on. Name the prize."

"I'll give you the rest of my chips for the night," I said.

"Please, don't insult me. I *bought* your chips in the first place, and you know I hardly have need of money," he said.

My skin crawled. I'd never opened my legs for a mark and I wasn't about to start. With how this conversation was going though, I guessed he might ask for it. If he did, the game would be up. I would have to get messy. And that would delay me more than I wanted.

I'd encountered so many terrible men in this town, some easier to correct than others. A few hissed words while their small cocks went soft underneath the blade of my knife and I would get a promise that they'd leave town and never be seen again.

But men like Richard...I found them irredeemable. I saw them as depraved monsters who deserved to have their throats sliced open. I acted as judge, jury and executioner. An unwilling witness to his many crimes. As much as I relished the thought of his eyes going glassy beneath my blade, as much as I longed to do it, I knew that if I had to kill him today, it would get messy and I'd have to slow down. Lay low for a while.

The longer I had to wait, the more women would get hurt.

I gave him a stony look and he heaved his own long-suffering sigh.

"Briar, what kind of man do you take me for?" he asked. "I'm a gentleman. I only want a kiss on the cheek."

I doubted that.

"Really?" I said. "Just a kiss on the cheek? Doesn't seem your speed." I hoped the derision in my words remained suitably hidden.

"With you, a kiss on the cheek will be like being touched by a woman for the first time all over again."

Disgusting. He always acted so crass.

"Well fine. A kiss on the cheek, then. But I don't know what you could do to prove this so-called magic of yours." I picked up the cards that slid across the table to me, checking my hand and setting it face down on the table again before throwing another handful of chips on the pile. "You better not try to pull a coin out from behind my ear."

"Oh no, my magic trick is much more impressive," he said, his smile sharpening. "It's a sort of...hmm...clairvoyance, or perhaps a clairsentience. An innate *knowing*."

The other gamblers at the table called their hands and left the table as I looked at Richard. "Well," I prompted. "Go on. What do you know?"

His smile faded and his eyes went flinty. "I know that you're the only high-end whore with her maidenhead still intact," he said.

I froze. I'd not expected that answer. Not at all. My poker face fell and my stomach clenched with nausea and my head pounded.

"Well, Briar?" he said as he drew closer. "Where the fuck is my kiss?"

* * *

I woke up with a start, disoriented.

I had no recollection of falling asleep, and falling headfirst into a vivid memory while I slept was doing nothing for my clarity. I still held Cassandre to my breast, only we both leaned back against the stone wall of the cave we'd been locked up in.

Groaning with discomfort, I shifted my shoulders slightly. The slight movement made my leg explode with the sensation of pins and needles.

"Cassie," I said, jostling her gently. "I need to move."

She didn't rouse. She didn't even move. I almost panicked, thinking she'd caught her death from the cold, but her body warmth enveloped me as she breathed slowly, steadily.

In fact, the entire cave was near silent except for the steady breaths of the other slumbering captives.

Had we all been drugged again? Had we been moved?

My eyes were no more adjusted to the darkness than they were before, but I strained them anyway, trying to see anything; an outline, a slice of dim lighting. Something coalesced as I watched, a sort of darkness.

No. That wasn't right. We sat in darkness. This was...nothing, the void, the abyss. Not so much darkness as the embodiment of absence.

"Cassie, Cassie–wake up." My heart pounded against my sternum so hard it surprised me when it didn't wake the girl sleeping against me. "Diana. Atreya. Bella!" Each call that went unanswered became louder, more panicked.

"They will not wake," the nothing said.

"What did you do to them," I asked.

"They slumber. They rest."

It sounded like...like *me*. Was I talking to myself? Was I going mad?

I stretched my neck and shook my head. Unease flooded me at hearing this voice disembodied. Not that it was strange to hear the voice without seeing a face to go with it; more like it was strange to hear this voice outside of myself. Even in the chamber, the sound of it didn't reverberate off the stone the way mine did. It sounded both within me and outside of me; simultaneously the sound of my voice and not.

"Are you what took us?" I asked.

"You know that I am not," it said.

Its voice changed; the timbre dipping deeper, the smoothness fraying into a rumble.

"What are you?" I asked.

"A guardian," it–he–said. "You know this as well."

That void came closer and it shrank. I almost had the feeling it–he–knelt before me. My heart was still pounding, but the rhythm remained stable. It didn't fumble or falter. It was the same steady thrum I felt when my marks were under my knife. A sort of intrepid purpose that steadied my hand while the men beneath me wept and soiled their trousers.

I'd always assumed it was my resolve. My intuition.

"My sweet carver, my blessed render of flesh, my priestess of carrion. Are you ready to become?" he asked. A hand curled around my still-numb leg. It was too large to be human, wrapping itself fully around the lower half of my calf. A single pointed nail on his thumb drew a line up my stocking. I heard the sharpness of it catch the delicate fabric and tear; felt a popped thread run all the way up my inner thigh to where the clip of my garter kept it in place.

An unfamiliar heat built in my lower belly. "What are you talking about?"

Another hand, large and warm, cupped the side of my face. No, not just my face. My entire head. One large finger curled a lock of my hair around its sharp talon of a nail. It made the skin on my scalp tingle. I leaned into the touch, finding it strangely comforting even though I knew I should be afraid.

Shouldn't I have been afraid?

"Too long they have ripped and shredded with greedy claws. Too long have they bound, beaten, and berated when they were created to protect and *cherish*."

He said the last word with the tenderness of a doting lover, his large thumb brushing the side of my cheek with covetous sweetness. "They have forgotten that they spring from very well they are poisoning."

"That's a lot of poetry and I'm a simple girl," I said.

I could almost hear the grin in his voice. "The *men*," he said. "They stole your shiny Penny, but first they shattered her, didn't they, sweet carver?"

Shiny Penny? I hadn't heard that nickname in...*years*. I'd had no reason to speak it. "How do you know about my sister?" I sneered through gritted teeth.

"You cried for me then," he cooed. "Called out for a bargain, asked to bring her back. She was so pretty. You always told her so. That she was prettier than you even though you wore the same face— shared the same womb."

His large thumb brushed away the hot tears that ran down my face.

"I'm sorry. I was sorry then, too. I could not give you what you wanted. I could not mend the broken threads of a life cut short. I could only give you the means to avenge it. For that is Her dominion. Retribution, wrath."

I knew he didn't mean Penny. I could hear the reverence in his voice.

I blinked in the darkness as that large hand settled at the base of my throat. His palm covered my decollete with the weight of a jewel encrusted bib necklace.

"What are you, exactly?"

"A servant to Her," he said. "The Forgotten One."

"The Forgotten One?" I balked, recognizing the name that was shared with a cult making headlines lately. "The Forgotten One is a *man*. And one whose followers think they can help themselves to whatever bride or body they *please*."

I could hear his smile again as the weight of his hand slowly faded from my shoulders. Panic rose as I realized he was *vanishing*. The nothingness in front of me faded before my eyes. "That is what they think, isn't it?" he asked.

The growl of stone dragging against stone tore through the tiny chamber and light spilled into it, blinding me and waking the other women. There was a chorus of panicked chattering and whimpers.

Cassandre's limp body went rigid and she clawed at my dress as if she were a child fleeing to her mother.

I faced our host and forced my eyes to focus, taking in the figure rimmed in golden light that bounced off the damp walls of the cavern and lit the planes of his face ghoulishly. He looked a phantom in garish cultist robes that would have been funny if the situation wasn't so dire.

"Ladies, ladies," the familiar voice said, his smile ominous as his eyes fell on me. "No need to be upset, girls. In a few short hours you will know the peace of submission, the cradle of *obedience*."

Richard's smile went feral as it spread with zealous glee on his face. "And of course, the pleasure in *fear*."

The creature's voice echoed in my mind.

That is what they think, isn't it?

Chapter Three

Briar

Reluctantly, we left the chamber and followed our captor to another group of women dressed in scarlet ceremonial robes. They kept their eyes pointed down as Richard made his commands: strip us, bathe us, feed us, and clothe us for the sacrificial rite.

They left us in a bathing chamber that acted as a prison to the twenty or so women there. I didn't want to think about the implications of that, of what purpose men like Richard would keep a group of cowed women in a bathing room for.

Once the door slammed shut and the click of a formidable-sounding lock clanked, the strangers swarmed us like bees to honey.

Cassandre hid behind me despite the fact that she neared half a head taller. Her pale blonde tresses fell all the way to her hips in soft, undulating waves. Her fingertips curled into the bustle of my skirt as she shrank herself from the ghost-like women. I merely stood still and let the women start unfastening the buttons of my bodice and pluck the hair pins out of my hair.

Diana was similarly cooperative, her ebony skin ashen as she looked through cracked spectacles at nothing in particular. I couldn't tell if she was deep in thought or if she had forced her awareness out of her body.

"This is good," Lily, the orphaned girl, said as she tore off her threadbare clothes and scratched a dirty hand through her mouse-colored locks. "Eating will help us replenish our strength. There's a lot of us here. We could overpower them."

Freya was also undressing herself, waving off the hovering hands of the other captives. "I just desperately want a bath. I haven't had one in weeks." She scooped her oily, raven hair over a bronze colored shoulder, her body already bare despite only removing one garment.

My stomach twisted. I always heard the men at the tables talking baudily about Vidalgan dress, that they basically walked around in their underthings and no wonder they were so promiscuous. Ignoring the fact, of course, that Vidalgo was right on the equator and hotter than the lakes of hell.

"I don't know if these girls are ready to fight," Bella said warily as she grasped a twiggy wrist belonging to one of them. "They're covered in bruises. They seem catatonic."

The woman's arm she held shook her head and opened her mouth wide. Bella gasped sharply, but I didn't get to find out why until I heard a scuffle in the corner of the room.

"Back the *fuck off*," Atreya screamed as four women coralled her like a wild mare. "I'm not letting you fuckers touch me."

A forelock of her copper-gold hair fell in front of her face, the rest of her hair bound in a series of bejeweled braids that I was sure were much tidier before our captivity. Priestesses of Atreya wore their braids as a sign of devotion to their goddess.

"Atreya, relax," I said.

"Fuck *you!*" she screeched. "I'm not getting sacrificed to some *fucked up god* of men getting their cocks wet."

Cassandre whimpered behind me.

"Atreya, it's going to be okay," I said. "They're probably not going to kill us. Look at all the girls here. If we survive, we can find a way to get out."

"Don't be *dense*," Atreya said. "What do you think they'll be sacrificing if it isn't our *lives?*"

"I know. More than you realize, Atreya," I said.

Her hard exterior cracked and and tears spilled out of her eyes, carving paths in the dirt on her cheeks, revealing amber freckles. "You don't understand," she wept. "My goddess will forsake me."

"No one is forsaking *anyone*," I snapped, my words echoing off the walls. "We are going to fight and we are going to get the fuck out of here."

Atreya's eyes blinked more tears out, but she wiped them quickly away with her linen sleeve. "Alright," she said. I could tell she only wanted to believe me.

In truth I didn't know how we were going to accomplish that.

"Bella, you alright?" I asked as she tied her long brown hair into a knot at the back of her head. The movement was practiced, like she did it every day.

She was opening the mouths of all the servant girls, one by one. A fresher one–one with a little more meat on her bones, quietly cried as Bella cupped her face with maternal care. "All of these girls have had their tongues cut out."

"What?"

Marguerite spoke for the first time since the stone door opened. Her voice sounded reedy and absent as she stepped down into the water. "Pa always did say women were better seen and not heard."

Diana sniffled and the woman helping her brushed away her tears with such tenderness that my own throat tightened. Diana stood fully nude, but enveloped the woman in a tight embrace anyway.

"I'm so sorry. I'm *so sorry*," she said.

"Don't you *dare* apologize."

I growled it with such ferocity that I didn't at first realize that it had come out of me until the room went quiet and everyone looked at me.

I knew I should be frightened. I knew I should be *disconsolate*. Instead, black, depthless, molten *rage* consumed me, body and soul.

Are you ready to become?

No longer would I apologize for the cruelty of *men*. I tired of tutting cautionary tales of girls who showed too much skin, or gave kisses too generously. I tired of laws that left sweet girls like Cassandre at the mercy of men like her brother because she couldn't simply inherit her father's wealth herself.

They stole your shiny Penny, but first they shattered her, didn't they, sweet carver?

The memory of Penny's broken body and glassy eyes flashed in my mind. Her sweetheart's relieved tears as he hugged his solicitor when the judge let him go *home* after he killed her and left her to *rot* in an alley. Her pretty white dress with the eyelet lace...it soaked up the piss in the alley. Blood and skin stuck under her nails. She'd fought. She'd cried. And he'd killed her anyway.

I was a coin without a face. Unfinished and stripped of all worth. But I didn't do that to myself.

I looked around the room and saw women of every color and background. Atreya's anger and abrasive nature couldn't protect her, nor could Marguerite's obedient gentleness.

Diana's illustrious writing career didn't save her, even though she spent most of her time at home. Bella, all altruism and hard work—the smartest of all of us probably, and she'd still been had.

Cassandre's wealth didn't save her. Lily's poverty didn't either.

And me? I hunted these men. I carved them up like roasted pheasants. I rejoiced in their terror and danced on their graves. I didn't fear them. *They feared me.*

And yet here I, too, had been captured.

They have forgotten that they spring from the very well they are poisoning.

A pawn. A sacrifice. A *possession*.

That is what they think, isn't it?

Yes. Thought that. But I would prove them wrong.

For that is Her dominion. Retribution, wrath.

Are you ready to become?

Chapter Four
Briar

At least the bathwater was warm. It felt good to soak the sweat and bile off of my skin.

In the end most of the women in the bathing chamber refused to fight. They were either too frightened or too weak from hunger and neglect. I didn't blame them for their choice; I could only guess at the nightmares they'd experienced in their captivity.

The ones who hadn't yet been broken got tips on how to defend themselves from Atreya, who proved as scrappy as she was cranky.

Cassandre had allowed me to undress her after I calmed her down. She sat next to me in the steaming waters and cried softly as a couple women brushed through and washed her hair.

She didn't say anything to the effect, but I thought she looked a little more at ease as the two women gently coaxed their fingers through the snarls in her hair.

A curl of unnamable discomfort had me stretching my neck again as Cassandre sighed and Diana carefully worked cleansing oils into deftly divided hair, focusing her lathering on the roots of her dense, curling tresses. I didn't have the mental faculties to keep track of the rest of our virginal cadre as the sensation inside of me deepened.

The same feeling as when I spoke with the entity in the cell. The hair on my arms stood on end as I closed my eyes and a warm wrongness swept through me before his hot breath brushed the shell of my ear.

"You've chosen," his voice rumbled as clear as my own thoughts inside my mind. It wasn't a question. He paused then spoke again. "The fighting won't work. You must become."

"I know," I responded.

A large, warm hand settled on the upper part of my back, shifting my buoyant weight until I lay on my back, floating. The warm water flooded my ears, the resonance in the room going silent. His hand was still warm even compared to the water, as if some sort of hellfire kept his body at a feverish temperature. I marveled at the size of his hand again, tracing how it spanned across the distance between my two shoulder blades, his sharp nails pressing against the ridge of my spine in a way that made a shiver course from my head to my toes.

After a few moments, his hand receded and I missed it. I opened my eyes and found myself alone in an expanse of... well I struggle to describe it.

It was neither dark or light, neither hot or cold. The lighting in the expanse held the same subdued quality of newly burgeoning dawn or dusty twilight. Like waking from a blissful nap I couldn't remember falling into, I couldn't tell which it was without the context of what came before.

I rose from my reclined posture and dropped below the surface of the water when my feet didn't touch the bottom I expected. I clawed at the water, surprised by how much stretched above me. No matter how much I kicked and swam, I couldn't break the surface.

My heart thudded loudly in my ears as fear overtook me. Was I swimming the wrong way? How could I find the surface? How long could I be without air? That strange, watery light–the expanse of the void around me–made it impossible to know.

"Be calm." His voice sounded steady. Comforting. "You don't need to breathe here."

I stilled, my nude body suspended in the expanse, my hair drifting like a cloud around me. I looked around to the left, to the right. That endless expanse of gloaming encompassed all I saw.

I felt a stirring in my hair and looked up.

Floating above me, the lock of hair in question entwined in his fingers, drifted the nothing from before. The angle of his face mirrored the angle of mine, his body pointing down where mine pointed up. Or at least I thought so, I still couldn't be sure which was which.

The nothing was no longer absence, but he certainly wasn't human. He appeared enormous, almost twice my size. We were almost nose to nose. His skin was the color of charcoal, which made the bloody crimson of his irises almost glow like jewels. Two sets of horns curled back from his brow, one set longer than the other, and both of them that same charcoal color with sharpened points of bone white. Silken strands of hair billowed out around his face, shorter than mine, perhaps cropped just past his pointed ears when it wasn't floating buoyant.

"Who are you?" I asked.

"I told you," he said, his full lips revealing two sets of over-large canines. "A servant of the Forgotten One. A vessel."

He released the strand of hair he had twined around his large finger and set himself to rights, coming to face me right side up. He stayed eye level with me, but his large body extended far past the soles of my feet. He scooped his hand around my back, his sharp nails pressing into the sensitive skin of my waist and just beneath my breasts.

I suddenly grew aware that I remained naked. My skin rippled with gooseflesh and my face flushed with heat. The vessel smiled, his sharp nose wrinkling with mirth as he cupped my face in his other hand. "Little carver, how your blood blooms like roses beneath your skin," he said. "Such a vicious little creature, yet you demure to be bare before me?"

That wasn't the only reason I found myself flushing. I could not ignore the fact that he also wore nothing.

"You said I have to become. But what does that mean? What does it entail?"

He gathered me closer to him and I found myself placing my hands on his sculpted chest. His skin almost burned beneath my hands. My heart raced in my chest in a way that was different from the way that it did when I was alight with the thrill of violence. My thighs squeezed as the hand cupping my face smooth down the back of my legs, covering the space beneath my seat all the way to the crook of my knees. He almost fully enveloped me in his large hands; almost entirely cradled against his muscled abdomen.

"The Forgotten One placed her power within me, but it is a seed encased in ice. It cannot grow within me. I have to pass that seed to you." He smoothed his thumb over the crest of my hip bone. "Yours is the fertile soil it needs to take root."

Despite the flowery language, I knew exactly what kind of seed he meant to expel and just where the fertile soil would be, too. My skin blazed, but not with arousal. With anger.

"Of course," I spat. "The promise of everything I could possibly need, the promise of protection, but only if I *fuck you* for it."

I pushed against the creature but his hands tightened around me, not painfully, just enough to keep me still. "No." His voice came out as a snarl. "Not protection. Power. Not given. Returned. Not fucked. *Worshipped.*"

His ruby eyes burned with fervency as the strong line of his nose brushed mine. "Allow me to worship you, little goddess. Let me kneel at the altar of your bloodlust, baptise me in the waters of your retribution, let me devour the fruit of your pleasure and I will forever be at your beck and call. Just as I always have been. Just as I always will be."

I closed my eyes and shuddered, leaning my forehead against his, feeling the smooth ridges of the roots of his horns against the planes of my brow. "I... I'm frightened of it," I said softly.

"You don't have to be." His voice was a gentle purr reverberating through his chest, his breaths almost as labored as mine. "Let me show you."

I opened my eyes, finding his irises still glowing–burning into mine. He was waiting for permission.

"Alright," I said. "Show me."

His hand on my back smoothed along the line of my spine, nails dragging enough to bite but not enough to break the skin. He cradled my neck, my hair billowing out as I let my head fall against the soft pads of his fingers. His thumb and forefinger gently curled to hold the edge of my jaw, the bend of his thumb pushing underneath my chin, granting him more access to my neck.

I closed my eyes again as hot, soft lips pressed against the place where my neck met my shoulder.

It was chaste at first–at least as chaste as a demon's kiss could be. But after that initial contact, his lips parted and brushed a wet path from my pulse point to the edge of my jaw. One of his canines caught the lobe of my ear and dragged with delicious slowness.

I whimpered and was rewarded with a kiss on the other side of my neck. Teeth nipped and captured the skin. He suckled on the captured bit of skin and I gasped as that unfamiliar heat coalesced between my thighs.

"Kiss me," I whispered.

He released the skin on my neck and captured my mouth with ravenous fervor. His tongue, I learned, was split down the middle. It brushed the seam of my lips, requesting entry. I obliged him, parting my mouth and relishing the overwhelming fullness as his tongue overtook my mouth, the two halves of his tongue wrapping possessively around mine.

I gasped, my body arching against his.

His hand supporting my legs shifted.Oh so easily, those massive fingers and palm supported my seat, allowing his thumb to brush a questioning path on the line where my thighs squeezed together.

My skin blazed as I leaned back into the hand supporting me, opening my legs to him. Then, with savoring slowness, the pad of his thumb slicked across the outer part of me. He broke the kiss to look into my eyes as he held me aloft. His thumb brushed a circle over a spot that caused a spasm in my thighs and a sharp gasp to escape me.

A low laugh rumbled through him, his smile sharp as he watched my face with rapt attention. "See, my priestess of carrion? See how your body sings for this? No man has stirred you like this, because no man can worship you as I have. I am devoted to you." He pressed a little harder as he circled again, my thighs clenching around his thumb. A tightness began to coil in me, like a snake preparing to strike. Slick, wet sounds came from between my legs as his circling shifted into a rhythmic slide from that sensitive tip down to my opening.

He didn't press into me, just kept stroking me as that tension wound tighter and tighter. My eyes were locked on his as he kept coaxing my pleasure. I rested my hands on his neck, smoothing one over the thick cords of muscle and into his hair.

"There is nothing to fear from me, beautiful monster," he said. "I will make you bleed but once so that you can bathe the world in blood."

I pulled him closer to me and he lathed the sensitive skin at my neck with his split tongue as I ground myself against his thumb. There were sounds coming out of me the likes of which I'd never heard before: whimpers, moans, pleas.

"Let go," my demon said. "Come undone and be made anew."

My toes curled as I did just that, my body going loose and my head falling on his shoulder as I shattered under his ministrations. I gasped against the heat of his neck as he slowed his stroking, letting the sensation taper off at a deliberate pace.

"You see? There is nothing to fear," he murmured against the shell of my ear while shifting me again, cradling me in his arms with surprising sweetness after such a carnal display.

"What am I supposed to do?" I asked, still breathless as I lifted my head.

"You need not do anything," he said. "The arrogant men will serve their purpose, they will call me forth from where I'm locked within you." His large thumb settled between my breasts, over my heart, as if to show me exactly where he was imprisoned. "I will come to you and your power will be yours again. No longer will you have to stare into darkness to find me, or quiet your mind while I whisper your will. I will have a form as solid as yours, and you will never be alone again."

My vision blurred and I swallowed tightly, looking away from him.

This man–this creature–was far more destructive than any man like Richard. With a simple promise of companionship I was sundered apart, my shattered heart laid bare.

He made a perch of his bent arm and wiped tears away with large, clumsy fingers. "No," he cooed softly. "Do not despair, little goddess. By the night's end, you will no longer be forgotten. The cruel and the greedy will tremble to know your name."

Chapter Five
Briar

It was almost laughable, how theatrical these men were.

Leave it to a self-important man to be completely deaf and blind in matters of taste and style. Richard did always struggle with dressing himself. He got by because of classic good looks, but when the man paired black shoes with a brown tie, it was no wonder that the venue for the sacrificial rite looked more like the set of a penny dreadful than a proper ritual space.

The room lacked the earnest austerity of a cathedral, but it made its best attempt at mimicking one. A large platform at the center of the room stood laden with white flowers: lilies, roses, daisies, carnations–seemingly whatever could be found on short notice. I wondered if any of them had been purchased from Marguerite, and a cursory glance her way told me they had been. She appeared almost green as she looked at her personal captor.

In the center of all of the foliage stood a stone altar; the most ancient thing in the room, with archaic etchings depicting figures of ambiguous gender in the midst of various carnal pleasures. To my newly elucidated eyes, it was clear that one figure appeared in each panel; a goddess with long hair and sharpened horns. I wondered if the men were blind to this because they were idiots, or simply because they were arrogant.

Encircling that ancient altar were eight other altars, newer in construction, each inhabiting the point of an eight-pointed star. One for each of us.

"Welcome, girls," Richard said from where he stood, still wearing his stupid looking robe and his feral smile. "Welcome to the first day of freedom."

In the end, the plan we'd come up with to fight hadn't amounted to much of anything, just as the demon had promised it wouldn't. Turned out that our hosts had picked up a magic trick or two, including some chant delivered in tongues that made the women in the bathing room fall to the floor like marionettes forgotten by their puppeteer.

When the shoddy plan failed, I'd expected Cassandre to fall apart. But she remained silent as she clasped hands with Atreya.

Somehow we all...lent each other strength in the moment of reckoning. It felt good to be silent and still as we were led down the halls in our pristine shifts and our bare feet. It felt good to not give these pigs the satisfaction of thinking we anticipated the violence awaiting us.

It felt good to know that, encased in my beating heart, was a monster that would tear them all to shreds.

I couldn't be sure, but I thought I heard the rumble of dark, satisfied laughter bounce off the walls of my skull.

"The time is nigh, men. Take your chosen brides to their marital beds," Richard bid the other eight men in the room. They swarmed us and each took the arms of the women they'd drugged and dragged here. I didn't take my eyes off Richard, but I heard quiet hissing and soft gasps. I even heard soft-spoken Diana bark at her publisher not to touch her.

Standing ahead of me, the ancient altar between him and myself, Richard offered his hand out to me. I strode slowly, taking my time. Richard's smile did not fall, but I watched it tighten. Apparently I wasn't scared enough for his liking. I came around the altar and placed my hand in his, pleased to learn that it felt no more vile than it normally did. I didn't fear this man. I hated him.

"So unschooled in the ways of seduction that you have to ritually claim your bride, Richard?" I asked.

"Please," he said through a chuckle. "Where I'm headed, I'll have no need for a *bride*. All women will be available to me. I will merely need to speak a whim and it will be fulfilled."

"Oh? And where is it you're headed? A wax museum? I hope you have plenty of firewood, I can only imagine how hard and unforgiving the wax is in the winter."

"I'm heading," he seethed, "to godhood. And soon will be freed of your incessant needling and acridity."

I smiled at his fraying temper. It was hard not to laugh, in all honesty. "I do love a bit of dramatic irony," I said.

His eyes narrowed. He hovered halfway between striking me or pitying me, unsure whether I was mocking him or descending into hysteria. "Are you going to lie down willingly or will I have to force you?"

Shrugging, I said, "I wouldn't want you to sweat on your pretty little robe."

His lip twitched with distaste, but he said nothing as I picked up the hem of my shift to step over the mass of flowers. The altar took up a larger space than I thought from a distance. The stone on the surface stretched carved and inlaid with shining obsidian in the shape of my demon. The only difference between this shadowy rendition and the real thing was that he was missing one set of his horns.

Richard held onto my hand like a proper gentleman as I settled myself onto the altar. Where I lay, my hands gently rested on the large, clawed fingers of obsidian. I realized with dark humor that they assumed this image–the image of a huge, clawed beast–depicted the Forgotten One.

I couldn't wait for them to find out just how wrong they were.

Once I settled with my hair spilling off the edges of the altar, Richard made an embarrassingly theatrical gesture with his arms. "Men! Prepare for your consummate relations," he called into the room. I looked around me as each of the men dropped their robes to the ground, revealing their pink, wrinkled bodies and their shrinking members nestled in unkempt nests of pubic hair.

I couldn't hold it in then. I sputtered a guffawing laugh. Cassandre looked back at me, the terror on her face melting into a curious, questioning expression. I gave her a knowing look before Richard grabbed my chin and brought my gaze to his.

He still wore his robes, which I found strange. Was the sacrifice not meant to be our maidenheads?

"You won't be laughing for long, you little witch," he sneered, inches away from my face.

He released my face and lifted his other hand, revealing an ancient, dull blade that I hadn't seen him pick up. My mind focused on that detail, trying to figure out when he must have grabbed it, or if he'd had it in his robe somewhere. Anything to avoid the distressing reality that he intended to use that blade on *me*.

He raised the blade over my chest, his other hand pressing down on my throat, clamping me there, crushing my windpipe. My ears started ringing as he called out to the room—to the unseen sky—with zealous fervor.

"O, Forgotten One! Behold your dark disciples. Behold their strength and their wisdom. Behold the sacrifice they bring to you. Too long has the world forgotten the *rightful way* of things. Too long has the world forgotten that which gives them their lives; the origin of their *power*. Come back into the world, Forgotten One. Remind the lost and the foolish where wrath resides and what *true* dominion looks like. Take this blood and use it to fuel you. Use it to once again take physical form. Your vessel awaits you."

I could no longer look at what happened around me, but I could hear things faintly through the pounding of my pulse in my ears as I gasped for what little breath I could manage with Richard's sweaty mitt on my throat.

I heard the tearing of cloth, the soft gasps and cries of Cassandre and Diana. I heard Atreya growl, *"Get off of me you disgusting swine."* Then came Bella's whimper of, *"Doctor, please."*

I hated myself for the fear that pounded in my heart when I stared at that dull blade covered in verdigris.

I will make you bleed but once so that you can bathe the world in blood.

Richard brought the blade down with all of the strength he could muster. I felt it in the weight of his hand on my throat, felt the twitch of his fingers as he stabbed, again and again, with that ancient blade.

It was pain like I'd never known, and I found myself feeling regret as he cracked through the thin bone at my sternum and into the sinuous tissue of my heart. Not regretting what I'd done, no. Regret that I had only ever used a knife so sharp that flesh parted for me as easy as opening a well-loved book. I should have been using a dull knife. It hurt so much more.

Hot, sticky blood spilled out over my breasts, across the altar, gluing the white linen of my shift to my skin. It sputtered out of my mouth, its coppery tang coating my tongue and teeth.

My ribs caved against this brutality, but I did not die. I almost wished that I would as he stabbed and stabbed and stabbed again.

Then as he went to pull the blade out of my ruined chest, it stuck. I watched as his expression crumpled with consternation. I thought that maybe he had stabbed me with such brutality that he'd managed to get the blade stuck in the stone beneath me, but I was certain that carving through my spine would have rendered me paralyzed or at least numb. Then again, the pain had subsided–all that remained was the dull force of his closed hand thudding into me.

He released my throat and tried to pull the blade out with both hands. He was like a fucked up retelling of a heroic myth; only he failed to pull a blade from a woman, rather than a stone.

His eyes met mine and I grinned at him, knowing my teeth must be garish with the sheen of blood and saliva.

"What's wrong, *Dick?*" I rattled wetly. "Having performance issues?"

"You little—" he started, but he didn't get to finish.

A huge, dark hand exploded from the gaping wound in my chest, charcoal-colored and covered in viscera. It grasped Richard's jaw with violent strength and I heard a sickening crack of bone as it squeezed.

Another arm clawed out of me, bracing on the bloody surface of the altar to give him the leverage he needed to wrestle the rest of his enormous form from the confines of my heart.

The men's voices all coalesced into a chorus of terror and shouted questions as my demon left my body. He held onto Richard's collapsing face as he turned to look at me with those beautiful ruby irises. With his other hand, he brushed bloody hair away from my face with such tenderness that I was enamoured. Who knew that a creature capable of such tenderness had such savage strength hiding beneath his too-hot skin.

"You were so brave," he cooed. "Allow me, little goddess."

He rose to his full terrifying height, and grabbed onto Richard's shoulder with the same hand he'd just used to brush my hair from my face.

He tore the man in two as easily as if he were made of paper.

Richard's entrails fell to the ground with a sickening, wet splat.

I looked weakly around the room, finding the naked men scrambling at the stone door that wouldn't open for them. Their would-be sacrifices were in various stages of getting up, most of them holding their shifts around their bodies after their captors had ripped them open. They watched my demon with fearful hesitance as he discarded Richard's corpse with careless abandon.

He stood, turning to the women who had become my sisters in this terrible experience.

"You may leave if you wish." He approached my side, crushing white flowers beneath bloodied feet. "Or you may join us. Your sacrifices await your retribution."

With one hand, he scooped my torso up toward him. With the other, he snapped his fingers. The men were rendered motionless, collapsing into disgusting, weeping heaps of hairy flesh on the floor.

Quiet reigned for a long time. Atreya was the first to speak.

"Will she die?" she asked.

"No," my knight said immediately, no hint of worry in his voice that was just so pleasantly reverent and resonant. He watched my face with rapt admiration. I smiled at him and brought a hand up to cradle his face. His sharpened teeth appeared in a smile as he cupped my cheek in turn.

"Good," Atreya said. "Can you help us with one more thing, creature? Help us get these disgusting pigs into the bathing room. There are some women in there who would like a *word.*"

"Bring them here," he said, scooping me up into his arms with tender care. "There are more tools for them to use. I need a moment with my goddess."

Atreya met my eyes over his shoulder as he turned and walked away with me. Her brows quirked, as if in question. I mustered a small nod, letting her know that I was okay.

My demon walked through the chamber as if he knew this place well. I'd assumed that the altar which I was laid upon had been found and moved here. Only now did it dawn on me that the caverns themselves may have been ancient as well.

Warm blood spilled down my front, soaking into my white shift like a glass of wine spilled on luxurious, white carpet. Or maybe an entire bottle.

"This looks as if it should be fatal." I leaned my head against his chest as I looked down at my ruined, sunken rib cage.

"It is."

So casually did he deliver this information that I thought I may have misheard him at first. His crimson eyes met mine as we passed behind a stone wall that I hadn't realized had an opening. "The

Forgotten One strikes fear into the hearts of many. Even Death himself will not disrupt your will."

"I'm not the Forgotten One," I said.

"Not yet," he said. "But you will be soon."

We passed under a stone archway where a long-haired woman reached for a two-horned demon, joined hands over our heads. "Is that you?"

He looked up at the sculptures and nodded. "Yes." His voice carried a quality that sounded almost wistful. He did not elaborate.

He placed his large hand over my chest where gore and viscera still gaped against the ruined front of the shift I'd been dressed in. His thumbnail caught and severed the soaked tendrils of linen with gentle care. I watched with the same detachment I always felt when I disposed of the butchered flesh of one of my marks. The only moment marked by cognitive dissonance was when the pad of his thumb brushed the sensitive skin on my sides and tickled.

I wasn't numb, then. Something just divested me of my pain.

"You've really been with me since Penny died?" Warmth spread across the space around my ribs. Light bloomed. My flesh and sinew reached across the cavern of my ruined heart.

"Yes."

I watched on, not missing that my heart did not reform as the cage of my ribs canopied my lungs again. For some reason...that felt right.

"Why didn't you save her?"

His eyes were ruby-like in their vigil over me as skin, new and pink, covered the fibrous muscle moss growing over stone. "It was through your loss of her that I found you," he said. "Once Death claims his bounty, I cannot get it back. But I could protect you. Strengthen you."

"Why me?"

"Asking such things is like asking why your sister went through the cruelty that brought me to you." His hand brushed into my hair, his thumb brushing my cheek bone. "Some questions have no answers."

That wistful quality returned to his eyes as he carefully set me down on soft cushions that smelled stale but felt clean. He tore through the remaining sheds of my shift, baring me to him with ease. When he removed the blood-soaked fabric from my body and discarded it like refuse, like he wouldn't abide the reminder of the man he'd ripped in half.

Blood still clung to my new skin. I was healed, but not clean. His eyes roved down my body, pausing at the peaks of my breasts, the curve of my stomach, the silken-haired mound between my legs.

His voice was rough, almost reverent, as he asked for the final time. "Are you ready to become?"

"Is there a choice?" I wanted to hide my face where I felt the flush of hot blood gathering there.

How your blood blooms like roses beneath your skin.

"There is always a choice," he crooned.

I knew this, somehow. And yet it felt good to hear him say it all the same. In truth, I had already made my choice. I made it when he came to me in the darkness, made it every time I sliced into sweating, hairy flesh. I made it the day I looked into the mirror image of my own face and found nothing behind Penny's eyes.

I will make you bleed but once so that you can bathe the world in blood.

No more girls dying at the hands of cruel men. No more sisters weeping. No more mothers burying their children. No more girls dying, sweating and vomiting in beds after unwanted life was carved out of them. No more brothers, uncles, fathers, taking what they wanted from sisters, nieces, daughters.

"I'm ready," I said, reaching up and cupping the side of his face.

He closed his eyes in comfort before kissing the inside of my hand, his mouth just about as large as the span of it.

Another kiss followed: the inside of my wrist.

The belly of my forearm.

The swell of my upper arm.

The curve of my shoulder.

The valley of my collar bone.

My breaths came in sharp gasps as his split tongue circled around my small breast, sinuous movements winding around the soft flesh before converging on my hardening nipple. I let out a whine as he took the bud between his teeth and increased pressure.

My hips bucked and he released it, pressing the gentlest of kisses to the affronted flesh.

"You will tell me if I hurt you." It wasn't a question.

"I like that it hurts," I sighed.

He smiled sharply against my breast before moving to the other to give it the same attention he gave to the first.

"You are a most beautiful violence," he said as he licked the blood from between my breasts, from the edge of my lower-most rib, from the well of my belly button. "How I crave to give you this *petite mort.*"

He lowered himself between my legs and I found myself pressing my thighs together. He tutted, brushing his thumb between them as he had the first time. "Let me worship, little goddess."

Not fucked. Worshipped.

My face and chest blazed with internal fire as I opened up my legs to him. The cold air hit hot wetness there. He pressed one kiss to the tufted softness of my pubic hair before descending lower.

My hips bucked involuntarily as he drew a line from the base of my opening to the tip of my womanhood. He pressed a large hand down over my hips, pinning me in place as one half of his tongue parted my folds and the other brushed impossibly delicious circles around that opening.

He moaned as if getting his first taste of a decadent meal. I moaned as that new-yet-familiar tension started to coil in my low belly again.

"Oh...*god,*" I rasped.

He chuckled warmly against the wetness growing between my legs. "You flatter me, goddess."

Where his tongue was once circling the well of my pleasure, now it broached within, filling me in a way I didn't know I could crave. As it brushed and tasted and coaxed and fucked, the other half drew lazy circles at the pinnacle of my sex, winding me tighter and tighter.

I reached down for purchase sightlessly, hands grasping onto the first thing they could find; his horns. I pulled instinctively, wanting more of this feeling. He didn't falter. He closed his lips over the entirety of the space between my legs, molten mouth and silken tongue lathing all across me. In and out, around, down. Across the tightness of my backside.

I gasped, eyes flying open as I looked down at him. His crimson eyes curved with mischief as half of his split tongue speared against the forbidding muscle between my haunches. My skin went hot and cold all at once as he worked both holes in a torturous, alternating rhythm. Just as the wave of pleasure from one penetration ebbed, the other crested and crashed into me.

My hands tightened around his horns as my toes curled. Sounds came out of my mouth that I'd never heard myself make as release barreled into me. I could feel the satisfied curve of his full lips as he savored every drop of the wetness between my legs.

He hummed, the sound vibrating against me as I went boneless under his hand. He raised his head, tongue snaking out to clean the milky sheen still clinging to his coal-colored skin.

"You're doing so well," he said as he brought his hand up from my hips and bit through the pointed claw on his thumb, blunting it. "How I love to watch you come undone for me."

He moved to his index finger, biting through that nail with a snap.

"What are you doing?" I asked.

He chuckled, blunting his middle finger, then his ring finger, before answering. "It helps that you're feeling good—it helps," he said, voice rumbling in his chest. "But if you're going to take me, little goddess, I have to prepare you."

He blunted the nail on his little finger with a final, decisive bite before dropping that same hand between my legs.

He rubbed two fingers in slow, agonizing circles over the sensitive flesh before curling all of his fingers but his pinky. He tickled gently at my opening before slowly, steadily pushing that fingertip into my body.

I gasped, covering my mouth with my hand as he watched me with hooded, hungry eyes. The sensation was so different from that of his tongue; it was rigid and unforgiving in a way that already had me stretching around him.

He groaned, his long lashes fluttering as his eyes moved to watch the pursuit and retreat of his little finger.

"Waiting for you these years has been agony," he grunted as he withdrew his little finger completely and replaced it with his ring finger. "I cannot wait to spear you upon my cock–to feel you twitch and entrap me, to feel your hot breath against my ear as you cry out my name."

My focus zeroed in on his finger as it slid in and in and into me. He swirled his fingertip inside of me, brushing against some secret place in my body that even I didn't know. He waited there, drawing circles inside of me until the feeling of overwhelming fullness softened to a comforting touch.

I looked up at him as those fingers continued their drugging circles inside of me. "What is your name?"

The words came out with too-soft edges, slurred and heady.

He smiled. "My old name died with you the last time, when you decided to rest and place your power within me for safe keeping. Choose a new one for me."

Another fingertip joined the other, leaving me seeing stars as he slowly stretched me around two of his large fingers. I could think of nothing else as he teased and coaxed and pressed.

"It's too much," I whimpered.

"Shhh," he soothed as he brushed the thumb of his other hand across the peak of my breast. "I thought you liked that it hurt?"

"I–I do."

"Just breathe, little goddess," he said as he pushed those fingers in deeper.

Such divine pressure spread inside of me, such exquisite pain as my back arched and my head pressed back into the old cushions. Once he almost bottomed out, he drew his fingers out of me again and started thrusting them into me, first slowly, then faster and faster until wet sounds echoed off the stone walls around us. My moans joined them at the same tempo, keening higher and higher until they were all but desperate sobs.

I reached a hand out toward him and he leaned over me. His nose brushed mine as I linked my arms behind his neck.

I felt so safe dwarfed beneath his huge frame. His hellfire warmth enveloped me as he increased the speed of his fingers one more time, the edge of his palm brushing just enough on the sensitive nerves at the apex of my core that I cried out with blissful finality as I came again.

He closed his mouth on mine, devouring the sound as I devoured him. He tasted like darkness and decadence and *me*. His fingers retreated, leaving me feeling woefully empty. I made a sound of protest in his mouth and he parted from the kiss to laugh darkly.

"You will soon have more than you ever dreamed inside of you, sweet goddess; patience with this servant to your will," he said.

I bit down on my lower lip and yelped with pain. Wonderingly, I tongued at the edge of my teeth, finding that my canines were longer, sharper–like fangs. He grinned at me, brushing blood from my lip and licking it off his thumb.

He only had one set of elongated canines, now, where he had once had two.

"Teeth to match your bloodthirst, goddess," he crooned.

He reached down between us and I followed the path of his

hand. His dark trousers were suddenly gone and his cock was a monstrous thing in his hand as he palmed himself.

It was slightly darker than the rest of him, almost soot-black against the muted charcoal of his hand. My mouth went dry as he pressed the silken head of it against my opening. His breathing turned rough and ragged as he slowly, patiently slipped inside of me.

The work he'd done preparing me made the sensation, at most, mildly uncomfortable. My legs twitched faintly as a series of raised ridges slipped past the sensitive threshold. He gritted his teeth in a snarl, as if this act of restraint required great effort on his part.

"I want to *fuck you* mercilessly," he growled. "My entire body screams for it."

If I still had a heart, I was certain it would be thudding.

"O-oh?" I gasped.

His eyes appeared dark and ravenous as they met mine. "Yes, goddess," he said. "I want to ruin you. But I won't. Not yet. Not in this."

Despite saying so, his control seemed to slip as his hips rolled and he buried himself deeper inside of me. He dropped his head down beside mine and growled into the cushion. "You are so exquisite. Better than I remember."

He drove in deeper; deeper than it felt possible. I watched the mound below my stomach distend as he finally bottomed out, his sharp hipbones flush against my inner thighs, forcing them wider apart and tightening his fit.

"*Goddess,*" he moaned as he slipped back out, ridges catching and making my unfamiliar teeth clatter as I gasped against his shoulder.

He thrust back into me, only slightly after this time. One large hand slid under me, angling me up a little higher at the small of my back. That little shift opened new depths to him and he retreated again before plunging even deeper.

This time we moaned together.

"*Bite me,*" he commanded.

I obeyed, opening my mouth and sinking my sharpened teeth into the spot beneath his clavicle. His hips bucked and I rolled my eyes as I tasted his blood, warm and sweet in my mouth. I lapped at the wound I'd inflicted as he started his rhythmic thrusting into my body.

My brow ached as he sat back, his other hand scooping beneath my upper back as he brought me up with him. My legs were shaky and loose as he tightened his hands around back and kneeled back. Instead of thrusting into me, he sat still while he moved my body, raising and lowering me onto his perfect, swollen cock.

"Name me," he growled.

"Mmn," I sighed out. My head was empty of everything but the perfect union of pain and pleasure.

"*Name me,*" he insisted again, bucking his hips at the same time that he slammed me down onto his cock. I gasped loudly, hands pressing against his chest.

"*Wait,*" I said uselessly.

He used his thumb to hook one leg higher as he ground his hips in a circular motion and plunged into me again.

I tried to make my brain think of anything. Anything that wasn't this divinely punishing cock driving into me again and again. I went boneless in his hands as he continued his delightful torture, turning me over and cradling me in his hands as he fucked me from behind.

From this new angle I could see all the etchings on the walls around us. Distantly, I scanned our entire life story in pictures as his tempo quickened. My brow ached as the imagery went from abstraction to memory in a seamless river of information.

"I missed you," he said behind me, his voice close to my ear. "I waited while everyone forgot."

I closed my eyes and a fever-dream of fragmented memories spilled into me. Or perhaps they were just recovered. I didn't know.

A man that looked like him, only without the horns and teeth; without the enormous size. His clothes were out of date.

The silken tug of colorful ropes bound around our hands before we smiled and kissed each other.

Dancing around a maypole when he was much younger. I was younger too. Smaller.

A long night at his mother's bedside with my herbs and tinctures.

Strange men in strange clothes coming into town and making camp.

Giving a girl a bundle of herbs and instructing her on how to unburden her womb.

The roughness of his hands as he brushed hair out of my face while I failed to carry another pregnancy to its end and dealt with the fever accompanying my miscarriage.

Prayers called out to the sky to take the strange men and their strange clothes away.

Being locked in a cage, stripped bare, checked for marks. *Touched* by these men. Snarling, biting, fighting them off; trying to.

"I couldn't stop them then," my demon said behind me. I reached up and smoothed my hand around the back of his neck, eyes still unseeing as this past self spilled into me.

The acrid smell of smoke. Fire. Fire. Fire. FIRE. FIRE. **FIRE.** Pain doubling, then tripling, then numbing. Numbing everything except for the rage. Gods there was such rage in me and rage in Rowan's face.

Rowan. That had been his name.

"Rowan," I sighed.

His pace stuttered and I came back into my body as he nuzzled against my neck. His thrusting continued, only now it was slower and more tender. His lips brushed against the sweaty skin of my neck.

"You remember," he said. "Your first becoming. You remember it."

My eyes rolled as another collapse into pleasure loomed. "They burned me," I said.

"Called you a witch," he growled. "My beautiful wife. Our precious healer. Protector of all that was good, all that was right. And they cast you out and called you a demon. Burned you while they made me watch."

"I want to see you," I said.

"Soon," he breathed against my ear.

I could feel him against every surface inside of me, but I didn't think I had another release in me. I feared I might break. As if sensing this, he became even gentler, his movements focusing on his own pleasure while simultaneously brushing his hands in soothing strokes down the length of my body. Touches meant to pacify, rather than titillate.

"I cursed them," I said, recalling the words I'd uttered.

"And I sealed that curse with their blood," he panted as a moan left his throat. "I tore them apart with nail and tooth and blade for you."

Yes. It was getting clearer. I was all but ash when the sky poured rain down on us all, extinguishing flame and creating rivers of blood that carved through our once-peaceful village.

"You came to me," I said softly.

"*Yes*," he moaned as his body trembled with effort.

"You held me in your arms as I soaked in their blood," I said.

"*Yes. Fuck*," he gasped.

His hips slammed into haunches as he curled over top of me, laying me face down in the old cushions as he fucked me into them. The tightening angle seemed to push him over the edge as he let out a snarl.

He slowed his thrusts, milking his cock into me. I felt the hot liquid fill me before it ran out of space and slipped out past the tight fit of him inside of me. His breathing slowed, he sounded like a powerful beast that had just led a stampede.

He laid next to me and I let a moan out into the cushions as every ridge and bump of his cock brushed on the over-sensitive surfaces of me. I rolled onto my side, my legs and body achy from the first and likely hardest fuck of my life.

He pulled me into his chest and started brushing his fingers through my hair, his hands painfully gentle. I tilted my chin up to look at him, but something...caught. Something painful.

A chuckle rumbled in his chest as he lifted his chin. "They will take some getting used to," he said.

I wasn't sure what he meant at first, then he grasped the tip of my chin and adjusted the angle of it so I could look up at him. When I did, I found he was down to only one set of horns: the larger set. Earlier I'd grown fangs where he lost two of his, so that could only mean...

I reached up to the spot on my forehead where I'd been feeling discomfort while he'd been fucking me, feeling a bulge and swell of bone before it extended up another four inches and tapered to a razor sharp point.

"Horns," I said.

He brushed a hand down my back. "Everything has been returned to you, my love," he said, leaning forward and kissing my forehead. I wondered if he'd done some magic, because the soreness abated after that simple show of affection.

"But we were just human," I said softly.

He didn't falter, picking up on the conversation we'd been having before he finished. "We had been once, yes," he said. "Servants of Atreya. Not priestesses, like the other one. But we followed her teachings. The missionaries came with their books and their rules and before long they had one half of the village turned against the other."

I closed my eyes, remembering the smell of blood and ash, remembering crying as I smeared soot that had collected on my own burnt limbs over his face. I'd wanted to memorize the feeling of it. The feeling of him. The feeling of love. Knowing that I was dying and that there was nothing I could do about it.

A single tear escaped my eye as this memory went hand in hand with the utter devastation of losing Penny. There was almost too much loss. A much smaller thumb brushed the tear away and I opened my eyes to see Rowan almost nose-to-nose with me. Roughly man-sized rather than the towering creature of before.

"You're smaller." I sniffed.

"You willed me to be," he said softly. "Before you needed me to be larger; stronger. You craved protection. Now you only need me to hold you as a man holds a wife; as an equal."

"Where did I go?" I asked. "Why did this all have to happen?"

He smiled knowingly at me, brushing tears away. "You were so tired," he said. "After doling out retribution again and again and again, seeing the darkness in men's hearts again, and again, and again. You are so vicious when angry, but inside of you is still this gentle, tender heart."

He placed his hand over the spot where my heart should be, but it was still.

"Do you feel rested now, Briar, Queen of Thorns?" he asked.

Queen of Thorns? Wasn't that some Atreyan minor goddess?

I placed my hand over his heart and felt two different heartbeats. He put his free hand over mine. "You gave me this for safe keeping," he said softly. "But you can have it back whenever you like. For the task ahead, it may be better not to have it."

Outside of the room a chorus of anguished screams and demented laughter rose and echoed against the walls.

I smelled the blood and bile, a stench that had become as well known to me as my favorite perfume.

"It sounds like they have already handled it," I said.

"It sounds like these arrogant fools have provided you with your very first priestesses," he said, his grin going wicked. "And that you need to teach them the best way to make use of those knives and just whose flesh it should rend."

"There are so many men like them." I sighed. "Our work will never be done."

"Fear can do so much to inspire good behavior, my love," he said.

I met eyes with him for a moment before struggling to sit upright. He braced his hand on my back to help me. I held my hand out in front of me, examining the brutal claws at the tips of my fingers, then looked with awe at the wavy hair falling well past my hips and pooling in black puddles around my body.

I was still me. But I was also *her*: She who grew tired and chose to be forgotten. And the creature beside me had waited so very long for my return. I wasn't sure if it was love that I felt for him, but I knew I felt gratitude and loyalty. Loyalty both to him and to the women destroying the men out in that ritual chamber.

"We need to get dressed," I said. "And we need to get started."

He cradled my hand in his and kissed the back of it.

"Of course, my love," he said obediently. "Let us rid the world of this scourge."

As the cries of dying men quieted to blissful silence and the drifting silk of fine garments enrobing my skin, I leaned in to kiss him before responding, "Sounds like fun."

The End.

Want more fiction from Amanda Cessor? Consider reading A WALTZ WITH THE BONE KING on kindle unlimited. Or learn more about what they're up to at http://amandacessor.com.

About the Author

Amanda Cessor (@amandacanwrite) is a genderqueer, pansexual author living with their husband and their pets in the San Bernardino mountains. She loves anime, unhinged dark romances, tabletop gaming, and singing songs to her cat. You can find more of her work in Merciless Mermaids Tails from the Deep and Full Mood Mag. You can also read longer form fiction like A Waltz with the Bone King on Kindle Unlimited and With Love, Juniper from Inked in Gray Press.

A Taste of Venom

By: C.B. Frey

About A Taste of Venom

Broken and stripped of her virtue, left to rot in the cruelty of the underworld, Rue Bennett emerges from the slick darkness, no longer a victim, but a vengeful force. Her thirst for retribution insatiable with each calculated step driven by pure rage of everything that has been taken from her. When an ex-con and asylum escapee with his own agenda finds her, their destinies entwine in a dangerous alliance as their shared thirst for vengeance sparks an undeniable connection. In a world where loyalties mean nothing, Rue must decide how far she is willing to go, and if this unexpected ally is the key to finally reclaiming her power.

Content Note:

Mature content for 18 years and over. Rape, Breath Play, off page SA, physical abuse, violence, blood and gore, exhibitionism, dismemberment, sexually explicit scenes, questionable ethics surrounding human remains.

Relationship type: M/F

Editing and Proofreading: Emma Morales

Chapter One
Rue Bennett

It's at night that I wonder if this will ever end, because I don't have time to during the day. When the sun is up, all we're forced to do is obey.

Don't move...don't look at any of the men.

And god forbid...don't *ever* have an opinion.

But the one thing they don't know is who I am. It doesn't matter that I come from a wealthy family, or have people who will hunt for me because that's what they are counting on. They feed off it, like fucking vultures, pressing and prodding their beaks into every single nook and cranny of your body just for a slice of fresh meat.

In their case, it's for a dime.

Tomorrow is another day in this filth and I must be prepared. Not just for my sake but for the others. Every day there are newcomers, some as young as thirteen.

Never been touched and never been kissed.

I close my eyes and focus on the sound of my heart beneath my chest, pumping angrily, not just at my situation but at myself.

How could I let them do this to me?

How could I sit there and take it?

I take a breath, expelling the last thoughts as I blow out the air through my lips and retrain my focus.

This isn't just about you, Rue.

This is about every woman that's stepped through those doors.

The voice in my head echoes, and almost as if she's heard my thoughts, Hope meets my gaze from her cell. Funny, her personality nary matches her name one bit.

"I don't know why you bother, Rue," she whispers through her matted brunette hair, now knotted beside her face as she leans on the bars separating us. "We're going to die in here."

I admit, I did think like her at one stage when they first took me, but I refuse to sit here and take it any longer. I know she prefers not to risk her life, but I'd rather die with my hand in a fist, drawing blood.

"I'm going to get us out," I say with conviction, and she pauses fidgeting with her torn nightgown.

"All three of us?" she questions with undeniable doubt in her tone.

"Make that my first promise." I grip the bars, formulating the plan further in my head, calculating all the right steps we need to take to ensure our freedom. "My next one..."

I peer over my shoulder at the large steel door before whispering in her ear, "...I promise you *revenge.*"

* * *

The clock ticks on the far-right wall, each chime louder than the last as Hope stands beside me, both our heads bowed, eyes to the floor. Heavy footsteps vibrate through the floorboards as two men stomp into the room.

"Don't you think it's about time we recycle and get something fresh in?" one of them snorts as he brushes up against my back, the stench of his cavity filled mouth pouring out onto my cheek. "Or we could sell them...I reckon this one could buy us a Rolls-Royce."

It takes everything in me not to bite back because I know better now. My bruises are a testament to the fight I put up when I first got here but as they've healed and faded, the rest of me withers away at their every touch.

"Liam will want them in good condition. Get them cleaned up before the opening ceremony and for fucks sake...cut that one's hair."

I don't have to look at him to know he's talking about Hope.

The man behind me grunts as his hand circles around my upper arm, he violently shoves me forward and my hands come out to stop my fall but before I can hit the ground, his knee drives into my stomach. Blinding pain travels through to my core but I don't make a sound. I refuse to give them the satisfaction of my pain and discomfort. Instead, I get back onto my feet.

"I think this one might be broken." He laughs as he shoves me toward the open showers. The cool air slaps against my skin as he tears the little clothing I had on, leaving me naked and barefoot on the frozen tiles. I don't make eye contact and stare directly ahead to the shower head, wishing the water would pour into a heavy river and drown me in it.

"Go. Under the water," he speaks as he turns the rusted knob, the water bubbling as it makes its way through the pipes. I brace myself before it hits my skin, steeling my jaw shut to stop the shivering as I stand, curling my toes to avoid showing any emotion on my face. "You know, the entire time you've been here, I have not once seen you smile."

Fuck you!

"You think you can muster one up for me, pretty lady?" I stare at my feet, his large black boots now filling my vision as he steps closer to me, the water dripping onto his clothes. I shudder with disgust internally as he grips my chin, forcing my head up. "Look at me."

I'm going to kill you first.

I raise my gaze slowly, meeting his brown eyes.

"Smile," he draws out the word in a sinister tone, but my face remains still, then a sting erupts on the side of my face and I come down hard onto the tiled floor. He picks me up and forces me against the wall. "You think you're tough don't you..." he grunts, sliding my legs open with his boot as his zipper sounds and I shut my eyes because I know what's coming. "...How tough are you now?" I will the tears not to come as they sting my eyes and I draw my focus to the painted tiles, scratching it off bit by bit, the remnants wedged beneath my nails as he has his way with me.

I disassociate because it's all I can do for now, until I have everything in place to make them pay for everything they have done, for who they are and what they believe. I won't rest until their bones have been crumbled into dust and I have taken every ounce of joy they have stolen from me and other women.

I won't rest until they've all had a taste of my *venom*.

Chapter Two
Elias Cross

Feverish. That's the word that comes to mind when I think of busting out of this mad house. Only then I wonder, who can stop me? The answer is no one. Not a soul can keep me grounded in a world like this where everyone deserves every horrific thing coming for them and it's going to be me who delivers it.

Does it make me crazy that I get hard every time I think of thick, red, blood painting my skin? If so, I don't fucking care. I'm ready to serve them their sentence with violence, even more so than the last time. I'm fucking turned on at the thought of them all begging at my feet for mercy.

The doctors here believe my thirst for blood is fuelled by my mental condition, but the only mental condition I have is the crazed desire to destroy. To take it all from them. Every. Single. Fucking. Thing.

"Mr Cross, time for your meds." The guard nudges me forward in line to the window where they dispense our medication to keep us numb and stabilised. I've been waiting for the window of opportunity to present itself to me and I think tonight might be it. The guards will all be in a meeting and all I need to do is steal one of their security tags.

How hard can it be?

"I've seen a big change in you Elias." The nurse smiles, her freckled face beaming with pride. "We rarely see anyone with this much of a drastic change in such a short period."

Yeah, if you can call two years a short period.

"Doing my best." I pick up the cup of medication she slid over to me and wedge the pills between my teeth and gums. I've become a professional at this since I've had time to practice and now, they're none the wiser.

"Let's see." The guard pries open my mouth, I lift my tongue then push him away.

"If you want a kiss, there's a nicer way to go about it, Jones," I spit, giving him the finger and walking into the community room. It's always so fucking quiet in here, everyone clearly high off their fucking faces. Some staring at the walls and speaking nonsense, others picking at their skin.

Just watching them makes me sick to my stomach. I know that feeling, when the fuzziness coats your entire body, and the only sensation you have is bugs crawling over your skin.

"It's light, and it's dark all at the same time." Mendez looks up at me, a man I shared a cell with the first few nights I got here. "They want you, Elias. They call out your name in the middle of the night," he whispers, and I kneel to his level.

"Tell them I'm coming."

"Th...th...th...they want your soul," he stutters, his face contorting with fear.

The hard truth...they already have my fucking soul, but they can keep it because where I'm going, I don't need it.

I don't have room for compassion or empathy.

I will never care for others, the same way they did not care for me or my sister.

The world be damned.

"Mr Cross, so good to see you're well." Dorris speaks as she walks by in her white coat, observing the room and I try to blend in. I don't respond, pretending to fidget with an item on the table, something I probably would have done if I was destabilised from the drugs.

Most people wouldn't return to the place that caused them harm or discomfort but I'm not most people.

When I'm done, everyone will come to know the name *Elias Cross*.

Chapter Three
Rue Bennett

*T*his is it, Rue. All you have to do is find a way to get the fuck out.

Looking around the room, I observe the women who have been paid to get us ready. One of them has luscious auburn hair, which extends past her ribs, and the other has glasses that are too large for her nose. They keep sliding off. Both are pretty in their own way, and I doubt they know who they are employed by.

"Close your eyes please, miss." The one with the glasses smiles and I do as she asks, her vanilla perfume still clinging onto her sweater as she swipes makeup over my lid. "This will suit your outfit perfectly."

From her comment alone, I realise she knows nothing about these people, and maybe it's for the best. I wouldn't wish this on someone I hated, let alone someone who is just doing her job. I haven't spoken to anyone besides Hope for the last month...at least that's how long I think I've been here...and honestly, I don't think I want to. After being beaten and forced into sexual activities with multiple men and sometimes women, I don't *want* to speak.

What could I say that would hold any value after what I had been through?

Who would take me seriously?

"You have beautiful skin." Her minty fresh breath fans over my head as she continues to work on my face and I want to thank her for the compliment, but I don't. My reality is my beauty has been stripped from me, taken with force, and moulded into a dark, sickening trauma. "I'm almost done," she whispers as she paints my lips.

I look over at Hope who now has a long bob cut, her dead straight strands shining beneath the lights. As her eyes find mine, I see the hesitation behind them because tonight is the night we will be separated. The ceremony is where the richest of filth gather to bet their millions on girls and women to have and keep, to do *whatever* they want with. It's where the women who have no one go, after their ransom requests haven't been met.

"Okay! I think you're ready." The woman with the glasses grins from ear to ear, looking to her colleague for approval and when the other woman nods, she reaches for a mirror. "Would you like–"

"No." I stand abruptly, the sharp ends of my outfit almost cutting my skin as I refuse to look at my reflection. The two women stare at me, then look at each other, unsure of what to say. Leaving everyone else in the room, I enter the attached bathroom. It's small, but it has everything you need. I avoid the mirror and shut my eyes, taking in a few deep breaths before everything begins. I don't know what to expect, and everything inside me screams with anxiety, but I can't focus on that. Looking down at my outfit–if you can call it that–I reevaluate my plan. It consists of sharp mirror like pieces, connected by mesh. One piece is a mini skirt and the other a bra. I was instructed to be bare beneath, so it really leaves nothing to the imagination.

Finding a long piece of mirror, I peel it off the mesh slowly, being careful not to make it obvious a piece is missing. Holding it in my hand, I test it on myself, gently pricking my finger until a dot of blood appears, then I slide it delicately into the bra, hooking it onto the mesh and pressing it to my skin so it doesn't fall. A loud knock vibrates the door, startling me and I turn the tap on to wash the blood off my finger before opening the door.

I keep my gaze low, knowing exactly who is behind the door and he chuckles. The searing memories from countless nights of his disgusting breath on my face and calloused hands on my body at the forefront of my mind every time he's near. When he's not, there's a voice inside my head. His voice.

"You think you'll ever leave here?"

"Not even your own parents want you."

"You're stuck here...forever..."

"I'll use you until your cunt can't take me anymore, and then I'll shove my hand so far up your pussy, I'll force you to smile, like my own personal puppet."

A shiver rolls through me at the echo of his voice as he nudges me forward. "They're waiting. It's almost time for the *main event.*"

A quick scan around the room reveals Hope has already gone but I pray I still have a chance to see her again. Stepping out the door with *stink breath* behind me, the corridor seems like it's getting smaller and smaller the longer we walk. My throat constricts the closer we get to the end, the black door mocking me like it's the final chapter of my life. It just might be.

Stink breath—or Teddy as they like to call him—opens the door before whispering in my ear. "If I was them, I wouldn't waste *piss* on you."

I grit my teeth before stepping out into a dark room filled with mirrors and my heart jumps into my throat as I snap my eyes shut.

No, no, no.

I don't want to see who I've become. I want to remember the woman I was before they turned me into a slave for their sick pleasures.

The microphone feed crackles as it turns on, a womans voice fills the room, vibrating off the mirrors. "This is our last prize. Gentlemen, we have Rue Bennett..." A bright spotlight shines on me, illuminating my vision with the red of the back of my eye lids.

"Open your eyes." A man's voice travels through the feed as my stomach does a summer sault, threatening to throw up the bile that's been stagnant in my belly for days. "I said open your eyes, girl!"

The thin, blade-like mirror presses tighter against my breast as I swallow and slowly open my eyes, my gaze trained onto the floor.

"Look at the mirror in front." Another command comes from behind me, *stink breath*, reminding me how much I need to get the fuck out of this place. Saliva pools in my mouth as I look at myself in the mirror and I purse my lips. The light from my eyes no longer there, instead, all I see is hate. My hair, wavy and neat, representing everything I once was. Spoiled with the comfort of money, able to afford all the finer things like being able to get my hair done every three weeks. My roots have grown out now, the dark blonde blending with the highlights I had.

A faded bruise, covered up with makeup, on the side of my chin from when *stink breath* shoved me into the tiled wall. I feel like I could throw up when my attention is stolen from the mirror above, diffusing as someone behind it comes into view. I can't see their face, only the outline of the body as they sit in a chair with two men beside them.

"Fifty thousand," he says as the red light flashes on his screen.

Are they fucking betting?

On me?

The disgust builds even more as I doubt my ability to escape.

"Seventy." Another man's voice echoes through my head as his light comes on and his mirror diffuses.

"Do a little twirl and show them that whorish ass of yours." *Stink breath* laughs from behind the door, and I wonder if they can hear us.

"Eighty." The other man bids again, and I curl my hands in a fist, telling myself to wait for the perfect moment.

It's not the right time yet, Rue.

"One hundred." Someone else's light turns on, the mirror diffusing. This time, I can see the man behind it. Dark eyes, blonde hair and a terrifying expression that tells me I need to stay far away from him if I want to live.

"Gentlemen, one hundred thousand dollars..." The woman over the speaker says as if auctioning off a possession. "...once...twice...sold to booth three. Your prize will be transported to your nominated address."

"Make sure she's wearing that when she arrives." The man commands, then leaves the booth, my blood immediately freezing in my veins.

I've been sold.

Chapter Four
Rue Bennett

The car rumbles beneath me as I hold Hope's hand. I'm relieved to see her again, but I'm devastated she's been bought by someone else. At least if she were with me, I could look after her. I see the pure fear in her eyes when she looks at me and I know the fear isn't because of where she's heading but what grows inside her.

She squeezes my hand tighter as a man I've never seen before sits in the passenger seat, scrolling through his phone, his gun placed in the middle compartment of the car. I've never seen our driver before either, so that makes things harder.

"We're getting out," I mouth to Hope as a tear glides down her face. We drive on the highway, the brightness of the full moon illuminating the road enough to see that wherever we are is a fucking wasteland. Not a house, petrol station or any buildings in sight. The car in front of us speeds up as our driver maintains speed.

"Catch up to them." The man in the passenger seat demands, fixing his glasses.

"I'm already doing one hundred and twenty. Do you want to

explain to Vaughn if there's an accident and something happens to them?" the driver retorts.

Vaughn.

That must have been the man behind the mirror.

"Fuck, you're a pussy."

The car jostles us every few metres, the terrain uneven and I'm forced to brace myself as a loud pop, then a scrape sounds from outside the car, slowing us down.

"You and your bad fucking juju! FUCK!" glasses yells in frustration, "You better change that fucking tyre quicker than you come, you limp dick."

The driver door slams as the other man walks out to inspect the damage and my heartrate picks up speed.

This is it, Rue.

I swallow as I slowly reach for the sharp mirror I stashed in my bra earlier, and grip it tight, the edges cutting into my skin, but I can't feel a thing. The adrenaline so fucking loud, pulsing through me like a waterfall crashing into a pool. I use all the energy I have left to hurl my arms around the passenger seat and plunge the sharp tip of the mirror into his neck.

"What the fuck!?" he screams and before he can get another chance to yell, I do it again, this time plunging it through his eye, my own voice tearing apart my throat as I do it again, and again, and again.

"Rue!" Hope gasps as I'm yanked from the backseat, my head hitting the dry dirt as the other man rolls me over onto my back.

"I've been waiting to have a second alone with you." His feral grin covers his scarred face and I cringe, writhing beneath him as he pins my arms to my chest. "Lucky for me, I don't have to waste my time with clothes since you're not wearing much." He chuckles, removing his belt with one hand and wrapping it around my wrists.

"FUCK YOU!" I spit, my saliva landing on his face. His fist meets my jaw, the pain travelling from the side of my face to my nose as he hits me again.

"I don't mind doing this with you unconscious," he says, hitting me again with a closed fist, my eye swelling up almost immediately as blood runs to the back of my throat. "In fact, I prefer it."

"Stop!" Hope's voice is like a beam of light to me right now as I struggle to open my one good eye, my hands working to tear off another piece of my outfit.

A gun sounds, then another when I finally tear off a piece of mirror, wedging it into his chest and toppling him over.

"MOTHER FUCKER!" I climb over him, grabbing the gun from his hand as he groans in pain, clutching at his chest. Aiming it between his eyes, I watch the terror in his build. "I'll see you in hell, you sick fuck." His head thumps onto the ground as the bullet enters his brain.

My legs barely lift me to my feet, and I stumble. "H-hope?"

I turn around to blood pooling on the dirt beneath Hope as she grasps at nothing, her breathing shallow.

"Hope," my voice shakes as I kneel before her, the pounding in my head now a faint buzz compared to the pounding in my chest. "No, no, no, no." The blood on my hand mixes with hers as she struggles to speak, one hand clutching the bullet wound in her belly.

"M-make...them...pay."

Chapter Five
Elias Cross

When you plead insanity, there is no erasing that from your history. It's embedded in it forever. Which is why no one ever does...because to plead insanity, you *must* be insane.

You can't fake it.

I know because some try and as soon as they see what's in store for the insane here, they beg for the system to imprison them instead.

It was easy escaping that place. The guards aren't the smartest or maybe they just haven't met anyone smarter than them. I left in the night, when they were all in a meeting discussing whatever the fuck they were, I snatched the pass off one of the nurse's trolleys as they all assumed we were all drugged off our heads, asleep. Threw on a white coat and walked out of the fucking place without anyone blinking at me twice.

Headlights approach from ahead and as they get closer, the truck slows to a stop and rolls the passenger window down.

"Aren't you far from home?" a man likely in his forties asks.

"Get out of the truck." I walk around to the driver's side and step up to open the door.

"Are you fucking crazy, man?"

"Just fled from an asylum actually." I pull him out of the truck, he yells as his body hits the ground and I take his seat.

Blood. Pain. No mercy.

I'm coming for you, Liam Schneider.

The hours don't feel like hours anymore, even the four I've spent driving this heavy fucking truck down a road more deserted than a cemetery at night. Funny, when you're free time doesn't feel as important, until it's being taken from you. Squinting, I try to make sense of the image in front of me and as I get closer, I stop.

Two bodies.

One in the passenger seat of the car and the other on the ground.

Don't involve yourself, Elias.

The voice in my head sometimes has my wellbeing in mind, but the other voice always wins.

Aren't you curious?

Stepping out of the truck, I scan the area and as I make my way around the car, I spot a woman in a pool of blood when something presses against the back of my head.

"Don't move or I'll do some more decorating," a velvety voice dances in my ears, and I smile, raising my hands in surrender.

"Don't shoot, I'm just passing through." As I turn around, I wince at the sight of her face. "Are you—"

"I'm fine. Get in the truck," she demands.

"No."

"I said get in the truck." She presses the barrel against my chest and all the blood in my veins rushes to my dick.

"Did you do that?" I ask, nodding to where the bodies lay.

She stays quiet, unwilling to engage.

"Why don't you just take the fucking truck then?"

"I..." She hesitates, gripping the gun tighter. "I can't drive a manual."

I smile, knowing that she needs me.

"Right. Well, it looks like we're in this together then."

She gives me a 'what the fuck' look and scoffs as she walks to the truck. "Take off that fucking coat, everyone who has a brain can tell you're not a doctor."

Climbing into the truck, she still has the gun pointed at me.

"Yeah, this isn't moving, so deal with it." She nods to the road. "One wrong move and I'll shoot you in the fucking dick, now drive."

Fuck, I should've readjusted my cock before getting in.

She is the most exquisite thing I've seen, with her scars, bruises and dried blood covering her face. I want to call up my dead mother and tell her I met someone who stole a piece of my crazy. I would say heart, but I fear I may not have one of those.

"Did you kill them?" I ask, starting up the truck.

"Yes, and I'm not afraid to add another to my list, so be quiet."

Oh mama. She's bossy.

I fucking love it.

"Where are we going?"

"There's no *we*." She keeps her eyes on me, and I smile, excited for what I'm about to find out.

Who did that to her face?

Where did she come from and how can I make her touch me?

She goes quiet, and I assume she's just thinking but when I look over, the gun is now resting on her lap, her hands shaking and the tears just falling from her eyes in silence.

A moment ago, I thought I didn't have a heart but in this very second, I can feel something beneath my chest move. I want to ask her what happened. However, I don't want to push her.

"It's okay, you know," I speak, hoping some of my words might comfort her.

"What is?" She sniffs, her tears mixing with the blood on her hands as she wipes her cheek.

"To kill." I keep driving, the empty road, just getting longer and longer. "I've done it and I'm going to do it again."

"What?" She holds the gun firmly with both hands and my laugh bellows through the truck cabin.

"Don't be worried, *slasher,* it's not going to be you."

The silence in the cabin tells me she's scared, and she shouldn't be. Not of me, because she's done nothing wrong by me.

"Some very inhumane people did some very bad things, and the police won't do anything about it because they're all being paid to keep their mouths shut. So, I'm going to staple their mouths to their asses...like a human centipede." I'm practically giddy at the thought. I have so many things I could do. So many lives I could destroy in so many ways and it makes me *horny* to think about it.

"Are you—"

"Insane?" I chuckle. "I've been called worse."

"No really, who are you?" she asks, still holding the gun.

"Elias Cross," I give her a sly smile. "Now are you going to tell me your name or am I going to see your face on a television somewhere?"

"Rue...Rue Bennett."

Chapter Six
Rue Bennett

I don't know what my plan is from here. I had hoped, but I didn't expect that I'd make it out. My luck, now I'm stuck in a truck with a fucking lunatic.

"I like *Slasher* better." He smirks as he mumbles something beneath his breath.

"Well, that's not my name."

As the adrenaline begins to wear off, my muscles become weak, my good eye beginning to close as I fight it.

"Whoa, whoa!" The truck swerves as my body gives up and blackness is all I see.

* * *

It's warm. Warmer than I've been in the last few weeks, and it feels nice. The pain is still there as I open my eye, my hand coming up to my face to touch the bandage now covering the other one. Panic sets in at the unfamiliar surroundings and I frantically search for my gun.

"Looking for that?" Elias speaks softly, motioning to the gun on the bed side table.

Grabbing it, I aim it at him, and he cocks his head.

"That bandage didn't magically appear, you know."

"Why?"

He shrugs as he walks past me unbothered, taking a seat on the motel bed. "Felt like it."

"Where are we?"

"Just south of the painted desert….a.k.a…*bum-fuck-nowhere.*" He looks at me expectantly, like he's waiting for another question, and I have several I'd like to ask but before I can, he continues.

"We're on Kempe Road and it's just a few hours drive to the nearest '*city*' If you can call it that. Motel's name is *Chancelor,* which is fucking odd if you ask me, and I went out to get us some breakfast." He holds out an oat bar and I fear he can hear my stomach rumbling.

"Why are you helping me? You could have just dumped me somewhere…"

"We'll call it curiosity for now, *Slasher.* Eat if you want your body to heal."

Grabbing the bar, I take a seat and unwrap it, this being the first real food I've had since I was taken. We eat in silence, and I begin to think about my parents.

How could they deny paying the ransom?

How could they leave me in the hands of those vile men?

"What happened to you?" he asks, taking the last bite of his oat bar.

"I'll show you mine if you show me yours."

He smiles. Not in the way someone does when they want to be friendly though…in the way that makes me regret saying what I did.

"In a nutshell…I escaped an asylum and now—"

I laugh nervously, "Wait, wait, wait, wait…an *asylum?*"

"Does that scare you?"

Does it?

"I plead insanity when they found me on top of my sister's killer with my hands around his neck." He waits for me to digest his words, studying my face.

"I'm listening."

"He raped her, killed her, and kept going when she was dead. He had her in his house for fourteen days before the police found him. She was fifteen."

A knot forms in the back of my throat, and I squeeze my eyes shut, bright lights flashing before me as *stink breath* shoves me into the wall.

"No! No! No!" I scream into the void.

"Hey...Hey!" Elias' voice breaks through the flashback and the pain from my nails digging into my thighs makes me draw back.

"I... It's... *fuck.*"

I can't formulate a sentence, the shock and trauma taking over my body.

"It's okay," he kneels before me, his dark hair falling beautifully over his eyes. The jumpsuit now hanging from his hips, his arms covered with tattoos. "It doesn't take a genius to put two and two together."

"I'm so fucking *angry,*" I admit.

It feels good to say it out loud. This is the most I've spoken to someone in weeks, and it seems *normal.*

"I just want myself back. I want to be the person I was before they did this to me!" My eye stings as the tears come.

"Hey. Look at me please," he says in a soft voice.

When I do, the green in his eyes ground me as he speaks. "Don't do that." He's careful not to touch me as he rests his hands beside my legs, looking up at me. "Don't diminish who you are right now. You don't deserve that. Not after what happened to you."

"I want to kill them all."

A slow smile spreads across his lips. "Don't be afraid to want it. That's the hardest part, I promise. Once you accept it, everything that follows tastes like a cool ice cream on a hot Sunday afternoon."

I smile back, feeling a little part of my *new* self starting to form.

Taking the last bite of my oat bar, I slide back onto the bed. "I'm sorry about your sister."

He nods, acknowledging the small bond that's starting to grow between us.

"This changes nothing. You're sleeping on the floor." I smile as I speak, watching him grab the thin blanket on top of the bed.

"I've slept on worse, *Slasher*, this isn't my first rodeo but I'm excited to be a part of yours."

Chapter Seven
Elias Cross

It's been a month since Rue and I met on that fateful night, and I've somehow convinced her to come with me as I gather weapons. I've taken her with me to a few houses now where I've killed the cops involved in my sister's case and each time I return to the car we stole, covered in their blood, I see a new smile on her face. She couldn't take her revenge in the state she was in and this way, I've been able to squeeze information out of the pathetic pigs before taking their last breaths.

I adjust my cock as I step into the car, the blood, the fear, everything about taking someones life, makes me harder than a rock.

"Oh my god, again?" Her bright laughter makes me smile. "Maybe you do belong in an asylum."

"I can't help it. It turns me on." Starting the engine, I pull away from the kerb.

"Okay, seriously, can I open it now?" She holds the box on her lap, the gift I gave her since finding out it was her birthday a week ago. I couldn't do much because I don't have a dollar to my name, but I know it'll make her smile.

"Go ahead, *Slasher*, open it."

She pulls the lip of the box open and her eyes widen. "Um..." She pulls out the handheld chainsaw and looks at me.

"Happy birthday."

"A chainsaw? Really?"

"Yeah. You never know when you might need it. Plus, I thought you could use it tomorrow." I test her, to see if she's ready to confront her parents and she sits up. A few days earlier, after some serious torture and unconventional coaxing, a cop admitted to being funded by a large organisation. One that deals with criminals of the human trafficking kind. As it turns out, it's owned by her family.

"You're right." She leans over and places a kiss on the corner of my mouth, dangerously close to my lips. "I can't wait forever."

"But tonight is your night. What do you want to do?"

"Hmm..." She taps her fingers on the box. "Let's go to St. Benedicts again."

I groan, "Fuck. I bring you there *once* and now you won't go anywhere else."

"Take me there or I'll shoot you." She playfully holds the gun to my head, the blood rushing to my cock again.

"Oh *Slasher,* don't tease me." I roll my hips, the friction from my jeans making me harder.

"You're sick." She giggles, trailing the gun down my chest, her hot breath on my ear as she whispers, "I think I'm sick too." Gliding the gun down further, she rests it right on my cock, her wet tongue travelling from my lobe, down my neck.

"*Fuck,*" I whisper as she slowly rubs the gun over my dick, the material of my jeans pulling the skin back and forth. "I'm going to crash this fucking car."

"Do you want me to stop?" she asks, knowing that I don't want her to do anything other than put her fucking hands on me. I'm being patient because I want her to do it in her own time and I want her to be in control.

"Keep going." I grind my hips into the gun, thinking about the two men she's killed, their blood on her hands and face as she stood over them. "You're fucking extraordinary," I whisper as she picks up speed, nudging the gun down to my balls and flicking off the safety switch. "Oh shit."

"Are you scared?" she taunts and I close my eyes for a second before gritting my teeth.

"No. But I think I might come," I confess, our gaze clashing as the light twinkles inside her eyes with excitement.

"You will." She glides the gun over my cock again, the safety now off, the adrenaline thick like blood in the air. Rolling my hips, I groan as my dick twitches, every muscle in my body tensing as I explode in my pants. I try to catch my breath as she steadies the steering wheel, snaking her other hand into my hair.

"That was the hottest thing I've ever seen," she says and her blue eyes make me question why we didn't meet earlier in our lives.

* * *

"One hour, okay? People will be looking for both of us," I warn.

"It's my birthday, Elias. I want to have some fun before I'm locked up in prison for murder."

She takes my hand, pulling me through the crowd of half-naked men.

"Two Tequilas, please." She pulls out a wallet I've never seen her carry before and slides a fifty over to the bartender, looking back at me shrugging. "What... it was literally hanging from his pocket."

"Not bad, *Slasher*. Not bad at all." We down the shots as she orders four more and we take them over to a table that's available at the back of the club.

"Quick ones. Your turn," she says, handing me a shot.

She decided she wanted to get to know me, so we came up with a fun way to do it.

"Last relationship and why it ended."

"Oh, so we're going for the hard questions tonight? Okay..." she throws a shot back, "Felix. He ended it because he thought I wasn't *emotional* enough." She laughs but I don't. I make a mental note of Felix and think of original ways to dismember him.

"Why did you help me?" Her question shifts the energy.

"I have a problem, *Slasher*, I can't let injustice go."

"Yet, you have no problem killing *cops*." She looks around, whispering the last word.

"Because they're dirty pigs." I shrug, "I'm far from perfect but I don't try to be."

She takes a sip of her drink.

"What are you going to do, Rue?" I ask.

I want her to tell me, in her words. I don't want to assume what she wants, I want to hear it come from her mouth. The same mouth I would die to have on my cock.

She stares at me, then closes her eyes for a moment. "I won't rest until they've all had a taste of my venom. From their leader, to their watch dog. I want every pound of meat pulled from their bones as they kneel before me, begging for death."

My cock springs to life at the way she describes her thirst for revenge, and I cannot think of a time I thought a woman to be so powerful.

"And as for my parents..." She takes the last shot, "I think it's time we introduce them to *Slasher*."

Chapter Eight
Rue Bennett

Slipping in from the back door, I don't even bother glancing around to see who's here because in my mind, it's just me and my parents. I couldn't understand why they would be involved with the scum of the Earth when Elias told me they'd been funding these criminals but as I look back, everything starts to make more sense.

My parents are wealthy, but they were never as involved as others in my life. They left me home alone since I was twelve to fend for myself as they partied and came home in the early hours of the morning, did coke in the fucking kitchen like crackheads before business meetings and did not attend my school functions once. Not even when I won the state title for sprinting.

"Mum and dad have a very important business meeting with very important people, dear. They're sorry they couldn't make it."

Our housekeeper would rattle off the same fucking sentence.

Elias hands me the chainsaw and it weighs less than I thought it would. Chatter comes through the closed french doors as we approach the formal lounge, my palms beginning to sweat. I made sure to time this during the guard's changeover, that way we wouldn't be interrupted.

"It's like they just want more and more. They never stop," my father says.

Kicking through the doors, they bang on either ends of the wall, their frightened faces looking from me to Elias.

"Darling?" My mother clutches at her chest.

"If you think *they* want a lot, you're not ready for what I'm going to want." I turn the chainsaw on, the two buttons easy enough to operate with one hand.

My father raises his hands. "Rue, we can explain."

"Explain?" I laugh, letting the manic rage take over me. "Young girls. Women. Children!"

The chainsaw in my hand vibrates as I step closer to them.

"The money you proudly sport on your wrist and hands might as well be covered with blood," I spit.

"Rue! Listen to me!"

"I'm done fucking listening."

I lunge forward and my mother screams, the chainsaw gutting her from the middle, her blood splattering over my face as my father makes a move to reach for his phone. Elias has him in a chokehold within a second as I twist the chainsaw, her eyes bulging from their sockets, the slick, warm blood coating my hands. She opens her mouth, but nothing comes out, her thick locks falling onto her face as I pull her intestines from her stomach.

"Good God! What have you done!?" my father yells as he struggles in Elias' arms.

Wrenching the chainsaw from her, she falls on her back, the blood pouring out of the six-inch wound in her stomach. Picking up the soft, jellylike organ, I throw it around my neck and sever the rest, wearing it like a necklace.

People say your first kill is hard, but that wasn't true for me. I took great pleasure in taking that slimy mother fuckers life and I'd do it again. The toughness is in accepting you *want* them dead. I used to be pure in my thoughts but when you're pure in your thoughts, the world takes advantage of you.

The horror on my father's face is the first I've seen it. He was always so damn serious, clutching his phone in his hand, plastered to his face, too busy to talk because he's always *doing business,* but not today.

Elias releases him, snatching and crushing his phone beneath his boot.

"Rue...please..." His bottom lip wobbles as his life flashes before his eyes, and fuck it feels good to be the one in power.

"Get on your knees," Elias demands, kicking him so he falls to the floor.

"Our father in heaven, hallowed be thy name," he sobs.

Wiping my mother's blood on my shirt, I step forward toward him and bring his eyes to mine. "Pray to your lord...but your soul is *mine* to keep."

He clutches his hands together, now sitting back on his heels, tears streaming down his face as he whispers, "I'm sorry."

"I hope it was worth it. The money, the cars, the life..." The chainsaw roars to life in my hands, like a wild beast, finally free from its cage.

"We didn't mean for this to—"

Brains, blood, and matter spray in every direction as the chainsaw meets the top of his head, my screams ripping my throat apart as I push against the resistance of his skull. I don't stop until it cuts through the bone, sawing down between his eyes, then nose and mouth. I want to keep going...to saw him in half, but the damn battery dies.

"Fuck!" I yell in frustration, the chain now wedged in my father's skull.

"We probably should have charged it," Elias jokes, stepping around to take a look at my artwork, adjusting himself. "That was a hell of a show though, shame it got cut short."

"Ugh!" I pull at the chainsaw, holding my father's body with my foot. "You couldn't have got something that runs on petrol?" I ask, yanking at the handle.

"And pollute the environment?" Elias laughs at his own joke and I turn to face him.

"Can you get it out or not?" I step aside and the body thumps onto the floor.

"Anything for you, *Slasher*." He winks, and with one pull, he frees the chainsaw. My father's blood and brains drip onto the expensive rug they purchased for their twentieth anniversary, and I cover my mouth as a smile creeps onto my lips.

"What?"

Elias stands there, tall, all black outfit with torn denim jeans, covered in my father's blood. At first glance, you wouldn't think he's crazy but if the last few weeks have taught me anything, it's that he very much is.

"I think I might be starting to understand why you're constantly rock hard after you kill someone," I admit, stepping toward him, our bodies mere inches away from each other.

"Miss Rue Bennett...are you flirting with me?"

The ridges of his muscles are like perfectly carved stone beneath my fingers. "I think I want to feel something other than rage tonight."

"Say it and I'll do whatever you want." He wraps his arms around me, pulling me in. "I'll *be* whoever you want me to be."

"I want *you, Elias*."

Reaching down, I unbuckle his belt and undo his pants, freeing his hard cock.

"If you touch me, I'll never be able to erase it from my memory," he speaks just as I wrap my hand around his length, thick and long.

"I didn't know you were a romantic." I smile.

"No, *Slasher*, I mean I won't ever stop thinking about it..." He gulps as I stroke him. "I will obsess over it...and when I obsess over something, it usually leads to carnage."

"Now *you're* flirting with *me*, Mr Cross."

He's not gentle in the way he kisses me, and I don't want him to be. I spent years thinking something was wrong with me because I didn't get along with the rich kids my parents knew. They always said I was weird, and they never once tried to understand me. Now, I have someone who wants me because of it. He wants me because my crazy matches his.

The chainsaw falls to the floor as Elias lifts my shirt over my head, revealing my bare breasts.

"Are you sure you want this?" he brings my eyes to his as he cups my face, "As much as it turns me on watching you unleash, I would rather chew my dick off than cross a line with you if you're not ready."

"Elias..."

His eyes fall to my mouth, his hard cock pressing into me.

"I want our first time to be now."

"In your family living room?"

"Yes." I smirk. "In front of my *dead* parents."

"Fuck," he whispers, his eyes rolling back as he falls to his knees, taking my breast into his mouth, sucking, biting, and licking. He doesn't waste a moment as he removes my shorts and panties, nearly tearing them in two. Lifting my leg over his shoulder, his tongue is everything I imagined and more. Wet, rough, and relentless. Flicking my clit, he teases me with his finger as I tighten my grip in his hair, yanking his head and rolling my hips over his face.

The gleam in his eyes can be seen from fucking Mars as he sucks me into his mouth, then flattens his tongue.

I moan at the sight of the slick blood on his hands, gripping my thigh as he devours me, and it feels like I might explode. Whether it is the sense of power from this position, him submitting to *me*, or the way he fucks me with his tongue... I'm never going to be the same again.

"Do you deserve the air you breathe?" I ask, tugging his face away from my pussy an inch as he licks my arousal on his lips.

"Not if you don't want me to." He smiles like a child in a playground, and I chuckle. "Sit on my fucking face and take your throne, *Slasher*."

I do exactly that, grinding my hips slowly at first, covering his mouth and nose as his tongue enters me and it's incredible. I whimper, unable to hold back my arousal and his eyes darken at my approval. Pressing me onto his face harder, he grasps my ass, digging his fingers into my skin. I feel the intensity begin to overcome me, as I curl my toes, almost ready to finish when he sucks my clit one last time.

"Elias!" I groan, shuddering over his face as he braces me, keeping my body upright as I ride the wave of pleasure.

He comes up for air, the blood now transferred from his hands to my thighs and now to his mouth. When he smiles, I don't think I've ever seen someone look terrifying and attractive at the same time.

Setting me down on the couch, he removes his clothing, his dark tattoos now on display as he strokes himself. He stands there, his dark strands falling over his face, the scars he's endured from countless kills covering his body.

"I'm addicted," he whispers.

Too spent to formulate words, I wait for more as he approaches me, nudging my knees apart. Two months ago, I thought I could never let another man touch me and when I met Elias, I never thought I would open myself up to him. He did everything in his power to get me to be comfortable in my own skin when all I wanted to do was rip it off. Now, I don't dare hide myself from him because I know the more I show him, the harder we both fall.

"I'm obsessed." He hovers over me, the tip of his cock beginning to stretch me open. "And now..." he pushes in further and I gasp, "I will show you how good it feels to give in to the voices until the only one you can hear is mine."

He thrusts into me, placing his hand on my throat. When I don't flinch, he smiles, tightening his grip. "Take a deep breath because for the next few minutes, I'm going to show you what it feels like in my head every time you look at me with those eyes."

He thrusts harder, jerking my body as his hand closes firmly over my throat, the blood in my face pulsing with nowhere to go. I open my mouth to speak, only to roll my eyes into the back of my head as he pounds into me.

I don't know if I've ever felt like this. To be fucked by someone who worships you cannot be compared to having sex in a regular relationship because now, I understand when he said it's all he'll be thinking about.

This moment will always be ingrained in my brain. I will train it not to forget what he feels like inside me because it's the most powerful I've felt in my life.

"You look sensational, *Slasher*." He chuckles as a sharp zing spreads across my breast, his teeth grazing my skin. "Taking all of me so fucking well."

I gasp as he removes his hand, sucking all the air back into my lungs.

"Is that all you've got?"

Grinning, he increases the pace, holding my knees apart as he watches himself slide in and out of me. "I don't know if you're ready for it all just yet."

"Don't make decisions for me." I glide my hand down and grip his cock.

"Fuck," he hisses, pulling out of me as I stroke his length. "If that's what you want, I will give you everything."

Spitting down onto my pussy, he coats it and begins massaging my clit with his thumb. My toes curl at the added sensation, every muscle in my body focused on the release that's imminent. "I can't wait to have *all* of you."

He flips me over, my face now beside the chainsaw covered in blood. Luckily it has a safety system in place where it cannot be operated unless the two buttons are pressed simultaneously, otherwise I fear the potential accidents.

My pussy stretches again, accommodating his size as he hovers over me, licking from my shoulder to my ear. "Did you enjoy it?"

I stare at the droplets of crimson, falling from the blade of the chainsaw as he enters me to the hilt. The sting in my skull makes me smile as he gathers my hair in a fist, pulling back.

"Tell me, *Slasher,* how much you enjoyed taking their life and how much you want to do it again."

I moan, my breasts rubbing against the material of the couch, the pool of blood getting bigger as it drips from the chainsaw. Pushing my hips back, the tip of his cock hits the right place, over and over again as he drives himself into me, the sound of our skin slapping against each other.

"I loved every single second," I whisper, still staring at the chainsaw.

"Yes," Elias groans, his cock hardening. "Such a *killer.*"

His hand lands down hard on my ass and my nipples harden at the contact.

"Oh, does my little *Slasher* like that?" He questions at my visceral response.

"Yes," I say breathlessly.

Again.

Harder.

He grips my hips as I struggle to think, thrusting into me as he groans, "I'm so close."

So am I.

The words don't come out as my body shudders again, tightening around his cock. White spots appear in my vision as I work to come down from my high, Elias still chasing his.

"I want you inside me when I'm taking my vengeance."

"Fuck!" he yells, exploding inside me, his fingers bruising my hip as his hot come runs down my thigh.

His breath fans the nape of my neck as he rests his head on mine. "The next time we fuck, I want you bathed in their blood."

Chapter Nine
Elias Cross

A dream. That's what I thought it was when my dick was inside her because that's what it felt like. Her warm, wet pussy gripping me as I focused on making sure she had hers first. This new obsession is highly addicting, like flammable liquid dangerously close to fire...all it takes is one spark and it's all up in flames. It doesn't matter that the whole world might burn, as long as I burn with her.

"How many do you think we need?" she asks, holding the solvent in one hand and a large black bag in the other.

"You need different chemicals to dissolve certain parts of the body." I smile at her innocence, and she frowns.

"There's too many of them to dissolve them all and I don't want to be digging graves either."

"We could always burn them?" I whisper and her eyes light up.

"That's brilliant."

Grabbing the lighter fluid boxes, she throws them in the cart, her hood and hat covering most of her face. It's extremely risky being out here with her, but I didn't want her to be alone in this. After the *party* at her house, the police are on high alert. Even though we cleaned up, the bodies were still there when we left and no doubt some of our DNA.

We pay for the items and leave, getting into the new ride we managed to steal from one of her rich neighbours.

"Don't think I've ever sat on leather seats in a car before."

The soft thud of her door sounds as she enters, closing it behind her.

She shrugs, looking around the interior of the car. "It's nothing special. Let's go. I want to get ready for tonight."

I feel her excitement radiating through her smile and my cock tents in my jeans.

"You have to stop doing that," I warn, pushing the start button.

"Doing what?"

"Talking dirty to me."

She giggles, playfully slapping my arm and I pin her to the back of the chair with my hand around her throat.

"I'm serious, or I won't be able to control myself."

Her mouth falls open, her eyes dropping to my lips as she grabs my hand and guides it into her panties. "Self-control is overrated."

Slipping a finger into her, I groan, my cock now painfully hard.

"You're teasing me."

"No..." Removing my hand, she places it in my mouth and the taste of her buzzes on my tongue, heightening everything around me. "I'm warming you up for the finale."

I'm fully aware that there is only two of us. I'm insane, not stupid. I know they're greater in numbers and I know this most likely won't end well for us. The gravity of the situation might be enough to throw some people, but I haven't sensed an ounce of hesitation or heard a sound of regret in her voice.

"*Slasher*, let's agree on one thing before we head in, okay?" I level with her because for the first time in my life I'm afraid of something.

"Don't tell me you're scared." She scoffs, shuffling her feet and grabbing the handles of the plastic bags.

"I am."

She whips her gaze to me, surprised.

"I'm fucking terrified of losing you."

Her expression goes from shock to awe. "Nothing's going to happen to me," she reassures me and I admire her for it. "They should be worried about what's going to happen to them."

Grabbing the chainsaw onto her lap, she strokes it like a pet. "*Spike* and I are charged and ready. Let me know if you need a breather."

I remain bewildered by her as she gives me a peck on my lips and slips out the passenger door, waiting for me.

"Fuck, I think I'm in love," I murmur to myself before reaching for the axe in the backseat.

Guns are too mainstream. Too easy. One pull of the trigger and they're dead.

Where's the fun in that?

Where's the savouring of the moment?

The sweet pause right before they realise they're about to die is one of my favourite seconds. As they draw their last breath, knowing my face is the last one they'll see, it makes me want to take a photo of them to create an album.

"If they touch me, I don't want you to intervene." She gives the chainsaw a test run, the blades whirring beside her.

"No fucking way, you can't ask that of me."

"Elias. I need to do this myself." She walks in before I can agree, which is probably a good thing because there is no fucking way I will let them touch her. She's mine and always will be.

Walking past the gates, we enter the yard in the middle of nowhere, nothing but a lone warehouse in sight as goosebumps rise on my skin, covering my neck, back and arms. The moonlight casts a shadow on the various abandoned vehicles by the building, only one of them looks like it's in working condition.

A thud vibrates the metal doors of the warehouse and we both take cover behind a wrecked car.

"How many people do you think they have in there?"

"I don't know, it could be from five to fifteen but when they had me, I saw five men. Two were outside keeping watch and the others were inside with the victims," she explains.

"I'll follow your lead."

I don't follow anyone, I don't even listen to many people but for her, I'll bend over backwards, offer myself up as bait or be the grim reaper at her service.

Edging closer to the door, we spot a man in all black putting a cigarette butt out with his boot, carrying a pistol in the back of his pants. Just as I'm about to speak Rue saunters off in his direction, the chainsaw resting on her shoulder, her denim shorts barely covering her ass with the way her hips sway when she walks.

Damn it. I'm hard again watching her.

"You!" He reaches for his gun as he spots her, my stomach almost falling out of my fucking ass but before he can grab it, she saws his hand off. "Ahhh! You crazy fucking bitch!"

She laughs as I approach them, his eyes now on me.

"Actually, he's the crazy one." She kisses me as he falls to his knees. "Have fun, baby." She trails her hand down my shirt and steps aside.

There are so many ways I could kill him and yet I can only think of one that would satisfy me right now.

"Are you curious to know what your spine looks like?"

The scent of his fear makes things so much more arousing as he whimpers, the adrenaline no doubt coursing through his veins.

"What's the matter with you, man?" He sniffs, the end of his radius and ulna now exposed to the air. "What do you want?"

"Well, the simple answer is your life."

He begins to pull himself along the dirt, glancing back and forth from me to Rue.

"Hold still." Rolling him over to his front, I remove my shirt and force it into his mouth. "You might feel a little pinch."

Lifting the axe above my head, I swing down hard on his back, his muffled screams barely over a decibel as I remove it and do it again on the other side of his spine.

It's ridiculous just how strong the human body can be. I know, I studied human motion and physics. The body can be the most dangerous weapon if you train it correctly or it can be the biggest, useless sack of meat if treated poorly.

"I might need that." I point at the chainsaw in Rue's hand, and she gives it to me.

"All this blood is making me thirsty." I chuckle, shoving my hand into the axe wound, the firm muscles beneath his skin unwilling to move as I feel my way round for his spine. Sawing into the other side, I almost slice my finger off.

Looking up at Rue, I notice the look on her face, the same one she was giving me in the car earlier.

"I told you not to look at me like that."

"Maybe you can make good on your threat when I finally kill them all." She takes the chainsaw from me and places the blade on my throat. "I'm getting impatient."

I hold her gaze as I pull at the man's spine, the vertebrae dislodging from the disc and muscle surrounding it. Opening her hand, I place it in her palm.

"A souvenir for your growing collection."

"What collection?" She rolls it over in her palm, the blood dripping from her fingertips.

"One I'm about to start."

Chapter Ten
Rue Bennett

I thought I might feel something odd being back here, like I'd somehow shrivel up into myself and become immobile, invisible like I always was, but it's the opposite. I'm free. Physically and mentally free to take whatever I want from them just like they took from me. Instead, I want to make them *hurt*. I want to not only take their freedoms, but I want to steal everything that makes them happy.

As I walk into the warehouse, the cages have doubled in numbers since I was last here, showing me that there's no sign of this slowing down.

Not unless someone does something about it.

One of the girls in the cages spots me and the light in her eyes is enough to brighten up the darkest depths of hell.

"What the fuck?" A man's voice sounds beside me and it's a voice I've come to know too well.

Stink breath.

"You came back?" He laughs, motioning to his men to grab me. "You're more fucked up than I thought."

"I came back to see what your heart tastes like." Flicking the chainsaw, blood splatters onto the floor, his eyes now on Elias.

"Wait. H-how do you two know each other?"

Elias smiles, practically giddy at the thought of someone knowing who he is.

"I'm after your boss, *Liam Schneider,*" Elias says, lifting the axe to point it at him, "But *you*...sadly your life is not mine to take."

I take a step forward, dodging the axe Elias hurls toward the man who reaches for me and *stink breath* takes a step back.

"Holy fuck!" he screams as the axe lands in the middle of the man's eyes, his body plummeting to the ground. He reaches behind him but before he can, I raise the chainsaw to his balls.

"Make another move and say goodbye to your appendage."

Raising both hands, his jaw tics.

"What's the plan here, huh? Kill me then what?"

"Taking things day by day, *stink breath.*" I remove the gun tucked behind his back and flick the safety switch off, then point it at him. "Open your mouth."

A man's screams echo through the partially empty warehouse and I look back at Elias jerking himself on top of a guard who now has the axe wedged in his thigh. "Yeah baby, give me another scream."

Returning my attention to *stink breath*, I slide the barrel into his mouth. "Sit down."

He does as he's told, kneeling before me, the power within me beginning to grow as I slowly take it back.

"Elias, bring both the bodies here."

"*Slasher,* I was enjoying myself." He huffs, stuffing himself back into his pants.

"I know something else you'll enjoy a lot more than pulling yourself off over this bastard."

His lips curl into a twisted smile, thrilled, waiting for his next order.

"Pile them up here."

When the bodies are placed beside me, I remove the gun from *stink breaths* mouth and place it in his hands, holding the chainsaw by his neck as I stand behind him.

"Shoot them all."

He hesitates, swallowing as I wait for him.

The chainsaw roars to life in my hands like a warning as I yell, "Are you fucking deaf? I said kill them all!"

Rapid gunfire explodes as the bullets sink into the bodies, the screams of the girls in the cages rattling off the metal doors.

The magazine clicks, indicating an empty round. Throwing the gun onto the ground, he directs his gaze to me. "Liam won't let this go. This is his best producing warehouse."

"I'm counting on it." I whisper, motioning him to move toward the bodies.

Elias grabs the rope from one of the walls and wraps it around *stink breaths* wrists. Pushing him onto the bodies, he knees him in the face.

"Your blood is like an aphrodisiac." Turning him around, he removes his belt, then pants and briefs, exposing him.

"What are you doing?" I ask the question before *stink breath* can.

"Giving it back to him."

"What!?" *Stink breath* protests, trying to wriggle out of Elias' hold. "No! Are you crazy!?"

"Why does everyone ask me that?" Pushing his arms up, *stink breath* wails in pain. "Now hold still, princess, this is going to hurt a lot."

I cover my mouth with my hand as he places a condom on himself.

"Look at her." He yanks his head up and I see pure fear in *stink breaths* eyes.

"Please don't do this! I'm sorry! I'm sorry!"

Elias looks to me for approval when a flash of white fills my vision. My own voice in my head yelling, pleading for all of it to stop when he was inside me multiple times. It didn't matter that I never said anything and just took it, he would still make it hurt as a challenge to see how much I could take. No matter how much it hurt, or how badly I wanted to die in those moments, I never said a word or made a sound.

"You don't have to do this! I can tell you where Liam is!" He tries to bargain.

I nod to Elias and turn around, blocking my ears and closing my eyes. Sounds of struggle are muffled in my ears and I try to think of the last moment of joy I remember, but I can't seem to find one. Sighing, I turn around.

"Just kill me, please, just kill me!" He sobs, his face now pressed against the dead bodies.

"How does it feel?" I crouch so he can look me in the eyes.

His lip wobbles, giving up in his struggle.

"Every time you were inside me, I wanted to scream. I wanted to claw your fucking face off when you hit me." I twist his ear and bring the whirring chainsaw beside his face. "Just know what you're feeling won't ever amount to the times you tortured and killed innocent women and children."

Sawing his ear off, I throw it aside like litter and just when I think he might pass out. I watch as the life in his eyes dies right in front of me, until there is nothing left but hatred for himself.

"That's enough."

Elias stops and removes himself as I lean into *stink breaths* face, I whisper, "I'll hang your teeth around my neck, like you wore my dignity beneath your boots."

A tear rolls down his cheek, his eyes absent from the present moment, clearly disassociated. A wave of calm rushes over me at the sight of my him immobilised.

"We should clean up," Elias says, discarding the used, bloodied condom on top of the pile of bodies.

"First, we let them out."

I head over to the cages and swing the axe onto the lock of each of them. The girls gather beside me, thanking me and Elias for rescuing them.

"There's a car parked just outside the gates, can any of you drive?" I ask the one who looks to be the eldest and she nods. Handing her the keys, I give her a small smile. "Don't stop, okay, there is a police station an hour drive from here and the car has plenty of petrol to get you there."

"Thank you," she says, ushering the rest of the girls out the door. When I turn around, Elias has already gathered the bodies into black body bags.

"Where did you find those?" I ask, watching as he zips the last one halfway, *stink breath* still breathing inside it.

"Does it matter?"

I shrug, making my way over to him. "Guess not...but..." pressing my thighs together, I notice the sweat beads rolling down the side of his neck and onto his blood-stained shirt.

He smiles as I meet his gaze. "Tell me what you want, *Slasher,*" he purrs, the back of his fingers brushing the exposed skin on my stomach.

"I want you to fuck me on top of them."

He chuckles, whirling me around and pressing me on top of *stink breath.* "Anything for you."

Stink breath stares at me absently and I think he's accepted that he'll die here because when he looks at me, the scary man that used to force me down is no longer tall and mighty. He's meek and immobilised.

Elias removes my shorts and panties as I turn my head to look up at him.

"Show this fucker how to properly fuck a woman."

Elias grins as he strokes himself behind me, his thick cock as hard as a wooden board.

"Well first," he gets down to his knees, "You taste her..." licking me from my clit to my ass, he grasps two handfuls of me. "*All* of her."

His tongue twirls around my ass and my breath hitches, my pussy pulsing, needy and hot.

"*Fuck.*" I breathe, pushing my hips back, as his tongue travels to my pussy, my arousal now plentiful as he enters me with two fingers, my eyes still on *stink breath.*

He watches, but I don't think he sees, so I slap him across the face and his jaw tenses.

"Are you watching how to fuck a woman properly, *stink breath?*" I moan when Elias inserts another finger, fucking me with them as I hover over another man's body.

"You're fucking soaking, *Slasher,*" Elias says.

Leaning in, he sucks my pussy into his mouth, then releases, extending his tongue onto my clit and flicking it back and forth, making me grip onto the body bag. He lifts my leg for me, placing it over *stink breath,* so I'm left straddling him.

"You're both *fucked,*" I hear him mutter beneath his breath as he looks away.

I force him to look at me, viciously sinching my nails into the skin of his cheeks.

"Right here big guy, this is what I want you to see." I smile as Elias slides into me, filling me up with his hard cock. "Mm."

He gives me a few slow strokes, waiting until I adjust, and I roll my hips back into him.

"Harder," I whimper, now ready for him to fuck me like it's our first time.

He listens, thrusting into me harder so our skin slaps together in rhythmic movements. His hot breath fans my neck as he leans over me, his tongue licking from my neck to the bottom of my ear.

"You'd look like a million dollars with his teeth around your neck."

He chuckles when I whimper at his dirty talk, the head of his cock hitting the perfect spot deep inside me.

"Shame they're all probably rotten." I breathe, pulling his face to mine as I bite his cheek.

He groans, gripping my hips harder as he pumps into me. Gliding his hand beneath my shirt, he plays with my nipple as I stare down at the man who abused me.

"Sick fucks," he cries, struggling with our weight on top of him.

I want to laugh but the building orgasm has other plans for me. My legs tighten as I curl my hands into fists, gathering the plastic in them.

Elias' hand comes down hard and I yelp, smiling at the sting left behind on my skin.

"Just like that..." I pant, "...Yes!"

"Oh yeah, *Slasher,* come all over my cock."

I do just that. Quivering, shaking and pulsing, I squeeze his cock inside me.

"Taking notes down there, dickhead?" he asks *stink breath* who is clearly not enjoying this.

Turning around, I kneel before Elias and take him into my mouth, pushing myself deep until I can't anymore. I make a point to exaggerate my choking because I never did that with *stink breath* when he would force himself on me.

"Fuck." Elias hisses as he thrusts deeper, holding my head in place. "Your throat is my second favourite hole."

He doesn't let me breathe as he continues to stick himself further until I gag, and he yanks himself out. My ragged breaths make him smirk as I blink, the water build up in my eyes now sliding down my cheeks, no doubt leaving a mess of mascara behind.

"So fucking pretty." He slaps my face lightly, jerking himself off with his other hand.

"On my face. I want it on my mouth."

I watch him rub the tip of his cock, his eyes never leaving mine as he reaches his climax, the hot spurts of his come now all over my face and lips.

I could have gone about this a different way. I could have shot everyone in this disgusting place without leaving a trace of evidence but where is the fun in that? Why should I end it so quickly for them when they had no mercy for me?

No. Even in a body bag, I want to make him suffer and rethink everything he's ever done; to make him realise he deserves all of this.

Turning, I smile at *stink breath* and lean over to place my lips on his.

Elias cackles manically as *stink breath* tries his best to wipe away the come from his lips.

"A goodbye gift," I say, gathering the come on my face with one hand and forcing his mouth open with the other, but he fights me, his jaw snapping as he tries to bite me.

Elias laughs at his pathetic attempt and holds his jaw open so I can slide my fingers into his mouth. "Delicious." I pat his cheek when I'm done.

"Now..." Standing, I put my clothes back on.

When I look back, Elias already has pliers in his hand. "I've never crafted jewellery before..." Placing the pliers on one of *stink breath's* molars, he pulls and gurgled screams echo through the near empty warehouse.

Chapter Eleven
Elias Cross

A pinch of salt. That's what I forgot. It's fine though because the broth tastes great. I cannot wait for her to taste it; I just know she's going to have seconds. Stirring the broth, I take in the delicious scent and almost hit my head on the rangehood when she enters the room.

"I think I'm going to die," she whines, my hoodie sitting just above her knees as she wipes her nose.

"Soup is almost ready. I promise it'll make you feel much better."

Giving it another stir, I scoop some into a bowl with a ladle and add the precooked noodles too. She takes a seat on the stool beside the breakfast bar as she tries to take a whiff of the broth but remains frustrated because she's congested.

"What flavour is it?"

I smile. "Is vengeance a flavour?"

She laughs and tastes it with the first spoon.

"Wow." She looks down at the bowl. "This is actually really good."

I place my hand on my chest in mock hurt. "Ouch."

"I know you're great at fucking, so I figured you might not be great at cooking." She giggles, sniffling as she wipes her nose.

"I'm a man of many talents, *Slasher.*"

Propping my elbows onto the counter, I lean into her and place my lips on hers. "Mm, the sweet taste of vengeance is the only thing that comes close to the taste of you."

She smiles, her messy hair up in a bun.

"Elias..." she looks at her bowl, "...did you not cook the lamb bones properly?" she asks.

I try to hide the twitch in the corner of my mouth and her eyes widen, spitting out the soup.

"No. You didn't." She looks at me, then the soup. "Are they..."

"Don't lie. It tastes better than chicken soup."

She tips the contents of the bowl into the bin and I can see the small smile on her lips. "I cannot believe you."

"What do you take me for?" I deny it even though she's discovered my secret ingredient.

Stepping closer, she places her hand on my cheek.

"Someone who would kill for me."

I place my lips on hers, the scent of her blueberry shampoo lingering around her.

"*Slasher,* I would not only kill for you, I would become the worlds worst nightmare if anything ever happened to you."

About the Author

C.B. Frey, the category bestselling author of The Casella King, thrives in the dark, finding beauty in the twisted and the forbidden. She writes with a raw edge, crafting stories of brooding anti-heroes, dangerous villains, and love that burns with obsession.
Her characters are messy, flawed, and irresistibly compelling—just like the stories she weaves. When she's not writing about the kind of love that haunts you, you'll find her seeking out thrills that match her characters' intensity—whether it's an adrenaline fuelled ride or just a cappuccino to fuel her next story. Her books are not for everyone, but for those who dare to dive in, they're a thrilling ride you won't forget.

www.cbfreyauthor.com

Son Of Sin

By: M.M. Riott

About Son of Sin

Sin: I've been watching them. Their perfect relationship is cozy, but I take what I want. And I want them... I want a *family* with them.

Kieran: I've never wanted kids, but what am I supposed to do when that's forced on me? Not take that shit lying down... that's for sure.

Noah: I only need her... or that's what I thought. But maybe I just needed someone to brake through my barriers and all the hatred my father instilled in me.

Content Note:

Mature content. For readers 18 & older. Explicit language, violence, description of gore and death, noncon (not on page, but is mentioned), forced unwanted pregnancy, kidnapping with the use of drugs, dubcon, homophobia (not on page, but is mentioned). This book contains explicit sexual content.

Relationship type: MMF

Prologue
Sin

They have no idea about the monster that lurks outside their windows. The monster that watches them through cameras hidden in their apartment.

He is loving and caring. She is beautifully tempting sin. Months ago, I saw them in the crowd at a concert, and I swore they would be mine. And soon, they will be.

It was easy to figure out their routines. The very fact she volunteers at an animal shelter only made me more determined to make her mine. She is great with the animals and her patience is unmatched. There is this one dog in particular, a brown and white brindle pit bull. I've watched how she cares for the dog, the love she has for it. She's a social butterfly, when she's at the shelter she's always talking to an older woman. Her laugh is like music to my ears; every time I hear it, I feel the way my stomach clenches. But I also see the tension in her, the way she shuts down when anyone mentions her past.

They'll both have everything they ever wanted once they're mine. I'll make sure of it.

I imagine Kieran's flat stomach round and full with our baby, her perfect tits swollen so they fill my hands. And don't get me started on her round ass. I want to see it red with handprints and full of bite marks. Her long blonde hair makes me want to wrap it around my fist and tug until her sapphire blue eyes fill with tears. She looks like an angel.

Looks can be deceiving though, because I've seen her on her knees with Noah's dick so far down her slender throat, I'm surprised she didn't choke. The memory of what I watched them do earlier through my hidden cameras has my cock twitching in my pants.

Noah's dark hair, beard, and caramel brown eyes are hard not to admire, and his tall, slender build is such a contrast to my muscled strength, I can't wait to feel him pressed up against me. His dick is the perfect fucking size, even if he doesn't have any piercings. He wouldn't even know how to use them if he did. I've thought about making him get one, once they are under my control.

I've seen the things Kieran likes to look at on her phone when Noah is not home. She goes online and watches videos of masked men while she pleasures herself. She wants to be dominated. She wants somebody to take her choices from her. She wants to feel used and degraded. She wants to be treated like the little slut she is.

I would love to pretend to be a good guy and act delusional, but I'm not. I can't pretend. Not when I broke into their shared apartment two months ago and flushed her birth control, and then again when I snuck in two weeks ago and slipped her a pill that made her delirious.

She leaves comments under some of the videos, they started out innocent enough. The first comment she left was on a video of a shirtless man who was covered head to toe in fake blood, licking more of it off a butcher's knife. Her comment was... 'I'd lick you clean.' That one made me laugh. She's gotten more bold as she kept commenting, her latest comment was on a video of a masked man in a towel slung low over his hips, showing a prominent V, he was tying a knot in a rope and hooking it to his bed. Now that comment, if I remember correctly, was 'I wish you would come and tie me up and use me anyway you'd like.' That one made me hard just thinking of all the ways I was going to have fun with her. I may have discreetly hacked into his account and reached out to her, asking her about her deepest fantasies and asking if she wanted to play some of those fantasies out. She said yes, probably thinking I wasn't serious. That was her mistake. She responded instantly, and that's how I ended up playing out her fantasies, exactly as she described them. She hasn't said anything to Noah about it either. She's such a dirty, dirty girl.

I have a plan though. Tonight, I'll make them both mine.

Chapter One
Kieran

Noah thought it would be fun to watch a movie in bed tonight, since our last date was a concert four months ago.

So, we decided to change that tonight, he doesn't have work tomorrow and I haven't worked in a couple years. Noah always said I didn't have to work if I didn't want to, because he's a tech guy and makes decent money, so when my boss decided I should earn my money by doing him in the break room, I walked out. I didn't want to just sit at home and do nothing, so I volunteered at the local animal shelter.

"Ma'am, are you still there?" The lady from Gio's pizzeria asks.

I jump from the sudden sound coming through my phone. "Oh, yes, sorry, I'm here."

"The meat lovers you ordered will be there in fifteen minutes."

"Thank you."

"Kieran, baby, what do you wanna watch?" Noah yells from our bedroom.

"Something scary," I call back.

After heading to the kitchen and grabbing us some glasses, I pour us some wine we've had sitting in the fridge. A knock sounds at the door, which must be the pizza arriving. I grab my purse and get out some money. When I am back in the kitchen, the pizza guy— I look at his name tag— Carl is leaning against the counter on his phone, looking bored. I stand in front of him and clear my throat. His storm gray eyes look up and lock on mine, a slight smirk on his face that takes my breath away. Immediately, guilt rushes through me–I shouldn't be looking at any man other than Noah, no matter how chiseled his jaw is, or that he looks at me with an intensity that makes me want to drop to my knees and do just about anything he asks. His strong hands twitch, and I imagine them around my throat before banishing the thought to the darkest depths of my mind. I never would have thought a hand could be a turn on. Shit. I'm a horrible person.

I love Noah. And that's enough.

Shaking away the feelings he stirs inside me, praying he doesn't notice the way I was looking at him, I hand him the money, refusing to meet his eye. "Keep the change" I rasp.

Carl nods his head and exits the apartment. I gather up the wine, the glasses, and the pizza, carrying them to the bedroom where Noah waits, still off center from the handsome delivery guy. While I set the drinks and the wine on the nightstand beside him, he reaches over and grabs the pizza.

"Man, this pizza smells delicious," he moans out. Smiling, I climb over Noah on the bed and get comfy. I hold my hand out for a glass of wine and he obliges. He takes a big mouthful from his at the same time I chug mine. I do a happy little wiggle, because, well... I'm happy–the man I love, a movie, pizza, and a glass of red wine. What else could I ask for? I ask myself, ignoring the quiet voice in the back of my mind that reminded me I'd just ogled the pizza guy. Grabbing the bottle, I refill my glass, setting it on my table. I burrow into Noah's side and watch the movie he chose.

As Halloween starts to play, I glance up at Noah through my lashes. What would he say if he knew about how turned on I was by the idea of a masked stranger fucking me?? What would he think if he knew someone broke into the apartment, and not only drugged me, but fucked me too? I basically cheated on him. The person did drug me, but I also haven't done anything about it. I'm not even scared now and in the moment the fear is what turned me on.

I think about that night often–his big cock, the way he covered my entire body, making me feel small and delicate, how I felt what he did to me for days after He haunts my dreams, then I wake up and have sex with Noah, drowning in guilt for using him to get me off after fantasizing about someone else.

Noah kisses me on my head as we continue to watch the movie, unaware of the turmoil in my head.

When a particularly scary part comes on and I jump, I feel myself growing damp. I've always been turned on when I was scared. When I admitted that to my high school boyfriend, at fifteen, he was so disgusted by it, he broke up with me and told the whole school I needed to be locked up. Ten years later, the humiliation and shame haven't gone away.

My eyes start to grow heavy. Just before they close, I see the shape of a man at the foot of the bed, wearing the same mask as the man who drugged and fucked me. Noah's hand is on my leg, heavy, as if he's feeling the same sleepiness. My eyes close and I feel something being tied around my wrists. Then it all goes dark.

* * *

I awake to the sound of a door closing. My head aches, like someone is taking a hammer to it. Hands are on my arm, helping me sit up. They are warm, but the finger tips are rough. They feel familiar, calloused, like they are used a lot. I look up into gray eyes. Wait...I remember those eyes! I jerk my arm back, scooting up the bed.

"Where am I?" I ask on a shaky breath.

"At my safe house," Carl the distressingly hot pizza guy replies. "Don't worry."

What the fuck does he mean 'don't worry'? I'm definitely

worried. This motherfucker kidnapped me. I'm alone in this room with a crazy person!

"Where is Noah?" I question.

"He's around," he replies vaguely, tossing a small box at me. "Take this." It's a command, not a request, but I ignore him anyway.

"What do you mean, he's around?" I yell.

Before I can ask anything else, he exits the room, I hear the lock click into place from the outside. Finally, I look around the room, trying to see if there is any way out. I see another door across from the bed, so climbing out of bed, I make my way towards the door. Opening it, I see a full bathroom. Turning back around, my eyes catch on a window on the far-right wall. When I pull back the curtain, the window is barred up.

"FUCK!" I yell into the dark. I cross the room and pick up the small box he threw at me, examining it, shocked when I realize what it is. Why would I need a pregnancy test? I've been on birth control since I started having sex.

Some people don't deserve to have kids, and with my parents being the way they are, I don't think I would make a very good mother. I never wanted kids, and Noah's never pushed me to have kids. He even wears condoms when we have sex for extra protection. There's absolutely no chance that I can be pregnant. Wait...

I scream. The masked man. FUCK.

Chapter Two
Sin

I walk into the room Noah's in, he should be waking up soon. It's right next door to Kieran's, but neither of them know that, because the rooms are soundproof.

A groan pulls me from my thoughts, and I make eye contact with Noah. If looks could kill, I'd be dead.

"Welcome to my home," I taunt.

"Go fuck yourself," he growls.

"Now where's the fun in that when you're lying right there, ready for me to fuck instead?"

"Don't fucking touch me!" he snaps. "Who the fuck are you? What do you want?"

Oh, Noah. I want you. And Kieran. He loves Kieran, that's clear as day, but I've seen his search history, just like I've seen hers. He wants to be dominated like Kieran. He watches videos of dominant and submissive men together.

I grab his throat. "I want you," I growled. "And I want you to admit that you want me."

I bring my lips down on his, electricity crackling between us where we touch. He resists, not wanting to open up to me. I squeeze his throat again, trying to get him to submit. He whimpers into my mouth.

I bring my other hand up to palm his rock hard cock before wrapping my hand around it and squeezing. Noah bucks his hips. Losing his focus enough from the pleasure, he slightly parts his lips and kisses me back. He needed this just as much as I did.

"Up," I rasp against his lips, before working my way down his throat, loving the scratch of his beard against my lips. When he doesn't move, I tighten my fingers around his throat and lift. He follows, fury snapping in his golden eyes.

Once he is standing, I grab the waistband of his sweats, tugging on them.

Noah breaks the kiss and shoves at my shoulders. "I'm not gay," he rasps, defensively, as if I give a fuck whether he thinks he likes men or not. I want him and he wants me.

"It sure seemed like you were enjoying yourself a moment ago."

His face turns red and he sputters, "It's because of the drugs!"

"It's most definitely not, they're out of your system."

"What did you give me?"

"I mixed GHB with your wine when Kieran ran to grab money to pay for the pizza." The moment he realizes I'm telling the truth. His eyes drop to the floor and his shoulders slump.

He glances back up at me, concern in his eyes. "Is Kieran okay?"

"She's fine," I answer, surprised it took him this long to ask about her.

"Take me to her," he demands.

"Absolutely not!" He still needs time to process that, I can and will give him anything he wants. All he has to do is submit and be mine. I want to be the man who fulfills their fantasies. In all honesty I would never let them touch anyone else. From the moment I claimed them they can only have me and each other.

I walk to my office with Noah's refusal to admit he could want me–a man–heavy on my mind. I could give him everything, if he would just accept that about himself.

I flip on the camera installed in Kiren's room to see if she's taken the pregnancy test yet. Even if she doesn't want kids, I'm determined to give them to her. Just because her parents were shitty people doesn't mean she won't be an amazing mother herself. I know she's scared. She doesn't need to be.

Kieran grabs the test off her bed and walks to the bathroom, her face ashen and her hands trembling, as if she already knows why I left the test on her bed. I switch cameras and pull up the view of her taking the test, my heart pounding and every muscle in my body straining with the need to rush in and be with her, to reassure her that everything will be okay.

She waits, staring blankly at the wall, her eyes growing damp. I set a three-minute timer and wait. It's the longest three minutes of my life. After three minutes, Kieran snatches the test up off the counter, sucks in a deep breath, and then flips the test so she can see the results. Her face fills with a look of pure agony.

She's pregnant.

She tosses the test and curls into a ball on the floor, sobbing. She's breaking before my very eyes, and she's never looked more beautiful.

I would get up, go to her, and comfort her, but I think that would do more harm than good. So, I stay sitting at my desk and watch her fall apart. I also might be online, gleefully shopping for baby stuff, but that would be better kept to myself. I get all gender-neutral stuff for right now.

Noah needs to learn about this new development. Then he will finally realize they aren't going anywhere. They are mine, and I am never going to let them go. A small part of me knows he needs to be the one to go and comfort her. They already have such a strong connection. He will know exactly how to piece her together.

I get up and walk back to his room, opening his door. He looks up at me and stands. "Let's go," I order.

"Where?" he questions.

"To Kieran."

I gesture to the now unlocked door. "Go, she's in there!"

He opens the door and slams it behind him. I lock them in there together and make my way back to my office, so I can watch through the cameras. He's on his knees next to her in the bathroom. She says something that has him tensing, so I turn on the audio. "How can you be pregnant? You're on the pill, and I use condoms?"

"I've been keeping a secret," she admits on a shaky exhale. "One night, he broke in wearing a mask, he drugged me a-and h-he took me."

"He?"

"The same guy who kidnapped us," she whispered.

"Why haven't you done anything about it?" Noah questions. "Did you go to the cops?"

"No."

"Why?" He asks, sounding bewildered.

"Because I liked it," she whispers, so quietly that the mic barely captures it.

Noah's face is scrunched up like he genuinely doesn't understand why she wouldn't report me. "What?"

"I SAID I LIKED IT, OKAY?" she cries. "I'm crazy and a slut; I wanted it. I wanted the masked stranger to fuck me! I like the fear," she sobs. "I wanted it."

Noah jumps away from her like she slapped him. He better not say anything negative about her or to her, or, as much as I want him too, I'll have to punish him... severely. It doesn't surprise me when he grabs her and pulls her to his lap. He knows what it's like to spend your life repressing who you are, even if he won't admit it. Noah holds her, rocking her back and forth, trying to soothe her.

Chapter Three
Noah

I'm rocking Kieran back and forth in my lap, holding her while she's crying. "Kieran, baby it's okay, we will figure something out. I promise," I soothe.

I will help her through this. Kieran is the most amazing person I've ever met. Being around her is intoxicating, she's a ray of sunshine. That bastard took her light. He hung rain clouds above her head. I hate him for that, I want to punch him. I've never been one for violence, but Sin brings that side out of me.

"Y-you're not disgusted by me?" Kieran's shaky voice pulls me from my thoughts.

"No baby, why would I be?"

"B-b-because I'm sick, there's something wrong with me and I'm a slut."

"Baby, you're not a slut, and there is nothing wrong with you," I admit. When she first told me what happened and that she liked it, I was horrified, but I realized something very important–I've been hiding myself too. How can I judge her for something she likes, when I would want her to still love and accept me for what I like? Just because she likes something that I don't understand, doesn't give me the right to judge her. "I've been told I needed to be locked up in a padded room, and the key needed to be thrown away," she whispers, "so I would understand if you wanted to leave me."

I look down at the small blonde in my arms, vulnerable and scared. "Kieran, I love you, I promise I'm not going anywhere." *No matter what, I vowed silently.*

She falls asleep shortly after I reassure her that I love her and won't leave her. I stand up, carrying her to her bed, and then I can't put it off any longer. I turn to the camera I know is there and mouth the words, 'we need to talk'.

I know he is watching. I'm not stupid. This means the masked man is also a tech expert, and man, he knows what he's doing.

The door finally opens and I come face to face with the bastard who took advantage of Kieran. The moment we're in the hallway, I punch him in his face. My fist connects with his nose and he stumbles back a step. I get ready to hit him again, when he pushes me into my room next door. I fall to the floor with him on top of me.

He pins my hands together above my head. My dick starts to get hard from Sin restraining me. Fuck, what does he do to me? He keeps making me feel things I thought I never would. I know he feels it because he laughs and shifts his hips so he is sitting right on my cock. I try to break his hold on my arms, but he's huge. He is probably six inches taller than me and maybe fifty pounds heavier.

He leans in. "You want me, baby."

"I don't," I lie.

He adjusts so both my hands are in his one, then he wraps his other hand around my throat. His threat, along with the heat of his body drags a moan out of me before I can stop it. He laughs again and moves his hips so he's rubbing on my dick. He lets go of my throat to grab my hard cock, before leaning down and sucking on my neck, stealing another throaty moan from me.

The kisses he trails down my throat leave me breathless, then he kisses up the center before he bites my Adam's apple. I buck my hips, and when my throbbing cock hits him just right, my eyes roll in the back of my head. It's a heady rush when the stinging pain from my neck mixes with the pleasure.

Fuck I need him off me. I'm feeling things I shouldn't be feeling. I'm into women, not men, but my traitorous body didn't get the memo.

He laughs and sucks harder before finally releasing my hands. I'm sure he left a mark, and I hate how much that thought turns me on more. He stands, offering me a hand to pull me up, which I refuse. Pushing myself up, I flip him off. The bastard just laughs and laughs and laughs.

"Why did you do that to Kieran?" I growl, before he can make another comment about how much I clearly want him.

"Do what?" He furrows his brows.

"Don't play fucking dumb, asshole, you know what."

"Watch how you speak to the man who holds your life in his hands."

I laugh, I just can't help it. He wants *me* to be worried about *my* life? My life.

"What's so fucking funny?" he snarls.

"Kill me then," I taunt, stunned at my bravery. Except, something about this man screams he won't hurt us. Maybe it's the fact that he drugged us and didn't hurt us, but I just don't believe he will.

I may be wrong, and damn do I hope I'm not, but I think he wants us alive. Why else would he get Kieran pregnant? She was on birth control, so either her birth control failed, or this fucker tampered with it. Suspicious, given that he gave her the test the moment she woke up.

He moves so quickly, I don't even have time to flinch before his hand is wrapped around my throat. "Don't fucking push me, Noah. You won't like the consequences when you do."

He tightens his hold, cutting off my breathing for a moment, before releasing my throat and stepping back.

I gasp in deep breaths. "Let us go," I demand.

"No, you are both MINE," he growls out.

"You're crazy."

"Maybe, but I'm keeping both of you." he shrugs before walking out of the open door to my room.

"Kieran doesn't want kids; she won't keep it!" I yell after him.

When he turns around to lock me in, I see the look of finality on his face. It's then I know we are never getting away, and Kieran is keeping the baby. She doesn't have a choice.

Chapter Four
Kieran

I startle awake to the sound of the door closing, only to fall back down into my pillows, grabbing my head. I have a fucking migraine. He won't get away with this, I vow to myself. No matter how much I liked it when he snuck into my room and fucked me before, I don't want *this*.

I crawl out of bed, shoving a pillow under the blanket and bunching it up some, to fool him into thinking I'm peacefully sleeping. I grab the top sheet off the bed and try to rip a strip off. I struggle for a few minutes before saying 'fuck it' and deciding I'm not gonna be able to do that. Searching the room, I don't see anything I can use against him until I spot the towel rod on the wall of the bathroom.

"Perfect!" I whisper to myself.

It wiggles some but seems sturdy, so I grip it tighter and pull harder until it snaps off the wall. Now it's just a waiting game.

I stand by the bedroom door, rod in hand, for what feels like forever. When I'm just about to say fuck it and try this another day, the door opens. He steps through the door, eyes locked directly on the bed. He takes one more step and I strike. I hit him right on his temple with the rod, and he drops to the floor instantly. Smiling triumphantly, I search his pockets for the keys to the rooms.

Fuck yeah!

I search his pocket, taking the keys, as well as a pocket knife and his gun. I set the gun on the dresser and grab the knife. I grab the sheet from the floor and cut two long strips. I try to move him and fail miserably. So, I do the next best thing–walk out of my room to search for Noah.

I try the doors across the hallway first. When I try the door next to mine, it opens and I see Noah sitting on his bed. His eyes flick to the door before he looks back down. I stand there for a second smirking as his eyes shoot up again and he jumps from the bed.

"Kieran, how? What are you doing?" he says in one breath.

"I need your help. Follow me."

I go back to the room directly across from mine and grab the chair I saw when I was looking for Noah, dragging it back to my room.

"Noah, can you help me get him into the chair?"

"I'm on it." Together, we get our captor in the chair and tied up in no time. I walk to my bathroom and fill a cup up with cold water, then I throw it on him.

He gasps awake and struggles in the chair, trying to get free. His eyes find mine and they light up with fury. He's pissed.

Well you know what I'm pissed too!

Might as well add insult to injury. "I don't want it."

"Don't want what?" he questions, eyes on Noah now.

"The baby," I answer. "I don't want the baby."

He turns his head towards me slowly and his eyes lock onto mine.

"Do you know what your name means in Irish?" he asks, completely switching the topic, giving me whiplash.

"No," I say hesitantly.

"It means 'little dark one' and I think that fits you."

"Why?"

"Because you have some darkness inside you," he answers. "Your darkness calls to mine, just like our darkness craves Noah's light. We need each other to feel whole."

I stare at the man tied to the chair with furrowed brows, seeing the shadows swirling in his eyes, the darkness he was talking about. "I don't want to have this baby," I blurt out again.

A dark look crosses over his face. "I don't care."

"It's MY body, it's MY choice!" I scream at him.

"See sweetheart, that's where you're wrong," he replies with a sardonic laugh. "It may be your body, but it's MY choice, and I've decided you're keeping the baby."

I let out a growl. "How can you sit there and force a pregnancy on me and take away all my choices?"

"Because, sweetheart, I can," he answers with a cruel smile.

"I'll just leave, and take care of it on my own."

"I'll find you, Kieran. Anywhere you go, I will find you," he promises.

"You have to understand."

"Understand what?" he snaps.

"This baby, you love them already, right?" I ask, pleading with him.

"Yes," he answers. "I'll do anything I can to protect them, even if it's from you."

"How would you feel if the baby's a girl and someone did this to her?" I question with an urgency I hope he picks up on.

He stares at me with an unreadable expression. "I'd kill them."

"Would you honestly think it's her body, but it's someone else's choice what she does with her body?" I ask, with a pointed look.

"No, I'd want her to make the choice for herself," he admits, his eyes falling to the floor.

"Do you see how hypocritical you sound? You want the baby if she's a girl to decide for herself, but you won't grant me the same respect. As a woman I need to have the right to decide what to do with my body. We fought so hard for our rights, and for them to be taken from us... it feels like a huge loss in the progress we've made."

"But what about me? What about what I want?" He says.

"We can have that conversation, but when I told you how I felt you just shut me down, no conversation or anything. YOU decided. Not US. WE need to decide together. You already took the choice of if I wanted a kid in the first place. You can't take this choice from me too." I let out a helpless sob, wondering if my breath was wasted on trying to explain why this was so important.

"Okay," he sighs.

"Okay?" I question, hopefully.

I release a heavy sigh, It feels like a weight was lifted from my shoulders.

"Me, you and Noah can talk about this."

My stomach does a little flip because he wants to include Noah in the decision. Now I need to make him understand why I can't have this baby. That's the hardest part. I hate talking about my past, even Noah only knows a very small part. Now I'm gonna have to come clean and tell him everything.

"Do you know anything about my history?" I question. My stomach roils with tension—I don't want to have this conversation, and I'm furious that he's making me dig up old, unhappy memories.

"Some," he answers. "I know you lived in foster care from ten until you aged out at eighteen. You bounced around from home to home, never staying longer than a year," he says. "And I know your parents had a terrible marriage, at least until your mother killed your father then took her own life."

Yeah, years of abuse will make you wish you were dead, I think bitterly.

"So you see why I can't have a baby now?" I answer sadly.

"No, I don't," he replies. "Just because you were raised like that, doesn't mean you'll be a shitty parent."

I stare at him with my mouth agape and eyes wide. He doesn't understand the trauma of having to watch your mother kill your abusive father then herself. My eyes drop to the floor and I hear a crash. When I look back up, I see the chair he was sitting on in pieces on the floor and he's climbing to his feet.

"You two will not see each other for a while," he says.

"Carl," I call out.

"That's not my name," he snaps.

"What? That's the name from your name tag," I say slowly.

"I stole the uniform from the one who was gonna deliver your pizza," he admits, like it's perfectly normal to steal clothes from someone and act like a delivery driver. This man is deranged.

"So, what is your name then?"

"You can just call me Sin," he replies, grabbing Noah's arm and walking out of the room, leaving me to think about everything we talked about.

Chapter Five
Noah

We have been locked up in our separate rooms for weeks, since the whole tie up the kidnapper incident. Sin is the only human contact I've had since I held Kieran in my arms, when she found out she's pregnant. I agree with Sin that her childhood doesn't define her, but I also see where she's coming from. The trauma would be hard to overcome, especially because she doesn't talk about it much. I ask to see Kieran every day to check on her, but every day I get the same response.

I'm getting sick and tired of hearing it! I need to see how she's doing, because it's irritating me that she might need me and I can't get to her.

"What's with the look on your face?" Sin questions.

I jump–I didn't hear him come in my room. "I want to see Kieran,"

"Not yet, it's not time,"

It's pissing me off. Sin is so much closer to getting me to admit that I want him. I've come to terms that I'm not straight, but I'm still not sure I'm ready. He's such an asshole. The only time we've ever got close to anything was when he let me into Kieran's room. Since then, he hasn't touched me and I haven't touched him.

Sin walks up to me, his gray eyes, staring into my soul. He reaches down and touches my face. "When are you gonna admit you want me?"

"I don't," I admit on a soft whisper.

"Why are you still lying?" Sin growls. "It's been weeks, and I've seen your search history."

That statement startles me. I whip my head towards him. "Excuse me?"

He looks at the floor rubbing the back of his neck.

"When I was watching both of you, I went through your search history. I saw what you were searching for. Why would you deny yourself for so long? What happened to you that you think this is the right way? Why are you still pretending to be straight?"

I stare at him. His face is as blank as the mask he wears. I should feel violated, but I feel immense relief and a little bit of shame. The relief is what catches me off guard. Why am I relieved that someone knows about this? "Do you know what it's like to have all sixty-four bones in your arm broken?" I ask while he stands there silent. "Because I do."

He blinks at me slowly, an unreadable expression in his eyes, and I take a deep breath, hoping that he'll understand what I'm about to say.

"So, I'm so fucking sorry if me being unsure about my sexuality is such an inconvenience to your stupid ass, but no; I'm not just going to jump into bed with you."

He takes a step back, like I slapped him. I look down at his hands and see them trembling. My eyes slowly travel back up to his face, his whole body is visibly shaking.

"Are you okay?" I question, taking a step closer. "You're shaking."

"I'm fine," he answers carefully and calmly. "Who did that to you? Who made you question yourself?" he says with a growl.

"It doesn't matter, it was a long time ago."

"It does matter, especially if it still haunts you," he replies. "I'm gonna ask you one more time, and if you don't answer or you say some bullshit, you won't like what happens." He drives the point home with a feral look. "WHO DID THAT TO YOU?"

I look at Sin, weighing my options. If I tell him it will dig up old feelings that I want to keep buried. I haven't even told Kieran about my past.

Sin clears his throat, tapping his foot on the floor. "Now, Noah!"

I take a deep steadying breath, needing to buy myself a few extra seconds. Closing my eyes I picture the only thing that will bring me any peace– Kieran. While I relive the worst moment of my life.

"When I was fifteen, I had a friend. He was my best friend really. He was on the football team or—well, I guess that's not important, but anyways, he came over to my house a lot, and one night my father walked in while we were kissing and—" I trail off.

"And what?" Sin presses.

"And my father ripped us apart and beat him so bad he had to leave in an ambulance. And me? Well, he broke every bone in my arm and hand. I was in a cast, I had to do years of physical therapy to regain my movement back." I raise my arm showing him my scars.

"What happened to your father?"

"Nothing. He has friends in high places who were able to sweep it under the rug."

"I'm sorry, Noah. I know what it's like to have a shitty father. I have a brother, I haven't talked to since I was ten. He left and fell in with bad people," He admits, with a pained look, "but a part of me knows he left because of me. Looking at me just reminds him of what happened to his father and our mother."

My heart squeezes for him.

Sin steps forward and hesitates before saying, "Can I touch you?"

I nod my head yes, and he wraps me in his arms faster than I can blink. I take a shaky breath and exhale slowly. I feel a wet spot on his shirt, so I pull back and blink, feeling a line of wetness on my cheek. When did I start crying?

Sin runs his hand through my hair and holds me while I release decades' worth of pent up hurt and sadness against his chest.

"I'm sorry I've been trying to push you, baby, but you need to let go of everything that vile man told you," Sin says, sadly.

I look at him. And I mean *really* look at him this time. He's just a sad broken man. I don't know what happened to him, but he needs help too. That has to be why he's doing the things he's doing.

He's walking a very thin line between me hating him and feeling so bad for him, and I'm willing to give him anything he asks for. I vow to myself that I will try to understand him. He needs that.

Chapter Six
Sin

Noah's father is a vile man who deserves everything I'm going to do to him. I don't believe for one second that his father stopped at breaking bones that one time. He abused his kid for something he had no control over. For something that is perfectly normal.

I've known since I was fourteen that I liked men and women. My parents were supportive of that. I may be fucked up, but it's not because I was lacking parental support or guidance. My issues stem from something else. I plan to check into his parents later, but for now, Noah needs me.

"Sin, I want to be okay with who I am," he says softly.

"I know, baby, I know," I say, stroking his head.

"I–" he stops, as if he's not sure what to say. "I want you," he says softly. "But I don't know how to be okay with that. Can you help me?"

Yes, I know I should ask follow up questions, like if he's sure and if he's really ready, but I've never pretended to be a good man. I grab his jaw and kiss him. The kiss starts out soft, tender and quickly turns to more, turning feverish, our teeth clashing. By the time we pull away, our breathing is ragged. Both of us suck in deep breaths.

Noah is the one who makes the move this time. He crashes his mouth back onto mine. I grab the hem of his shirt, pulling it over his head. Reaching behind my back, I pull mine off one handed, before grabbing the waistband of the sweats I left in here for him. They look fucking fantastic on him. I love seeing him in my clothes. Once I free his hard cock, I take a step back and admire the view. He is tall and lean with muscles that are like a runners. His cock is long, thick and curved, with a vein that runs up the side, it's swollen and already dripping precum.

Looking at Noah's sexy body has made my own cock so hard it hurts. I feel the precum leaking out of the tip and smearing on my boxers. I free my own hard shaft, watching Noah's eyes roll up and down my body, before his eyes go wide, stopping on my piercings. His dick twitches, and with the look in his eyes, I know he's a little terrified but he's enjoying the view. When I take a step forward, Noah takes one back until the backs of his legs hit the bed. He falls back on the bed in a sitting position. I walk back to my pants on the floor, fishing out the packet of lube I have in the pocket. I was planning on taking him today regardless of how he felt. I ran out of patience.

I walk back up to the edge of the bed and grab Noah's jaw, bringing my lips down onto his. I push on his chest, making him lie back on the bed. Once he is lying down, I kiss and suck my way down his chest and stomach, kneeling as I do it. When I reach his shaft, I open my mouth and swirl my tongue around his tip. Noah releases a loud moan, the noises he's making encouraging me to take him deeper. I take deep breaths through my nose before hollowing my cheeks and taking him all the way down my throat. I hold him there, before pulling back up and circling my tongue around his tip again. He bucks his hips, trying to make me speed up, but he's not leading this, I am. I pin his hips to the bed and keep my slow torturous pace.

Noah groans. "Please, I need to come."

I laugh and pull off him completely.

He sits up and scowls at me.

"Calm down, baby," I playfully reprimand. "I'll make you come so hard you'll see stars."

I spread his legs and rip the lube open with my teeth, before I squeeze some on my finger and rub it on his tight hole. Noah tenses, clenching his ass cheeks.

"Relax, baby," I soothe.

My heart jackhammers. Noah's finally giving in to me. I'm totally caught off guard, but when I'm done with him, he'll never question himself again.

I feel him relax ever so slightly and I slowly press my finger into him. Once my finger is inside his warm hole, I add some more lube and press another finger into him. No matter how much I finger him, this is going to hurt. I'm big, I should have prepped him more but I'll make this as painless as I can.

I reach up with my other hand and spit into it. I wrap my hand around his cock trying to distract him some before adding a third finger. When my third finger breeches his tight puckered hole, Noah sucks in a deep, shuddering breath. I slowly spread my fingers inside him and stretch him out some more. I feel Noah tense before he shoots ropes of come onto my hand and his stomach.

I rise up off my knees and line my cock up to his tight hole. Noah releases a shaky breath and nods, letting me know he can take it, that he's ready. I push in an inch slowly, then pull out. Keeping that agonizing pace, I finally have about half my cock in. Noah relaxes further, so pulling out, I slam all the way in.

He lets out a loud, "Holy shit."

"Fuuuuuuck," I moan out, "baby, you're tight as fuck, the way you're squeezing me."

He lets out a guttural moan at my words.

"Baby, you feel so fucking good, you're so perfect," I praise.

Just as I thought—he's a slut for praise, if his swelling cock is any indication.

"Are you gonna take my cock like a good boy?" I ask.

Noah just moans at my question.

"Answer me," I growl.

"Y-Yes."

"Yes." I punctuate with each thrust. "You. Are. Because. You're. Such. A. Good. Fucking. Boy."

After a few more hard thrusts, I feel his body lock up again, and his come paints both our bodies. That pushes me over the edge, and my release fills his ass. I thrust a few more times before pulling out. I look down to see my come leaking out of his ass, so I reach down and push it back in. Noah moans from the feeling of my fingers sliding inside his abused hole.

I collapse on the bed next to him, pulling him on my chest. When his head is on me, I run my fingers through his hair, falling asleep.

Chapter Seven
Kieran

Sin still hasn't let me see Noah. It's been weeks since he's kept us separated. I don't regret what I did, and I haven't apologized. I'm not sorry, but I need to see Noah. I've never thought of myself as codependent before. I'm going stir crazy. I can't tell I'm pregnant other than the test on the stand by my bed and my missed period. I still can't believe Sin forced this on me. I don't want kids.

I startle out of my thoughts when the door is opened. Sin and Noah walk in. I guess we are finally having that talk after weeks of silence.

"I'm leaving for a couple of hours." Sin says, distractedly.

I see the flicker of something like anger in his expression. What pissed him off this early? It's barely even nine in the morning. Sin walks out slamming the door behind him.

I turn to Noah with a sigh. "What did you do to him?"

"Why do you think it was me?"

"One, you walked in here with him. And two, as soon as he opened the door, he looked pissed so I know it wasn't me."

"I swear it wasn't me; he woke up like that."

The 'he woke up like that' piques my interest. I look at Noah with a curious expression. What does he mean he woke up like that?

"Did Sin stay with you last night?" I question.

He looks away almost shyly. *He so did.* I wonder if now is the time Noah will tell me he likes men. I've known for years now, ever since I saw Noah checking out a man when we were grocery shopping. I've never said anything because I was waiting for Noah to tell me. As the years passed, I thought maybe I was wrong until it happened again. Then I figured he hasn't explored that part of himself. *Did he explore it last night with Sin?*

Noah finally looks back at me "Would it bother you if I said yes?"

"No," I answer honestly, "it wouldn't."

He whips his head towards me and gives me a curious look.

"I already know, Noah."

"Know what?" he quickly asks.

"I know you're into men too," I reply.

His eyes go wide. "Wha— how?"

"There have been signs. I'm not mad about it."

His pupils dilate and I see heat enter his eyes. Damn I missed him. Just being near him again is like I can finally breathe again after being deprived of oxygen. These damn pregnancy hormones are gonna kill me. I feel my panties grow damp. Stepping towards Noah, I wrap my arms around his neck. He smiles at me and puts his hands on my waist.

"Hi," I say shyly.

"Hi, baby," Noah says back. "I can tell you want something. Tell me what you want."

I stare up at him. "I want—" I trail off, biting my lip.

"Say it," he growls out.

"I want you."

"Good girl," he smirks, picking me up by my waist.

I wrap my legs around his hips, locking my ankles behind his back. He places a hand on the back of my head, bringing my lips to his. The kiss starts out slow. I bite and suck on his bottom lip before releasing it with a pop. Noah moans softly before the kiss quickly turns hungry and feverish. He walks backwards until I feel the backs of his legs hit the bed and he falls on top of the comforter.

I straddle him, and we resume our kiss. Noah grabs the bottom of my shirt, tugging it over my head, starting to kiss down my neck and chest. I throw my head back on a moan while he grabs my waistband and starts to slide my pants and panties down over my ass. Noah flips me on the bed and pulls my pants off the rest of the way before kissing up my ankle to my calf and up my thigh. He pauses with his mouth directly over my core. He lowers his head and in one long motion, licks from my opening to my clit.

I put my hand over my mouth and let out a strangled cry. Noah must hear how muffled the sound is, because he reaches up and grabs my hand, pinning it against the bed. My hips lift off the bed while he continues his licking and sucking. With every scratch of his beard on my upper thigh, I fall closer to the edge. With my free hand, I reach down between my thighs and grab a handful of his hair. Noah moans into my core. The sensations are almost too much, so I press my thighs against the sides of his face and try to slide up the bed more, away from his mouth. With his other hand he wraps it around my thigh and pulls me back down to his mouth.

"No-Noah," I moan out.

He lifts his head just enough to look at me. "Let go and come for me."

Noah resumes eating me out, biting my clit hard enough for the sting of pain to shove me over the edge.

"Oh my god, Noah," I cry out.

He climbs up the bed, then he's kissing me. I wrap my legs around his waist, noticing he took off his pants. The shirt's gotta go too. I grab the hem, and Noah breaks the kiss long enough to let me pull it over his head. I feel him reach down between our bodies and line his hard length up with my drenched center. He rubs it up and down my core before sliding into me.

I gasp as he stretches me. Noah is big—every time we have sex I feel him the next day. He starts out slow, but he picks up his pace and starts pounding into me harder. I feel another orgasm building. Noah lowers his head and takes my nipple into his mouth, sucking on it. He grazes it with his teeth and I shatter again. My body feels heavy and sated, but Noah isn't done yet. His pace turns punishing and he starts rubbing circles on my swollen nub. The sensations are too much, it almost hurts.

"Noah, I can't," I cry.

"You can and you will. Now come for me again."

His thrusts are brutal and he's still circling my clit, but when he leans down and bites my neck hard, I am hurled off the cliff. I scream so loud; I'm surprised I don't shatter our eardrums. Noah thrusts once more before going completely still. He comes with a grunt, falling on his back and pulling me with him, so I'm lying on his chest, his softening cock still inside me.

Noah is still breathing heavily while he comes down from his orgasmic high. He kisses my nose and closes his eyes, falling asleep. I follow him into darkness moments later.

Chapter Eight
Sin

I finally pull in the driveway after a long ass drive. Why do Noah's parents have to live five hours away? The drive let me think of every way I was going to make his dad pay for his treatment of Noah. Patrick Wilson is going to regret ever laying a hand on him. By the time I'm done with him... Well, let's just say he won't be recognizable.

I think I should be worried about my psychopathic tendencies, but it's not like I go around killing animals. I definitely don't just look at people and think 'oh shit I would very much like to kill them'. I'm not *that* crazy. If someone fucks with something that's mine, then they die. It's simple really, Noah and Kieran are MINE. His father made him feel like he was doing something wrong... like he was wrong. I'm gonna show his father why that was a mistake.

When I get out of the car, I walk to Patrick's front door. His wife is at work, still. I checked.

I knock on the door three times in rapid succession. While I'm standing there waiting, I hear footsteps approaching the door. It swings open, revealing an aging man with thinning gray hair and a sneer on his face. He is shorter than I am and looks nothing like Noah. He has age lines all over his clean-cut face.

Maybe thirty years ago, he would have resembled his son, but now not even their caramel brown eyes are the same. Noah's are friendly, with a light in them so bright it chases away darkness. His father's eyes are pure darkness that chases away the light. This man has no good in him. I've looked into his file. I pulled Noah's medical records after our conversation. He spent a couple years in and out of the hospital, they say he "fell". I call bullshit. His rap sheet is longer than mine, but it pays to have friends in high places.

"Who are you, and what are you doing here?" Patrick snaps.

"I'm your son's boyfriend," I answer with a smug smile. "Nice to meet you, Pops."

His sneer turns into a sadistic smile. "Oh, how lovely, come in."

I plaster on a cheery smile. I know how this is gonna go—only one of us will be alive when this door opens again. It's gonna be me. I step into the house. The foyer has white walls with oak trim and oak floors and leads to a big living room with the same walls and floors.

"What brings you here—" he trails off, realizing I never gave him my name.

When I don't supply my name, he turns and looks at me with a raised brow. "Well? Your name?"

"That's not important for why I'm here," I growl. "I've been informed that you were a shitty father."

He glances at me and continues walking through the living room. "So, Noah's crying about his childhood?"

"No. He doesn't even know I'm here. I just didn't like what he had to say about you."

"So, why are you here; to tell me I was a shitty father?" he asks with a disdainful expression.

"Wrong again," I smirk. "I'm here to kill you."

I'm definitely not one to beat around the bush, I like to be direct.

His expression turns to one of shock before revealing his true face again. "I'm not scared of you, boy," he says, mockingly. "What do you think you're going to do to me?"

I laugh at him. While he scowls at me. What can I do to him? I have about sixty pounds of muscle on him, I'm three inches taller, and I'm twenty years younger.

"What's so funny, boy?" Patrick snarls.

"Nothing," I say as I step closer and draw back my fist. He tries to dodge, but I bring my other fist up and it connects with his temple. He falls onto the floor in a heap. He's out cold. I grab his leg and drag him to the kitchen. I saw it as soon as we stepped into the living room; he has an open concept. I leave him on the floor and walk back to my car. Opening the trunk, I grab the backpack from it and head back inside.

I brought rope and knives and a tarp; I'll call a cleaning crew when I leave. With my hacking skills and no evidence left behind, they will never know he's dead. When I walk back into the kitchen, he is still lying where I left him. I drag him off the floor and put him into the chair, tying him up. When that's all done, I go to the sink, get a cup and throw water on him, waking him up.

He groans and looks around, struggling to get free. Once he realizes he can't, he looks up at me with pure terror and a little rage. He was all talk earlier, but now he's a scared little man. He uses his words to try and intimidate people–the type of man who thinks just because I'm into men that I must be weak. He's wrong of course.

I grab the piece of paper and pen out of the book bag and place it in front of him on the counter.

"What is this?" he questions.

I untie one hand and give him the pen.

"Write a letter to your son, apologizing," I demand. When he doesn't move, I add in a loud snarl, "NOW!"

Patrick scrambles to grab the pen. He starts writing. The letter ends up being short and to the point.

I snatch it off the table, folding it and putting it in my pocket.

Grabbing the book bag, I get out a big tarp, laying it out. I grab the chair Patrick is sitting on and tip him over onto the tarp. He groans and curses under his breath, that terror bleeding back into his expression.

I grab the knife from my pocket and start cutting him, watching his blood coat my hands and the knife. He screams so loud; I have to grab a rag from the bag and shove it in his mouth. He starts to choke on it from how far back it is in his throat. I don't wanna kill him right away; I want him to suffer first, like Noah had to do all those years ago. Muffled whimpers come from his gagged mouth. Only when his skin is split open and he's bleeding all over the tarp do I reach for the gun in the waistband of my pants. I press it to his temple and pull the trigger. Good riddance.

I grab my phone and dial the only man I'd trust to get rid of the evidence in this house—my brother Sean. I haven't seen him in years; not since he started working for the Cosa Nostra but Sean always said If I ever needed him just call. I think he feels obligated, since he's older than me by eight years.

He answers after the fourth ring.

"Hello?" Sean asks.

"Hey big bro, I need a favor."

"Okay?" he says, hesitantly.

"I need you to get a clean-up crew to the pin I'm sending you now."

"What did you do?" he questions.

"What I had to, so... clean-up crew?" I ask, impatiently.

"Yeah, I'll send some men to you," he sighs in resignation.

"Nah, I won't be here, but the wife will be in three hours," I smirk.

"Fuck, Sinesio! Okay, fine—I'll call the crew right now," he replies, sounding annoyed.

"Oh, and Sean, don't call me that!" I snap, grinding my teeth.

Our mother named me that after my piece of shit father. Sean had a loving father, the one who would pick him up and taught him how to drive. Until he died in a horrible accident.

After I end the call, I gather all my stuff and head home. Home, to Kieran and Noah.

Chapter Nine
Noah

I wake up to the sound of the door opening. When I glance down, I see Kieran sleeping on me, a heavy, but comorting weight on my chest. She looks so beautiful. I look to the door that opened moments ago, watching as Sin stumbles in, looking exhausted and covered in blood. Wait, what?

I crawl out of bed, moving Kieran to lay her flat. Once I'm up, I move to Sin's side.

"Are you okay?" I ask as my breath hitches and my heart rate speeds up.

What happened to him? Where was he?

"I'm fine, baby," Sin answers.

"Why are you covered in blood? Who did this to you?" I question in rapid succession.

"It's not my blood. Now calm down, and quiet down," he orders. "Kieran is sleeping, and she needs it."

"Yeah, you're right, I'm sorry," I reply.

"I need to shower; you coming?" Sin says on a sigh.

We walk to the bathroom connected to Kieran's bedroom. As soon as the bathroom door closes, Sin starts taking off his clothes. I walk to the shower and turn it on, adjusting the temperature until it's just right. Sin steps in, and while he washes the blood away, I undress. I step into the shower, grabbing the loofa from Sin and washing his back. If the blood really wasn't his, I bet he wants every inch of his body scrubbed clean.

When I'm done, he turns around, letting the water rinse the soap off. Sin grabs my jaw and brings his mouth down onto mine. The kiss is hungry and soft at the same time. Sin is hesitant to take things further, I can feel it. I drop onto my knees and wrap my hand around his semi hard dick. I bring my mouth to his cock and lick from base to tip, over every piece of metal in his dick, flicking the piercing on his head with my tongue.

I swirl my tongue around the tip, that always drives me wild when Kieran does it. It has the desired effect when Sin reaches down and drags my head forward, slipping his now hard length in my mouth. I hollow my cheeks and let him thrust into my mouth at his own pace. He pushes to the back of my throat. I gag when the bar hits the back of my throat, causing Sin to pull back.

I've never done this before; I just know what I like done to me. I'm just mimicking Kieran right now, but it's hard with his piercings. Sin slows his pace some, and I start sucking and swirling my tongue. He grunts and bucks his hips. I grab his balls and squeeze them a little. I suck one more time and release him with a pop.

Bringing my hand to my mouth, I suck my finger, getting it nice and wet before placing it at his asshole. I grab his shaft with my free hand, then bringing my mouth to it, I start licking and sucking on him.

I slowly push my finger into his tight hole. Sin gasps and bucks his hips faster while I finger his asshole. Sin starts coming and I swallow every drop. I stand slowly. He grabs my chin forcefully. Sin turns my head and brings his lips onto mine.

Breaking away he looks into my eyes. "Thank you."

"You needed it; you seemed stressed."

"No, not for the head, however amazing it was. I meant the trust you showed by dropping to your knees and letting me be the first you've done that with."

With that, he climbs out of the shower and dries off. I stare after him. surprised a man like Sin would thank anyone for something like that. I following him out of the shower and to Kieran's room, hurrying to dry off and pulling on my clothes on my way into her room. She cracks open her eyes when Sin gently shakes her.

"We need to talk," Sin requests.

"What time is it?" Kieran asks while stretching.

"It's nine-thirty," Sin answers.

"Where have you been all day?" Kieran snaps at Sin.

"Jealous, baby?" Sin taunts.

She scoffs at him. "Me? Jealous? Please."

"What if I told you I was out with another girl?" he asks.

I watch as her face twists with anger. I think Sin is joking, but I've been wondering where he's been all day too. Kieran sits up in bed and folds her arms, pushing her tits up. With the tank top she's wearing, it makes her tits look big. They are definitely bigger than usual. Sin may have a troubled past but that is no excuse for what he's done to Kieran.

"Then go back to her!" Kieran yells.

"Calm down baby, I wasn't with anyone else," Sin rushes to soothe the angry woman sitting in bed. "I promise there's no one else for me besides you two."

Kieran searches his face, looking for a lie. When she sees nothing but sincerity in his eyes, she relaxes slightly.

"Then where were you?" she tries again.

"That's what we need to talk about," Sin announces. "Noah, you may want to sit for this."

I look at him quizzically, but walk to the bed and sit.

"I killed your father."

'I killed your father.'

Those words spin around in my head. My father's dead. He's gone forever. I want to feel bad. I want to be sad, but I can't. He was never a father to me—cold and heartless. My heart thumps, slow, steady, even, as always, shocked at my lack of feeling. No, that isn't true. I take one deep breath and then another, trying to identify the emotion crawling up from the depths of my soul.

Freedom. I'm free. Sin freed me.

"Are you mad?" Sin asks.

"No, I'm not," I answer honestly. "I feel like I should be, but I'm not."

"I have a clean-up crew that took care of the scene, so no one will know he's dead. I will cover the tracks and make it look like he's over-seas," Sin informs. "This cannot leave this room, okay?"

"Yes, Kieran says at the same time I say, "I understand."

"We need to talk about the baby," Kieran blurts out, pushing her lip between her teeth.

She's nervous. That's proven further when she starts tugging on her hair.

"I know," he agrees with resignation.

"I've thought about it," she says with a sad smile. "I want to try. I want to have the baby."

Me and Sin exchange a surprised look, and our eyes shoot to Kieran.

"You didn't have a choice. I wasn't gonna let you hurt them," Sin grumbles.

"What changed your mind?" I cut in, before he can say anything else as stupid as that.

"Sin was right, my past doesn't have to define me," she sighs. "I can be the type of person I've never had in my life."

I smile at her, "You know I'll support any decision you make, but can I just say I'm so fucking happy you want to have this baby." I admit, "I've always wanted a kid."

"Why didn't you say anything?" she asks, shocked.

"Because, you were so adamant about not wanting kids," I answer, sadness lacing my tone.

She sits there, eyes wide and mouth agape staring at me.

Chapter Ten
Kieran

S in is the one who makes the first move, effectively putting an end to the conversation. He grabs Noah's head and kisses him. I see Noah tense and freeze up. Sin must notice too, because he pulls back with a scowl.

"What's wrong?" Sin questions.

Noah glances at me, with a shy look on his face. I know exactly what he needs.

I lean forward and cup his cheek. "Noah, it's okay; do what makes you happy."

I feel honoured Noah wants to share this with me. I believe Sin and Noah could be amazing for each other. Just like Sin said we both need noah. He centers me.

Noah leans towards me and claims my lips. I match his pace and kiss him tenderly. He pulls away, with a gentle, "Thank you."

Noah leans towards Sin and kisses him feverishly. Sin reciprocates, and before I know it, I clench and rub my thighs together. Watching them together has me wet and needy. I sit there waiting, biting my lip, not wanting to interrupt their moment.

Sin reaches out a hand, blindly grabbing mine and pulling me forward. I go willingly. Sin pulls away and looks at me, then, leaning forwards he claims my lips in a brutal kiss, teeth clashing. I feel hands on my shirt, tearing it off my body. Once my shirt is off, my bra is next.

When I'm completely bare from my waist up, I feel a mouth on my boobs. Noah licks and sucks on my breasts while Sin is kissing me. I reach my hands out and put one on Sin's face, the other finding Noah's hair. When Noah bites my nipple hard, I let out a mix between a moan and a scream. Sin and Noah switch places; it's Noah's turn to claim my lips and Sin's to ravish my body. Something starts tugging on my pants, then I feel a rush of cool air on my heated skin. I look down and see Sin with a knife, cutting off my panties next.

I gasp. "What are you doing?"

"Be still, baby," Sin growls.

With two flicks of his wrist, the only thing left on my body falls away. Sin pushes me flat on my back. I watch as he drops between my thighs and flicks my small nub with his tongue. I throw my head back, which Noah takes advantage of by sucking and biting on my neck. It feels so good. I don't know where one sensation begins and the other ends. It feels like my body is a live wire. Electricity is zapping every nerve ending in my body. Sin does something with his tongue that has my hips shooting off the bed. With one more flick of his tongue I shatter with a scream.

"I want Noah in your mouth, baby," Sin commands, looking at me.

Noah moves so I can sit up a little. Looking at Sin, my eyes go wide. This is the first time I've seen him completely naked without being drugged. He is sexy. He has a big grim reaper tattoo on his right shoulder that trails all the way to his breast bone. The rest of his chest has small crisscrossing scars. What happened to this beautifully broken man? My eyes trail lower to his stomach where a big puckered scar sits. I follow the trail of hair to his dick. OH MY GOD. There is no way that thing is coming near me sober. His cock is like eleven inches and thick enough that I don't know if my fingers will be able to wrap around it. He has a Jacob's ladder and a Prince Albert. I only remember the stretch that followed the days we had sex the first time, not the actual sex.

"That isn't going inside me," I whimper.

"Baby, it's already been inside you, and you took it really fucking good," Sin laughs. "Now suck Noah's cock."

I let out a choked noise and lean back, taking Noah's familiar length into my mouth. I hollow my cheeks and suck Noah to the back of my throat while Sin adds a finger into me, watching me suck Noah. Every time I stop sucking Noah's dick, Sin removes his finger. I groan around Noah and Sin chuckles. Sin must be getting impatient because he orders Noah to fuck my face.

Noah grabs the sides of my head and starts thrusting his hips, hitting the back of my throat. Where did this Noah come from? He's rougher, more dominant. I like it.

Sin lines his hard length up with my soaked center. Noah pushes to the back of my throat and that's when Sin starts to slide in.

I can feel the ridge of every piercing as he fills me, the sting only adding to the pleasure. He thrusts in all the way, stretching me, his piercings hitting a spot that has my eyes going unfocused and a scream ripping from my throat. Noah and Sin speed up, lighting up my already sensitive body.

When Sin rubs circles on my nub while pounding into me, and Noah releases one side of my head to pinch and twist my nipple, I come undone.

Noah tenses in my mouth before coming down my throat. I swallow every drop before Noah pulls out and lays beside me, stroking my side.

"Good girl," Sin praises.

My pussy clenches at the praise, and Sin moans, stilling as he releases his hot load into me. I gasp to catch my breath, and Sin flops down on the other side of me.

Our legs are all tangled; I can't tell where one of us ends and the other begins. Sin sets his hand on my flat stomach before rubbing gentle circles.

He sits up and plants a soft kiss right below my belly button. "I love you so much already, baby," he whispers to my stomach.

That brings a tear to my eye that I quickly swipe away. This baby, I realize, will grow up so differently from me. The baby will grow up with love and support, not just from me, but these two amazing men.

Chapter Eleven

Sin

Six months later...

I sit at the table drinking coffee, watching Kieran dance around the kitchen. She said she wanted to cook us breakfast this morning. She's making eggs, French toast and sausage, even though last night, she complained last night about how swollen her feet were and said she was gonna stay in bed all day today.

I was really hoping she would. I had plans to devour her. But when she woke up this morning, she was bouncing around with so much energy.

Poor Noah. He's upstairs looking for her comfy shirt. That's all she yelled when she looked in the dryer and didn't find it.

Her exact words were, "Noah, what did you do with my comfy shirt?"

When he asked what her comfy shirt looked like, she yelled back, "My comfy shirt, find it now!" So, he's been up there for an hour looking for her comfy shirt. We don't even know what the damn thing looks like. Her pregnancy hormones are killing us.

Noah stumbles down the stairs with a shirt balled in his fists. "Is this it?" he pants.

"Yessssss!" she yells as she runs up to him and jumps into his arms. "Where did you find it?"

"It was under your pillow," he sighs.

"Ohhh yes, I put it there last night so you two wouldn't steal it," she laughs.

That damn laugh has my stomach doing flips, just like it did the time I heard it at the shelter.

Now it's my turn to chime in. "Why would we steal it?"

"Because you two already tried to."

She grabs the shirt and holds it out for me.

Taking from her, I hold it up. It's a plain black t-shirt. We'd decided to throw it away since it doesn't fit either Noah or myself That's her comfy shirt? "Where did you find this? Noah was supposed to throw it away," I ask.

"I found it in the trash. I bought this shirt so it would fit over my belly. I'm huge; I can't fit into my shirts anymore."

I look up and down her body. She's in a pair of my boxers and a lacy little bra that her tits spill out of like a tasty fucking treat, just begging for my touch. She looks fucking sexy. She must notice the heated look in my eyes, because she pulls the t-shirt on with a scowl. "You're not touching me! I'm huge; I look like a whale," she announces, sounding annoyed.

I smirk, standing from my spot at the table. Walking over to her, I grab her chin. "You are the most beautiful woman I've ever seen," I admit, leaning down and claiming her lips.

The kiss quickly becomes heated. She pulls back, turning to go back to the food she's cooking. When she starts to walk away, I slap her ass. She yelps and turns, shooting me a nasty look. Her viciousness makes me laugh. She's come out of her shell a lot and turned into such a ferocious creature. I fucking love it.

The doorbell rings and I stand, knowing exactly what's here. I hurry to the door before she can, opening the door. I'm greeted by a friendly looking woman in her late fifties.

"Hi ma'am, did you bring him?" I ask in my friendliest voice.

"Oh yes sweetie, though I do have to say you're gonna make one of our volunteers very sad," she answers. "I'll go get him now."

She turns and walks back to her car. Opening the back door, she reaches for something inside. When she steps back, the most adorable brown brindle and white pit bull jumps out. The shelter lady walks back up and smiles at me, handing me his leash and the dog bed he loves. That's what she told me when we were talking on the phone.

"Sin, what are you doing? Oh hi, what are you doing here?" Kieran says, sounding confused, "Oh my god—Thor!" she yells, dropping to her knees next to the dog.

Thor walks up to her and licks her face. She wipes it with the bottom of her shirt.

The older woman gasps. "Oh my goodness! Congratulations, Kie!" she shouts.

Kieran looks up and smiled at the woman. The shirt hides her bump a little and the woman must have just realized she's pregnant.

"Uhhh, Sin, will you help me up?" Kieran asks.

I reach over and grab her hands, pulling her to her feet. She leans down and scratches the dogs head before looking back at the older woman.

"Thank you, Martha, but what are you doing here?"

"Well, this nice young man called and wants to adopt Thor!" she exclaims. "But I see now; he's for you!"

I look down at Kieran's face and see it light up. This was a great decision. She looks up at me and starts tearing up.

"What's wrong, baby?" I say, concern lacing my voice.

"I'm just so happy," she sobs.

I reach over and pull her to me. Leaning down, I plant a kiss on her lips. "Happy birthday, baby."

"Well, I'm gonna get out of here and leave you lovebirds alone," Martha says sweetly. "Bye, Kie, it was lovely seeing you again."

"Bye, Martha!"

Kieran turns to me with a twinkle in her eyes. "How did you know about Thor?"

"I was watching you in the cameras at the shelter."

"You know what— I'm sorry I asked," she says with a roll of her sapphire eyes. "Come on Thor, let's leave him and go play."

"What about breakfast?" I yell.

"Finish it yourself."

With that, her and Thor disappear into the backyard.

"I guess breakfast is up to me," I mutter, but when I walk into the kitchen, Noah's already at the stove

Man, Noah's sexy. He's standing at the stove in a pair of my too-big gray sweats, shirtless. I walk up behind him and kiss his shoulder.

He mumbles something about, "Stop that or this will burn."

I chuckle and step back, sitting at the table. Then, I just watch him. He's bulked up some since we met, not quite my size but bigger than he was. We work out together, and after Kieran has the baby, she will too.

Right now, though, she just watches. On those days, it always ends in us fucking her against the wall or on the floors. Life is great; I have the family I've always wanted with Kieran and Noah and the baby boy who is so close to being here.

Chapter Twelve
Noah

Three months later...

"NOAH! SIN!" Kieran screams for us.

I look up at Sin, who is currently beating my ass. We woke up this morning and were working out, when I had the fun idea to tell Sin I could take him in a fight. As he thoroughly proved, I, in fact, cannot beat him in a fight, if the bruising I can feel already forming on my body is any indication. It took him two minutes to get me on the ground and another three to get me to yield. Well, I guess that was Kieran's blood curdling scream.

Sin jumps up and hightails it out of the basement gym, and I'm trailing right behind him.

"Kieran, what's wrong, baby? Where are you?" Sin yells back, panicked.

"Nursery," she calls back.

Running up yet another flight of stairs, we turn left and bust through the door. We find Kieran leaning on the crib for support with a puddle of water underneath her.

"Kieran, what's wrong?" I ask this time.

"I'm in labor, asshole." She rolls her beautiful ocean blue eyes.

"Are you sure?" I ask dumbly.

"I mean, judging by the water, I don't know— YES!" she growls.

Sin's standing there, staring at her wide eyed, his mouth slightly parted. I'm not doing much better. She flicks her eyes between the both of us before snapping her fingers.

"One of you help me to the car, and the other one get the hospital bags... Now!"

That snaps us out of our stupor and we get moving.

It's happening! She's having the baby!

I think I'm going to be sick.

Sin rushes to her side. Walking past her, I quickly stop in my tracks. I turn towards her and kiss her temple before grabbing the diaper bag from the floor. I rush to our room and grab the duffel bag we packed with all of our clothes. Before long, we are in the car on the way to the hospital. Kieran is up front with Sin and I'm in the back. The drive to the hospital is filled with pained whimpers from Kieran and soothing words from me and Sin.

Once we arrive at the hospital, I rush to get a wheelchair for Kieran and Sin helps her out of the car. When I return with the chair, she's shaking.

"Are you okay?" I ask.

"No, it hurts!"

"It's okay baby, it will all be over soon," Sin says.

Kieran grabs Sin's shirt and pulls him down so they are nose to nose. "Shut up!"

A petite nurse rushes to us as soon as we get inside the doors. She has mousy brown hair, with glasses that look too big for her face covering honey brown eyes.

"Is she okay?" she questions.

"She's in labor," Sin answers calmly.

"Okay, follow me," she says quickly.

The nurse leads us into an elevator, hitting the button for the third floor. The ride is over quickly, then, following the nurse down the hallway we reach the room all the way at the end.

"Go in here and put the robe on, it's on the bed. The doctor will be in soon." With that, she's gone.

I help Kieran up.

"Raise your arms," Sin commands.

Kieran lifts her arms while Sin slides her shirt off, then her bra. Once he's done with her top half, he slides her leggings and panties off. He kneels to slide off her slippers, and I smile at the sight of this brutal, terrifying man, delighted to do anything to make Kieran more comfortable. Kieran places her hand on his shoulder as she steps out of her pants.

As Sin stands, he kisses her stomach, and slides the gown up her arms.

The doctor walks in as soon as Sin and I help Kieran on the bed.

"So, I hear the baby has decided to come today," Dr. Samuel says, sliding his gloves on. "Let's have a look."

Dr. Samuel grabs the stool and slides up to the bed. "Put your feet in these stirrups," he directs, covering Kieran's lower half with a sheet.

Nurses come in and start attaching Kieran up to monitors. The doctor lifts the bottom of the sheet. "The baby is crowning; it's coming now!"

* * *

I look at Kieran and Sin, my eyes filling with tears while watching Kieran trying to get the baby to latch. She said she never wanted kids, but I can see the love in her eyes as she holds our baby.

I'm happy to share the father title with Sin. He has shown us a million times over since he took us why we are lucky to have him. He really is a great person, he's loving and caring. I honestly cannot imagine my life without Kieran and Sin.

The nurse walks in. "Have you decided on a name?"

Kieran gave Sin the power to name him. The bastard wouldn't tell us what he decided on, until the baby was here. I'm not gonna lie, it irritated me to no end, I've never been a fan of secrets and surprises.

Sin looks down at the little boy bundled up in a blanket with a smile. "His name is Xavier."

"Oh, that's a lovely name, here's the paperwork for the birth certificate, I'll be back later for it," she says, setting it down on the table before exiting the room.

"So why Xavier?" Kieran asks.

"I chose a name that held meaning. I've been researching since we found out it was a boy. I chose Xavier because it means savior, and this little boy is my savior."

About the Author

M.M. Riott loves writing dark stories! When she's not writing you can find her cuddled up in bed with her two dogs. She's originally from upstate New York but lives in North Carolina!

Stay up to date with everything here.

PSA: THIS STORY WILL CONNECT TO R&R (Sign up for my newsletter to read the prologue)

PREORDER R&R here!

Good Villains

By: Jo Brenner

About Good Villains

Kara, Conor, Micah, and Luke have one job: to kill a powerful, wealthy rapist before he gains even more power by running for office.

And there's nothing more than the foursome loves to do than bathe in the blood of evil men...

Content Note:

Like the other stories in this anthology, this short romance is *dark*. And *pissed the fuck off.*

So, there's torture, murder, gore, violence (on page), references to past sexual trauma and sexual assault (off-page), references to past murder and violence (off-page), and MMMF consensual nonconsent. If *any* of these topics are triggering to you, please feel free to skip this story! You have my blessing—reading should bring joy (and sometimes, catharsis).

Otherwise, have a bloody good time.

Love,
Jo

Relationship Type: Why choose

Chapter One
Kara

I loved my job. Sure, it was challenging, and at times mentally taxing, and a therapist would have a field day if they knew what I did for a living. Not to mention that blood was hell to get out of fabric—especially the lace lingerie and silk robe I currently wore. But it turned out that writing highbrow fiction no one wanted to read—or creating marketing strategies for large corporations—were *not* my callings in life.

Killing evil men was.

It had only taken being kidnapped by three dark, handsome, near-but-not-complete strangers and pushed to take stock of my life as I was doled out orgasm after orgasm while fighting against a real enemy to figure that out.

And thank fuck for that—and for them.

"What are you smiling about, radiant girl?" Conor, one of said three kidnappers-turned-loves-of-my-life, asked into my earpiece as I knelt in a bedroom of the Austin, Texas townhouse that housed our target, careful to keep my posture timid and my face demure.

"You," I murmured, knowing the mic in my necklace would pick it up. Micah, another of my men, had designed the tech, camou-flaging it within the lab-grown diamond they had gifted me for Hanukkah.

There was silence on the earpiece, before Conor's voice turned warm. "You're the best thing that ever happened to me, Kara."

A throat cleared.

"To us," Micah corrected. He was in a van a few blocks away, keeping visual tabs on the location—and me. Even though my men didn't have to, they worried.

A low chuckle sounded. It was Luke, the final member of our foursome, who was on a rooftop nearby with a sniper rifle in hand in case things didn't go to plan. "I'm glad we're taking a moment before shit gets bloody to share our feelings."

"Fuck off," Conor murmured, but unlike in the past, there was no tension, no heat in it, just humor. Luke and Conor had worked through their shit, and what used to be an unspoken battle for power and dominance had become good-natured ribbing.

"Never," Luke laughed into my ear. I wanted to lean into it.

But I had a job to do.

"We can always do this differently, sweetheart," Luke said, his voice now sober. "You don't have to play the seductress to get this job done."

But I wanted to.

Micah laughed in my ear. "Our little badass baby wants to do this, don't you?"

I smiled to myself again. "Sometimes murder requires a feminine touch," I said.

At that moment, the door opened, revealing the target himself standing in the doorway, and I fell silent, swallowing back the bile that rose from seeing him—and calming the sick anticipation in my chest. Our target had done horrible things and was positioned to do more. He was a serial rapist who'd used his tech money to get away with his crimes, consequence-free. And now he was running for office —and our client refused to let him win: a cause I could get behind.

Some men, you can smell the evil on them. It's a stench they can't hide under their expensive cologne, no matter how hard they might try.

The short, slim man was in a robe, already erect from the fun he assumed he was about to have with me. But the sight of his pale bare legs calmed me, a reminder that, despite the power and influence he wielded, he was still human.

After all, even the most powerful men can bleed.

"Good, you're ready," he rasped.

I didn't speak. I didn't need to. Not yet, anyway.

"I paid a lot of money for this," he continued, lowering a hand to rub his penis. Once, the sight of a man thinking he could use my body for his own pleasure would have filled me with bile.

But I had my men in my ear, supportive, loving—ready to do what was needed to be done.

And I'd dealt with worse. So much worse.

"Get on the bed," he ordered.

Rising to my feet, I followed his orders, climbing up on the ostentatious furniture and facing him, letting my robe gape open to expose my cleavage, careful to make sure the X-Acto knife tucked into my bra didn't cut me. It was hidden in the underwire; the only way I'd gotten it past the heavy security.

He walked toward me, a hideous leer on his face, as he began describing to me what he planned to do—and how he wanted me to behave.

This time, I did almost throw up. But I steeled myself, inhaling slowly as he crawled over my body and stared into my eyes.

"What is it boys say these days?" he asked me. I slowly moved my hand to my chest in preparation.

I didn't answer him, honing my rage as sharply as the knife in my bra.

His eyes gleamed, evil blazing in them like a fire in hell. "Your body, my choice."

Staring straight into them, I withdrew the knife.

Quietly, I asked, "You sure about that?"
A moment later, he started to scream.
Like I said, I really, really loved my job.

Chapter Two
Micah

He was a screamer.

And I loved watching my baby make bad men scream.

I stood in the doorway, admiring Kara's handiwork. There was blood everywhere—on the white satin sheets, matching pillows, even dripping onto the hardwood floors.

Kara was crouched above the target, writing something with the small blade she'd smuggled in across his stomach.

Even in the dim light, I could see the words she'd carved:

This is what happens to rapists.

Tied to the bed post, a pair of men's briefs stuffed in his mouth, he looked over at me, Conor, and Luke. Even from here, I could see the relief in his eyes.

He thought he was being rescued.

"Help!" he tried to scream, the word muffled by his makeshift gag. "This bitch is trying to—"

Luke pushed past me, standing over the two of them. My massive lover looked terrifying, his red hair ablaze in the light.

"Careful what you call her," he warned. "Or the pain you feel now will become a distant, warm memory."

To Kara, he added, "I love when you get violent, sweetheart. It makes me so fucking hard."

Kara looked up at him, looking more beautiful than I'd ever seen her, wearing nothing but blood-soaked lingerie and controlled rage.

"I have an idea," she said, her voice husky. "Why don't we let this fucker bleed out while I see to that hard cock of yours."

Conor moved his way into the room, shaking his head. "I don't care that he's on death's door. No one gets to hear *you* scream but us."

I smiled to myself. Our other male partners were incredibly possessive. I personally didn't mind if a target heard the sounds Kara made when she came for us, but relationships meant compromise.

Kara growled. "You never let me have any fun."

Conor kneeled next to her, grabbing her head in his hands and pulling her into a long, dirty kiss that made my own cock go rock hard.

Fuck, I needed to be inside her.

Pulling away, he said, "Vengeful girl, you can have all the fun in the world you want—once the body goes cold."

At that, the target began to struggle, making high-pitched, fearful noises.

Rolling her eyes, Kara turned back to him, leaning over and saying slowly to him, "Turns out it was *your* body, *my* choice."

And with that, she drew the blade across his neck, and with a final, helpless gurgle, the target stilled in death.

Luke growled. "If he said to you what I think he said..."

Kara shrugged as Conor helped her to her feet. "He's dead now."

Stretching, she complained, "This shit is hell on my knees."

Striding forward, I nudged Conor out of the way, sweeping my baby into my arms and carrying her to the bed, grateful that I'd had the mental wherewithal to wipe Conor's, Luke's, and my identities and prints from any digital system that existed, so our prints or hair follicles couldn't be matched up to anyone. Kara's had been wiped by our long-gone enemies, and I'd kept it that way.

We were ghosts, and we liked it that way.

"You're a bloody mess," I said fondly before reaching down and tearing the bra and panties off her.

Kara grinned up at me, her eyes filled with the lust that often came after a good kill.

"You owe me a new set of these," she said.

"I'll buy you a thousand more," I promised. "But first I need to stuff my baby's juicy cunt full."

Too hard to bother with foreplay, I flipped her onto her hands and knees, unzipping my pants with one hand as I filled her with two fingers, testing to make sure she was ready for me.

But then she was always ready for me and the copious wetness on my fingers proved it.

"You're so wet for me, baby," I growled.

Kara moaned.

A big hand grabbed my hand before I could lick up my favorite taste in the world, and then a mouth was sucking on my fingers, making me even harder.

I turned to look at Conor next to me.

"Pick her up again," he ordered. "I want my mouth on her pussy while you fuck her."

"Whatever you want, boss," I said lightly, grabbing Kara around the waist while Conor slid onto the bed, his head toward the end, facing us.

"Ride my face," he told her. "And if you say a word about suffocating me, worried girl, Luke will paddle your ass until you scream so loud we fuck up this whole mission."

"Luke will do that anyway," Luke said as he joined us near the bed.

I lowered Kara over Conor's face, so she kneeled above his head. One hand on her hip to keep her in place, I grabbed my stone-hard and sensitive cock with my other hand, lining up with her dripping cunt.

"Keep her quiet," I told Luke, who was already stripping off his pants.

"I plan to," he said.

"Oh god," Kara gasped, then screamed as I shoved all the way into her, pushing her forward against Conor's face.

She squirmed against us as, with a growl, Conor went to town on her pussy and I pulled out only to shove back into the tight, warm, wet heat I called home. The positioning was a little tricky at first, negotiating fucking Kara while Conor licked her, especially as our girl writhed against both of us.

"Too much," she cried.

"Luke," I groaned.

"On it," he said, and then he was grabbing her head between his large hands and shoving his own cock deep into her mouth, turning her screams and cries into a muffled, garbled moan.

"Gonna fill you up, baby. From both ends. How's that feel, knowing you're going to fly home as my come drips out of you? Gonna breed you, baby—and when we get home, Luke and Conor are going to take their turns doing the same thing, over and over, until you're so full and so sensitive, you'll forget what it was like before."

Kara tried to pull off of Luke's cock to say something, but he shoved deeper, silencing her. And the way her cunt tightened around me made it clear: she liked what I was saying.

Good. We weren't quite ready for kids yet but preparing her for a time when we would be was fun as fuck.

Watching Luke choke her with his cock while Conor sucked and licked and ate at her and my own cock was swallowed by her sweet cunt had me way too close to the edge. And knowing she had no choice but to take what we gave her—and that she loved every second of it—made it near impossible not to fill her up with come.

I locked eyes with Luke, who grinned at me.

"I love you," he said.

"I love you," I said back.

Conor growled in agreement, his free hand working his cock. That was all it took: Suddenly, Kara froze, and then her cunt was squeezing around me in perfect, cock-strangling pulses as she came, and took me with her, making me go briefly blind with how good it felt.

Home.

I did as promised, filling her up with come until she was sloppy, messy full.

With two simultaneous groans, Luke and Conor came too, Luke into Kara's throat, and Conor all over Luke's stomach.

Sighing, I pulled out of Kara, who slumped over between Conor and Luke.

"I love you, baby," I told her.

"I love you," she groaned, "But one of you is carrying me out of here."

"Deal," Conor said.

Luke eyed the room—including the cooling body I'd briefly forgotten. "We should get out of here. This place freaks me out. It's worse than Marcus's many homes."

At the mention of my half-brother, I sighed.

"Yeah, and his plane is probably on his way to pick us up. Kara, don't you dare clean up your messy pussy," I warned.

"Wouldn't dream of it," she said, pulling her robe back on.

Usually, we'd clean up our mess—but our client had asked to leave things as they were. No one would find us or connect the dots, and we wanted the kill to serve as a warning to other oligarchs with political aspirations.

They could try.

But we would be waiting in the shadows, ready to make them regret it.

With our little badass baby taking the lead in their destruction.

"Come on, sweetheart, time to go home."

With that, Luke swung a sated Kara up into his arms like the bride she still was, and we headed off into the night.

THE END

About the Author

A lover of dogs, mountain adventures, and HGTV, Jo Brenner writes dark romances that are a little bit twisted, a lotta bit sexy—and always have an HEA. Stalk her everywhere to get publishing updates, book teasers, and other filthy and fun stuff.

Acknowledgments

First, thank you, dear reader, for picking up this anthology and for your solidarity as we express our RAGE at the never-ending restrictions on reproductive rights, including abortion. All proceeds from RAGE will be donated to the Chicago Abortion Fund, and we encourage you to donate to the abortion fund of your choice to help folks from places with abortion restrictions to receive vital reproductive healthcare.

Thank you to all the authors and artists who contributed creative works to this anthology.

Thanks to Danielle Romero, who generously donated covers for both the ebook and all of the paperback editions.

Thank you to Kelly, Jasmine, and Raeleen, whose behind-the-scenes support made this anthology possible.

An enormous thank you to the editors who either offered up their services for free or at a discounted cost to anthology participants: Raeleen Nelson with Book Witch Editing, Alexa Thomas with the Fiction Fix, A.N. Stauber, MP Starkweather, Ashley Oliver, Raven Heidrich, Kyla Lee, Rosie Sloane of All the Proof, Bookish Services by Kay, Fae Darling, Scarlett of Scarlett Pen Edits, Alexandra of Sinful, Nooks Editing, and Nikki Grant.

Our deepest appreciation to all the influencers and readers who volunteered their time and their platforms to get the word out about this important fundraiser.

And finally, once again, thank you for putting your foot down and saying, "ENOUGH." We are so grateful to each and every one of you for joining us in this fight. It's going to take all of us.

It's not over. We've barely begun.

Yours in solidarity,
    Poppy, MT, and Jo

Made in United States
Troutdale, OR
04/14/2025

30576395R00412